Dear Reader,

Do you judge your *Scarlet* books by their covers? Or do you choose your romances by the 'blurb' on the back of the book? Perhaps you pick a particular novel off the shelf because of its title, or maybe because of the author's name? You'll notice that each month we provide a list of forthcoming *Scarlet* books, with short outlines giving you a taste of each new story. Does *that* help you to make your selection? Of course, I hope you are buying all four titles each month, but I'd love to know how *you* make *your* reading decisions.

And by the way, how do you feel about sequels? A number of readers have already written to ask if we are planning to publish new books featuring popular characters from already published *Scarlet* novels. If you'd like to see a spin-off of your top-of-the-pops *Scarlet* romance, why not send me a letter for the author in question and I'll be happy to pass it along.

Till next month,
Best wishes,

Sally Cooper

SALLY COOPER,
Editor-in-Chief – *Scarlet*

JESSICA MARCHANT

LOVE BEYOND DESIRE

Enquiries to:
Robinson Publishing Ltd
7 Kensington Church Court
London W8 4SP

First published in the UK by Scarlet, 1997

A copy of the British Library Cataloguing in
Publication data is available from the British Library

ISBN 1–85487–925–1

Printed and bound in the EC

10 9 8 7 6 5 4 3 2 1

To Peter, with love and gratitude

CHAPTER 1

'Careful,' Amy said. 'You're pulling.'

Robert went on dragging her hair together in both his fists. When he had it tight, he pinned the two red hanks wide apart on the pillow and surveyed her naked body with satisfaction.

'Not a freckle anywhere.'

'Yes, well, I stay out of the sun, don't I?' Amy jerked her head uselessly. 'Let go, will you?'

'You didn't stay out of the sun in Corfu.' He kept her hair pinned, and went on studying her in the glow of his parchment-shaded bedside lamp. 'The first thing I noticed about you was the way this –' he straightened her hair to its full length, almost reaching the abundant curves of her breasts – 'shone across the beach . . .'

'Stop it!' Amy prised at his hands, trying to free herself. 'That bloody hurts . . .'

She hesitated, angry with herself for breaking her own rule. She had always been careful not to swear at all, first because of her younger brothers, then because of the young people she taught.

1

At least it seemed to have worked, on this occasion. He opened his hands to let her hair spring back to its usual tangle, and propped himself beside her on one elbow.

'Only playing.'

Only playing. The words struck an uncomfortable chord. When she caught playground bullies tormenting some smaller pupil they always said *Only playing, Miss*. I wonder why I never noticed it before, she thought.

But then, with Robert's looks it was hard to notice anything else about him. Such eyes, deep-set under straight, dark brows, yet even in this light they shone a brilliant, transparent amber. Such wide, smooth shoulders, still deeply tanned as when she'd first met him on that beach three months ago . . .

He must use a sunbed. The thought dropped unbidden into her mind and dug itself in. Not that she objected to sunbeds, not really. Only, then there was his hair. She knew he had it regularly washed and styled in the hairdressing department of Lang and Drew's, the multiple store whose Maidstone branch he managed, and why not? But earlier this evening, when she first arrived, she had noticed a lightness about the roots. He must have it tinted too. For some reason, the idea made her vaguely uncomfortable.

Yet why shouldn't a man take care of his looks as much as a woman? She pushed her doubts away, welcomed the hard male strength of him as he pressed against her, and felt with satisfaction the heat of his erection. When he lowered his head and swept each of her nipples with his long lashes, she closed her eyes and abandoned herself to the world of sensual delight.

'More, please . . .' she whispered, and let the words trail into the hot silence.

Robert didn't like her talking as they made love. Instead, to show her appreciation she put a hand on his chest and ran it lightly down to his flat, hard belly. Once there, she let it rest. Right at the beginning, three months ago, he had let her know that she must not take too much of a lead.

Which was fine with her, since he took it so expertly himself. She shivered and drew a long breath as his lips found each of her breasts in turn, then traced their tantalizing, tormenting, glorious path down her body, leaving flares of pleasure wherever they touched. Oh, that was so good, she couldn't bear it, she couldn't wait, he knew so well how to rouse her, how to hold her back, how to push her to what seemed like the very edge, and then further yet . . .

She let her own mouth explore his warm, satiny shoulders, tangled her hands in the hair on his chest, and presently, knowing that it was time, slid her arms round him and invited him in. How well we fit together, she managed to reflect, and then the whitewater journey of pleasure began and all thought drowned in the torrent of pure feeling which prolonged itself, climaxed, and at last dropped them each into their separate satisfaction.

'Robert,' Amy said at last, humbly voicing her gratitude, 'that was marvellous.'

You're marvellous, she wanted to add, but some-how, even at this time, she couldn't say that.

'We're good together,' he agreed, 'now I've got you trained.'

Oh dear. Determined not to react to his compla-cency, she sat up and lowered her feet to the white Wilton carpet.

'I made us a casserole last night. I'll go and get it from my car.'

'Not yet.' He put a hand on her upper arm, gripping it too tightly. 'We have to talk.'

'Couldn't we talk while it's heating?' She tried to free herself. 'It'll take most of an hour, what with getting the oven up to temperature.'

'Come back to bed.'

'But I haven't had anything to eat since . . .' She looked down at his hand, still pressing into her arm, and gave up. 'All right then.' She settled once more against the pillows, the duvet tangled round her feet. 'What is it?'

He glanced down at her body and quickly away. 'Cover up, there's a good girl.'

Amy tried to control her irritation, knowing it to be hunger-sharpened. Even so she felt her hackles rise as he slid the sunflower-patterned duvet up to her chin, and tucked it round her shoulders.

'I don't want to be distracted,' he told her.

'Oh well . . .'

She freed her arms – the right one, she noticed, reddened where he had grasped it – and put them

4

behind her head. The movement raised her breasts so that her sensitized nipples stirred against the cover, reminding her of why she came here, direct from the end of school in Canterbury, every other Friday. The thought mellowed her in spite of her nagging hunger.

'So what is this thing we have to talk about?'

He sighed. She waited, but he only propped a pillow against the bars of his brass bedhead, leant back on it, and stared at the silver-striped wallpaper on the other side of the room.

After a moment Amy wriggled upright next to him. Catching his disapproving glance at her bouncing breasts, she impatiently pulled the duvet up and tucked it beneath her arms. Her sweater and bra lay somewhere on the stairs, where he had thrown them when she first arrived.

'If you don't want to be distracted,' she said, 'why don't we put our clothes on?'

'Because I want you with them off,' he answered in that sexy growl she found so appealing.

'Already?' she asked in surprise. 'All right then, if you'll just let me go and get that casserole first . . .'

'Forget the damned casserole.' He spread his strong, manicured hands on the duvet, and stared down at them. 'I wish you'd let me have a cigarette.'

'It was your own idea to give up smoking,' Amy pointed out carefully.

'You moaned about the smell.'

'I didn't . . .' She stopped.

I didn't moan, she had meant to say, *only commented* – but that might lead to another argument like the one after the original comment. She found something else to say instead.

'I'm only here every other weekend.'

He didn't answer.

'So what *is* it?' Amy asked.

Still no answer. Had he run into his ex-wife again? That always upset him. The ex-Mrs Dawlish lived in the next village and shopped in Maidstone, so he met her far more often than he liked.

'You've seen Sarah?'

He shook his head, but scowled. 'I hear she passed all her exams.'

Well done, Sarah, Amy thought; there's a woman who's put her life back together and made something of herself. However, she knew better than to express that idea to Sarah's resentful ex-husband. Instead she offered him a crumb of comfort for his ex-wife's success. 'I suppose she'll go home to Cornwall, now she's a fully-fledged vet?'

Robert's beautiful mouth clenched. 'The local practice has taken her on.'

So that was it. Sarah hadn't merely qualified, she'd got a job locally. She would stay and flourish right here within Robert's sight, while he seemed as far as ever from his own goals of managing the Oxford Street branch and sitting on the board of Lang and Drews. Amy sympathized with his thwarted ambitions if not with his destructive hatred of Sarah, and sought for a way of cheering him.

'You'll feel a lot better after we've eaten. Just let me . . .'

'It's exactly like a conker.' He had lifted one of her curls into the glow of the lamp.

'Food, Robert!' Amy murmured as her stomach sent up hunger signals. 'It's high time . . .'

'Will you shut up about food!' He threw the curl back to her shoulder. 'In fact shut up about everything, and just listen for a change.'

So it wasn't Sarah he wanted to talk about after all. Amy closed her mouth and waited. And waited. And waited.

'I've got a niner somewhere,' he said at last. 'From when I was twelve.'

He glanced up to the calendar above the bedside table. Amy had often wondered why he would keep a calendar in his bedroom, and decided it was because of its Klimt paintings of beautiful, mostly naked women. October's girl, she noted for the first time, had red hair like her own but brighter and longer, streaming over pearly, naked breasts.

So that's why he pulled my hair, she thought, to make it longer so it would fit the picture.

In the continuing silence her mind wandered. On this year's timetable she had Year Seven Drama all Friday afternoon, a marvellous way to finish the week. The new eleven-pluses had such energy and enthusiasm. Today she'd taught them to circle sunwise for good magic, widdershins for bad . . .

'I suppose,' Robert said in what was for him almost an apology, 'I'm having trouble leading up to it.'

Amy found her fingers circling widdershins on the duvet, and willed them to stillness. 'So why don't you just say it? Whatever it is.'

He turned towards her, the light gilding the edge of one fine cheekbone, the rest of his face shadowy. 'I want you to marry me.'

'Oh, Robert . . .'

She turned to stare at him, confused by that sense of helpless dismay which always overwhelmed her when this happened. Why did none of them ever believe what she told them?

'You know why I don't want to get married,' she said at last in a low voice. 'I told you, right back at the beginning.'

'I know you had a lot of drudgery while you were growing up . . .'

'It wasn't *drudgery*,' Amy said. But she spoke without conviction because it had been, or some of it had. She hated to admit it when she loved her four brothers so much, especially little Gareth, whom she and her father had helped into the world on that snowy night seventeen years ago.

If only Moor Fell Farm hadn't been so remote. If only the snow hadn't brought the telephone wires down. If only her mother had been stronger, less worn out by childbearing, better able to fight for life . . .

Amy made an effort of will, and dragged her thoughts away from the familiar treadmill. She had

8

always found it best to think not of what she had lost but of what she had been given; dear Gareth to cuddle and feed and wash and change and shield from harm; David and Adam and Matthew to love and take care of . . .

'Of course it was drudgery,' Robert cut into her thoughts. 'The very idea of an eleven-year-old girl having to look after her father and four younger brothers . . .'

'We had housekeepers,' Amy said quickly, sensing the criticism of her dear, grief-stricken father. 'Only . . .'

'Only he wasn't very good at choosing them,' Robert finished for her.

'He did his best,' she retorted. 'With five children and a farm in the back of beyond, he had to take what he could get.'

The first had been slatternly, not keeping up with the work or doing it all anyhow. The second had fiddled the housekeeping, cutting down on food and putting the money into her own pocket. The third had seemed fine until sheep-shearing time, when sixteen-year-old Amy had arrived early from school to find five-year-old Gareth locked in his room, while the woman who was supposed to be looking after him lay in the barn under one of the shearers.

That was when Amy had persuaded her father not to look for a replacement. Thereafter she scrubbed and polished, marketed and baked, scolded and encouraged; did everything she could to see that her beloved brothers had the best possible start in life. Often it meant missing school, but Amy brought the same determination to her work there, and left with better exam results than she ever expected . . .

'You know perfectly well,' Robert went on, 'that our marriage would be nothing like that.'

'Yes,' Amy admitted. 'I know things would be easier. But . . .'

But there wouldn't be the love, she thought. I could never, ever love you, Robert . . .

She felt her eyes widen with surprise, almost shock. Mingled with it came another feeling, almost of panic, and then a full understanding of something she'd known for months and never wanted to admit, something that swept into her mind in this unguarded moment and refused to be denied any longer.

I should never have got mixed up with him at all, she realized, putting it into words. He's vain and cruel and self-centred, and I knew that, all of it, the first hour I spent with him. I could no more marry him than . . . than enter a heavyweight boxing contest. It *would* be a heavyweight boxing contest, with me on the losing end . . .

'But what?' He still had his head turned to her in shadowy half-profile. 'Come on, out with it.'

Now it was Amy who pulled the duvet around herself, as high as it would go. In the blinding light of her finally accepted understanding, she knew that she must on no account annoy Robert. And turning down his proposal would annoy him however gently and tactfully she tried to do it. She must play for time.

'G-give me a minute to think?' She knew she sounded almost pleading, and tried to put some strength into her voice. 'It . . . it isn't the kind of question I get asked every day.'

'I should hope not.' He turned to her in the bed, a new erection suddenly hot against her thigh. 'Let me help you make up your mind . . .'

'Not yet.' She moved away as far as she dared. 'Why do you want us to marry, Robert?'

'That's a damn silly question . . .' He mastered his frustration, and went on in a tone of forced lightness. 'All the usual reasons.'

The same reasons that had made him want to marry Sarah? But she didn't ask it aloud. 'There are all sorts of usual reasons,' she said instead. 'Which are yours?'

'Damn it, Amy, why does anybody ever want to get married?' He ran a hand through his hair, leaving it gorgeously spiky. 'I suppose I'm in love with you.'

Oh dear. What could she say to that? She racked her brains. 'Th-that's nice of you, Robert . . .'

'*Nice!*' He turned to stare at her in irritation. 'Don't be so bloody ridiculous.'

'I . . . I only meant . . .'

He flung himself out of bed and stalked across the room, as sleek as a racehorse. Amy noted with something very like terror that he was still rampantly aroused and it was with relief that she watched him throw on his blue silk dressing gown, belt it, and drop into his leather bedroom chair, all in one superb movement.

'I'm asking you to share my life, not inviting you to a bloody vicarage tea party. I take it you don't like the idea?'

'Well . . .' Amy began, then went on hastily. 'There's my job . . .'

'Where on earth does that come into it?'

Amy made no reply. In the three months they'd known each other he'd never let her talk about her work, so naturally he didn't realize how important it was to her.

It was understandable, she supposed, trying to make allowances. After all, she hadn't known herself before she started what an absorbing job teaching could be.

Seven years ago, David had married Jenny and brought her to live on the farm. At first Amy had been a little worried to have another woman in the house but she soon saw the advantages, especially when the woman was the capable, loving Jenny. Then Adam took up with Lynne, and somehow, though they never got round to marrying, presently Lynne too was living on the farm, revelling in the clean and quiet air and giving back far more than she took in practical affection. Twelve-year-old Gareth quickly took to her, and then, only then, did Amy start to wonder about that other life she longed for.

At last she could try her luck as an actress. She knew she had the voice, the presence, the study, the flexibility – hadn't she always had leading roles in school productions, and hadn't she always done them well in spite of her cares at home? But when she tried to discuss it with her ageing father, the idea had so distressed him that she had been forced to compromise. She couldn't abandon it entirely, but her application for teacher-training calmed him, and she could at least apply to colleges with good drama departments. She had finally been accepted by one in Kent.

'You can't,' Robert went on, 'want to teach in a grotty comprehensive for the rest of your life?'

'It's . . . it's a good school,' she answered, barely above a whisper. 'And . . . and yes, I do want to go on teaching.'

She had known it on her first teaching practice, the minute she stood in front of her first class. By good luck it had been a group of eleven-pluses, nearly as new to secondary school as she was herself. Looking from one small, eager face to another, Amy had realized for the first time that these weren't only pupils, they were people; this wasn't just a class, it was a collection of individuals, each with hopes and troubles and rights and talents.

They had liked her, too. The older groups had been more difficult, but the tenacity which had helped her master four turbulent growing boys at home came to her aid again, and all her classes ended up at least grudgingly respecting her. At the end of her four-year course, the headmaster of that same school offered her the job in their drama department and launched her on a happier, more fulfilled life than she had ever believed possible.

'All right then, we'll find you a part-time job in a private school,' Robert's impatient voice cut into her thoughts. 'Until the children come, anyway.'

'Children,' Amy repeated dully.

'You're twenty-nine,' he pointed out. 'It's high time you got on with it.'

'But Robert, I've already brought up a family . . .' She paused, remembering suddenly that he was six years older than herself. Was this what had brought on the proposal? Had he decided that he himself must 'get on with it'? Had he chosen her to bear his children? She suppressed a shiver at the idea, and spoke quickly, thoughtlessly, to cover her dismay.

'M-my house is so small . . .'

'For heaven's sake!' He sprang to his feet and strode across to her, six-foot-something of magnificently impatient male. 'You don't think you'd go on living there, do you? We'd sell it . . .' So that was her beloved cottage taken care of. '. . . and use the money to buy a flat for when we want to be in town.'

'I see you've got it all worked out.'

'I'd sell this house too, of course,' Robert went on. 'We'd want something bigger, with servants' quarters.' He warmed to his dream of married bliss. 'We'd need a maid, a nanny, an odd-job man for gardening and a bit of chauffeuring . . .'

'You didn't have all those things in your marriage with Sarah.'

It was out before Amy could stop it, and as soon as she'd spoken she could see it had been a mistake. He scowled.

14

'I didn't, no. Why do you think the marriage failed?' He spat out the last word, as if it tasted bitter in his mouth.

'Is that how you see it?' she asked softly. Of all things, to feel sorry for him! But heavens, what a view of the world he'd just revealed. To believe that you needed to be rich in order to have a good marriage, that was poverty indeed.

'Leave it.' His angry gesture brushed away his past. 'It's the future I want to talk about.' He settled by her on the bed, trapping her thighs uncomfortably beneath the duvet. 'Our future. Together.'

'It's . . . certainly . . .' Amy summoned all her actress's skills to hide a sense of rising panic. 'It's certainly very tempting,' she managed at last. Her tone sounded thin and phoney in her own ears, but it seemed to satisfy him. He took her hand, and cradled it between both of his.

'Look, we don't have to settle anything here, this minute. Tell you what . . .' The amber gaze met hers with a nonchalance so false that it made Amy feel like Sarah Bernhardt in comparison. No wonder he hadn't noticed her pretences, she thought, when his own were so transparent. '. . . Come with me to Weybridge next Sunday,' he continued. 'I'm playing golf with Tommy Drew, and lunching at his place afterwards.'

So that was it. Amy now knew with absolute certainty that she had reached the heart of the mystery, the real reason for his sudden proposal of marriage.

Her pupils called it 'creeping', this currying favour with the powerful, but Robert's word for it was 'networking'. And now Robert's networking, described in tedious detail over the three months she'd known him, had paid off. Perhaps, stimulated by anger at his ex-wife's success, he had worked extra hard at it. At all events he had at last achieved the longed-for invitation to the home of Tommy Drew, son of Julius Drew, chairman of Lang and Drew PLC.

What a lousy actor he is, Amy thought across the great, cold distance that now divided her from her companion. Any of my Third Years could have made a better job of being casual about it.

'A party?' she asked aloud.

'Family only.' He couldn't hide his triumph.

'And you want me there too?' Amy spoke slowly, putting off her refusal. 'A stranger?'

'You wouldn't be a stranger. You'd be my girl.'

Amy clenched her teeth, to hold down her newly-acquired horror of the idea. 'We only meet every *other* weekend,' she ventured to remind him. 'I . . . I'm pretty taken up with school affairs just now. The Christmas production . . .'

'Oh, come on!' He didn't have to act his outrage. 'I'm asking you to marry me, for heaven's sake.'

To marry him. Or rather, to meet the Drews, be vetted as a future company wife, and then marry him. Always supposing she passed, of course. It was so ludicrous, so hopelessly misjudged that Amy could find nothing to say.

Where on earth did they get these ideas? Last spring, Andy had wanted her to help run his vineyard. Before him, Australian Kev had wanted her to break her statutory two months' notice and travel the world with him in that rickety dormobile. And last year, Philippe had seen no obstacle to her living with him in Paris, maybe teaching a bit of English when she wasn't valeting his suits and cooking him superb French meals . . .

I must be doing something wrong somewhere, Amy thought. Giving out the wrong signals. But how could she give out the right ones? She liked men, understood them, knew from managing her five beloved menfolk how to get on with them – perhaps that was why so many of them seemed to like her in return. How could she ever tell any man how her heart sank at the very thought of living with him and running his home and looking after his children? She always made noises about how content she was with her present life, and how little she wanted to leave it, but they never seemed to believe her, any more than Robert did now.

'I'm asking you to marry me,' he repeated to underline his indignation, 'and you prattle on about a lousy school play?'

This really couldn't go on. Amy took a deep breath. 'It'll be a good school play,' she contradicted him firmly. 'And the reason it'll be good is that it'll be properly rehearsed . . .'

'All right, all right,' he broke in impatiently. 'I'm sure you're great at your job . . .'

'And one of the rehearsals,' Amy went on, refusing to be deflected, 'is scheduled for next Sunday.'

'You can cancel.'

'And let down all the kids?'

'They've got to come into the real world some time.' Here it was again, the gulf between them opening wider with every word they spoke. 'They're lucky to get you from nine till four, the money you're paid.'

'It isn't a question of money . . .' Amy sighed, and let it go. What was the use? This whole affair had been a mistake. She had been hoping to tell him so in a way that would spare his feelings, but the more she tried, the more she saw how hopeless it was. Far the best thing she could do now was to get away from here, away from him, as quickly and cleanly as she could. She took another deep breath, and spread her hands before her on the duvet to remind her to keep them still.

'Sorry, Robert. The answer's no.'

He stared at her, refusing to believe it.

'No,' she repeated, 'I don't want to marry you.'

'You'd rather go on *teaching*?' He sounded so incredulous that Amy opened her mouth for a hasty retort. It's a marvellous job, she wanted to say, a hundred times better than the awful, empty, overstuffed life that you think makes a good marriage. A thousand times better than *any* marriage when you've spent your childhood doing all the chores that wives do . . .

Still, that wouldn't get her anywhere. 'I like teaching,' she said instead with forced mildness. 'And yes, I intend to go on doing it for as long as I can.'

'But what about children?'

'I . . . I'm quite happy teaching them. And spoiling my nephews and nieces,' she added as an afterthought.

'You must want some of your own. All women do.'

'I . . . I suppose so.'

'Don't you like children?'

'Of course I do.' A collective vision of the new Year Sevens flashed into her mind. Such pristine uniforms, such clean little faces, such eagerness to please. How delightful they were then, and how they changed as they went on through the school. 'I like them very much,' she added. 'Only, I get all I want of them . . .'

'Other people's children. You can't possibly tell from that what it's like having your own.'

'You forget, I looked after Gareth from the moment he was born.'

'It's still not the same.'

'Maybe not, but it was enough for me. I love babies,' Amy went on carefully, 'but remember, I work with what the babies become.'

'That's different . . .'

'It certainly is. I'll leave out the teenage pregnancies and vandals and shoplifters, because they're the exceptions . . .'

'I'm glad to hear it.'

'So I'll just talk about ordinary kids.' She ignored his interruption. 'Clever girls who won't work. Nice boys who won't wash. Gigglers. Attention seekers. Little bullies. Little madames . . .'

'Ours wouldn't be like that.'

'They would,' she said, recalling the changeling each beloved brother in turn had become as he reached the age of fourteen. 'All teenagers are a pain, it's a stage they have to get through.'

'All right, for a year or two maybe . . .'

'And who has to see them through it?' she demanded, triumphant at the crux of her argument. 'Their poor old . . .'

'You're paid for it, aren't you?'

Cut off with the crucial word unspoken, Amy closed her mouth and stared at him in resigned silence. She might have known she wouldn't be able to make him understand.

'If you hate the job that much,' he went on, 'I'm amazed you're so set on keeping it.'

He really does believe I'm complaining about being a teacher, Amy thought with sudden weariness. He hasn't begun to think what it's like being a parent. I doubt if he ever will. Their poor old mum, she'd meant to say, that's who has to see kids through their teens. Except with ours, it was me . . .

'I don't hate teaching,' she said quietly, knowing she was wasting her time. 'I like it and I'm good at it. I want to go on doing it.'

'In spite of the kids being such a pain?'

'They always have a nice side . . .' She gave up. 'Look, just take my word for it. I'm not ready to get married.'

'I see.'

He didn't, but she let it go. His splendid shoulders had drooped as if she'd let the air out of him.

'I wonder,' he went on, 'how we came to be at such cross-purposes?'

'We wouldn't have been, if . . .' She bit off the rest. If you'd let me talk about my job. If you'd shown me only a little, tiny bit of the understanding partners need before they can think of making a life together.

Yet if they'd misunderstood each other, it was as much her fault as his. Perhaps she'd been too content to keep their relationship merely physical, something apart from the working world which in its own way she found so satisfying.

'. . . if we didn't live so far apart,' she finished lamely.

'This village and yours aren't exactly on different planets,' he told her, homing in at once on the lameness. 'We could meet far more often than we do.'

She shrugged. 'I need all my weekday evenings for school work,' she reminded him. 'And every other weekend for the play. I did say that, right at the start.'

'I know what you said.' He rose from his place beside her, rejecting the argument. 'That was before we started thinking about marriage.'

We. As if it were as much her idea as his. And yet, freed from his uncomfortable weight against her knee, she felt once more that urge to comfort him. Poor little lad, robbed of his winning conker. She put a hand on his arm.

'I'm so sorry, Robert . . .'

21

'Sorry!' He flung away, out of her reach. 'I should damn well think you are. What the hell have we been *doing* all these months?'

Amy looked down at the duvet, strangely ashamed.

'Just . . . copulating,' he savagely answered his own question. 'Like animals.'

'It . . . it didn't feel like that at the time.'

But it had, it had. She knew that now. She had always had a weakness for handsome, dominant men, but with Andy and Kev and Philippe there had also been affection, shared tastes, shared jokes, pleasure in their company. With Robert there had never been anything but enjoyment of his looks, his beautiful body, his skill at lovemaking. As she admitted it to herself, Amy felt a heaviness in her stomach, as if she had eaten too much of something disagreeable.

With an effort, she raised her eyes and met the amber gaze. 'I'm . . . I'm so sorry,' she repeated.

'All right, so you're sorry.'

The hauntingly perfect features took on an expression she had never seen before. Staring up at them, Amy was reminded of the transformation scene in a werewolf film.

'So,' he went on, 'what are you going to do about it?'

With an effort of will, she dragged her gaze away from his, flung back the duvet, and stood up. 'I suppose I'd better be going . . .'

She froze, realizing at once that it had been a bad move. But what else could she have done, she wondered desperately as she stood there exposed and helpless; she had to get out of here somehow. In the heavy silence he went on staring down at her body, the muscles of his lean jaw slack with desire. Unable to bear it any longer, she turned her head away so sharply that her hair swished over her shoulders.

'You bitch!' As if at a signal, he flung away his dressing gown and leapt at her, his greedy mouth pulling and sucking at her neck.

'Robert!' She struggled free and took a step back from him, one hand nursing her neck. 'Please, please don't be like this.'

'I'll be any way I damn well please.' He lunged again.

'Leave me alone.' She dodged to the other side of the chair. He gathered himself for a fresh attack, lithe, predatory, powerful as a god of battle. His amber eyes glittered with anger, his strong hands curved to take her . . .

Heavens, he's sexy, Amy thought distractedly. Maybe I'd better just let him . . .

Let him bite her? Pull her hair? Worse? She dragged her gaze from his aggressive, faultless body and cast about for ways of escape.

The bathroom, and lock herself in? Yes, and then what? The window? No, she'd hurt herself. The bedroom door had a key though, if she could only reach it and get it into the outer lock with him on the other side. Keeping him in her sights, she edged towards it . . .

And found a soft, slithery mass entangling her feet. She recognized his discarded dressing gown, then

23

landed on her back with a thud that drove all coherent thoughts from her mind. Before she could recover he was on her, crushing her to the carpet, pinning her arms to her sides while he bit that same place on her neck . . .

Too high to cover with a scarf, she thought on a new wave of pain which this time brought fury with it. Right mate, gloves off. But first she must think. Think, think, think, her mind repeated over and over while her lungs dragged at the air, in, out, in, out . . .

Then, suddenly it was all right. She could think, she really could, in spite of the pain, his weight on her, his teeth pulling relentlessly at her neck, her fear of what might come next . . . But no, forget what might come next; things weren't going that far. She summoned all her acting skills.

'Let's go, then,' she murmured into his ear. 'Have you any idea how hot you've made me?' He had, too. 'I'm steaming for you,' she informed him with relish. 'Streaming for you . . .' She turned a new gasp of pain into a convincing enough gurgle of pleasure.

It worked. He took his mouth from her neck and rose over her, his weight on his hands which ground her arms further into the carpet. Amy relaxed her jaw to stop herself wincing, and that pain too lessened as he went on rising away from her.

Was this the moment? Not yet. He'd only changed his balance, squatting now with a triumphant knee either side of her and pinning her hips to the floor with that small bum she'd once found so fanciable.

24

'So all this time you've been wanting it rough,' he observed complacently. 'I might have known.'

'A girl doesn't . . .' She paused, swallowing disgust at the ugly charade he was forcing on her. 'A girl doesn't always like to say these things.'

'Let's play then.'

Only playing, Miss. But no, she wouldn't let herself imagine what Robert's idea of playing might be. Instead she would stay limp, like this, and drop her eyelids, like this, and watch him through her lashes, and wait for her moment.

'Let's see, where shall we begin? There's this.' He buried his fists in her hair and pulled her head painfully up from the floor. 'Or there's these.' He dug his fingers into her breasts, twisting and squeezing. Amy gasped and thrust her tongue out with the pain, then set it to a slow, deliberate licking of her lips.

'Mm. That's nice.'

'Good, good.' He tweaked her pain-stiffened nipples. 'Then there's that mouth of yours.'

Oh God, now what? But she kept her head, and moved her abused arms to bring her hands together, suggestively stroking the air.

'I know something I could do with my mouth.'

He looked pleased. 'Why didn't I make you behave right from the start?'

Amy summoned a display of eagerness. 'Make me now.'

'Right. We'll do it there.' He pointed to his black leather bedroom chair, and she held her breath. Would he leave her, and get up, and sit in it? He would, he would, he did. The lifting of his weight from her hips brought a relief so exquisite that for a moment she could only lie there breathing out, in, out, the long, slow, calming rhythm she taught in her relaxation exercises.

'Kneel here.'

She raised her head to find him magisterially seated and pointing to the carpet at his feet. Slowly, slowly she leant up on one arm, and drew her legs under her. As she rose to her knees, her brain worked overtime and she fixed her mind on that key, that vital, all-important key . . .

'Come on!' He pointed again, impatient. 'Or I'll slipper that beautiful bum of yours. In fact I'll slipper it anyway, it should go a fine pink . . .'

'I'm here.'

And she was, coiled with her body pressed close to his thigh. Would he notice that she wasn't completely abject on two knees, but had one foot to the ground ready to spring up? No, he had leant round to pinch her buttock between ruthless, nail-digging fingers. 'And I'll have a go between these, in a minute,' he snarled.

Amy suppressed her outrage. 'They're all yours.'

'Plenty of time. Open your mouth.'

Amy obeyed, and with another insinuating, stroking gesture slid her cupped hands across his thighs. Here it was, the hot pillar of flesh which in the past had given her so much pleasure. How on earth could she do this to it?

'Get to work!' He boxed her ears with his open palm. 'This minute.'

She could do it. Down went her hands, stroking and teasing while her lips and tongue did the work which must put him off-guard. She heard the long, deep inhalations of his pleasure, saw his hands slacken on the arms of the chair, and at last could move her careful fingers towards his unsuspecting testicles.

For a moment her mind shuddered away from what she had to do. Then she summoned all her resolution and in one movement freed her bruised mouth, closed her fists with all her strength, and twisted.

His harsh cry of pain nearly defeated her. Only her aching breasts, her ringing head, her bruised neck kept her squeezing and twisting until he doubled and clawed at her arms. Then she shot to her feet, dodged behind his chair, put her hands against its back, and tipped with all her might.

Up it came and over, and there he lay in a heap on the floor with the chair on top of him. Amy grabbed the duvet from the bed, flung it over him and chair together, and made for the door. The key slid easily out of the inner lock, cold in her hand as she dodged out of the door and banged it shut. Now to fit the key into the outer lock, and turn it.

Did it work? It did. She breathed out in relief and sped down the dark staircase to the clothes she had so joyfully abandoned when she had first arrived. Her long Cossack coat was enough for the moment. Its unlined wool scratched her bare skin as she gathered the rest in a bundle, snatched up her handbag, and whirled through the front door to the biting cold garden. The burglar light sprang to life as she crossed its beam, helping her to find her keys and open her car.

'I'll get you for this, Amy Hammond.' His voice grated down to her through the dazzle of the light. She shielded her eyes and saw his silhouette against the open casement window, the closed curtains striped light-and-dark about him.

So I didn't hurt him too badly, she thought with relief.

'I'll get you, if it takes me forever.'

She scrambled into the driving seat, closed the car door, and thrust the key into the engine. Feeling the pedals cold against her bare feet, she eased round the asphalt half-moon before the house, down the drive, and out into the quiet, tree-lined street. She sped between the dark gardens, and only when she reached the sodium-lit main road did she begin to feel she'd really got away.

Before the motorway, she stopped long enough to slip her feet into her flat-heeled driving shoes. After that she kept going until, with the dashboard clock standing at midnight, she reached her own front door.

CHAPTER 2

'OK, so I'm pregnant,' Joanna said. 'So what?'

'You'll soon find out what,' Richard sneered. 'We're not having your Republican brat on this train.'

He signalled to Matthew and Tim, who grabbed Joanna's arms. Ella, until now frozen in horror, gave a wordless cry and sprang to her daughter's side. Tim beat her off, and she sank to her knees with her hands over her face. Joanna doubled forward, hands over her belly, straining against the soldiers either side of her. Slowly, deliberately Richard, their officer, drew a gun from his belt, reversed it, and curled his hand round the barrel. He raised its butt over Joanna's huddled figure, and the group froze.

'Marvellous timing, kids,' Amy said, scribbling in her record book.

Guer, she entered five times beside her list of names. It stood for *Guernica*, and would remind her, she hoped, how this group had based their test work on the great Picasso painting she had used as a stimulus for last week's lesson.

29

They shouldn't have. The exercise was to communicate the physical feelings of being on a train, and they hadn't tackled that at all. Still, *t A, s of d A*, she scribbled, which meant timing good, sense of drama good. And the final freeze was superb. 'Your final freeze was great,' she told them, still writing. 'And I liked the idea of the pregnancy.' Was it just an idea though?

'It's all right, Miss.' Joanna, a matriarchal thirteen-year-old, grinned tolerantly. 'I'm not really expecting.'

The rest of the class laughed. Amy smiled absently. 'The trouble is, you didn't show any signs of being on a train,' she resumed. 'No swaying about, no balancing.'

'See?' Joanna hissed at Richard. 'I told you we should've put that in.'

So he's the problem, Amy thought; I might have known. Trust Richard to go his own way.

'We'd stopped the train, Miss,' he assured her with his usual confidence.

'That's handy.' Amy gave him a look. 'You didn't work on being crowded into a narrow space either.'

He smiled, green eyes teasing beneath the thick blond fringe. 'We'd taken her into a barn for questioning.'

'Then you shouldn't have.'

'I told him we should've stayed on the train,' Joanna said. But her reproachful glance at Richard quickly changed to a doting fondness.

Lovesick, Amy noted in the slot by her name. By Richard's she put *wilful, uses charm*. And heaven knows, he has plenty of it, she thought. I do hope he doesn't hurt her too much. Or at least, not on purpose. She put her hand into the concealing folds of her hair, and felt the sore place on her neck. She had bought this sweater on Saturday for its high cowl-neck, and worn her hair loose this morning, but even so she feared that pupils might see the livid, tooth-marked bruise Robert had left on her. What a horrible, horrible man.

'Right, boys,' she said aloud. 'Your turn.'

This group had been whispering together. When they took their places she saw that they had learnt from her comments on the last lot. Crowded into an imagined narrow space between imagined train seats, they swayed with abandon in unlikely directions.

'Freeze now,' Amy told them, smiling, 'and start when I give the word.'

They stilled, and she opened her notebook. Predictably, this all-boy group had chosen to stage a fight scene, but they did it with Year Nine skill. Their final freeze had one holding himself up by an imaginary luggage-rack, two crouching in cramped aggression, and one lying dazed on the carriage floor.

'Well planned, boys,' she told them, and noted as much.

The third group, all girls, did something witty about trying to eat in a train moving at high speed.

The fourth, mixed, staged a family argument about tickets, and the fifth, all boys, went for an Agatha Christie-style murder.

One thing about this job, Amy thought gratefully, it doesn't leave me time to worry about my own troubles. She always had to be with her classes a hundred per cent, most of all on a Monday morning. Stimulating these sleepyheads with a game, calming them with relaxation, and talking them through work-alone movement practice had taken every spark of attention she could muster.

Improvisation time was easier, but not much. Normally she worked for a while with each group, helping them prepare their ideas for showing to the rest of the class, but today she couldn't. With school reports in the offing, she had to observe and make notes on each individual's skills of movement, voice, imagination, concentration, ability to work with others.

She closed her notebook for the last time, and glanced at her watch. She should finish with another relaxation exercise, but with morning break coming, they'd have time to run off the energy the lesson had generated in them. She would skip relaxation for once. 'Right,' she said. 'Change and collect your gear.'

Chattering, they flocked obediently to their coats, bags and outdoor shoes at the far end of the room. Amy dropped her notebook and pen into the documents section of the big shoulder bag she carried for work, then opened the cavernous maw of its main compartment and fished for her keys. Her questing hand found her scarf, her metal school whistle, a piece of chalk, her sandwiches, a wrapped toffee which, during last week's break duty, she had politely accepted from an eleven-year-old, a little cardboard box which her fingers shuddered away from – and here were her keys at last.

She fished them out, and the string which had tangled with them. She must have knocked the box apart in her searching, she thought with revulsion. At the end of the string hung a small pulpy lump, so battered it had almost flattened to a disc-shape, though its shiny, dark-red coating still clung in places.

'What you keeping that for, Miss?' demanded green-eyed Richard, strolling back to the workspace ahead of the rest of the class. 'Anybody can see it's a loser.' He peered closer. 'Must've been up against a good 'un, to bash it that bad.'

'I suppose you picked it up off the playground, Miss?' asked Joanna, never far behind Richard. 'These kids and their messy games.'

'Yeah, it's a kids' game really,' Richard announced, belatedly the superior thirteen-year-old.

Amy dropped the conker back into her bag and did her best to forget it. 'Do you want to go to break or don't you?' she asked of the returning, chattering group. 'Wait for it.'

The chatter stilled to the required silence. The bell shrilled through it, but the class waited.

'That's it, then,' Amy said. 'Off you go.'

They straggled to the door, and she checked round the room. Kate Campbell, the head of English who also taught a little drama, worked here next. Partly because she liked Kate and partly out of pride, Amy made a point of leaving everything in good order for her. Blinds up, lights off, blocks against wall, chairs piled; yes, everything was fine except for this piece of junk mail on the floor where it had dropped out of her notebook. She had no idea why she had put it there, but then she hadn't been herself this morning when that thing came in the post.

She stooped quickly and picked up the bold-printed envelope, then called to the last pupil drifting out. 'Jill!'

Overgrown, sallow Jill Gann trailed back, returning the packet of crisps to her bag.

'You know you aren't supposed to eat in here,' Amy reminded her gently. 'Is that your lunch?'

Jill nodded, narrow eyes stretched as wide as they would go. She didn't look charmingly pathetic as she intended, but that only deepened the pathos.

'I didn't have breakfast, Miss. I'm famished.'

Amy sighed. There would never be much breakfast, she guessed, for this eldest of five whose father had long disappeared and whose mother just about coped. The girl's knowing glance flicked to the side of Amy's neck, and for a moment pity soured; trust streetwise Jill to see and recognize the bruise and the efforts to hide it.

Still, that wasn't the issue here. 'If you eat your lunch now,' she pointed out, 'you'll be more famished than ever by four o'clock.'

Jill shrugged. Four o'clock could look after itself, if it ever happened.

'No breakfast, and a packet of crisps for lunch.' Amy bit her lip, then dived again into her capacious handbag and brought out her purse. 'Get yourself something at the canteen at dinner time,' she said, and handed over a coin.

Jill accepted the money but let it lie on her palm, looking across it. 'I got to go shopping dinner time.'

'Shop for a sandwich as well, then.' Amy almost pleaded, remembering her own harassed schooldays. 'You've got to eat or you'll be ill, and then where will your brothers and sisters be?'

The girl's head snapped up. 'Mum does her best . . .'

'Eat something, Jill,' Amy cut in, ending the matter.

'Yes, Miss.' Knowing herself dismissed, the girl trailed to the door, but once there, turned for a moment. 'Er . . . thanks, Miss.'

Amy only nodded in reply. Left alone, she felt a new wave of depression roll over her. She held it at bay and opened the envelope she had been clutching all this time; a firm in Windsor trying to sell her personalized stationery. She dropped letter and envelope into the wastebasket. Now to reassemble that horrible package. I should have put it all in a plastic bag, she thought as she returned the battered conker to its box. That would have preserved the evidence.

But evidence of what? He hadn't broken any laws. Doing her best to banish the subject from her mind, she sat on one of the moulded plastic chairs, took off her

35

trainers, and pulled on her high-heeled boots. When she put them on this morning she'd hoped that their soft autumn-gold would cheer her up, but they didn't. Nor did her moss-green tights, nor her heather-checked mohair skirt, and certainly not this new moss-green sweater she'd had to buy to hide Robert's bite.

As for her Cossack coat, she could hardly bear to touch it. The mere feel of its rough wool against her fingers brought back a host of unwanted memories. For two pins she'd have worn her old raincoat in spite of the sunshine . . .

Let's get out of here, Amy told herself.

Locking the door behind her with relief, she shouldered her bag and descended the stairs for the long walk to the staff room. Her class had already fanned out across the playing fields, mingling with groups from other classes. Ahead of her on the path two of the boys who had staged the fight scene described it to friends, adding dialogue they said they'd put in.

And so they might have, if they'd thought of it in time. Amy glanced after them with affection as they made for the tuck shop.

What a beautiful day. Low winter sun gilded the beech hedges, and leafless chestnut trees threw spiky blue shadows across the scarred grass. Amy breathed deep, then sprang forward and stuck out a boot to catch a passing football. She stopped it neatly with the side of her foot and nudged it back to the boy who approached from the playing field to fetch it.

'Not too near the windows, James,' she warned.

As she walked on, worry and anger hit her again. Mingled with both came the guilt, a needle-sharp self-blame which insisted that some at least of what happened last Friday must be her own fault. But how was I to guess, she argued yet again, that he was a . . . Her mind veered from the word *psychopath*, as it so often had during this wretched weekend. She mustn't overdramatize. Robert had shown himself an ordinary bully, that was all. Bullies were common enough, every teacher knew dozens, she could spot one a mile off.

And she had spotted Robert for one, right away, as soon as she met him. So why had she gone on seeing him?

A vivid picture rose in her mind from the lesson just over, Joanna doubled to protect her imaginary pregnancy, Richard raising his imaginary gun over her. After it came one less vivid but more telling, of Joanna trying to scold green-eyed Richard, and only managing to smile fondly at him.

Sex is why I went on seeing him, Amy admitted to herself. I liked going to bed with Robert, so he had to be all right. She'd let herself be taken in by charm, just like Joanna. Just like every woman in the world, now and again. Must she blame herself for that?

Yes, yes, yes. She should have known better. She who taught body language, who knew what people said without words, what they said with shoulders and hands and eyes, she of all people should have picked up the signs that Robert was a psych ... Was a particularly bad bully.

But I couldn't see straight, she argued with herself. I ... I *fancied* him.

Even unspoken, it had a hollow ring. To love a man was one thing. To get into a mess like that – like this – merely through fancying him was at best stupid, at worst masochistic.

No! The thought repelled her so much that she threw back her shoulders, and tossed her hair into the wintry air. Whatever else, she certainly wasn't a masochist. Hadn't she firmly rejected from the start all Robert's attempts to move her in that direction? Which from the start she had clearly recognized. Yes, she had. She couldn't deny Robert's tendency to sadism, even if she only now let herself admit it.

Hell! She entered the staff room at speed, flung her bag on a chair, and made for the bubbling comfort of the coffee urn.

'Steady on!' Kate Campbell gathered together her scattered report sheets. 'You'll blow us all away.'

'Sorry.' Amy filled her coffee mug and came to join her friend. 'Bad weekend.'

Kate finished writing a name and a date at the top of a report form. Then she put down her pen, looked up, and absently ran a hand through her short, greying dark hair. Her small, shrewd grey eyes shone clear and dark and reassuring behind their horn-rimmed glasses. 'Seriously bad?' she asked in her deep, soothing West Country voice.

Trust Kate to ask the right question. Amy pulled out another of the heavy, wooden-armed chairs and sank into it, wondering as she so often did why her friend's wisdom and strength and good nature went along with such lousy dress sense. If Kate hadn't yet achieved her hoped-for promotion to headmistress, it must be partly due to boring cardigans like that pink one she wore now, with a tweed skirt all wrong for her dumpy lines.

'Seriously bad?' Kate repeated. 'Or just ordinary bad?'

'Seriously bad,' Amy admitted with relief.

This, she realized at last, was what she had been hoping for. This was why she had put that thing in her bag; not to show it to the police, but to show it to her friend and tell what it meant.

'Your Demon Draper played up?'

'I wish you wouldn't call him that . . .' Amy trailed off. 'I suppose,' she went on, slowly and painfully, 'he really might be a bit demonic.'

Kate tidied her reports together and waited, calmly receptive. 'You'd better tell me.'

'Not here.' She glanced round the big, sunny room. The grey-haired head of home economics sat at the other end of the long table, counting attendances in her register. By the window a tweedy maths teacher discussed some classroom incident with the lanky student here on teaching practice this term. The student cast longing glances towards Amy. As soon as he could break free, he would be over here with his callow chat and immature opinions . . .

Amy looked away from him. She had enough troubles of her own this morning, without having to be brisk and motherly with a moony eighteen-year-old.

'The Crossed Keys?' Kate's voice soothed like cold water on a burnt finger. 'Lunch time?'

The Crossed Keys stood on the edge of the village of Davisham, seven or eight miles from Canterbury. It had white weatherboarding, a sign showing gilded Gothic keys, and an ample car park. Within, it offered real fires, real flowers, and good food, but for the staff of Oaklands High its best feature was its distance from the school. They sometimes met parents or ex-pupils there, but never current pupils trying to buy illegal, under-age drinks.

For Amy, in her present state of mind, it had other advantages. Its rambling bar, several small rooms knocked into one, offered a choice of secluded corners. On this quiet Monday the two women were able to have their favourite, a solid-walled alcove with a window overlooking the north downs.

'I suppose this used to be a cupboard,' Amy observed from her cushioned bench.

'Mm.' Kate sipped her tomato juice.

'With this view, what a waste.' Amy stared out unseeing at the sheep-dotted hills. 'I suppose that's why they . . .'

'What did he do, Amy?'

'Ah!' Amy accepted her oval dish of lasagne and its accompanying salad. 'That smells good,' she lied.

'All right.' Kate took her knife and fork to her grilled trout. 'But we only have an hour, and –' she consulted her watch – 'ten minutes of that have gone already.'

Amy ate a scrap or two of the pasta. She knew it was as good as usual, toasty and gold-brown on top, lusciously sauced within, but she could hardly taste it. She forced down a mouthful, and told of Robert's proposal of marriage. 'It made me suddenly realize all sorts of things I hadn't known I knew.'

'So you turned him down.' Kate removed another strip of rose-white flesh from the delicate bones of her fish. 'How did he take it?'

Amy played with her pasta, and stumbled on. The arguments, his violence, the distasteful charade she'd had to act to escape. She put her fork down by the half-full dish. Even without the details – perhaps specially without the details – the story made her feel cheap and small.

And that after all wasn't the worst of it. The worst had happened this morning when the postman delivered . . .

She wouldn't let him get to her, she wouldn't. But her hand, acting of itself, pushed her plate away.

Kate laid her knife and fork alongside the neatly cleaned skeleton on her plate. 'I hope you haven't been off your food like this all weekend?'

Amy shrugged. 'I suppose I haven't eaten much.'

'Why on earth didn't you get in touch?' Kate asked. 'You didn't need to be on your own with all this.'

41

'I did need to,' Amy said. 'I had to . . . to work through it in my own mind.' She also hadn't wanted to tell it, she knew that now. 'Besides,' she added, justifying herself, 'you're so busy with reports and all.'

'And have you?' Kate asked. 'Have you worked through it?'

Amy shook her head.

'Of course not,' Kate went on, 'how could you, without talking about it? It's a rotten thing to happen to anybody.' She glanced at her friend's abandoned meal. 'I take it you've finished eating?'

Amy nodded. 'Go ahead, enjoy your smoke.'

Kate drew her cigarillos from her handbag and lit one with deft, quick movements. 'Now,' she said, flicking out the match, 'say what bothers you most about this Robert business.'

'The . . . the . . .' Amy gave up, stared through the window at the cold, clear, pale blue sky, and tried again. 'The guilt, I suppose.'

Kate nodded. 'Is it any use telling you that's silly?'

'I don't know.' Amy forced herself to look through the twisting, aromatic smoke. She couldn't quite meet Kate's eyes, sympathetic though they were, but she could at least fix on the clean decisiveness of the gold-rimmed glasses. 'Didn't I,' she offered, 'bring it all on myself?'

Kate turned away to breathe out her smoke. 'Do you feel able to go on about that?'

'Well . . .' Oh, the clean, clean blue of that sky; so infinitely easier to look at than the smeared black shine of their table. 'I went to bed with a man I didn't love,' she managed in a rush, and was able once more to fix on those gold-rimmed glasses.

The eyes behind the glasses remained intent. 'You've done that before.'

'I know. I've been doing it ever since I left home.' Amy kept her gaze on the table. 'I suppose it's a kind of reaction from all those years when I was so busy, and never met anybody . . .' She trailed off, disgusted at her lame attempt to excuse herself. 'This time,' she admitted at last, 'it caught up with me.'

'It did?' Kate blew another cloud of smoke, then sat back on her narrow bench with a deliberate air of repose. 'Think it through again, only leave out the love.'

'But that's just what I did,' Amy insisted, refusing to spare herself. 'Left out the love.'

'Think,' Kate urged matter-of-factly, 'of what else was wrong between you and the Demon . . .' She bit off the nickname. 'Between you and Robert.'

'Is there anything else that matters?'

'You're talking like a cheap romance.' The placid voice came as near as it ever did to reproof. 'Of course other things matter.'

Amy straightened and looked once more through the smoke. This time she found the small grey eyes looking back at her, transparently bright and alive behind their polished lenses. At once she understood, as so often in this friendship, exactly what her friend meant to convey.

'Of course!' She shook her head, wondering why she hadn't seen it till now. 'It isn't that I didn't *love* him, is it? That's beside the point.'

Kate nodded, and waited.

'It's that I didn't *like* him,' Amy finished, enlightened. 'I should never have gone to bed with a man I didn't *like*. I always knew he was a bastard.'

'And thought it didn't matter.'

'It's worse than that. I thought it made him . . .' Amy broke off. *I thought it made him sexy*, she'd almost said, but after last Friday she could no longer utter the trivial, silly word.

She looked round the bar. It had more customers now, among them a man who had just arrived alone. There he stood, surveying the room with the flicking, predatory glance she knew so well. It reached her and lingered as that male glance so often did, and she returned it absently. One part of her noted his neat, fair head, the height of him in that smooth, expensive overcoat.

His eyelids drooped, signalling, and she looked quickly away. No thanks, not yet. Probably never again in all her life.

'The trouble is,' she went on, returning to the task of excusing and explaining her involvement with Robert, 'a lot of men have a bit of the bastard in them.'

Kate pursed her lips, not about to express an opinion.

'Which makes it harder to pick out the real *psy* . . .' she bit off the ugly word '. . . the real bastards,' she finished lamely.

44

'Well, anyway, you're clear of him,' Kate comforted. 'That's the main thing.'

'If only I could be sure!'

Kate blinked at the force of the outburst, then put her head on one side. 'There's more, isn't there?'

Amy nodded.

'More and worse?' Kate asked.

Amy clasped her hands tight on her lap, while Kate stubbed out her cigarillo in the ashtray. 'Whenever you're ready, my dear.'

'It . . . it might be nothing . . .' She told of what Robert had shouted from his window, his outline dark against the lit curtains.

'*I'll get you for this, Amy Hammond,*' he'd said. '*I'll get you if it takes me forever.*'

At the time she had felt nothing but relief, right through the tense journey home. Only in the sleepless night had the self-loathing started, and the misery, and the wondering about those last, threatening words.

'You were bound to have a reaction,' Kate said into one of the long pauses. 'It'll pass. Just don't let him frighten you.'

'I told myself that,' Amy agreed. 'I tried . . .' She broke off, and glanced down at the food she had failed to eat. 'But still I didn't sleep,' she added, and went on with her story.

Saturday had dawned pink and perfect. Helped by the bright, frosty weather, Amy had done her best to be positive about her unplanned weekend at home.

45

The bruise on her neck invisible under her outdoor clothes, she'd shopped for food, chatted with friends in the village's cosy, ancient high street, then gone on to Ashford where she had found and bought the moss-green sweater she now wore.

The afternoon and evening had been harder. She'd considered going swimming, until she remembered that livid, branding bite and quailed from exposing it to the world. Still, she'd done the housework, cooked for the freezer, tied up some Christmas parcels.

'And jumped every time the phone rang,' she added ruefully.

'Did Robert call?' Kate asked.

'No, but that didn't stop me worrying that he might. Or worse, that he might come and see me . . .' At last she had unplugged both her phones and watched a horror film on television. She had gone to bed in the small hours, regretting both the lateness and the violent, creepy images the film had left in her mind.

Sunday had been worse. The usual long call home had been so difficult, trying to sound normally cheerful, then blaming her depressed tone on fatigue and the time-consuming task of report writing. When she put down the phone, she had at once unplugged it again. Then she made sure the door was locked and bolted, before she started trying to prepare her Year Seven reports.

She had struggled on for an hour before she gave up. Heavy-eyed and heavy-headed, she finally admitted that her listed grades made no sense to her, and that

46

she couldn't think of a single comment to make even on her most outstanding pupils. So she tried the more automatic task of heading blank report covers with the names of her own form pupils, but had to leave that too.

'You should see all the scrunched report covers in my wastebin,' she observed ruefully. 'Could you let me have your spares?'

'Some of them.' With all her forbearance, Kate couldn't resist a glance at her watch. 'So what did he *do*, Amy?'

'I'm coming to it. I've never been so glad of a Monday – yes, really,' she said to her friend's raised eyebrows. 'All I wanted was to be in school and busy. Only, the post . . .' She broke off, hating to tell what the post had brought.

'Amy,' Kate said gently, 'We really haven't much time.'

'Sorry.' She took a deep breath. 'You, er, you have to understand that when I left Robert I, er, I hadn't anything on.'

Kate frowned. 'It's lucky you didn't catch your death.'

'It was all right, I'd left my clothes in his hall. I managed to get my coat on . . .' Memory overwhelmed her. She could almost feel the unfamiliar roughness of the coat against her misused body, the November chill on her ankles, the biting cold asphalt under her bare feet. She clenched her fingers as if they still held her car key, still aimed at the lock of her car door. Thank heaven it had opened so smoothly in spite of her shivery clumsiness.

'So what was in the post?' Kate prompted gently.

'My stocking,' Amy began in a rush. 'I must have dropped it in the drive or somewhere.'

'And Robert returned it?'

'All wrapped in Christmas paper.'

'That's a lot of trouble to take,' Kate murmured, giving her friend the time she needed, 'over one stocking.'

'In a neat little cardboard box,' Amy managed to go on, 'like it might have held a . . . a stapler, or a pencil sharpener.' She swallowed hard. 'Recorded delivery. A typed address label, or I'd have known the writing . . .' She trailed off, started again. 'I expect I'd have opened it anyway. I signed for it, chatted to the postman . . .'

She struggled on and told the rest. How, needing scissors, she had taken the innocent, gilt-wrapped package to her newly cleaned kitchen. How she had stood at her sink facing the garden, amid the scents of soap and spices, cut open the Christmas paper, and seen . . .

'It wasn't just your stocking, was it?' Kate asked, carefully matter-of-fact. 'It must have been something worse, to make you look like that.'

Amy nodded, unzipped her bag, and brought out the box. She set it on the table, a four-centimetre cube of strong cardboard with white paper glued to its top. On the paper an eye had been drawn in spidery black ink, the pupil a black blob, the iris coloured by felt-tip scribbles to a glaring yellow-brown.

Kate leaned forward to look at it. 'Not nice, I agree.'

'I suppose,' Amy said, 'he means it to be the same colour as his own eyes.'

'Did he write anything?'

'He didn't need to, did he? The message is clear.'

'I'm watching you?'

'Or an eye for an eye. Or the evil eye . . .'

'And your stocking inside?'

Amy nodded. 'All wadded round, to make a sort of . . . nest.'

'A nest for what?'

Amy opened the box, and tipped the conker on to the smeared black table. Too flattened to roll, it sat there in its sorry, shredded skin, its string curled round it like a snake.

'Is that so awful?' Puzzled, Kate picked it up. 'I can see that it's lost a few matches . . .'

'Look closer,' Amy said. 'It's been hit from top to bottom, the same way the string is threaded.'

Kate obediently peered down at the battered object. 'I see what you mean. Another conker would have bashed it on the side, not the top.'

'I think he did it with a hammer,' Amy affirmed. 'See that round dent where a hammer head could have squashed into it?'

Kate put the conker down, momentarily lost for words.

'He talked about having a niner somewhere, from when he was eleven,' Amy went on. 'Can you imagine him going to the trouble of finding it, and doing that to it?'

'It is a bit . . .' Kate began, searching perhaps for some not-too-disturbing word.

'Weird.' Amy said it for her. 'And nasty. Especially when I remember that he'd just compared my hair to a conker. Then there's this.'

Gingerly, with finger and thumb, she lifted the black wadding from the box and held it up. Slowly it dropped and fluttered to its full length, her stocking shredded to rags by what could only have been a knife or a pair of scissors.

'Not nice,' Kate said again. 'Not at all nice, I agree.' She gave her head a little shake, clearly turning her mind to more practical ideas. 'Have you kept the wrapping?'

'I have, yes.' Amy dropped the stocking back into its box. 'Though there doesn't seem much point. I suppose you're thinking of the police, as I did?' Seeing her friend's nod, she went on, 'And what do I tell them?'

'That you've been sent offensive materials through the post?'

'An old conker,' Amy said in a flat, leaden voice. 'A stocking. A drawing of an eye.'

Silenced for a moment, Kate chewed her lip. Then she spoke in a new tone, purposeful yet undramatic. 'You're well rid of him, Amy.'

'*If* I'm rid of him.'

'Come on, my dear. He vented his temper, that's all.'

'And if he has some more temper to vent?' Amy demanded. 'What if he s-s-s . . .' she stammered over the barely speakable word, 'what if he *stalks* me . . .'

'Now you're way off,' Kate's even voice interrupted. 'This is a man whose job takes up all his time, and who's ambitious to get on in it.'

'That's true,' Amy agreed, comforted. 'He's going to family lunch next Sunday, with the junior Drews.'

'Is he indeed?' Kate considered this new information, head on one side. 'Is that what brought on the proposal, then?'

Amy nodded. 'I suppose they told him to bring his girl along, and he decided I could be it.'

'What a pity you didn't just accept,' Kate said lightly.

Amy stared at her. 'The invitation, you mean?'

'Both. Taking you to the lunch would have changed his mind about marrying you.'

'I beg your pardon,' Amy mock-bridled, realizing she was being teased and trying to respond in spite of her worries. 'I don't eat my peas with a knife, you know.'

'You're no yes-woman though, are you? In fact,' Kate went on, pretending to consider the matter, 'you have a definite tendency to bossiness.'

'I haven't!' Amy said, nettled. 'No more than most teachers . . .'

51

'If he'd seen you in the ordinary world,' Kate persisted, 'instead of just in bed, he'd have found you out long ago.'

'It's only that I'm good at making boys behave when they're being silly . . .' Amy broke off, feeling muscles relax which she knew now had been clenched for days. Could she really be smiling, smiling as though she meant it, smiling because she had found something funny to smile at?

'I did, too, didn't I?' she said slowly. 'At least, if I didn't exactly make him behave . . .'

'You certainly stopped him messing about.' Kate glanced at her watch with the air of a job accomplished. 'Time we were getting back.'

Amy swept up the flattened conker and dropped it into its box on top of the shredded stocking. Picking up the lid, she studied the baleful eye. 'He can't draw, can he?'

'There are a lot of things he can't do.' Kate stood up, dropping her fat, clasped handbag into the shopping bag she used for her school things.

'There are, aren't there,' Amy answered softly, more at ease than she would have believed possible an hour ago. She returned the box to her bag, and drew the zip on it. Then she too stood, turning for one more view from the window to the sunlit, sheep-grazed hills. Somewhere out there in his dreary house, a dreary man had put himself to the trouble of trying to frighten her. He'd succeeded for a while, might be succeeding still if her friend hadn't worked this sunwise counter-spell and reminded her of her own power to resist him, her own effectiveness as a human being.

A final, ghostly image formed in her mind, of a hammer descending on a dark red conker. But even as it formed, it faded into the pale blue winter sky, and Amy returned to the relative dimness of the rambling bar.

'There's my cooking, too,' she observed. 'Far too plain for Robert's tastes.'

Kate smiled. 'I was coming to that.'

'You were going to make a list of reasons he would change his mind about marrying me?'

'I would have,' Kate said, 'if I'd needed to. You're feeling better, aren't you?'

'Much better.' Amy shouldered her bag. 'And . . . Kate?' She paused for one moment longer in the murmuring room. 'Thanks.'

CHAPTER 3

'MY sister goes to typing lessons now, Miss,' Tracy Norris announced, china-blue eyes accusing. 'An' she has to start all her paragraphs –' a dramatic pause – '*right up against the margin.*'

Amy tried not to be irritated by the girl's triumph at having caught out teacher. The trouble was, in these few English lessons she taught to fill gaps on the timetable, she was only too easy to catch out.

I never have these problems in drama, she thought. For one thing I know what I'm doing, and for another the class are always too interested.

'Not half an inch off it,' Tracy pursued her game, 'like you make us do.'

'That's how it's done in books,' Amy said, always ready to admit when she didn't know an answer, 'but I'll find out about it.'

She made a mental note to ask Kate. Treading as lightly as possible on the booming hollow floor of this hut which was her English classroom, she approached Tracy's desk and flipped open the story book which lay on it.

54

'Until I've found out, just do as it does here.'

Tracy studied the horsy text, unwilling to be convinced. 'The first paragraph starts against the margin.'

'And that's all.' Amy turned a page, and another. 'See?' She closed the book. 'Do get on, Tracy, or you'll never finish . . . Tim!'

'Me, Miss?' Tim Horner turned from his front desk, all rosy-cheeked innocence. 'I was only . . .'

'Only wasting time,' Amy cut in. 'As usual.'

The class waited, knowing the routine. Amy returned to her desk, this time letting her heels boom to add to the tension. 'That's seven minutes you owe me,' she informed Tim. 'Twenty-three to go.'

'Yes, Miss. Sorry, Miss.' Tim bowed his fair head over his scrawled page in good-natured resignation. He had the highest total of wasted lesson time in the class. That still left him well short of the thirty minutes which would earn him a lunch-time detention, but the threat kept him working. The rest of the class, having briefly enjoyed his defeat, settled back to their find-the-noun exercises.

'How d'you spell "saddle", Miss?' asked serious Jenny.

That meant she had finished her exercises and started her story. Amy sighed at the thought of having to read yet another piece about a horse, wrote the word on the blackboard, and turned to survey the rows of virtuously bowed heads. Now that she had them writing she mustn't hover and distract them. On the other hand they might need her help any time, so she couldn't begin any work of her own.

55

Half past three, she noted, and stifled a yawn. This was another thing that didn't happen in drama lessons, these spells when you couldn't do anything but watch the class working. Roll on quarter to four, and the final afternoon bell. Tonight she would go to bed early and sleep, sleep, sleep. Thank heaven for a friend like Kate, who could put things into proportion. After their talk, Amy felt able at last to forget Robert . . .

'Yes, Martin?' she said as the door opened.

Martin Sullivan glanced with scarcely veiled contempt at the hard-working, neatly uniformed class. Back in September he himself had tried to work for a while, and worn that uniform of dark red pullover and grey trousers. Now he sported faded jeans, checked shirt, and an over-large leather jacket. Outdoors he added a hands-in-pockets swagger, but he knew Amy better than to try that in the classroom.

'Phone.' He caught her eye, and hastily added 'Miss.'

Amy frowned. Friends and family never phoned during lessons.

'It's serious, Miss.' Martin's uncertain hardness gave way to his eleven-year-old sense of drama. 'Miz Brooke says I'm to behave and be nice to you, because of your trouble.'

Trouble? Amy's thoughts leapt to her family in Northumberland. Her brothers? David was a bit of a tearaway when he had the chance, and young Gareth had just got a motorbike . . .

56

'Keep working,' she ordered the class. 'I want you all to have this exercise finished by the end of the lesson. Come on then,' she said to Martin as she joined him at the door. 'Let's get you back to the office.'

Martin muttered something that sounded like 'Will if I want', but not loud enough to challenge. Indeed, once away from the class and his need to save face, he fell willingly into step at her side.

'I suppose you're waiting to see the Head again,' Amy asked, glad to be talking. 'Who caught you this time?'

Martin kicked a pebble. 'The filth.'

'Don't use that . . . the police?' She glanced sharply down. 'You're in trouble with the law?'

'I weren't doin' nothin'.'

'Only bunking off.'

'It's Monday. We 'ave maths Mondays.'

'If you went to maths you might learn something . . .' She broke off with a sigh. 'Where did the police pick you up?'

'I weren't 'urtin' their fuck –' he glanced anxiously up at her from under his coarse, sandy fringe, and went on with difficult restraint – 'their old cathedral.'

'Cathedral?' Amy wondered if she'd heard right. 'The police caught you in the cathedral?'

'Thought it might work better there, didn't I?'

'What might work better?' She had a crazy vision of shaggy little Martin trying out a defective video game before the high altar.

'Supposed to be good for sick people in there, innit?' He dragged along beside her, head down. 'People used to go there an' get well, didn't they?'

'You're ill?' She glanced down at him in quick concern.

'Not me.' Martin stuffed gloomy hands in his pockets. 'Bet it don' work anyway. It didn' when we done it in drama.'

In drama? Amy cast her mind back to last Friday's lesson, and the spells sunwise or widdershins. Martin had turned a spectacular set of backsprings and cartwheels which showed what an athlete he could be if he ever bothered. He'd later admitted, tongue-tied and scowling, that he'd gone sunwise to cure . . . somebody. And now he had taken this witch dance, which she had taught only to amuse and loosen up the class, into the hallowed quiet of Canterbury Cathedral.

'I were only in this little side place, not disturbin' nobody,' he said. 'An' this old geezer still comes up shoutin'. So I tell him to fu . . .' Once more he choked back the forbidden word '. . . that it ain't none of 'is business. An' 'e turns me in.'

'He wouldn't understand, Martin,' Amy said, appalled at the trouble she had brought on him. 'They're not used to . . . it isn't the way they do things,' she finished with a helpless glance down at his drooping head.

Dared she ask who he wanted made well? Or would that only worry him more, and push him further from being able to talk? Before she could decide, they had reached the office and the kind, bossy Irish secretary.

'Off to the Head with you,' Teresa said to Martin, and to Amy, 'I'm sorry for your trouble, Miss Hammond.'

'T-trouble?' Amy grabbed the phone, and heard an unknown male voice, muted and ceremonial.

'My sincere sympathies, Miss Hammond.' Amy clutched the phone tighter. 'This is George Kensing,' the voice went on with subdued authority. 'Funeral director. When may I call on you?'

'I . . . I don't know.' Amy sank to the chair. 'Wh-what's happened?'

'We have details to settle, Miss Hammond,' the voice soothed. 'Mrs Clark asked that you as her son's fiancée . . .'

'As what?' Amy interrupted in overwhelming relief. 'I'm not engaged to anyone.'

A pause. 'Not to Joseph Clark?' the voice enquired, 'who died this morning in St Bartelmy's after a road accident?'

'I don't even know him.'

Another pause. 'You are Miss Amy Hammond, of 27 Canterbury Road, Stribble?'

Amy admitted it.

'And there's no one on the staff with a similar name?'

'I . . . I don't think so.' She gestured to the fascinated Teresa, who could clearly hear every word. Teresa quickly scanned the staff list, then looked up and shook her dark head.

'Definitely not,' Amy said into the phone. 'Besides, that's my address.'

A long, long pause. When the voice spoke again, it had hardened to normal working tones. 'We talked to the hospital, of course. They do have a Joseph Clark in their . . . in those circumstances.'

Amy couldn't suppress her shiver that someone's death, some real loss, should be so heartlessly misused. She shut her eyes tight and shook herself, trying to gather her wits.

'Who . . . who spoke to you about it?'

'Mrs Clark . . .' The voice broke off, then went on with resigned, practical bitterness. 'A woman who claimed to be Mrs Clark, mother of the deceased.'

A woman? How had Robert persuaded any woman to help him with this silly, miserable, cruel trick? 'Are you sure it was a woman, Mr er . . .'

'Kensing,' the voice replied, clearly used to repeating it to the recently bereaved with their minds on other things. 'I'd better speak to our receptionist.'

'Could you ask her if there was anything . . .' Amy ran her tongue over her dry lips '. . . anything odd about the voice?'

'Odd?' Mr Kensing responded, 'I'll give her odd when I catch up with her. You wouldn't believe how many idiots try it on . . .'

'Ask her,' Amy interrupted, conscious of her waiting pupils, 'if it might have been . . .'

'. . . to get us to a stag night. A birthday party, even . . .'

'Perhaps I could talk to your receptionist myself?'

'Eh? Certainly not, Miss Hammond, you and your friend have wasted enough of my firm's time already.'

'I'm sorry, Mr Kensing . . .' And why the hell am *I* apologizing, Amy thought. 'But it wasn't I who wasted your time,' she went on, louder and more firmly. 'And at the moment, *you*' – she emphasized the word – 'are wasting mine.'

She might as well not have spoken. George Kensing was determined to have his say. 'You'd better tell your friend . . .'

'He's no friend of mine, Mr Kensing.'

'. . . that we at George Kensing have better things to do . . .' Something penetrated at last, and Mr Kensing paused. 'What was that you said? He?'

'I think it may have been a man I know.' Amy kept hold of her growing impatience, and spoke as carefully as she could. 'If you want to ask him, he's . . .' She broke off, baffled. 'It's no good, he'll only deny it.'

'I suppose there's no point in throwing good time after bad,' Mr Kensing conceded. 'Luckily we always check and double-check.' He didn't sound as if he felt lucky. 'But I advise you to speak to your friend in the strongest possible terms . . .'

'I repeat, Mr Kensing, he's no friend of mine.'

'Then you might be wise to report him to the police.'

And a lot of good that would do. Not only would Robert deny his hoax; he would also, plausibly and with authority, throw the accusation right back at Amy. Subtly or not so subtly, with a great show of good sense, he would hint that he'd always suspected her of being unbalanced.

'I'll keep that in mind. And now if you'll excuse me,' Amy added loudly into the renewed flow of complaints, 'I have a class waiting. Goodbye.'

When she hung up, Mr Kensing was still talking.

'The impudence!' said round-eyed Teresa, neglected letters spread on the desk before her. 'The black heartlessness! How could anyone . . .'

'Yes, well,' Amy stemmed the flow. 'I must go. If there are any more calls for me . . .'

'Holy mackerel,' exclaimed good, Catholic Teresa in the strongest language she allowed herself, 'is that the time?' She seized an envelope and thumped it shut. 'There'll be no more calls of any sort, my dear,' she assured Amy as she started on the next envelope. 'The switchboard closes in a minute or two.'

'There might be . . .' More tomorrow, Amy meant to say, but changed her mind. Tomorrow could take care of itself. Tomorrow she might have had some sleep, and be better able to think. For now, she had a job to do.

The bell rang as she crossed the school yard. Her long-suffering class still waited, even Jenny whose only bus went at four. Amy sent the girl on her way with a brief apology, and dismissed the others in short order.

Being first-years, some wanted to stay and chat. Amanda's sheltie had six pups, did Miss know anyone who would like one? Jane's family were organizing a charity boot sale on Saturday, would Miss like to come? Tim was now playing the hind legs of the dragon in the Christmas production – did he still have to do his homework?

'Sheltie pups, how nice,' Amy said, 'I'll ask around. Sorry, busy on Saturday,' she told Jane, 'but good luck; I hope you make lots of money. Of course you do your homework as usual, Tim.'

They trickled out, and Amy realized with surprise how sorry she was to see them go. She cleared her desk and packed her bag with unusual thoroughness, checking her cupboard twice for things she might have forgotten. If she waited a moment longer the cleaners would be here, and she could ask them about that window she couldn't close. Or she could go and see Kate, and tell her about this latest . . . You'll do no such thing, she scolded herself; you've taken up quite enough of Kate's time and energy for one day. No, you'll go right out there, and drive home, and not think another thing about Robert and his childish pranks.

Easier said than done. An eye for an eye, the engine sang as it carried her through the outskirts of the city and into the gathering November dark. On the main road she found her foot pressing the accelerator from sheer tension, and had to make a conscious effort to slow down.

He's done you no harm, she told herself repeatedly as she turned the car along the narrow road to Stribble. Only you can harm yourself, by letting him scare you.

She wouldn't let him scare her, she wouldn't, she wouldn't. But when Stodbean Wood closed overhead, a cage of darkness where goblin shapes glided in and out of the headlights and tiny phantoms drifted against her windscreen, she had to speak aloud. 'It's only trees,' she assured herself. 'Only trees and the last of their leaves dropping . . .'

A new shape, pale, blunt-headed and silent, swooped across the road. Amy jammed on the brakes but already the thing had made its purposeful way into the trees, a barn owl intent on its hunt. 'Bad news for the mice,' she told herself in the eerie quiet left by the stalled engine. 'But not for you. Not for you.'

Ashamed of the tremor in her voice she hastily turned the key in the engine, and relaxed a little as it restarted first time. A minute or two later the lights of Stribble blinked beyond the tunnel of trees.

Normally she loved this winter approach to the village she had made her home. Even now its cosiness cheered her, the street lamps beckoning, the flint walls of the church glinting briefly in her headlights, the houses of the Canterbury Road shedding coloured chinks of light through winter-lined curtains as she eased between them to where, on the white-lit inn sign further along the street, Lord Nelson clapped the telescope to his blind eye. Nearing the disciplined shape of her own hedge, close-clipped under the street light, she almost felt herself relaxing.

But not for long. Of all times for someone to steal her parking space. Worse, the battered blue van stood far too wide into the road. She had to bump round it, up to the opposite pavement and down again before she could park, uncomfortably tilted, on the rising ground at the other side of her own gate.

Harold Clark, said the lettering on the side of the van, *Heating Engineer*. Struggling to climb out of her car against the force of gravity, Amy pictured Harold Clark taking his ease in the cosy saloon bar. All right, so the inn's little car park was unusually full for this time of the evening but he could have found space by the church. Only then he would have had to walk a yard or two, the idle . . .

'Are you Amy Hammond?'

The inn door had opened, spilling yellow light over the tall, blurry figure which had emerged. The door closed and the figure crossed the car park in the fitful light from the inn sign. Amy put up a hand to shield her eyes from the street light, but still couldn't see the face clearly. The voice had been a man's, the figure was tall as a man. Amy put a hand behind her and grabbed the cold, reassuring curve of her wrought-iron garden gate.

He crossed the road towards her. 'Can I have a word?'

He sounded mild enough, his voice soft and slightly hoarse. As he came into the street light she saw that he was wearing a dark leather flying jacket.

'A word?' he repeated, a little reproachful now.

'What about?' Still facing him, she felt for the catch of her gate.

'My name's Clark,' he said. 'Without an e . . .'

'So it's you,' Amy interrupted wrathfully. 'Before we go any further, would you please . . .' She broke off, whirling to the tortured shriek behind her. She hadn't known she was opening her garden gate. I must oil the hinges, she thought as she propped it back and another high-pitched creak tore at her nerves. The noise sent her hurrying into the garden, too fast and too far. Before she knew what was happening her foot had dropped lower than she meant it to, and the darkness had come up to her with a jarring thud.

That damned step down from the gate. Her hands and knees throbbed where they had hit the concrete path, rods of pain shot through her arms and shoulders, and her head sang as she flopped over to one haunch and tried to regain her wits.

'Are you all right?' The man had followed her through the open gate.

Amy tried to scramble to her feet. 'I'm fine.'

But she wasn't. A sharper pain stabbed one knee as she unfolded it, and she hadn't put any weight on it yet. She gasped, dropped back to half-sitting, and tried to calm herself with a long, ragged breath.

'Let's see if I can help you stand.' He bent to her with hands outstretched.

'I'll manage.' She levered herself up with a huge effort. The chill concrete pressed her bruised hands and a fiery line of pain shot through her knee as, with the iron gate post cold beneath her clutching fingers, she stood lopsidedly upright. Casting round for support she found herself steadied by a leather-clad arm which had somehow got itself round her, its hand supporting her elbow.

'Have you got your keys?'

'Of course I've . . .'

'Right, then let's get you indoors.'

As she hobbled through the darkness, his arm at her back urging her forward, she wondered how on earth she had got into this. But she knew the answer. She had panicked, and now she needed help. She couldn't have gone anywhere without that supporting arm, and she absolutely needed to lean on this other hand which grasped hers.

Strange, pungent smells surrounded her, blocking out the wintry scents of earth and leaves. What were they? They mingled oddly yet somehow fittingly with the stronger tang of woodsmoke from the inn.

'Vinegar?' She sniffed again, reassured by the homeliness of it. 'Vinegar, and chemicals, and something else. Something foody . . .'

'What a winetaster you'd have made.'

'You don't need a winetaster's nose to pick this up. What is that stuff – paraffin? No, it's got perfume in it . . .'

'Easy now.' He urged her ahead of him into her tiny porch. 'Key?'

She fished it from her pocket, and managed to open the door without too much fumbling. Reaching into her dark hall she thankfully switched on the inside lights, and turned back to see at last who he was, this man who dressed in leather and smelt like a salad in a laboratory.

The thin yellow hall light shone down on dark-brown, close-curled hair, olive-dark skin, high cheekbones, full lips, a strong jaw. His high-crowned head conveyed a feeling both of elegance and of extraordinary power, and his eyes, set beneath arched brows, were a deep, astonishing, gentle blue.

Looking up into those eyes, Amy wondered why she had been so frightened. No one with such eyes could ever hurt her . . . You don't go by looks, another part of her mind argued.

'Shall we get you inside?' he suggested.

Amy stayed where she was, drawing strength from the light and her own territory. 'Thanks for helping me . . .'

'I'm not finished yet. In you go.'

Perhaps she wasn't as much recovered as she'd thought. She found herself obediently entering the cottage, her companion coming in after her and closing the door. At least she'd have more light, she decided, and propped herself against the walls of the tiny hall to press the switch just inside the kitchen. Its fluorescent tube blinked on-off, on-off in that way she found so irritating, then to the dimness of the hall added the flat, matter-of-fact brilliance she so much needed at the moment. If only her corridor-shaped kitchen offered even a stool she would go no further, but it didn't, and she must sit down. She hobbled on to the sitting room, switched on the ceiling light in its old-fashioned china bowl, flopped to the cushioned corner bench that ran round two sides of her pine dining table, and took another look at her companion.

He hadn't followed her into the room, but instead stayed in the doorway, his broad frame almost filling the space. He looked lithe and graceful, long-legged and wide-shouldered as he leant against the doorjamb.

'And now, what about a cold compress?'

Amy almost relaxed. He really wanted to help. She mustn't let her experiences with Robert unnerve her, above all not here in her own place. She glanced round at the blue curtains, the white walls, the report forms on the table, the oil painting of Lindisfarne Abbey she had found in a Wooler junk shop, all the signs that life went on as usual. In the cleaned-out hearth the fire she had laid this morning waited only the touch of a match. The two little blue armchairs stood before it as she had left them, and so did that coffee cup . . .

That half-full coffee cup on the mantelpiece, put down when she answered the postman's ring this morning. Amy shot stiffly upright, and winced as new pain radiated out red-hot from her damaged knee.

'Yes, a compress,' the man decided. 'And the sooner the better. You look awful.'

'Thanks!' she responded through pain-gritted teeth. 'Here, where are you off to?' He had gone, but she raised her voice and tried again. 'I don't want you to . . .'

No use, he was running a tap in the kitchen. Presently she heard a shower of light knocks like a spirit at a seance, and then he was back, his strange, chemical-domestic scents eddying before him as he approached her.

'Here you are.' He proffered her map of Kent tea towel, soaked and twisted lumpily together with the corners knotted into each other. 'Put that where it hurts.'

She accepted the dripping object and stared down at it. So this was how he'd made those knocking sounds, loosening the ice cubes he must have taken from her freezer. She fingered their cold squareness through the towel.

'Go on,' he urged in that soft, hesitant voice. 'Use it.'

She shrugged. 'Oh well. Seeing you've brought it.' She raised her skirt and applied the compress to the puffiness of her knee. The chill spread clammily over her stocking, but almost at once the pain eased to a more manageable ache.

'And you ought to have your feet up.' He glanced from her to the armchair, came to a decision, and stepped forward to take hold of her two hands. 'Let's get you organized.'

'I'll organize myself, thank you!'

But already he had her upright, the vinegar-and-food-and-chemical scent overwhelming as he guided her to the armchair he had chosen. Before she could protest any further he had settled her in it, whisked her raffia stool from its place by the wall, topped it with a cushion, and raised her still-booted foot to rest on it. She had to admit the relief was enormous, especially when she applied his cold compress once more to her knee.

Feeling almost human, she gazed up at him. That really was a remarkable coat, its leather worn and lived-in, a genuine flying jacket. It had cost someone real money, that coat, but a long time ago. It was the oldest garment she had ever seen outside a museum, its leather creased and discoloured yet still supple, giving out a sheen against the matt dark brown of the fur collar.

'Good, eh?' Conscious of her inspection he raised his arms expansively to show off the coat.

Amy sniffed at the new waves of pungency the movement released. 'What on earth makes it smell like that?'

'It hasn't aired out yet, then?' He raised an arm and sniffed the the leather. 'I suppose I've got used to it.'

'That's some getting-used.'

'Well, it's two days since I treated it. Which is worst, the mothballs or the oil-and-vinegar?'

'I knew it was salady,' Amy said, pleased that her nose had been so accurate. 'Why oil and vinegar?'

'It's Mrs Beeton's recipe for reviving leather.'

'You're sure you got the right page in the book?'

'*Linseed* oil and vinegar,' he pointed out with dignity. 'It's from her Household Hints. And you still haven't told me which is strongest.'

'The mothballs,' she said without hesitation. 'So that's what they smell like?'

'You mean you didn't know?' He seemed astonished. 'You never smelt mothballs before?'

'Now you know how the other half lives. Why are we talking so much about mothballs?'

'They're useful things,' he retorted, defending them. 'Years of mothballs is one reason why this –' he stroked the collar – 'is in such good nick.' He gathered the coat around him with pride.

But Amy had stopped listening. She had just remembered the van outside her gate, with this man's name on it.

'You realize,' she said suddenly at class-quelling volume, 'that your wretched van is in my parking space?'

He stared at her with those blue, gentle eyes. Then he turned to the dining area, took one of the two straight chairs that supplemented the corner bench, brought it to the fireside, and sat on it. What long, long legs he had, and how limber their action in spite of the restraining stiffness of those ancient tweed trousers . . .

What the hell's the matter with me, Amy asked herself angrily. After what happened this weekend. And he isn't even my type, too bossy . . .

'Do sit down,' she said acidly to cover her embarassing thoughts.

'What? But I already am . . . oh. Sorry.'

'Sorry doesn't get your van out of my parking space. Surely you must have seen that I've nowhere else . . .'

'That's not my van.' He sounded suddenly, unaccountably sober.

'Oh, come on, don't try and wriggle out of it that way,' Amy said, exasperated. 'I suppose it belongs to a different Harold Clark, Heating Engineer?'

'I'm not Harold Clark Heating Engineer,' he told her with persistent calm. 'I'm Paul Clark Antiques.'

Silenced, Amy surveyed him. That explained the coat, then; he took an antique dealer's pleasure in old things of any kind.

'That's what I want to talk to you about.' He shot her an enquiring look from under his arched eyebrows. 'There's something odd going on; we all need to hear from you.'

'Who all?' Amy felt the ever more familiar hollowness return to the pit of her stomach. 'Hear about what?'

'About why all us Clarks've been called here for different reasons.'

'All you . . .' She broke off. 'What do you mean? How many Clarks can there be . . .?'

'Well –' he held up a hand, counting on long fingers which broadened at the tips – 'Felicity's here to pick up your dog . . .'

'I have no dog.'

'I'd probably gathered that. Then there's Dave, who thinks you want driving lessons . . .'

'I don't.'

Paul Clark nodded. 'We all saw you do that tough bit of parking.'

Amy remembered the van once more. 'And I don't want anybody to engineer my heating, either.'

'Poor old Harold.'

'Poor nothing, if that's how he . . .' She stopped, struck by the tolerant, almost affectionate tone of long acquaintance. 'You know him?'

'He's my cousin,' Paul Clark explained. 'That's how we got talking, and the other two at the table joined in.'

73

He glanced at his watch. 'They're all waiting to hear from me.' But he showed no sign of moving.

'There was another Clark.' Amy remembered her talk with the undertaker this afternoon, and shuddered. 'Maybe that's what gave him the idea. Maybe he went on and picked Clarks out of the yellow pages.'

'Who did?' Paul Clark still spoke with that slow, deliberate calm. 'Do you know who's doing this to you? To all of us?'

Amy tried to gather her wits. 'I suppose he booked you all by phone?'

'He?' Paul Clark stared at her intently. 'Three of the calls were made by a woman claiming to be you.'

Amy revived a little, sensing a lead. 'Was yours one of those?'

He shook his head. 'Mine was from Darby and McMorris, Canterbury solicitors. Or that's what he said.'

'So he didn't bother to disguise his voice for you.' Amy tried to hold back her growing dread. 'And what were these solicitors supposed to be doing, that needed your help?'

'Valuing your cottage and its contents.'

'I was supposed to be selling it all?'

'You were supposed to be . . .' Paul Clark stopped, looked away, looked back, then leant forward, alert yet strangely gentle. 'You were supposed to be dead.'

CHAPTER 4

'Well, the fridge is all right.' Harold Clark edged into the living room with his stooping, apologetic air, deposited his gangly length on the dining bench, and reached for the padded shirt he had left there. 'Properly earthed,' he added, shrugging the shirt on over his T-shirt with the well-faded motorbike picture, 'as far as I can tell.'

'Thanks,' said Amy from her armchair by the unlit fire.

An unfortunate accident with a piece of electrical equipment, Paul had been told. Now he and two other Clarks were all over her home, checking every piece of electrical equipment they could lay hands on.

They wouldn't let her stir. They had even taken her coat off for her, permitting her to stand up one-legged for only the briefest moment so they could slide it off her shoulders. Dave had held her waist on the pretext of helping her balance; Paul had taken the coat and hung it in the hall next to his own remarkable garment;

Harold had settled her back in the chair with a plastic bowl from the kitchen to hold the dripping icepack.

That had been an hour ago, straight after Felicity Clark had left to take care of her dogs. Ever since then Amy had sat here, officially immobilized. She supposed it was for the best. She hated having to keep still for so long, but certainly her knee hurt less, hardly at all now as she shifted it on the cushion.

Harold bent to his canvas bag and carefully put away the circuit tester he had been using. Presented with the dark top of his head, Amy saw that his hair curled thickly like his cousin's, but he wore it longer and arranged into soft-rolled curls. He had the same olive skin as Paul too, but his eyes were different, dark and tilted in a way that might challenge devastatingly if he ever grew up and acquired some confidence.

'Of course,' he went on, emerging from the bag with a thermos which he set on the table before him, 'you'll have to . . .'

'Coasters,' Amy cut in before she could stop herself.

'Oh. Sorry.' He looked about for them.

'In the stand,' she said with what she feared was her classroom manner. 'There, in the middle of the table.'

'Cheers.' He took two of the woven straw coasters, one for his thermos, the other for its cup. After a moment's reflection he took a third coaster and placed it under the gadget, some special kind of screwdriver, which Paul had left on the table. Watching him, Amy was pleased to see him so careful.

What an old maid I'm getting to be, she thought. Yet still she hated to risk ring marks or scratches on the smooth greyish-gold of her table. Bad enough to have it littered with the three soiled plates which had held the suppers the Clarks had fetched over from the Nelson. Well, two plates at the moment, until Paul returned from the compost heap where he was taking, at her request, her half-eaten pizza.

Perhaps she should have asked him to take the conker as well, and the stocking, and the drawing of an eye. Oh, how she longed to be done with them and forget them. But no, the Clarks said she must keep them; that though they weren't in themselves criminal evidence, they might help later, if other, worse things should happen.

Amy shivered and felt queasy at the thought. Paul had wanted to take out Dave's chicken bones as well, but she had said no, some dog might eat them and hurt itself, or else the seagulls would throw them messily about. She wished now that she had let them go anyway; she could smell their greasiness from here.

Ah, that was better. Harold had poured delicious-smelling coffee from his thermos.

'I could have made you some fresh,' Amy felt bound to protest.

'This is as good as fresh.' Harold bent to his bag again, and came up with a tiny bottle half-full of milk. 'My mum buys it special. Besides,' he added, uncapping the little milk bottle and adding its contents to his coffee, 'Paul says you're not to move.' He produced the argument with such a clinching air that in spite of her worries Amy almost smiled.

'You're very young,' she said, 'to be running your own business.'

Harold paused, thermos cup halfway to his lips. 'It's my dad's business,' he said, mildly injured. 'Didn't Paul tell you?'

'He may have done,' Amy said. 'I've a lot on my mind just now.'

''S all right,' Harold assured her, blushing. 'Normally Dad would come himself when it's the chance of a new order, but he'd a job over Harbleden. Besides –' Harold sipped his coffee – 'he thought there was something funny about this call.'

'And how right he was.' A slashed stocking and a destroyed conker, gift-wrapped. A series of fake phone calls, one of which said she had died . . . Amy went on talking, too quickly. 'So you and your father are both named Harold?'

Her companion darted her a glance from those leaf-shaped eyes, then stared into his coffee as if seeking his fortune there. 'Call me Hal,' he mumbled, and at once made a great business of finishing the coffee and returning the cup to the thermos.

Amy sighed. Why did she attract so many of these very young, insecure men? Two years ago, when she'd first started at Oaklands High, some of the older boys had been a real nuisance. Luckily they had all gone, and the present generation, having known her so long, simply regarded her as one of the fittings. However, that still left odd characters like the maths student currently with them on teaching practice, and now Harold . . . Hal? She had a sudden inspiration.

'Is that what your mother calls you?'

'Well, no,' he admitted, puzzled. 'That's her name for my dad, see. Mostly she calls me . . .' He blushed; presumably he had almost given away some family pet-name. 'Well anyway, she often calls me Harold.'

'Then so will I,' Amy announced, and went on talking to smooth over the rebuff. 'Why hasn't your dad got "& Son" on the van?'

'He will have,' Harold said, pleased at her interest in this at least, 'soon as I'm eighteen . . .'

'Right, I've checked the bedside light.'

That was stocky, fair-haired Dave, erupting in the doorway with typical brashness. Strange how all these Clarks had such different natures; Felicity large and milky and slow-moving; this one punchy and determined to impress.

'An' I had a look in the bathroom while I was about it,' he went on, his deep-set blue eyes alight with conscious virtue. 'Cheers, mate.'

He returned Harold's screwdriver. Amy suspected it was typical of him not to keep such a basic tool in his car, and have to borrow it. He seemed somehow – she sought for the word – somehow uncommitted; as in the way that he hadn't even taken off that handsome sheepskin jacket for the job, let alone rolled up the sleeves of that dark blue sweater with the *Le Coq Sportif* embroidered on the chest under the little red silk rooster.

'Now then.' He clapped his hands together expansively. 'My turn to get 'em in . . .' He broke off, sniffing. 'You drinking *coffee*?' he asked as if naming a noxious poison.

'I am,' Harold responded stolidly.

He raised his bag to his knee and took from it a rolled-up plastic case. Unrolling it, he tucked the returned screwdriver into place with the caressing movements of a father putting a loved child to bed. When he had returned the case to the bag he repacked his thermos, which clearly also had its own proper place. Dave watched him with growing contempt.

'D'you take that gear everywhere with you?'

'Only on jobs,' Harold answered, and stood up. 'Sorry again,' he told Amy, 'about your parking space.'

'That's all right . . .'

'Off back to Mum now, are you?' Dave asked witheringly.

Harold looked down from his superior height with a composure which made Amy revise her ideas about his lack of confidence. 'I want my supper.'

'You could've eaten with us,' Dave pointed out; he had been through this already. 'Then you could've stayed, instead of pushing off just when we're ready to enjoy ourselves.'

Amy listened with dismay. So he did mean to settle here and make a night of it! She wondered how she could tactfully explain that she didn't feel in the least festive.

'What I'm going to enjoy,' Harold said as he shouldered his bag, 'is my mum's jugged hare. She's keeping it hot.'

So that was what his brief call on the cellphone had been about. 'I appreciate your staying and helping,' Amy said, meaning it. 'Many thanks.'

''S all right.' Harold checked off on his fingers. 'Stove, fridge, these lamps –' he gestured to where they shed their gold-shaded light from the television and the bookcase – 'wall-switches, toaster, clothes-washer . . .'

'An' don't forget the kettle I did,' Dave put in. 'An' the bedside lamp. And I had a look in the bathroom.'

'Mind now,' Harold went on, ignoring the interruption, 'you'll need to get a proper electrician straight away in the morning.'

'Speak for yourself,' Dave put in, nettled. 'My jobs'll be all right.'

'Can't be too careful, Dave.'

This was Paul, returned through the hall with Amy's now empty plate. Loose-limbed and unhurried in the yellow polo-necked sweater and old, fine tweed trousers which had appeared when he took off his coat, he moved to the table and stacked the three plates in one neat pile. The scent followed his movements, fainter than the coat but still detectable, linseed oil and vinegar.

'Though I'm sure you've done a great job,' he added peaceably to Dave.

Amy wondered if all of that branch of the Clark family were as good-natured and even-tempered as he and Harold seemed.

'You're off then, Harold?' he asked.

'Back to his jugged hare,' Dave said. 'What a bashdamper.'

Bashdamper? Amy, who had never heard the word before, decided it must mean somebody who left the party early. Poor Dave, his bash would be damped a whole lot more when she had convinced him that this wasn't a party at all. What a pity he didn't have dogs waiting for him, like Felicity, or a mother with dinner, like Harold.

In the event he proved unexpectedly easy to dislodge. She started the process right after Harold's departure by refusing to have a drink fetched for her from the pub.

'Not even now?' Dave asked incredulously. 'When we can relax?'

Speak for yourself, Amy wanted to quote back to him. Then she recalled his disapproval of what Harold had been drinking, and knew what to do. Putting her foot cautiously to the carpet, she gripped the arms of her chair and started to rise.

'That's right, let's relax. I'll get us some coffee.'

'Stay where you are,' Paul said at once. 'I'll get it.'

'Thanks, but it's hardly hurting at all now . . .'

'It will again, if you use it too soon.'

'Oh, all right.' Amy flopped back into the chair with unadmitted relief, and kept up the good work on Dave. 'D' you take milk and sugar?' she asked him.

'Eh? Oh. Don't bother with any for me, thanks. I'd better be going.' He looked ostentatiously at his watch.

'I hadn't realized how late it is . . .' He broke off as a rhythmic bass thump, muffled but relentless, made itself heard through the thick old walls of the cottage. 'Is that from the pub?'

Amy nodded. 'It's karaoke night.'

'They only have it on one special night?'

She shook her head. 'They run it all the time,' she told him with regret; she often found the noise troublesome when she was trying to work. 'But on Mondays they have a kind of karaoke happy hour, every fifth number free.'

Dave's foot had started tapping. 'I wonder if they've got "*Tiger Lil*"?'

Amy had never heard of '*Tiger Lil*', whatever it was, but didn't ask about it. 'They might have.'

'Maybe I'll just look in for a minute and see.'

He left so quickly that Amy barely had time to thank him. The music thumped louder as he opened the front door, softer as he closed it after him, stopped for a moment or two presumably between numbers, then pounded on as before. Paul went to the window and parted the blue curtains, letting in the yellow light of the street lamp and the white light of the inn sign.

'Will it go on for long like that?'

'It stops around ten,' Amy told him. 'Earlier – or they turn it down, I suppose – if somebody complains.'

'Odd to have a happy hour on a Monday.'

'I think the idea's to boost trade when it's otherwise quiet.'

'Well, I hope Dave gets his "*Tiger Lil*".' He spoke as if he meant it, dropping the curtain and gathering up the plates from the table.

'Seeing he was going to the Nelson anyway,' Amy commented, 'we should have asked him to take those back.'

'Oh, I don't think so.'

Paul spoke softly, without malice, but Amy knew at once what he meant. Never in life would Dave have agreed to turn up at the pub with his hands full of greasy plates.

Wondering why she hadn't seen it herself, she watched Paul disappear with them towards the kitchen. She heard the rubbish bin rattle, then the tap swished into the sink, a clean, companionable noise to hold off this feeling of darkness and danger which clamped down on her the minute she was alone in the room. Even that karaoke thump helped, she realized in surprise; at least it showed that other people weren't too far away.

'I've found your cafetiere.' Paul stood in the doorway, his yellow sweater lighting the air around him, his scent eddying its comforting domesticity into the room. 'Do you really want coffee?'

'I don't know.' Amy glanced up at him, surprised and oddly pleased that he had recognized her get-rid-of-Dave ploy. 'Decaf, maybe. I wonder where I put the beans . . . how about you?' she added, belatedly conscious that he was supposed to be her guest.

'Can I have some of that camomile tea in the cupboard?'

'Of course, what a good idea.' Amy sat straighter at the discovery of someone who shared her taste. 'So few people like that kind of stuff, I didn't think of offering.'

'So you'll have it too? Good,' he went on when she agreed, 'now all we need is the kettle and a couple of those mugs off their hooks.'

She saw what he meant. No decaf coffee beans to be located, no need for her to give laborious descriptions of where to find the grinder, no fuss with milk or sugar. She didn't have to explain a thing. What a nice man he is, she thought, with his sun-yellow sweater and Mrs Beeton smell, his quiet voice and soothing ways. Already she felt calmer, safer . . .

At that moment, without warning, all the lights went out. Amy froze like a hunted creature in the darkness. It wasn't a power cut; she could still hear the thump of the karaoke, woven now with the new, loud, irregular beat of her heart and the surge in her ears which must come from her fear-quickened pulses.

Ideas tumbled one after another through her mind, a catalogue of horrors compressed into a single second like the Bible on a grain of rice. Had Robert come here at last? Had he found a way to disconnect her power supply so that he could reach her in the dark and really hurt her? Must she wait here helpless . . .

'Get a grip!' she hissed aloud to herself, and drew a ragged breath. 'P-P . . .'

The breath whispered out again and she let the name die away unspoken, a new set of fears racing through her. She didn't know that man in the kitchen at all, had only met him two hours ago, had nothing but his own word for who he was and what had brought him here. Maybe it was all lies. Maybe he'd come here to help Robert. Maybe he was in Robert's pay . . .

Well, he wasn't going to find her just sitting here, waiting for whatever had to happen. She breathed in again, deep and slow this time the way she taught in drama relaxation exercises, in, out, in, out. That was better, her heart had quietened and her eyes adjusted to the dark. In fact it wasn't dark at all; light filtered through the curtains and showed shapes against the paleness of the walls; her picture of Lindisfarne, her bookcase, her television on its stand, over there by the door her dining table set into its corner bench with the chairs tucked into its other two sides.

It would make a useful weapon, a hard chair. Better than this foot stool she was pushing aside. She levered herself to her feet and stood for a second judging the distance to the nearer dining chair, testing her injured knee to find out how much of her weight it would bear. Then she set off across the floor . . .

Hell! How could she have forgotten the spindly occasional table Paul had set by her? He'd said it was to hold her tray, but she hadn't used it at all and now she had knocked it over with a bang and a rattle that sounded deafening to her pulse-maddened ears. She was lucky she hadn't tripped over it herself, and fallen again.

'Amy.'

A torch shone from the doorway, its scanning, yellow-white beam picking out the fallen table. Amy bent over, snatched the table up by the legs, raised it as best she could, club-fashion, and brandished it at the darkness beyond the torch.

'Don't come near me.' She tried to make it a warning growl and almost did, though she warbled once into the wrong register. 'Or I'll brain you.'

'Calm down.' The soft voice from behind the torchlight didn't sound in the least threatening, only amused. 'Tell me where your fuse box is, and I'll mend whatever's blown there.'

Amy lowered the little table but held on to it, still suspicious. 'Is that all it is?' she asked, her voice wobblier than ever now she had lowered it to normal speaking tone. 'A blown fuse?'

'Several, I should think. Fuse box?'

'In that little flat cupboard just inside the back door.'

'And wire?'

'The fuses are the push-button kind.'

'Right.'

The torch beam turned and disappeared, leaving Amy still waveringly upright, still clutching her table. She realized that she was holding its legs far too tightly; their corners had dug into her palms. She loosened her grip and blinked, dazzled, as the lights came back on.

So it had been fuse trouble, just as Paul had suspected. She placed the table carefully, over-carefully, by the arm of the chair where she had been sitting, and looked at her curled-over, red-marked palms.

'There.' He was back in the doorway, waving what she presumed was her own heavy black torch. 'I took this from the kitchen window sill. D'you want me to put it back there?'

Amy nodded. 'I . . . I keep it there . . .' Oh dear, if only her voice would settle down and sound normal '. . . for emergencies.'

'How sensible . . .'

'Don't condescend to me!'

There, that was more like it; she had managed to speak with real fire at last. And she had impressed him, she could tell by the way he blinked. For a second he stared at her, his placid brows drawn together in a small frown. Then he spoke, softer than ever.

'I wasn't condescending, honest. Only admiring your common sense. Now,' he went on before she could answer, 'do you trust me enough to sit yourself down and give that knee a chance?'

Amy stayed on her feet, holding on to her new hardness. 'Why did the lights go out?'

He shrugged. 'It happened when I plugged in the kettle.'

'But Dave checked that . . . Oh.' Almost she wanted to laugh, maybe with reaction, or maybe Dave's incompetence was really funny. 'He said the jobs he'd done would be all right.'

Paul shrugged again, accepting the ways of the world and such as Dave who peopled it. 'Are you going to sit down, now the panic's over?'

'I didn't panic!' Amy said, still venting her undirected anger. 'After everything that's happened . . .'

'It was only a way of putting it.' He raised his spread hands before him like a shield, but his voice continued soothing. 'C'mon now, sit.'

Still shakier than she would admit, Amy lowered herself reluctantly to her seat. Once there however, she strained forward. 'You're *sure* it was just the kettle?'

'When I switched on at the wall, the plug flashed like a firework,' he told her with a decisiveness which contrasted with his usual easy ways. 'I haven't looked yet, but I'd guess it's been rewired wrongly.'

He advanced towards her. It was all she could do to prevent herself cowering away in her seat, but he only put the foot stool and its cushion in place, and then looked at her expectantly. She returned her booted leg to it, and as if he recognized her fears he immediately moved back from her. Perhaps because of that, perhaps because she was now resting it at last, she realized that her knee had been hurting, and that now, in its new position, it hurt less.

'Dave said . . .' She tried to remember it over the black gulf of her recent fears. 'He said something about having done the bedside light as well.'

'I'll have a look at it presently, if you like. Now,' he added on a business-like note, 'supposing I rewire the plug of that kettle, and we have that camomile?'

'Yes . . . no . . .' She floundered to a halt, hating the weakness in herself which made her so indecisive. Another deep breath, hands deliberately loose on her lap, and she was enough in control to know what was worrying her.

'If I touch that lamp barefoot, I might get a bad shock.' And if it plunged the house into darkness again, leaving her alone and defenceless? 'Could you check it now, please?' She managed the last word as if she meant it. 'In case we forget.'

'I won't forget . . .' He broke off, his placid gaze recognizing something in hers. 'Ma'am.' He sketched a mock salute, right finger parallel to his thick-curled temple. 'Did Dave, er, fix anything else while he was up there?'

She had to admire his refusal to judge. After that small hesitation, he had put only the tiniest hint of irony into the question.

'He said something about having looked in the bathroom as well.' Recalling Dave's vagueness, she frowned. 'I wish I'd asked him what he meant. Electricity going wrong in a bathroom can be really dangerous.'

She marvelled that she could say it so easily. Could that be because she was speaking only of Dave, who with all his faults wished her no harm? Yes, she realized, she found it almost a relief to think of Dave's ordinary, human bungling rather than . . .

'Can you check?' she asked quickly.

'Sure.' Paul took up his screwdriver from the table. 'But you will call a proper electrician in the morning?'

'I certainly will,' Amy agreed at once.

'Right,' he said, and disappeared.

She heard his light tread on the stairs. The old boards hardly creaked under his weight; he must be taking several at a time and missing the noisiest. Once he reached the upper floor his footfalls sounded equally smooth through the ceiling.

He walks like an athlete, she thought. Or like a thief . . .

He had gone into the bathroom; she heard the little penetrating click of the string-pull light. She set her teeth for another plunge into darkness, but no, the room stayed tranquilly gold from her two lamps, and through the wide-open living-room door the white neon glare from the kitchen still lit the tiny hall. Maybe Dave hadn't done quite so much damage after all, she thought as she heard the cistern flushing. Paul must have taken the chance to use the bathroom while he was up there, and so far, nothing had gone wrong.

What was that? A sliding, rattling noise filtered down through the ceiling, something medium-heavy like metal against something hard and slippery and echoing like . . . like what? It wasn't too loud, not frightening in itself but unnerving in its unfamiliarity. Amy flung her head back and strained her eyes at the ceiling as if she might see through it, but the noise stopped abruptly and was not repeated.

After a while, she became aware that the pull on her throat muscles had drawn her mouth open; she must be gaping like a fool. She leant against the back of her chair and closed her mouth, careful not to let her jaw clench as it wanted to. And here were her fists balled up tight again, she must do something about that, and about her breathing, in, out, in, out . . .

Where *was* he? What was he *doing* up there?

Thump thump went the karaoke. Out in the street voices called and others answered, just as she heard them on any normal evening when people came to the pub or left it. This lot must be leaving; if they had just arrived she would have heard a car arrive and pull up. And yes, they were leaving, there went their car engine starting up and driving away. And there went the throaty diesel of her neighbours' car, also driving away; perhaps some of the voices had been theirs.

In and out went her breathing. She set herself to visualize a tidal river rising and falling; then thistledown lifting and settling; then flowers opening and fading; then she ran out of soothing images and just went on taking deep breaths, unnumbered and unmarked. Her electric wall-clock fussed away the seconds, the minutes, the five-minutes, the ten, the twenty.

Another car arrived; that would mean more voices in a minute. The engine of this last car had a different note, bangier, scratchier, less regular. It stopped, and the karaoke beat on. With the help of those everyday noises in the street her deep breathing was beginning to work; she felt calmer with each slow change-over from in to out, from out to in. And here was Paul coming down the stairs; she would show him how calm she could be.

'Where the hell have you been . . .' She stopped, abashed at her own hectoring hysteria, and closed her eyes for another deep breath. It changed midway to a questing, open-eyed sniff. 'Why is your jacket's smell so much stronger?' she asked, glad of the diversion.

'Is it?' He raised an arm to his nose, releasing a new wave of pungency. 'I expect it's because of my being so wet.'

'Wet?'

Why, so he was. The cable-stitch of his sweater clung to his lean frame, its yellow wool darkened with a great, irregular patch of wetness, and his hair curled more than ever. Individual strands of it, plastered against his temples and forehead, shone as he moved through the different circles of lamplight.

'It is just water?' she asked, unable to suppress her renewed fears. 'Nothing worse?'

'Nothing worse,' he assured her

He pulled one of the dining chairs up to the radiator and sat on it. Then he produced a towel from somewhere, and draped it over his head.

'That's my bath towel,' Amy said. 'You'd have found a clean one in the cupboard.'

He ignored her complaint. 'I'm wetter than I'd realized,' he said, muffled by the vigorously rubbing towel. 'I hadn't got round to doing anything about it yet.'

'What happened?'

'Nothing awful.' He emerged from the towel and bunched it round his neck. 'Dave must have fixed the cold tap at the wash basin.'

'It did drip a bit,' Amy admitted. 'Has he made it worse?'

'Not so much made it worse as jiggered it entirely.' Paul squinted ruefully down at his soaked sweater. 'When I tried to wash my hands, the turning bit of the tap fell in the basin.'

'So that's what the noise was.'

'You heard it? Well, after that the water shot up like a fountain.'

'Damn and blast Dave!'

'It's all right, I got the tap back together. And your bathroom isn't too wet. Most of the water –' Paul mopped at a drop which had trickled down his forehead – 'went over me.'

'I'm sorry about that.'

There I go again, Amy thought, apologizing for something that isn't my fault. But no, this wasn't an apology, she was just sorry, genuinely sorry he'd been made so uncomfortable. 'You'd better take that sweater off,' she suggested, 'and we'll dry it.'

Immediately, uncontrollably, shamelessly, a tantalizing, half-complete picture flashed into her mind of Paul without his sweater. Was he wearing a shirt under it? If so, that also would be wet and best taken off to dry. Would that olive skin be paler over his shoulders, or darker? Would his chest have more of that curly hair, or would it be smooth like the rest of him . . .

Stop this, she told herself angrily, it's nothing but adrenalin from all the upset. She watched him dab at the sopping sweater, and found something to distract herself.

'We could hang it over a radiator, but it might dry felted,' she told him. 'Let's light the fire, and put the airing rack in front of it.' That was better; now she could think of ordinary, domestic things. 'You'll find the rack in the shed to the right of the back door, and the gas poker's there too . . .' She broke off, her worst fears pelting back as a new noise penetrated their small, lamplit world of indoors. The tortured shriek from outside mingled weirdly with the karaoke beat, like the sound track of a horror movie. It stopped for a moment, then sounded again. This second noise was worse, a wail of grinding agony, yet it took away Amy's first, primaeval panic.

'It's my gate,' she said. 'Somebody's just come into the garden.'

At once the panic was replaced with a new, all-too-rational dread. She strained her ears, but the only thing she could hear was a car starting up, the same bangy, scratchy engine she had noticed while waiting for Paul. It puffed and snorted for a moment at some kind of manoevre, then changed gear and bang-scratched away into the distance. In the comparative peace it left behind Amy strained her ears, but not a footstep could she hear, or any other out-of-place sound.

'The gate was propped open.' Paul too had been listening, his head alert above the twisted bulk of the towel. 'You left it like that after you fell.'

'And nobody closed it later on?'

'We were all coming and going to our cars . . .'

'But that means the noise just now was somebody closing the gate, not opening it,' Amy half-whispered. 'Why would anybody do that?'

To make it harder for her to get away? To make it harder for other people to come in and help her? To have longer to do whatever he, she wouldn't name him, meant to do to her? Or to her home? Perhaps he meant to set fire . . . She pushed away the tumbling, terrified images and tried to listen to what Paul was saying.

'. . . a neighbour being helpful?' But he too kept his voice low, as if someone out there might be listening.

'They never have before,' Amy hissed back at him. 'Besides, I heard the neighbours go out a while back, and old Mrs Lambe on the other side . . .'

'Listen!'

She listened, and heard only stillness. The karaoke had stopped; she glanced at her watch and saw with surprise that it was eight o'clock, time for the half-hour rest they always gave it. No sounds came from the street or the car park either, no engines, no voices, nobody arriving or leaving. The village street beyond her garden must be as peaceful as it would ever be.

'I can't hear . . .'

'Shsh!'

He leant forward in his seat, raising his hand in a tense, quick gesture that made her catch her breath. Then she heard the noise that had prompted it; her gate rattling back and forth on its hinges as if someone were pushing against it, trying and failing to open it.

'But it doesn't lock,' Amy breathed. 'He only has to lift the catch.'

'Sounds like he can't.' Paul's brow creased in thought, and his voice almost regained its normal volume. 'Maybe he's hurt.'

Burnt with his own matches? Fallen into his own mantrap? Cut with his own blade, choked with his own fumes . . . Amy crushed down the ever-more-lurid pictures, and tried to make sense.

'He's right outside in the garden. He surely couldn't have done much without our hearing it?'

Couldn't he? Couldn't he just! But no, she wouldn't think of all the things which that unknown person might have done in stealth out there in her garden, just on the other side of that blue-curtained window . . .

Half with dismay, half with relief, she saw Paul remove the towel from his neck, dump it beside him, and rise to his feet. At any other time she might have asked him to take that wet towel off her table, but at the moment nothing could have mattered less.

'You're going out there?' she asked.

He nodded. 'That's the only way we'll find out what's going on.'

His voice had returned to its usual relaxed huskiness, but Amy was not comforted. 'You might get hurt.'

'I doubt it, but I'll take that torch of yours. It's heavy enough to make a useful weapon . . .'

The last word acted on Amy like a spring released. Before she knew it she was on her feet, not even thinking of her twisted knee, let alone feeling pain from it. 'I'm coming with you.'

'No you aren't.' He still spoke quietly, not arguing or ordering but simply stating a fact. 'You'd only be a liability.'

Amy's temper rose. This was her house, these were her problems; who was this stranger, this interloper, to tell her she would be a liability? Somewhere at the back of her anger she sensed a reluctance to be left alone any more, but then, why should she be? Why should she consent to be kept out of the action and not know what was going on in her own garden? She tossed her hair back over her shoulders, and summoned the hard-edged voice so well-known to troublemakers at Oakland Comprehensive.

'I'm coming . . .' She was tempted to go on, to reason and justify, but no, that would only waste time. '. . . and that's that,' she finished.

Paul opened his mouth to argue, looked down at her, and shrugged. 'OK. Wait till I get the torch . . .'

He got no further. At that moment a new noise arose from the garden, high and chilling and inhuman. Listening to the long baying howl, Amy stared at Paul and remembered how, when she first saw him from a distance, his furry, loping walk had made her think of a werewolf.

CHAPTER 5

'You see.' In the howl-filled dimness outside the front door, Paul had to shout close to Amy's ear. 'It's only a dog.'

'Are you sure?' She peered down the garden, making what she could of the shadow by the gate. 'It looks more like a wolf.'

The creature had quieted, she supposed at the sound of their voices. Its blackness merged with the rustling, twig-fretted dark so that she could see little of its size or shape, but the odd glimmer here and there showed it sitting on its haunches, its great wolf-head silhouetted against the pallor of the inn car park and weirdly framed by the wrought-iron patterns of the gate. It must know they were there; it seemed to be turning towards them.

'I suppose,' Amy observed from her knowledge of the Moor Fell dogs, 'it sees in the dark far better than we do.'

'I should think so.' Paul didn't sound at all disturbed at the idea.

'So it can see us better than we can see it.'

'Smell us, too, of course, given what a keen sense of smell dogs . . .'

'I know about dogs, thank you.' Ashamed of how irritable she sounded, Amy took a deep, deliberate breath and carefully controlled her voice before continuing. 'In short, it's got every possible advantage.'

Whatever the dog saw or smelt of them, it wasn't satisfied. Its muzzle thrust skyward again and a new, long, liquid howl, terrifying in its strength and wildness, curdled out of it.

As if the sound drew him, Paul started towards it.

'Where are you going?' Amy called after him, horrified.

'To quieten it, of course,' he called back over his shoulder.

'Don't be silly, it's bound to be dangerous. We should get the police . . .'

She trailed off, not sure he could even hear her in the dismal row. For a moment she watched his loose, easy movements, dark against the beam of the torch which he was now shining downwards to light his way along the concrete path.

What long, long legs he has, she thought. Are they the reason for that special way of walking, so fluid and strong and somehow carefree?

That walk seemed familiar to her, though she couldn't pin down why. After a moment she gave up and, with a confused feeling that he would need help, limped after him.

The dog had finished one howl and immediately started another. Amy caught her breath as Paul, well ahead of her on the path, reached the little step inside the gate and dropped to one knee. How could he dare to go so close to the dog, leaving himself so open should it choose to attack? He still shone the torch beam on the ground, but by the light that filtered upwards she could make out a shaggy black pelt, a broad greyish-yellow chest, and muscular greyish-yellow forelegs.

Not a wolf perhaps, but certainly some kind of alsatian, or at the very least a mongrel with alsatian blood. Remembering stories of how unreliable and occasionally savage this breed could be, she hurried down the path as fast as her lameness allowed

The wild, sky-pointing head seemed to grow ever more wicked and terrifying as she approached it. Yet Paul was actually reaching out to it, offering his open hand palm upward as if for a civilized introduction. Now he had even switched off the torch.

Amy shuddered, expecting to see him mauled or worse, but no, the dog stopped in mid-howl. In the blessed quiet that followed, broken only by ordinary street noises and ordinary garden noises, she saw the shadowy head sniff at Paul's fingers.

'Here, boy,' Paul said in his soft, soothing voice. 'What's all this about then?'

Amy had often smiled when she heard people talk to animals as if the creatures could understand and answer. Nobody did that at home, where the dogs were loved and valued fellow workers, often petted or praised or given commands but never asked questions.

Listening to Paul questioning this dog, Amy didn't feel in the least like smiling. 'Are you expecting it to *tell* you what's the matter?' she asked on a new surge of exasperation.

The dog looked towards her and snarled, an impressive set of teeth showing white in the gloom. She took a step backwards.

'Your tone worries him,' Paul said, keeping his own voice low and soothing. 'I expect he can smell your fear, too.'

'But . . . but it's *meant* to frighten me.' Amy struggled to express what she knew must have happened. 'That's why it's been brought here . . .'

She broke off. And if I let myself be frightened, she thought, he – or whoever it is – will have succeeded. And it's only a dog, she told herself, straightening her shoulders.

She knew dogs. All right, so this one was bigger and stronger than the border collies of Moor Fell, but it was still just a dog. She could rely on it to have all the usual loyalties and affections and enthusiasms of its race.

Paul had understood that at once, she thought wonderingly. He'd also seen that it was unhappy, which of course it must be or it wouldn't be howling like that. How clever of him, and how brave to have gone so unflinchingly close to it.

'Paul . . .'

'Sh!' In the near-dark he raised a hand with conscious smoothness, silencing her.

Too late; the great head lifted for the next howl. Here it came, a mournful funnel of sound which at this short range echoed louder and more chilling than ever.

Under it Amy heard Paul making more of those soothing noises. This time the dog ignored them, and presently he gave up and hissed back over his shoulder.

'If I knew his name it would help, but he hasn't a collar.'

'Of course he hasn't a collar,' Amy said. 'He'll be a stray that Robert's got hold of . . .' She broke off, partly in regret at having spoken Robert's name, partly to note that she had picked up Paul's attitude to the dog and called it 'he'. Across the road the pub door opened, shedding a new yellow light, a burst of voices, and a loose knot of figures which started on a more-or-less purposeful course across the car park.

'Great,' Amy said. 'Now we've got the Nelson regulars in on the act.'

One of the figures crossed the road well ahead of the others. 'What's he done now, Amy?' it shouted above the noise. 'Is that a dog he's dumped on you?'

Amy felt fear and irritation alike sink under a huge wave of depression. The usual topers would have been bad enough; she really could do without Dave just now. From his casual willingness to discuss her problems at the top of his voice, she guessed that he had already given an account of them to anybody in the bar who would listen.

'I suppose so,' she called back shortly. 'Somebody did.'

That, she realized for the first time, explained the gate creaking a few minutes ago. The intruder hadn't been entering her garden but leaving it. He must have closed the gate to keep the dog in, and the rattling which followed must have been it trying to get out. For the first time she felt true pity for the poor creature, caught up in human conflict far beyond its understanding.

Perhaps the dog picked up and understood her change of attitude. At any rate it stopped in mid-howl and its head swung once more in her direction. In the sudden silence, Dave's footsteps sounded light and brisk on the pavement as he arrived to stare down into the gloom over the gate.

'Sssww,' he whistled through his teeth. 'The size of him.' He raised his voice to one of the three men still approaching on the other side of the road. 'Come and look at this, Jim.'

'Keep your voice down,' Paul hissed from where he half-knelt by the dog. 'You're disturbing . . . Wait a minute.' His tone changed. 'Look at him.'

The dog had raised its head towards Dave, ears peaked forward.

'Jim,' Paul almost whispered, experimentally. 'Here, Jim.'

The dog's head swung round to him.

'Whassat?' Dave's friend had rolled over the road, a fat man with a bush of curly hair. 'You talkin' to me?'

'Good boy, Jim.' Paul offered his hand again to the dog. 'Who's a good old Jim, then?'

The dog nosed at his fingers as it had done before. Then it opened its mouth. The tips of its white, terrible teeth showed, but only for a moment before its pale tongue emerged to lick Paul's hand.

He leant closer to it, murmuring soothing nonsense. Presently he put down the torch so that he could lay his other hand on the wicked head. Watching him stroke firmly between the peaked ears and down the shaggy neck to the bunched shoulder-muscles, Amy sensed, rather than saw, that the muscles loosened a little. Certainly the ears stood less to attention.

'That dog ain't no savage,' said the man called Jim. ''E's as Christian as I am.'

'Same Christian name too, eh Jim?' Dave laughed his high, nervous laugh.

The dog's ears went up again.

'I'd appreciate it,' Paul said, quiet as ever, 'if you'd let us alone with him now. He isn't going to give us any trouble.'

'Yeah, I gotta get back to the bar,' said another of the figures, speaking for the first time and revealing himself as the son of the Nelson's landlord. 'I promised Dad I'd do a stint while he had his supper. 'Night, Amy.'

Amy responded to the various leave-takings, and stood watching the group wander back across the road, through the car park, and into the inn. The door spilt its brief yellow light, and once more they were alone in the gloom with the dog . . . with Jim.

'Hi, Jim,' Amy murmured experimentally.

Jim whined softly in response, while something thumped on the path and set the leaves of the nearby fuschia shaking and rustling.

'He's wagging his tail.' Paul switched on the torch, shining it down towards the fringed tail spilling over the path and into the bushes. 'Hang on.' He leant closer to the dog. 'What's this?'

He held the beam full on the black-and-tawny hind leg, which had caught his attention. In the yellow-white light it showed dark and matted, and Jim whined again.

'Oh God!' Amy felt suddenly sick. 'He wouldn't do that, would he?

But he would. She knew he would. She was sure now that it was Robert who had brought this poor animal here and left it in her garden. That in itself was bad enough, but either to make it more dangerous, or to frighten her with ideas of what might happen to herself, he had deliberately hurt it first.

'So how did you do this to yourself, eh?' Paul was asking in his soft voice. 'No wonder you were howling, poor old lad.' He gave the dog another strong, expert caress, and rose from his crouching position. 'Let's get him indoors,' he said to Amy, 'and see what we can do for him.'

Amy might have protested that she wasn't organized for a pet of any kind, let alone a huge one like this. She might have offered to ring the police, or the RSPCA, or a vet, or even Felicity Clark who ran a kennels, and ask them to take Jim away. She might even have pointed out that he would be better off with an organization which knew how to look after him.

But she couldn't do any of those things. In the tiny space of time they had all been together here at her garden gate, the dog had become . . . a friend? A responsibility? A way of not letting Robert succeed in frightening her? Whichever it was, she couldn't turn Jim away. Without a word, she led the way back to the house.

Maybe Paul's right, she reflected as she went. Maybe Jim just had an ordinary accident.

But if that were so, how like Robert to use the injury to harass and scare her. Hearing Paul's light footsteps following her, and Jim's uneven pattering, she felt grateful for their company.

'He can't be all that badly hurt,' Paul said as they reached the cottage. 'He can still get along, though he's limping.'

That makes two of us, Amy thought as she passed thankfully through her front door. Robert has a lot to answer for.

She hobbled straight along the hall to her living room, and was surprised how glad she was to drop into the armchair by the unlit fire. But heavens, what a mess, she thought as she looked about her. The plastic kitchen bowl still stood on the hearth where she had left it; the map of Kent tea towel by this time floating in a puddle of melted ice cubes. And there on the table was the towel Paul had been using . . .

'I clean forgot,' she said as he followed her into the room. 'You're soaked.'

'It's drying,' he assured her.

'Do take it off,' she urged, 'and we'll light the fire and dry it.'

'All in good time.' He took up the plastic bowl from the hearth. 'Before I do anything else, I'm going to fetch some clean water, and wash that paw.'

'But you'll get chilled . . .'

No use, he had already disappeared to the kitchen. Amy lifted her foot to rest on the cushioned raffia stool, sighed, and closed her eyes. When she opened them she found Jim standing before her, his round brown eyes gazing expectantly up into hers.

What a huge, strongly-built creature he was, to be sure. Her little room had shrunk about him; he stood almost as high as her dining table and made it seem spindly in comparison. Now that she could see him in the light, she realized that she had been deceived by that first sight of his silhouetted head with the standing-up, pointed ears; in truth he hardly looked alsatian at all. For one thing his head was too broad and rounded between the ears; for another his hair was far too long and too fine. It was beautiful, that hair, hanging like dark-gold silk from his body and legs and tail, and shining like jet over his back.

He stood before Amy, gazing up at her. 'Sit?' she offered experimentally.

Jim limped round and turned his back on her. So much for obedience to orders, Amy thought. Should

108

she try another? Give him another chance? But wait, he *was* sitting after all, on his haunches, cuddled against her good leg. So that was why he'd turned away, to snuggle up to her and make himself comfortable. Amy felt absurdly flattered, and with that living, trusting warmth against her knee came a wave of anger against Robert, who had so mistreated this splendid animal.

'He's a *good* dog,' she exclaimed on Paul's return. 'He knows how to behave, and he's . . .' She broke off, strangely self-conscious. *He's loving*, she had meant to say, but somehow couldn't. 'He's nice-natured,' she finished instead.

She needn't have worried, Paul was paying very little attention. 'Come on, Jim.' He knelt by the dog, and put the bowl back on the hearth. 'Let's be having that paw.'

Amy saw that the contents of the half-filled bowl steamed a little. 'You're using hot water?'

'Only with the chill off. And I took this –' he lifted out and wrung the green disposable dishcloth – 'from the packet under the sink.'

Amy looked down at Jim. 'Stand.'

To her delight he slowly came to his feet. Monumental on her multicoloured woven hearthrug, he limped round to face her and waited for her next order. She reached out and stroked his silky head.

'Let's keep him up like this,' she said to Paul, 'so you can ease that paw into the bowl.'

Jim allowed it, only whining a little as Paul cautiously lifted the hurt paw.

Once in position he stood like a little gentleman, as Amy's father would have put it, while Paul worked gently round the hurt paw with the cloth. The water in the bowl turned slowly red, and presently Paul fetched more water in another bowl. Transferring the wet paw to the new bowl was tricky, but Jim seemed to sense they were doing their best for him, and stood quiet.

Paul fetched water for a third soaking. This time it stayed clear, so he lifted the paw out and stood it on Amy's bath sheet, which he had fetched from the table.

Ah well, Amy thought, it was due to be laundered anyway.

'Lie?' she ventured to Jim, not too sure if anything would happen. Jim lumbered round and settled himself once more against her leg, this time reclining like a heraldic beast.

'What a good dog you are,' she said, stroking him while Paul carefully lifted the back leg and examined the hurt paw. The cut, visible now that the dried blood had soaked away, proved to be right on the pad, a wavery dark streak in the swollen flesh.

'Not as bad as it looks,' Paul said, gently lowering the paw to the towel. 'Jagged, but shallow. He must have stood on broken glass . . .'

'Or somebody slashed him,' Amy put in, seething for Jim's suffering.

From his kneeling position Paul looked up at her, a small frown between his arched brows. Caught by the full light of the standard lamp, his eyes glowed unexpectedly brilliant.

His cousin Harold's eyes are beautiful, but not like these, Amy found herself thinking. So blue . . .

'It looks far more like an accident to me,' he said.

Amy gathered her straying wits. 'Like all you Clarks coming here was an accident?' she countered. 'Like that conker in the post was an accident? Like what happened to me on Friday . . .'

She let the words trail into silence. In telling her story to the Clarks she had spoken of Robert in the vaguest possible terms, presenting him as 'someone I've been seeing, who got angry when I broke it off.' She had said nothing even about the proposal of marriage, let alone about what had followed.

Now, with those deep blue eyes searching hers, she found herself not just reluctant to speak of it, but passionately hoping she would never need to. In spite of her healing talk with Kate she still felt contaminated, she realized, and guilty too, because however you looked at it, some of what had happened was her own fault. She had leapt into bed with Robert almost as soon as she'd met him, and from then until this weekend, a whole three months, she had refused to let herself think about all the things she knew were wrong with him.

And still Paul's dark blue eyes held hers. 'Are you saying,' he began slowly when he was sure she didn't want to continue, 'that you think Jim was deliberately hurt, and then brought here to upset you, by that same man? By –' he thought for a moment – 'by Robert?'

111

Amy felt her eyes widen. 'How do you know his name?

'You mentioned it out there in the garden.'

So she had, and immediately regretted it. At the time her regret had seemed mere superstition, like not wanting to conjure up the devil by naming him, but now she knew there had been more to it than that. She hadn't wanted Paul to know anything at all about Robert, not even his name.

And now he did. In spite of all that had been going on at the time, he had noticed the name and stored it in his memory, and now he was one step nearer to finding out all the ugly facts which she so very much didn't want him to know.

'So you think Robert did it,' he repeated. 'That'd be some trick, you realize, to damage a dog as big as this one?'

'He could do it. And worse.' Amy shuddered, and found her hand, which rested on the arm of the chair, suddenly covered by one of his. She glanced down at it, and felt the blood racing in her ears. To distract herself she stared at his long, capable fingers, his clean, square nails, his strong wrist disappearing into the yellow cuff of the sweater where she knew the rest of him would be smooth and muscular, just like his walk . . .

I must stop thinking like this, she told herself.

But still she couldn't take her hand from under his. Instead it was he who moved first, casually lifting his own hand from hers and setting it on

Jim's ruffed neck. While he unfolded from his kneeling position by the dog to a sitting one on the hearthrug, Amy shifted and settled in her chair, trying to ignore the tiny chill within her at the small separation.

I must stop thinking like this . . .

'You've got to stop thinking like that, you know.'

'What?' Amy stiffened in dismay. Had she been so transparent? Were her beating pulses so visible, her confusion so obvious? And heavens, to make everything worse she was flushing, she could feel the heat in her cheeks.

'Like . . . like what?' she stammered.

Seated below her, he drew his long legs together and put his arms round his knees. 'Like the way you're talking about this Robert.'

Amy breathed out a quiet sigh of relief, and gladly took up the argument. 'You don't know him.'

'I do in a way – he messed me about too, remember.' Further from Amy now but still lit by the lamp, the dark blue gaze returned to hers. 'He must be a right toad.'

'Well then . . .'

'A toad,' Paul repeated firmly. 'Not a monster with superhuman powers.'

'You don't have to be superhuman to hurt a poor dog,' she said stubbornly, setting a hand on Jim's head to show him he was safe now, 'and then leave it where you know it'll frighten somebody you're trying to get back at.'

'No,' Paul agreed. 'And you may be right, it could be Robert who brought Jim here. But it could have been a lot of other people too . . .'

'Like who?'

'Like all the sods who . . . sorry,' he interrupted himself as he took in her startled expression at his unusually strong language. 'The . . . the sub-humans who get tired of their dogs and dump them.'

'Poor Jim,' Amy said, caressing the thick, soft fur. 'Whichever way it happened, it was rotten for him.'

'I'm told it's a particular problem in Kent,' Paul went on. 'People going abroad just tip the dog out of their car and drive on.'

'But Jim wasn't dumped just anywhere, he was left out there, in my garden.'

Amy's hand left Jim to gesture out of the window. 'Somebody went to the trouble of finding Stribble in all these narrow roads . . .'

'Maybe they didn't want him hurt by the motorway traffic.'

'He was left in *my garden*,' Amy repeated, so emphatically that Jim stirred and turned his great head to look up at her. 'With the gate shut,' she added in a carefully softened voice.

'With the gate shut, exactly,' Paul answered calmly. 'To keep him penned up till they got away.' He leant forward and put a hand on Jim's neck, quieting him. 'It could have been anybody who did that, and it could have been anybody's garden.'

'If that's so –' Amy strove to match his calm '– it's a huge coincidence that it was my garden they picked.'

'Coincidences happen . . .'

He let the idea trail into silence, his dark blue eyes thoughtful while his hand still soothed Jim. She had convinced him at last, Amy decided, and felt strangely disappointed. He had no answering arguments, and no wonder, seeing there weren't any, but somehow she would have liked him not to give in so easily. Still, she might as well pursue her victory.

'You know as well as I do that it was probably Robert.'

He moved a little on the rug, sitting straighter. 'I shouldn't have let you sidetrack me.'

So she hadn't defeated him after all, she thought with an odd pleasure, he'd merely been regrouping. Why was she so glad of that? Was it because she wanted him to convince her, really wanted to believe she had less to worry about than she feared? Or was it some other, deeper reason? Was it that she had hoped he'd be strong enough to master her?

For heaven's sake, woman, she inwardly scolded herself, haven't you had enough of masterful men even yet?

'I started by saying you mustn't think like that,' his soft voice continued, drawing her mind thankfully back to their theme, 'and whatever else is right or wrong, that still applies.'

Yes, that was how this discussion had begun, Amy realized. She had misunderstood him and been needlessly embarassed, which was probably why she had argued so passionately, but in her heart she knew now what he meant, and knew also that it was true.

'I said much the same to myself, out in the garden,' she admitted. 'That if I let him frighten me, he's won.'

'Exactly. And he's also won,' Paul pointed out, 'if you blame him for everything unpleasant that happens.'

'But Paul,' she almost pleaded, 'how can I not, when they keep happening?'

'That's how life is, sometimes good, sometimes bad . . .'

'Spare me the philosophy.'

'If you conjure him up every time it's bad,' he went on, ignoring the outburst, 'you'll never be rid of him.'

Now it was Amy's turn to be silenced. She knew so exactly what he meant. Robert's aim was to bother her, and here she was letting herself be bothered, blowing him up in her mind from . . . from draper to demon, she thought, borrowing and adapting Kate's nickname.

As if he sensed he had said enough, Paul made no further effort to persuade her. Instead he braced his arm against the floor, and with his usual easy grace sprang back to his kneeling position next to the dog.

'I wonder,' he said, 'if we can get a sticking plaster to stay on this paw?'

'There's one in the medicine chest in the bathroom,' she answered, relieved to be back with ordinary, everyday things, 'that I think might work.'

116

It did, a strong but fine webbing with unusually firm adhesive. Jim held still while it was stuck in place, one piece lengthways over the cut, two more crosswise over the first. When it was done he inspected it and licked it once.

'No!' said Amy firmly.

The great head swung round to face her with a guilty air, and Jim licked no more.

'He *is* a good dog,' Amy exclaimed, impressed. 'Now, what shall we give him to eat?'

They decided on bread, leftover cold meat and milk, which Paul said he would mix in the kitchen. Amy instructed him to use one of the stainless steel bowls he would find in the lefthand cupboard, and listened to the comfortable noises of the food being taken out and prepared, followed by a grateful rattling and gulping which indicated that Jim had accepted it.

'He's certainly getting round it, no trouble,' Paul reported back with satisfaction. 'I gave him some water as well . . .' He broke off, and sneezed.

'You see?' Amy reproached him. 'I told you about that wet sweater.'

'I'm still not cold,' he said dismissively. 'I expect it's dog fluff or something.'

'At least light the fire. The gas poker's . . .'

'. . . in the shed to the right of the back door,' he finished with her.

What a good memory he must have, she reflected as she looked up at him. Away from the direct lamplight his eyes had gone back to being just dark, no particular colour. To show their full beauty they had to be brighter lit than they were just now . . .

'So go and get it,' she said, pulling her mind back to the subject in hand. 'It hangs over a hook next to the gardening tools.'

He made no move to obey. 'Isn't it a bit late to be starting a fire?'

Amy glanced at her brass wall-clock. Heavens, ten already, where had the time gone this evening? Tomorrow she would be rehearsing the Christmas play until late, so it was vital she get some work done now.

'Not that late,' she countered as briskly as she could. 'I have I don't know how many reports to write before bedtime . . .'

She let the words trail dismally away. Bedtime. Another night of tossing and turning and shaking out her pillows, too tense to sleep, too tired not to wonder what new, dreadful thing might happen. This night would be worse though, because dreadful things had already happened and unimaginable others might follow.

'And now we're on to bedtime,' Paul's careful voice penetrated her gloomy thoughts like a welcome shaft of sunlight. 'It's a bit hard to know how to put this, but –' he paused, choosing his words with care – 'but if you'll trust me, I think I ought to stay the night,' he finished in a rush.

Trust him? Amy glanced up at him with sudden suspicion. Was he after all just like the others, a man on the make? On top of her other worries she found herself struggling with the disappointment of it.

He read her uneasy thoughts. 'That's why I said if you'll trust me,' he went on. 'If you will, and if you'll put up with me, you'd feel happier having someone here with you.'

'But didn't you say,' she began slowly, 'that I was to stop letting . . .' she hesitated, still reluctant to name Robert '. . . letting all this bother me?'

He nodded. 'If you have company you'll find that easier. And I expect the shop'll be all right for one night . . .'

'The shop? Oh yes, of course, you're Paul Clark Antiques.' She sniffed at the ghosts of linseed oil which still floated about that damp pullover, reminded how little she knew of this man . . . 'So you have a shop?'

'Isn't that the normal way of selling things?'

Amy stared at him, stung by his abrupt, ironic comment. 'You might have been an auctioneer or . . . or whatever.'

'Well I'm not,' he said shortly. 'I run a shop and live over it.'

Amy tried to picture it, and couldn't. Something about Paul – the subtly well-cut old tweeds, the air of ease, even the old flying jacket – hinted at a much more spacious life.

'I can't imagine you living over a shop,' she said. 'Harold, yes . . .'

'Harold,' he cut in frostily, 'lives in a very nice house in Hythe.'

'Well, I can imagine that too.' Amy refused to be

119

repressed. 'Come to think of it, you and Harold look a bit alike but you're very different really . . .'

'No we aren't, we're very alike,' he announced in a voice that forbade further probing. 'As for where I live, it's handy and it's good security . . .'

'OK, I'll lay off.' She realized she was responding to his tone rather than to anything he had said. It wasn't his austerity which had persuaded her either; she could cope with far worse than that. Rather it was what she sensed behind it, a barrier raised against . . . pain?

Yes, she decided, this thing he didn't want to talk about was something which had hurt him. She was dismayed to note that she now felt more inquisitive about it than ever. To distract herself, she changed the subject.

'Good security,' she repeated. 'So what you sell is valuable?'

'Some of it, very.'

She pictured rosewood tables, marquetry cabinets, carved Chippendale chairs. Yes, that was much more what she would expect of him. Moreover, it now seemed only natural that he should want to live near his treasures, the better to look after them.

And here he was offering to desert those same treasures in order to keep her company. He was willing to risk having them looted or vandalized because he knew that tonight threatened to be a bad time for her, and he knew his own presence would help her through it. Thinking of the sacrifice, she felt curiously humble.

'If you did spend the night here,' she ventured, 'you'd be leaving your stock unguarded.'

'And if I don't,' he answered promptly, 'I'd be leaving *you* un . . .' He stopped in mid-word, and Amy knew exactly why. I'd be leaving *you* unguarded, he had been about to say, and then had realized that, after all his efforts to persuade her otherwise, he had now spoken as if he thought she was in danger.

'I'd be leaving you here on your own,' he said instead, 'to imagine all sorts of nasty things that are never going to happen.'

Well saved, Amy wanted to say, but she didn't. She felt grateful for the reassurance even though she couldn't believe it. She thought of her last two nights here alone, exhausted yet unable to sleep, barricaded in yet never feeling safe, urging herself to be sensible yet listening unawares for any unfamiliar noise.

'There'll be Jim, too,' Paul interrupted her thoughts, and stood listening with his head on one side. 'He's very quiet in there – I hope he's all right. I'd better go and see.'

He made for the kitchen. Amy heard him murmur doggy nonsense to a background of conversational wuffs and of doggy claws clattering on her kitchen lino. They returned together, man and dog side by side. Paul came back into the room, but Jim stayed on the threshold, looking from Paul to Amy and back again. She held out her hand to him.

'Come and sit, Jim.'

Jim limped happily in, arranged himself in his preferred place with his back resting against her knee and sat.

'He was sitting there in the kitchen, waiting to be told what to do next,' Paul said. 'I don't know who's trained him, but they've done a great job.' He paused, looking at her tentatively. 'I thought I might take him home with me?'

Amy felt a pang at the idea of parting with him, a need to raise objections. 'He's . . . he's very big . . .'

'Great for guarding the shop. And I'll see he gets plenty of exercise.'

Amy gave herself a little shake. What was she thinking of? She couldn't keep Jim or any dog, with all the hours she had to spend in classes and on school activities. 'I think that's a marvellous idea,' she said. 'I'm sure he'll have a good home with you. Could I . . .' She hesitated, then went on, 'Could I perhaps see him from time to time?'

'Whenever you like,' Paul assured her. 'And for tonight, we're both here with you.'

'That's . . . that's very good of you,' she said humbly. 'I appreciate it.'

CHAPTER 6

'What kind of breakfast would you like?' Amy called through the open door.

'You're up already?' Paul sprang from the second last stair into the hall and hastened to where she stood at the table in the dining area. His hair, still wet from the shower, curled close and neat as ever, and the scent of her lemonflower soap mingled with his usual scent as he approached.

'I thought when you said I could have the bathroom first, it meant you'd want to lie in a bit,' he added as he joined her. 'It isn't seven yet.' He studied her with an enquiring frown between his thick, arched eyebrows. 'I hope you didn't sleep badly?'

'I slept very well indeed, thank you.' Her response sounded stilted and schoolgirlish in her own ears, so she added hastily, 'I never seem to need more than six hours – I always get up early.'

'Why so do I.' A smile lifted the corners of his mouth and eyes, as if he recognized a friend. 'I think early mornings are the best part of the day, don't you?'

'Well, er . . . yes . . .' She had always risen early at Moor Farm, sometimes absurdly early, to have a little time to herself before the family needed her. Now that she lived alone she had kept the habit, pottering around in her dressing gown for an hour and easing gently into her day. This morning, with her routine already altered by having to let Jim out into the garden, she had hoped to wake and gather her thoughts before she had to start being sociable, but she could hardly tell Paul that.

'I hope you slept well?' she said instead, still awkwardly polite.

'Beautifully, thank you . . .'

A brief wuff at the back door indicated that Jim wanted to come in. Amy turned towards it but Paul was already on his way.

'Will you put off the outside light when you close the door?' she called after him, a little irritated that he had forestalled her. 'You can leave the kitchen one on, I'll be needing it.'

'Will do.'

'Oh, and don't forget to relock the back door. Not the mortices, I won't turn those till we go.' How fussy she sounded. She hoped she wasn't turning into a spinstery schoolteacher. But if only he'd let her get on with things herself . . .

She heard the kitchen door open and close, and the clatter of dog claws on lino mingled with Paul's murmured greeting. No doubt he would be stroking the silky fur, and Jim would be accepting the caress with his usual alert good manners.

All very well, she thought, but I haven't heard that door being locked yet.

Fretted by having such an important job taken out of her hands, she waited with her head on one side, listening. Ah, there it went, the unmistakable click of the back door lock as its key turned. So Paul had done that right. A little mollified, she waited until man and dog reappeared together at the entrance to the living room.

'Have you looked at his foot?' she asked. 'I did when I first got up, and I'm sure it's better than it was last night.'

'Let's see,' said Paul. 'Lie, Jim.'

The dog sank obediently by the door, and Paul crouched on one knee to examine the hurt foot. Amy noted that his yellow sweater looked none the worse for last night's soaking, and decided that his tweed trousers, though ancient, must be of the very best quality judging from the way they adapted with casual elegance to his long, folded legs. Moreover he must have hung them and smoothed their creases as part of his nightly routine before going bed; they seemed as crisp and refreshed as the rest of him.

She pushed self-consciously at her unbrushed hair. Her sea-green cotton nightdress, chosen last night for its up-to-the-neck modesty, felt suddenly shabby, and she had to resist the urge to tighten the belt of her dark blue, long-skirted wool dressing gown to hide her favourite scuffed felt slippers.

Don't be silly, she silently scolded herself, he's dressed for the day, that's all. He had the bathroom first . . .

'Yes, the swelling's down,' Paul said, and with Jim rising unbidden to follow, he rejoined Amy at the table.

Why did I never notice before how tall he is, she wondered. And how clear his eyes are, even in this light . . .

Instinctively, hardly knowing what she was doing, she put her hand to the pull-down lamp she had lowered over the table and pushed it back up to the ceiling. The rosy gloom of its red shade lifted, and in the unscreened glare of its hundred-watt bulb she noticed for the first time the day's growth of stubble which shadowed Paul's jaw.

So he isn't all that perfectly turned out, she thought, and felt a little more on equal terms. Then she saw how the shadowing enhanced the hollows under his cheekbones, and added a husky, outdoor air to his otherwise impeccable grooming. She quickly stooped to the damp, garden-and-dog-smelling Jim, and patted him until she realized that Paul was speaking.

'. . . shouldn't you be sitting down?' His voice held a certain patience, as if he might be having to repeat the question. 'Resting that knee?'

'It's fine, thanks.' She detached a dead leaf from Jim's fur. 'I hardly feel it at all this morning.'

'Glad to hear it, but do be careful.' He watched her lift a folder from the table. 'How did the report writing go?'

'Splendidly. I expect that's one reason I slept so well.' Reminded that she had succeeded last night in preparing draft reports for a whole class, she took up her school bag and unzipped its paper section with a new optimism. 'It's such a relief to have made a start.'

The previous night she had worked sitting in the armchair rather than in her usual way at the table, but that had been all right. Paul had set her school bag by her on the carpet, and brought over her father's recent present, the big, glossy *Illustrated Garden Flowers*, for her to use as a makeshift desk.

'You're sure there's nothing else I can help with?' he'd asked. 'Ten fifteen at night seems late to be starting.'

'Just leave me to it,' she had answered, taking her mark book out of her bag and setting it handy on the spindly table. 'The spare room bed's made up, I always keep it ready . . .'

She'd trailed off, glancing up at him in sudden uncertainty. He was being so kind and helpful, and she was so grateful to him for staying to keep her company, yet here she was dismissing him from her living room, ordering him off to bed without a thought about whether he was ready to go there.

'You don't mind going up?' she asked belatedly. 'Only, I need to concentrate . . .'

'You get on with it,' he told her, equable as ever. 'I'll read, if you can lend me something.'

'There's all sorts of books in the spare room, and a good bedside light.' But she was only half-reassured.

'I'm so grateful to you,' she added haltingly. 'Staying here without any of the things you need for the night.'

'I have the new toothbrush you gave me, and I never wear pyjamas anyway . . .'

At his sudden pause Amy glanced up, and saw his eyes suddenly darken. She looked away from him, and coped as best she could with her own disturbing vision of that olive-dark, rangy body naked in one of her spare room's chaste twin beds.

'I'm still grateful,' she muttered, and opened her mark book.

She had known that if she really worked at it she could will her mind back to the much delayed reports. *Richard Ablett*, she wrote with great deliberation in the name column, and gave green-eyed Richard a C for effort and a C+ for achievement. That bit was easy; it was the comment which would be difficult. How to convey tactfully to Richard's mother that her boy tended to be wilful and to use his charm?

'Good night, then.'

'Hm?'

Amy looked up, and realized with relief that she had done it. She had got her mind away from Paul, and all the implications of his spending the night here, and on to her job.

''Night,' she responded more absently than she felt. 'Sleep well.'

Left alone in the quiet room, she wrote, *Richard is too inclined to go his own way*, and rested her pen. It was enough. Poor Mrs Ablett should understand the comment seeing that her husband, Richard's father, had gone his own way two years ago with an eighteen-year-old girl.

They're all alike, Amy had thought, pen in hand. All, all alike . . .

Just then, a sigh from the rug at her feet had brought her gaze down to Jim. While he stretched and made himself comfortable she remembered Paul's kindness to him, and to herself, and common sense returned. Some men behaved badly but she knew lots who didn't, including her father and her brothers, and now Paul. That thought strengthened her to go on with her task, and with Jim's sleeping, silky bulk guarding her, she had worked swiftly and well.

And here this morning was the result, the task of reporting finally, seriously started. She took the papers from the table where she had left them overnight, and zipped them into her school bag.

'So what time did you make it to bed?' Paul asked.

'Not so late.'

Amy found herself unable to meet the clear, dark blue gaze. She had decided to let Jim sleep on the rug by her bed, and had thought she might tell Paul so as she went by his room. Yes, face it, she had very much looked forward to talking to him again before she settled for the night. But when she passed his door his light was out, and now at the breakfast table she relived for a moment her brief, unreasonable disappointment. Then she resolutely banished it, and opened the table drawer.

'I think it was about a quarter past midnight,' she said. 'The little grille over your door was dark, so I take it you'd gone to sleep?'

'I suppose I must have.'

Amy drew from the drawer one of the green-and-gold placemats she used for breakfast. This morning she would need the other as well, she realized, and took an odd pleasure in setting it out.

'Now what about breakfast?' she asked. 'I have eggs, and there's bacon in the freezer that I could defrost in the microwave . . .'

'Thanks, but I prefer toast and marmalade. Or just bread,' Paul added, 'if toast is any trouble.'

'It's what I always have,' she said, and departed to fetch it.

The kitchen felt cold after the heated living room. So much the better; it always woke her up coming in here in the morning. In the neon-lit brightness she took the favourite leaf-patterned tray Gareth had given her last Christmas and set about loading it. Two knives, two teaspoons, two green Denby plates; she ticked them off in her mind as she put them on the tray, then turned to the row of mugs which hung under the wall-cupboard.

I'll have the Japanese flowerbell this morning, she decided, enjoying the choice, and he can have – he can have *this* one. She unhooked her favourite, eggshell-fine mug with the bands of mauve, dove-grey and mandarin-orange. She liked it so much she hardly dared use it, but today was special.

Idiot, she said to herself as she lowered the mug gently to the tray, what on earth's got into you? He's another man, that's all. You know lots of men . . .

Yet still it continued, this inexplicable feeling of happiness that she and Paul were to have breakfast together. She never would have believed she could feel so good about having a man here in her beloved cottage.

She so much enjoyed living on her own after the rough-and-tumble of Moor Fell farmhouse. Her living room stayed tidy, her carpets needed sweeping only once a week, and this tiny kitchen seemed unbelievably spacious when she only needed to cook for one. Until this fateful weekend her privacy and independence here had always exhilarated her, and though she had entertained her lovers to meals she had never, in spite of broad hints, invited any of them stay the night.

Her father and younger brothers came down for visits, and she welcomed them. But always she was aware of how heavy they were for her little chairs, how substantial their feet between her and the fire, how bulky their clothes in her little spare room wardrobe.

And now here she was welcoming a man, a stranger, so much that she had set out her best porcelain coffee mug for him. A man. One of the tribe who left the lavatory seat up, and shaving foam unrinsed in the wash basin. Who said they didn't want her to take any trouble on their account, but looked so disappointed with omelette or risotto that she felt compelled to cook

131

the substantial meals they were used to. Who crowded her little kitchen in well-meant efforts to help but only got in the way, and who never washed up after themselves.

Wait a minute though. The tumbling ideas pulled to a sudden halt in her mind. Paul must have washed up. Though she had never been in here last night, the kitchen this morning was as neat as she would have left it herself. She opened the cupboard under the sink and yes, he had put the washing-up bowl back where it belonged; she presumed he had also put the other bowl back where he found it in the little understair cupboard. Her map of Kent tea towel hung on its rail almost dry, and the mugs from which they had drunk their belated camomile tea were back on their hooks. Even the crockery from the Nelson stood shining clean in a neat pile beside its gleaming cutlery, all ready to be returned whenever the pub should be open and available for it.

And he only wants toast and marmalade for breakfast, she reminded herself. The same thing I always have myself . . .

'Is everything all right?' Paul had come to the door, the inevitable Jim at his side. 'No more nasty surprises?'

'Nasty surprises? Oh.' Realizing what he meant, she felt her exhilaration ebbing away. The events of yesterday came flooding back to her, and she wondered how she could possibly have forgotten them. Why, they were the very reason Paul was here at all.

She glanced down at the clothes washer, then let her gaze travel round the room to the radio, the refrigerator, the stove. Could Robert possibly have got in here and tampered with something to make it dangerous?

Jim's silky warmth brushed past her where she stood at the worktop. Turning, she found that he was following Paul who had already edged by her. He must have pressed against the wall in the narrow space to avoid touching her in passing, she decided, and was still wondering what to think about that when he picked up the kettle.

'I know this is all right,' he said. 'I rewired the plug myself after it fused the lights.'

'After Dave botched it, you mean.' Amy felt so relieved to be talking about the ordinary, everyday problem of Dave's poor workmanship that she almost smiled. She nodded at the toaster, which she had just lifted on to the tray.

'Do you remember who checked this last night?'

'That was Harold, it should be all right.' He glanced down at the half-loaded tray. 'Shall I carry that to the table?'

'It isn't ready yet.' She surveyed the tray, checking. 'I keep the butter in the living room in winter so it's there already. Marmalade –' she took it out of its cupboard – 'honey, oh, and bread of course, for toasting.'

She opened the refrigerator where she kept it, then remembered that they had cut up the heel of the loaf last night for Jim's supper. She closed the refrigerator and, belting her dressing gown tighter, moved towards the solid block formed by Paul and Jim.

'Can I come past you, please?'

'Where are you going?' Paul asked.

'To the freezer. In the shed,' she explained, waiting impatiently for them to move. 'I need a new loaf, and I've got one out there.'

'Let me fetch it for you.'

'Thanks, but I'd just as soon . . .'

'Sit, Jim.'

Obedient Jim settled on his haunches, filling the narrow, corridor-shaped kitchen like a cork in a bottle. Blocked on the wrong side of him, Amy had to watch while Paul unlocked the back door and stepped outside into the still dark November morning. As the cool garden-scented outside air washed over her, she felt another surge of irritation at not being allowed to get on and do things in her own way.

'No, don't close the door,' she said. 'It's mild outside, and I like the morning air.'

Paul let his hand drop from the door, and reached down to where her rosemary bush lay on its side with compost spilling out of its pot.

'Jim must have knocked this over.'

'It's top heavy in that pot,' she said, excusing Jim. 'I should have planted it out long ago, but it's so handy having it by the kitchen.'

'I'll try and be more careful than he was.' He rose, stepped between the other random pots of bay and thyme and basil by the back door, and made his way towards the dark garden.

'Hang on,' she called after him, 'If I can just get round this dog I'll put on the outside light for you.'

'Don't need it,' he answered over his shoulder. 'It's much lighter out here than you'd think when you're inside.'

'You'll need the light in the shed, though.' If only he would let her do things for herself! 'The switch is just inside the door. Oh, and it's locked . . .'

But he was already far advanced into the obscurity beyond the kitchen door's oblong of light. Probably he didn't even hear her; before she finished speaking she had disappeared round the corner of the wooden out-house which leant against the end wall of the cottage. Not for the first time she regretted the impractical way its door faced the road, as far from the kitchen as it would go.

Oh well, Paul would be back when he found he couldn't get into it. Amy sighed, remembering his kindness last night, and her happiness a moment ago just because he was here.

You can't have it all ways, she told herself, and opened the bottom drawer of the kitchen unit. Somewhere under the clutter of string and clothes pegs and free samples and rubber gloves lay the giveaway key-ring, absurdly decorated with a miniature plastic bunch of bananas, on which she kept the key of the padlocked shed.

Ah, here it was. She lifted it out, closed the drawer, and turned back towards the open door. Jim, still massively seated between her and the outside, raised his head and cocked his ears to an interested angle.

'Good lad,' Amy said absently, and stared past him.

Jim sighed, and relaxed. Small rustlings and stirrings and faint earthy scents drifted into the kitchen on the damp November air. Was morning here, or was it the moon which lightened the blackness? Amy tossed up the keyring and caught it, passing the time until Paul should have found the padlock and returned for the key. He was trying the door now, she recognized its characteristic penetrating creak . . .

No, that was wrong. The door only creaked when it opened, and he shouldn't be able to open it. Unless she had left it unlocked? Maybe she had forgotten to replace the padlock after her last visit to the freezer. That would be yesterday morning, at breakfast.

Almost at the same time as the door creaked a soft thump, hardly noticeable, had sounded somewhere out of sight in the garden. It had been a very gentle noise, as of a sweater or a cushion dropping, but it seemed to have worried Jim. She saw that he had stiffened, his great wolf-ears forward.

'It'll only be a fox or a squirrel rummaging in the compost heap,' she told him, but his ears stayed up. 'I suppose you're right, it's nearer than that,' Amy conceded. 'I expect a clump of moss has fallen from the roof, then. The birds peck them for insects.'

Jim's handsome wolf-muzzle went on pointing through the darkened doorway.

'I agree it sounded a bit heavy for moss, but it could have been a specially big clump,' she said. 'And it's early for birds,' she added with a glance out at the just lightening sky, 'but they'll be about, looking for their breakfasts . . .'

Jim shot to his feet, growling.

'Quiet . . . my God!' Amy half-whispered as a weird figure came into view round the corner of the shed.

Her first startled impression was that someone had taken Paul's clothes and sent them out to walk towards her on their own. The brightness of the yellow sweater shone through the gloom but she couldn't see anybody wearing it, and the sweater itself was horribly misshapen. Its shoulders and upper chest had disappeared, its arms had somehow withered to crooked twigs, and the rest of it held scattered speckles and drifts of black as if the last of the night had settled over it in a cloud.

Jim's growl turned to deep-chested barking.

'Wh-who are you?' Amy quavered through the noise, her hands bunched into fists. 'Wh-*what* are you . . . oh.'

The creature drew near the light from the kitchen. 'Quiet, Jim.'

As soon as he heard the familiar, husky voice, Jim stopped barking. He must have been objecting to that acrid, dusty smell, which his sensitive nose would have picked up long before it came within human range.

'It's only soot.' In the surrounding blackness of his face Paul's eyes seemed bluer than ever, their whites a

137

startling blue-white. 'Your friend's idea of a joke, I suppose.'

His head and hands were covered with the dense, matt blackness; no wonder they had been invisible from a distance. The first impression of grotesque, twig-like arms had also been caused by the soot, which had settled on the upper parts of his sleeves and merged them like his head and shoulders and hands into the night.

'Bloody hell,' Amy exclaimed, shaken into breaking her self-imposed ban on strong language. 'He's not here, is he?'

The matt-black head shook reassuringly. Even in the midst of her dismay, Amy couldn't help noticing how the blackness suited Paul. Under the tight powdery-black curls his eyes seemed larger than she had realized, and a little tilted, like Harold's. Yes, he did look more like Harold, the same straight, flaring nose and firm, full mouth . . .

'No, there's nobody there,' he assured her. 'There didn't need to be.'

'What do you mean?'

'It's a popular schoolboy trick.' Paul raised his hand to show the smallish paper bag he carried. It too was almost invisibly blackened, which must, Amy decided, be why she hadn't noticed it before. 'You open the door a little way, and balance your bag of soot over the top of the opening,' he explained. 'The next person to come along pushes the door further open, and . . .' He finished with an expressive gesture which released more soot from his clothes. Amy watched it drift down from him like black snow, and shook her head in disbelief.

'All that, out of that little bag?'

'It doesn't take much.'

'But how did he get the door open?' she asked, chilled at this evidence that her tormenting enemy had prowled round her home. 'I keep it locked.'

'Maybe you forgot, and left it open?' he suggested, echoing her earlier thoughts. 'Or maybe he knows how to pick locks.'

Amy hugged her arms tight to her body and shivered. 'If that's so, he could have got in the house as well.'

'We checked everywhere last night,' Paul reminded her gently. 'And you're pretty thorough and careful about locking up in general, aren't you? All those mortices and things?'

She nodded, a little comforted.

'I don't know if this will be any good for fingerprints.' Paul flourished the paper bag which had held the soot, keeping it carefully upright. 'But we might as well look after it, just in case.'

'Though it's hardly a police matter,' Amy said gloomily. 'Soot.'

'As part of a general campaign of harassment . . .' He broke off and sneezed, a small explosion which set more soot drifting from his clothes and hair.

'You're catching a cold,' Amy said, conscience-stricken at keeping him standing here talking.

He shook his head, and sneezed again. 'Soot up my nose.'

'All the same, do come indoors. Out of the way, Jim . . .'

'Let me get this off first.' He stepped back well clear of the door and its clustered pots of herbs, and peeled the blackened sweater up over his head. Amy saw with what she refused to admit was disappointment that he had under it a perfectly respectable, short-sleeved, crew-necked black cotton T-shirt. She also saw, though she tried not to, that the arms he freed from the sweater were strong, smooth-muscled, and only lightly downed, and that the T-shirt covered wide shoulders and a well-proportioned chest which tapered to a long, narrow waist.

'You'll want the bathroom all over again now, won't you,' she said for the sake of saying something.

He nodded, dropping the sweater to the concrete path and holding up a spread hand to indicate the lightening sky. 'There's still plenty of time though, isn't there?'

Amy glanced at the kitchen clock. 'It's only five past seven,' she said in amazement. 'So much has happened, I was sure it'd be much later than that.'

He smiled, a dazzling display of white teeth in the black face. 'Only one thing's happened. And that's nothing serious.'

With that special, graceful suppleness which distinguished all his movements, he doubled over from the waist, right to toe-touching position. He didn't touch his toes, but ran his fingers through his close-curled, upside-down hair, to rid it, she supposed, of as much soot as possible before he came indoors.

He really is very agreeable to look at, she thought, watching him. Not conventionally handsome, not conventional at all, but very, very agreeable.

'Now,' he said, straightening. 'Supposing we get ourselves sorted out, and have some breakfast.'

'Breakfast.' The word recalled to Amy the reason Paul had gone out to the shed in the first place. 'I'll fetch the bread, then, while you have your shower.'

'You will not,' he said calmly. 'If your friend . . .'

'Don't call him that.'

'If the . . . the low-life who did this,' Paul corrected himself with an air of restrain, 'could get into the shed, he could have fixed other little surprises in there.' He turned and moved back the way he had come. 'I'll go and check.'

'Thanks,' Amy said humbly. 'Er . . . I hope it'll be all right.'

'I expect it will be.'

'If it is,' she called after him, 'could you fetch the bread this time?'

He did, five minutes later, with a report that everything else in the shed seemed exactly as it ought to be. Then he went up to shower again, and Amy went out to check the shed for herself. She found the lawn-mower still in the corner where she stowed it for the winter, the spade and fork and trowel and broom still on their hooks, her folding chairs still against the wall, and the spare plant pots still piled on the work bench, everything as far as she could see just as she had left it except for the little heaps and smears of soot round the doorway. After she had swept them together, picked them up on a dustpan, and emptied them into her dustbin, the place looked as it always did.

She could find no sign of the padlock. If Robert had broken or picked it to get in he must have taken it away with him, she decided as she walked back to the kitchen in the growing daylight. Then, opening the living-room curtains for the day, she found it lying on the windowsill.

Picking it up and weighing it in her hand, she felt for a moment almost light-headed with relief. Robert wasn't after all a sinister lock picker who could reach her anywhere, merely an opportunist who had taken advantage of her carelessness.

'I remember now,' she told Paul at breakfast. 'I was just going to lock the shed yesterday when the postman rang.'

A picture flashed into her mind of what the postman had brought, the gift-wrapped, battered conker. Robert might not have broken into her shed but he had still found his way into it, and now he was still out there making trouble for her. She looked down at her toast, and wondered how she was going to eat the rest of it.

'I must have carried the lock into the house in my hand,' she went on. 'I . . . I wasn't quite myself, yesterday.'

Paul reached for the bread, and put two more slices into the toaster. 'You've relocked the shed now?'

She nodded. 'I hope you can eat both of those?'

'I could, but one's for you.'

'I don't want any.'

'One piece of bread isn't much to take you through the day.' He glanced down at her plate. 'And you've only eaten a quarter of that.'

She rubbed at a smear of soot which had mysteriously appeared on her placemat. The damned stuff got everywhere; she would probably be coming across traces of it for weeks. She raised her gaze to Paul's and saw that his hand was still suspended over the toaster, waiting for an answer.

'I'm . . . I'm not hungry,' she told him.

The dark blue eyes narrowed, holding hers. 'Would you eat to please me?'

She stared back at him in surprise. None of the men in her life, not her father nor her brothers nor her lovers, had ever bothered about whether she ate or not. Rather it had been the other way round; she had always been the one to worry about what she should provide for them.

Of course, she thought, until now I've always had a healthy enough appetite.

'Would you?' he persisted. 'Would you at least try?'

'I suppose so,' she said ungraciously. An old memory resurfaced of the time when Gareth, recovering from some illness, had lost all interest in food. 'If you promise not to cut it up and pop it into my mouth when I'm not looking.'

'That's better.' He activated the toaster, and she realized with surprise that what had pleased him was to hear her making a joke, however weak. And after all, a little piece of toast wasn't so difficult to eat, and another.

'Now,' Paul said over their second and final mugs of coffee, 'I'll tell you what we're going to do about this pest.' He drained his coffee, and put down the mug with an air of decision. 'We're going to go and see him.'

'No!'

Amy spoke with far more force than she had intended. Heaven knew what Robert would say about her if he had the chance, and the very idea of Paul hearing such things set her teeth on edge. Afraid of having given herself away, she took a deep breath and carefully controlled her voice before she continued. 'It's . . . it's my problem . . .'

'Mine too,' Paul reminded her. 'That soot was meant for you, but I'm the one who got it.'

Unable to argue, she stared at him in silence.

'And Dave, and Harold, and Felicity have all been affected,' he went on. 'Not to mention that undertaker chap – what did you say he was called?'

'You're surely not suggesting you all go and see Robert?' Amy stifled a nervous giggle.

'Only you and me. That'll be enough.'

'Please no, Paul. It . . .' Amy sought a reason, and found none she could give. 'It wouldn't help,' she finished weakly, and lowered her gaze, aware of those dark blue eyes scrutinizing her face.

'We'll see about that,' Paul said.

CHAPTER 7

'What d'you mean, our horses are broken-down jades?' Joanna's strong voice echoed with a splendidly raucous edge through the cavernous depths of the Yates Centre's drama studio. 'I'll broken-down jade you . . .'

'They're the best horses this side of Canterbury,' a penetrating pipe interrupted.

Shading her eyes against the spotlight, Joanna turned her matriarchal head to the distant part of the acting area from which the voice had emerged. Tracy Norris, self-important as a miniature magistrate behind the table which would eventually be her apple stall, went on being helpful.

'That's what you should be saying, Joanna.'

'Gimme a chance, little Trace.' Joanna, though still easy to hear, had reverted to her usual good-natured tone. 'I haven't had time to learn me lines yet.'

'Miss said we should all know our lines by this rehearsal.' Tracy appealed to where Amy sat on the second step of the dim, red-carpeted audience area. 'Didn't you, Miss?'

'Tracy,' Amy said, 'has anyone ever told you what a know-all you are?'

The child's eyes widened in . . . bewilderment? Dismay? 'No, Miss.'

'They will,' Amy predicted. 'Now get back to those apples, and stop interfering.'

Tracy lowered her head. Doll-like in the stage lighting, she picked up an imaginary apple and polished it on an imaginary napkin. She mimed it well enough but all the bounce had gone out of her, and her china-blue eyes shone watery-bright.

Oh dear, Amy thought, now I've hurt her feelings. She's only eleven.

'This is the first full-cast rehearsal, or you'd know,' she added in a gentler tone. 'Joanna's only just begun this part. She had to take over from . . . somebody else.' She refrained from naming Jill Gann. At the casting session back in September Jill had pleaded for the part of the ostler's wife, and it wasn't her fault she'd had to drop out, not really. Her undernourished, fourteen-year-old body had turned out to be far gone in pregnancy. By Christmas she would have her own baby to take care of as well as all those younger brothers and sisters.

'But, Miss, Joanna does have to remember that bit about the best horses this side of Canterbury.' Carl Stevens disentangled his huge knitted scarf from his guitar, and turned his lordly dark gaze on Amy. 'I need it to cue in my song.'

Amy was tempted to tell him what he could do with his song. He had written it himself in music lessons, or

146

so he believed. The music teacher had persuaded her to use it, and now he gave himself airs like a pop star.

'What's the scarf for, Carl?' she asked. 'You're supposed to be a pilgrim, not a football supporter.'

''Tisn't a football scarf. Somebody knitted it for me.' A besotted fan, Carl hoped to imply. 'I'm using it till I get my cloak.'

Amy noted the boy's glistening forehead. 'It's making you far too hot.' She fanned her own face with her rehearsal notes. Usually when she was to rehearse in here she remembered how overheated the place could be, and dressed accordingly. This morning however, what with Paul and the booby trap, she had been so thrown out of her routine that she had clean forgotten. Luckily her black skirt was fairly lightweight and her black velvet jacket removable, but her high-necked moss-green sweater, still necessary to conceal the bruise on her neck, clung most uncomfortably. One more black mark against Robert.

'I'm not too hot, Miss,' Carl protested, shaking his sweat-damp hair out of his eyes. 'Honest . . .'

'It's also getting in the way of your guitar.' Amy used the tone that brooked no argument. 'And you could trip over it. Take it off. Now.'

'OK, Miss.' Defeated and probably relieved, Carl unwound the long strip of multicoloured knitting from his neck. 'Could you keep an eye on it for me? Just till rehearsal's over?' He came forward to lay the scarf carefully on the first step of the audience tiers, by her foot. She waited with stony patience until he remembered what she required him to say next.

'Er . . . please,' he added belatedly.

'It won't run away,' she said. 'Now get back to your place.' She peered down at her watch, and could just make out that its hands stood at quarter past five. 'We haven't got all night.'

They had in fact fifteen more minutes. There were limits to what one could expect of pupils after a tiring school day, and she always sent them off to tea and homework at five thirty.

Carl hurried back to the spotlight and placed himself on the chalk mark where the stable door would be when the scenery was built. When he raised his guitar for action, Amy stared in disbelief. 'You're supposed to be facing the audience, not the market square.'

'He wants to show off his profile, Miss,' Joanna said with a grin. 'Mind you it's a lovely profile,' she added in an undertone.

Ella, the innkeeper's wife and Joanna's accomplice in everything, gave her newly sex-conscious, thirteen-year-old giggle and agreed. 'Great nose he's got . . .'

'*Quiet!*' Amy barked. '*Carl, face the way you're supposed to face!*'

Carl shot her an apprehensive glance, and whirled to the correct angle.

'And don't you forget,' Amy added to Joanna, 'it's important to feed in the bit about the best horses in all Canterbury.' She glanced down at her notes. 'Let's take it back to where the traveller comes asking for a horse.'

The rehearsal continued, Carl went into his song, and Amy briefly relaxed. Let the audience of fond parents work out why a pilgrim passing through a medieval Kent village should accompany himself on the guitar and wail about the environment.

It had been one of those days. Her twisted knee had turned out far more troublesome than she had expected, and she had been forced to sit down as much as possible. In English lessons this just about worked, but in the drama lessons which made up most of her timetable she found it a serious handicap. Drama was an activity where pupils moved about all the time, and when she couldn't move with them, advising and demonstrating, she felt she was short-changing them.

That alone was bad enough, but there was worse. No more tricks had emerged yet, but she couldn't help worrying that they would. Disturbed by Robert's malice, wondering where the next blow would fall, she knew she had been – was still being – distracted and bad-tempered both with pupils and with colleagues.

The argument at breakfast hadn't helped, though at least she had won it. Paul might insist they go to see Robert, but he didn't know where Robert lived. Amy did, and would decide in her own good time, she grandly announced, whether she thought it a good idea. With that she had leapt to her feet and started to pile plates on the tray, preparing to carry it to the kitchen.

'Wait a minute,' Paul said from his corner bench. 'There's a lot to be sorted out.'

'I must wash up.' She glanced at the clock. 'I have half an hour to shower and dress, and I must find some breakfast for Jim.'

A shiny black nose poked out from under the table, where Jim had taken his place at Paul's feet. Clearly he recognized his name, maybe also the word 'breakfast'.

'It won't hurt him to wait until I've bought some proper dog food.' Still Paul made no attempt to rise. 'I'll make it the first thing I do when I leave here.'

Amy, poised with the marmalade jar she had just lifted from the table, found herself clutching it tight. She so much disliked the idea of Paul leaving that she could find nothing to say. His intriguing looks, his comforting strength, his gentle good humour had become so much a part of her life that she couldn't believe she had only met them for the first time last night. Now in less than an hour she would have lost them. Even Jim would be gone . . .

At least she could talk about that. 'I'd very much like to hear how Jim gets on.'

'First things first.' Still seated, Paul grasped the marmalade jar from below and took it from her. She didn't know whether to be sorry or merely relieved that he contrived to do it without touching even the tips of her fingers.

'We need to talk.' He set the jar on the tray. 'I'll clear away and wash up while you're showering.'

'Oh. Yes, I suppose you could.' She remembered what a good job he had made of it last night. 'Er . . . thanks. I really am grateful for all you've done,' she added, more awkward than ever with the prospect of their parting hanging over her. 'It's made such a difference.'

'Glad I could help. Now then.' He spread both hands palm-down on the table in front of him. Amy wondered what it was about those hands that made her feel so safe. Was it the long fingers, or the sheen of health on the gentle, olive-pink nails, or that spread-out gesture which partly offered, partly compelled?

'I suppose,' he went on, 'you have your own reasons for not wanting to visit this scum who's bothering you.'

Amy glanced again the clock. 'I'd better go . . .'

'It's all right, I'm not prying.' The dark blue eyes regarded her with a mixture of sympathy and resignation. 'If you won't see him you won't. So what will you do about being alone here in future?'

She felt her knees weaken, and quickly sat down. When she put her own hands on the table it was more for steadiness than from any idea of asserting her will. It seemed incredible now Paul had mentioned it, but she simply hadn't thought of the future at all. In depressed silence she pictured the long winter nights she must spend here, wondering what Robert would do next.

'The police?' Paul suggested without much conviction.

'Practical jokes,' Amy countered gloomily. 'Soot, for heaven's sake.'

'It isn't just soot.'

'Anyway, what could they do?'

'Question him?'

'He'd only deny it all.' Amy didn't add that she found the idea of having to talk to the police nearly as bad as the idea of confronting Robert.

'Just a thought.'

'Surely,' Amy spoke almost pleadingly, 'he has to get tired of this silliness sooner or later?'

But she didn't know if she could hope for that. She didn't know anything very much about Robert. One of the things that had depressed her in the last few days was discovering how little she had ever understood of his character. She had seen him – coupled with him – every other weekend for nearly three months, and never once had she remotely imagined that he could behave as he had last Friday.

Nor could she ever have predicted yesterday's practical jokes with their mixture of menace and schoolboy silliness. And now, she couldn't begin to guess how long he would keep them up.

Paul broke into her despondency by turning away from her with an air of resolve. Jim's shiny nose appeared again from under the table and this time the rest of him followed; Paul must have disturbed the dog's favourite leaning position by swinging sideways to stand up. He bent and stroked between the high, sensitive ears, then straightened once more.

'I suppose I'd better get used to the hygiene rules of having a dog,' he observed without looking in her direction, 'and wash my hands before I handle the food.'

He vanished to the kitchen, followed as usual by Jim. Amy listened to the sound of the tap running, and glanced at the clock. Yes, she must soon go up and change, but with Paul taking over the clearing of breakfast she had time in hand. She also had a very strong feeling of something unfinished between them, something not yet spoken but implied by that last, subtle change in his manner.

Now why, she wondered, does he seem so much less decisive all of a sudden? More than that, why do I get the feeling that he means to be decisive, but can't quite manage it?

He returned to the table so quickly that she suspected he hadn't dried his hands properly. 'I'd offer to stay on here.' He kept his face averted, carefully wrapping the bread together in its plastic bag. 'But I sleep over the shop, and I don't like leaving it for too long.'

'You mustn't think of it,' Amy quickly agreed.

Still he wouldn't look her way. Now it was the ceramic butter dish which seemed to engage all his attention. However, while he lifted it to the tray as if it were Ming porcelain, his soft, diffident voice made the contact his eyes refused.

'Some of my stuff's quite valuable.'

'I do understand.' Amy tried to keep her tone light and cheerful. 'You've already done far, far more than I could have expected.'

So this is what it's like, she thought, to be the one who needs help rather than the one who gives it. I never realized how difficult it could be. 'After all,' she went on, 'you have your own life to . . . leave the butter in here, it gets too hard in the kitchen at this time of year.'

'Sorry, I forgot.' He returned the butter dish to the table with the same exaggerated care, still not looking at her. 'What about you coming to stay with me?'

She stared at him, ideas and feelings chasing each other like butterflies through her distracted mind and nerves. Such kindness, to offer to take her into his home with all the disruption that would involve . . . And why should she let Robert drive her out of her own home . . .? And what might Robert do to this place while she wasn't in it . . .? And Paul was right, the sensible thing now was to confront Robert . . . And still she couldn't bear the thought . . .

And through all the shifting, confused images, something else shone with the steady brightness of sunlight. She didn't know what it was and wouldn't examine it too closely, but she felt its certainty strengthen her as sunlight strengthens a plant.

He wants to go on helping me. The words beat in her mind so that she couldn't tell if they were thoughts or feelings. He wants to treat my troubles as his own, he wants to take care of me, he wants to see me again . . .

No, she wouldn't think any more about that. To avoid thinking any more about that, she said the first thing that came into her head.

'Oh Paul, that's so good of you!'

'Not at all.' Perhaps it was his stooping to unplug the toaster which made it sound so stilted and conventional. 'My spare room's all right. Nothing marvellous, but all right.'

'I . . . I just don't know if that's the answer.'

His silence said more than words. They both knew what the answer was, or at least what the next step should be. If only she could bring herself to face seeing Robert.

The tray loaded, he lifted it and made for the kitchen. 'Maybe you'll have a better idea about things when you've dressed,' he said over his shoulder.

There he goes again, Amy thought in irritation. Not exactly instructing me, just pointing out what I ought to do next.

To make it worse he was proved completely right. Twenty minutes later, showered and dressed, hair brushed into something resembling its usual guitar-curves and eyelids subtly shadowed the same hazel-green as her eyes, she felt she had put a protective coating between herself and the world. She even thought she could find the strength to make her own move in this strange, reluctant pattern she and Paul were weaving round each other. She limped to the kitchen, where true to his word he stood at the sink washing up.

'You rinse all the detergent off in cold water, then leave them to air-dry,' she instructed automatically.

'Bossy boots.' But he took each plate from the rack and rinsed it under the cold tap.

'It's my kitchen.' There, that felt good, she had been wanting to say it all morning. Pleased to have got it out at last, she could easily summon the acting skill to seem casual about what she really wanted to discuss. 'Now about me staying with you.'

Did she imagine it, or had his hand stilled on the tap? With the water gurgling and splashing in the sink, she found it difficult to tell.

'I wonder,' she went on, approaching the crucial words with care, 'if we could meet this evening and talk? If,' she added hastily, 'you haven't anything else . . .'

'It's what I was going to suggest myself.'

'Were you?' The world seemed suddenly brighter. 'Well then . . .'

They agreed to put off any further discussion until this evening. Paul told her that he was attending an auction in Canterbury this afternoon, so he could quite easily come on to the Yates Centre at half past five.

Which, thank heaven, it nearly is, Amy thought now with another glance at her watch.

'It's no use, we 'aven't a metre of space to spare,' Ella proclaimed as the innkeeper's wife. 'We got people sleepin' on the floor, in the cellar, in the . . .'

The other places where the inn had people sleeping were lost in the discordant row which at that moment broke out in the music room. Behind the scarlet wall which separated it from the drama studio, someone was crudely banging the piano with great force, several notes at a time, so loudly that even those close to Ella couldn't have heard much of what she was saying. She struggled on gamely for a word or two, then gave up.

Amy sighed. It was all very well for architects to design a prestigious building for officials and advisers to admire, but it had problems, and here was one. The scarlet wall was really two huge doors which could be slid back to expand the acting space. It must have seemed a good idea to somebody, but it meant the music room wasn't soundproof.

Besides, whoever was punishing that piano might be damaging it beyond repair. She rose to her feet, disdaining to shout in competition with the noise, and clapped her hands briskly instead. When she had the cast all looking her way she pointed to her watch and made a shooing gesture of dismissal. The various groups in the different parts of the acting space broke up, chatting and comparing notes as they straggled to the glass outer door which led to the lobby and cloakrooms.

Amy limped in the opposite direction, down the stairs at the side of the audience tiers and across to the music room to investigate. She pushed at one of the scarlet doors and it opened on a blast of noise which entirely swamped its usual luxurious sliding murmur. Blinking in the sudden brightness of neon top-lighting she saw a small, thick-set figure in faded jeans, a checked shirt, and an over-large leather jacket, standing between the piano and its pushed-back stool, banging at the keyboard with doubled fists.

'Martin!' Half-deafened, Amy put her hands over her ears. 'What do you . . .'

No use, he couldn't hear her. He didn't know she was here, hadn't noticed the great door opening to admit her. He went on banging, sometimes with one fist after another to make a non-stop jangle, sometimes with both at once for a clanking climax. So great was his enthusiasm, his venom, that his coarse sandy fringe bounced frantically above his pale, unformed little face.

Amy limped across to him. 'Martin . . .'

Rather than bellow in his ear she touched his shoulder. He dropped his hands from the keyboard and whirled on her.

'Leave me alone!'

She slepped back in surprise. The blunt, childish features had distorted to a mask of ferocity, the eyes narrowed to grey slits, the lips pulled back in a snarl. It crossed her mind fleetingly that he could be dangerous, but heavens, he was only a little boy.

'It's all right, Martin,' she said gently. 'I'm not going to hurt you.'

Instead of answering he covered his face with his hands. The next moment he was crying loudly, wetly, shoulders shaking, tears squeezing through his fingers.

Amy's first reaction was to return to the sliding door with all the speed she could muster, and push it shut. The cast had left the drama studio, but any of them might be inquisitive enough to glance through the glass outer door. With the intervening studio so dim and this room so bright they would easily see into it, and she knew Martin would be humiliated if they did.

She limped back to him in growing dismay. After the events of the last few days her nerves were none too strong, and the sight of this tough little boy so abandoned to grief almost pushed her over the edge. When she felt her own eyes burn with threatened tears she acted on purest instinct, sinking to the piano stool and putting an arm round the heaving shoulders of the clumsy leather jacket.

'That's it, cry it out,' she murmured, hardly knowing what she said. 'That's the best thing to do. There's nobody here but me . . .'

The sobs slowed and quietened, the tears dried. Presently he gave a huge sniff and wiped his nose on his leather sleeve. She wished she had a tissue to offer, but her supply was in her bag back in the studio.

'Listen, Martin,' she said, choosing her words carefully. 'If you feel you can tell me what's wrong . . .'

'None o' your business.' His voice was still thick and watery, but came as near as possible to his usual macho growl.

'I know it's not. But sometimes it's better when you tell somebody. Besides –' Amy stood up, not wanting to embarass him now that the worst of his tears were over – 'maybe I could help.'

'You can't,' Martin said. 'Nobody can.'

'I'm sorry about that.' Amy stared down at him, wondering what to do next. From the stubborn set of his jaw she knew that further questioning would only alienate him. Tomorrow she would ask at the morning meeting if anyone knew what was making Martin so unhappy, but it seemed a roundabout, hopelessly inadequate response. Still, it was all she could do.

She gathered her thoughts. 'You know you're not supposed to be here by yourself, don't you?'

He shrugged angrily.

'But seeing you are, why don't you . . .' Wait till the others have gone, she would have suggested, then go to the cloakroom and splash your eyes with cold water so people won't know you've been crying.

Perhaps it was just as well he didn't stay to listen; he would probably hate to have his tears mentioned aloud. Before she could finish he had turned his back on her and slouched over to the glass-panelled door that was the fire exit.

So that's how he got in, she reflected as she watched him pull open the door and disappear into the evening darkness. I must tell the caretaker.

Like a child playing hide-and-seek she counted to ten to give Martin plenty of time to be well away. Then she limped over to the door and replaced the locking bar which the caretaker must have overlooked. As she did so she heard the red sliding door reopen, followed by a familiar voice whose husky notes at once made her feel better.

'They told me you'd be in here.'

'Who did?' she asked, making her uneven way towards him.

'Little fair girl who giggled a lot, and a bigger bossy-looking one.'

'That'd be Ella and Joanna.'

'They offered to come with me in case I got lost. Which doesn't seem likely,' he added, indicating the space behind him, 'seeing you were just the other side of this theatre or whatever it is.'

'Studio. And they didn't think you'd get lost.'

'That's a relief; so I didn't strike them as a complete idiot.'

'They just wanted to come with you.'

'Out of nosiness?'

Amy nodded. 'Plus I expect they fancy you.'

'I'll try not to let it go to my head.'

'They do run after everything in trousers,' she agreed. 'On the other hand,' she went on, liking his self-ridicule, 'you're quite . . .' She broke off, angry with herself. Telling him he was quite fanciable was almost the same as saying she fancied him herself, and she didn't, didn't, didn't. She was through with fancying men she hardly knew. '. . . quite well-preserved for your age,' she finished instead, 'as they'd see it.'

With a mock preening gesture he straightened his tie; Amy wondered if its muted swirl of greens and violets were hand-painted on silk. He wasn't wearing the aromatic coat; she presumed it would be too hot now the weather had turned so mild. His moorland-brown tweed suit, though old-fashioned, fitted him with a fluid elegance which spoke of expensive tailoring, and his dark green shirt united suit and tie by picking up the undertones of both.

'I'll take their interest, if that's what it is,' he said, 'as a compliment to my auction outfit.'

'It's certainly a sight to behold.' She looked him over. 'Is it so you can catch the auctioneer's eye?'

'Something like that.' He glanced back into the dimness of the studio. 'Is that your bag, over there on the steps?'

She nodded, and indicated the lighting box under the roof in the top corner of the audience tiers. 'I must go up there and switch off the stage lights before we leave.'

'Let me.' There he went again, taking over. He didn't wait for her assent, but moved at once to the studio. By the time she had put out the music-room lights and limped after him he was already rising through the audience area, disdaining the stairs and letting his long, springy legs take him smoothly from one red-carpeted tier to the next. Watching him, she had to admit to herself that she was glad to be saved the climb. After the day's exertions, her knee was troubling her quite seriously.

'Be sure to put the on house lights so we can see our way out,' she called after him. 'We can turn them off at the door.'

'Ma'am.' His voice echoed down from the roof as he sketched a salute. 'Heavens,' he added, fanning himself, 'it's hot up here.'

'Isn't it,' she agreed. 'The caretaker says he can't do anything about it.'

'I bet he could if you rang the council offices about the wasted fuel.'

'I can't do that,' Amy objected, horrified. 'I don't want to get him into trouble.'

'You wouldn't have to.' Paul pulled open the door of the lighting booth. 'Just showing you were thinking of it would do the trick.'

It probably would, too, Amy thought as he vanished into the smoked-glass cubicle. And after all it's true, this overheating *is* a shocking waste of fuel.

She resolved to try what he had suggested, but not now. I must be getting old, she thought as the spotlights dimmed away and the house lights blinked on. I really feel I've had enough for today. Twenty-nine and I'm past it.

But when Paul rejoined her at floor level, his enthusiasm cheered her like a tonic. 'It's fun up there, isn't it? Who works the lights for your shows?'

'On this one, a couple of sixth-formers.'

She stared up at him. For some reason the house lights made his tie seem bluer, and brought out the blue of his eyes. His hair had curled tighter and his olive skin shone a little, from the heat trapped under the roof she supposed, but it looked like sheer good health.

The blue eyes sought hers. Thinking how haggard and worn she must look, she refused to meet them. If only he didn't always make her feel at a such a disadvantage.

'Supposing we find somewhere to eat?' he suggested gently.

At least he hasn't said I look as if I need it, Amy reflected. She knew she did need to eat; she had skipped lunch today. Aloud she asked if he knew the Crossed Keys at Davisham. He did, and they agreed to drive there in convoy. She hoped she could do better justice to its food than she had managed the last time she ate there – was it really only yesterday?

'I'll carry this.' He lifted her bag from the audience bench where she had left it, and Amy opened her mouth to protest, then bit her lip, and instead muttered her thanks.

He was right – again. What with English exercise books to correct, plus two sets of the final, formal report sheets to which she must transfer her drafted gradings and comments, her bag was heavy tonight. With the need to keep weight off her damaged knee, she was lucky to have someone else to carry it for her.

She picked up her jacket, and shrugged into it. Paul took a step towards her as if to help, then seemed to change his mind.

So at least he thinks I'm fit to put on a coat by myself, Amy thought. She knew she was choosing to be grouchy rather than examine what she really felt about his reluctance to come near her. Did he think her bad luck was contagious, and he might catch it from her?

To distract herself she checked round the cavernous studio for anything she or the cast might have forgotten. Finding nothing, she turned towards the glass outer door.

'Let's go.'

Side by side, not touching, they made their way out of the studio, through the lobby with its little counter that could be used as a coffee bar, past the now-deserted cloakrooms, through the centre's main double doors and out into the soft, damp, black air of the fitfully-lit car park.

'Which of these is yours?' Amy asked. She found herself mildy surprised that she shouldn't already know, when in other ways she felt she knew him so well. But his car had spent the night outside the Nelson, and she hadn't thought to look for it when she set off this morning.

'It's over there . . . hang on.'

His long stride quickened between the dimly outlined shapes of the cars. Amy limped after him, cross at being left behind, crosser when she saw him presumably reach his car and dump her school bag on the wet asphalt. Why, for all she could see from here he might have put it in a puddle . . .

No, at least he hadn't done that. Her indignation waned, gradually replaced by surprise as she approached near enough to see that he was standing by a battered blue mini-van exactly like the one run by Harold Clark Heating Engineer. Whatever kind of vehicle she had expected him to own, it wasn't this.

The van's back door was raised. So that was why he'd been in such a hurry just now; he must have spotted it from a distance.

'It's been broken into,' he called across to her.

'I'm surprised Jim let anyone do that,' Amy said as she finally reached him.

'Jim isn't here,' he told her. 'I took him to Felicity's kennels to be looked after while I was at the auction.'

'I am sorry,' she said, momentarily forgetting her own troubles. 'Has much been taken?'

'I don't know yet, but they've damaged this lock.' He indicated the handle of the lifted door. 'I'll have to tie it up somehow before we set off.' He peered into the van's black interior, then gave up and moved forward along the van to try the driver's door. 'This one's all right.'

'I'm glad of that,' Amy said, meaning it.

Perhaps after all it would turn out to be not too bad, just one broken lock. She glanced round him to the lit phone box near which she had parked her own car. Paul had unlocked his driving-seat door and switched on the interior light and headlights, which made it harder to see into the gloom outside, but she could just make out the caretaker's banger in its usual space. Next to it stood the off-road vehicle that belonged to the centre's supervisor, and the Oaklands PE teacher must be training in the gym; there stood his sporty white coupé on this side of the phone box.

Paul had lowered himself into the van's driving seat for a look round the little lighted space. Now he got out of it, straightened, and reached Amy in one stride. When he spoke his voice was low as ever, but it held a menacing growl she had never heard before.

'My coat's gone.'

So at last this good-tempered man was angry, and rightly so. The coat might seem an irrelevance to some, but he treasured it, had worked on it, and would never be able to replace it.

'Oh Paul,' Amy exclaimed, conscious of the inadequacy of words. 'And you were so fond of it. But why on earth would a casual thief . . .' She broke off, her troubles returning and multiplying until they filled her horizon with sickening familiarity. 'Do you think,' she asked, dry-mouthed, 'that it was a casual thief?'

'There's nothing else missing.' He spoke with grim neutrality, suspending judgement. 'And no damage except for that one lock where they broke in.'

'Where *he* broke in,' Amy amended from the depths of her renewed depression. 'So my bad luck really is contagious.'

'Bad luck?' He considered the idea. 'I suppose you might call it that . . .'

'No, we'll call it what it really is.' She faced him in the thin spillover from his headlights. 'Robert's still persecuting me, and now he's started on you as well.'

'We don't know that . . .'

'We can give a good guess.' She sought in her tired brain for words to explain what she meant. 'Nobody else would do anything so . . . so hurtful, and yet so . . . so pointless.'

For a long moment he was silent. When he finally spoke, his voice had regained its usual soft good humour. 'If you really think that, there's only one thing for us to do.'

'Yes,' Amy agreed. She had no choice. It was one thing to refuse to tackle Robert when he was making a nuisance of himself to her alone. But now he had started on Paul, and for no better reason than that Paul had gone out of his way to help her.

It has to stop, she decided inwardly, and took out her car keys.

'I'll drive ahead,' she said aloud, 'and show you the way.'

She moved beyond the glare of the van's headlights and made for her own car. Here was the phone box, here a motorbike that hadn't been there earlier, and yes, here it was, her little red Polo . . . No, wrong, that was someone else's red Fiat; her Polo must be further along than she remembered.

But it wasn't. Blankly disbelieving, she walked along the row of parked cars and then back to the Fiat that wasn't hers. Then she returned to the blue van and knocked on its window. When Paul wound it down she spoke less to him than to the black, whispering hostility of the night.

'My car's been stolen.'

CHAPTER 8

'Damn and blast Robert,' Amy burst out as they reached yet another snarled-up queue of vehicles. 'May he burn, may he rot, may he . . .'

'Careful,' Paul interrupted. 'Don't put . . .' He broke off to nudge the van through a gap in the stream of cars. 'Don't put wishes on people,' he went on as he reached the lane he needed. 'They always come back on you.'

'Like radishes, you mean?'

He didn't respond to the joke. 'What you send out, you get back. Always.'

She glanced sideways at him from her place in the passenger seat, but he was intent on the intricacies of the Canterbury traffic system, and didn't return her gaze. His profile, steady and dark against the shifting lights of the city, showed no sign of relaxing into a smile.

'What you send out, you get back,' she repeated, considering the idea. 'You sound very serious about it.'

'It's a serious subject,' he assured her in a matter-of-fact tone.

Amy stared past him, to where a part of the cathedral's lit façade glowed at the end of a narrow street. She was remembering the time when a fifth-year boy, normally sullen and uncooperative, had walked into her classroom defiantly wearing a checked tweed cap and clearly expecting it to cause trouble. Because her father always wore that sort of cap, she had smiled at it. To her surprise the boy had smiled back, and taken the cap off without a word. That had happened early in her time at Oaklands, and she had learnt from it.

'If you treat a class properly they'll always do their best for you, even the baddies,' she said slowly. 'So it certainly makes sense in teaching.'

'It makes sense in everything.'

'Then you have to be careful to give out only good?'

'If you can.' He nosed the van across another cluttered junction. 'It isn't easy.'

'No,' she agreed thoughtfully. 'I don't suppose it is.'

Could this be why Paul was so endlessly good-humoured? In the brief time she had known him she had seen him soaked by a badly fixed tap, then covered in soot which had probably ruined his beloved yellow sweater. Though he surely liked clothes and took care of them, neither incident had ruffled him in the slightest. Even discovering the theft of his beloved coat half an hour ago had upset him only for the briefest time. The moment's fury past, he had at once become his old, easy-going self.

Or that was how she had thought of it at the time. She had assumed that he was blessed with an unusually even temper, hard to provoke, quick to recover after a mishap. She realized that unconsciously she had almost dismissed it as a weakness in him that he showed so little anger.

Now she saw that in truth it was a strength. In those few words, 'what you send out, you get back,' he had outlined a philosophy which made his good nature seem no mere natural trait, but a positive act of will.

'So Robert behaving like this,' she speculated aloud, 'is damaging himself more than me. That's a comforting thought.'

'Not really.'

Amy didn't ask what he meant by that. As she stared out at the city's massive, flint-built walls, the comment began to explain itself. If you get back what you give, she thought, you can't find comfort in anything bad that happens to someone else, however much they deserve it.

No, wait, it wasn't for her to say what other people deserved. That would be judging, and in Paul's philosophy the only person you could judge was yourself. Not a comforting thought at all.

'Anyway,' he said as they slowed for yet another traffic light, 'whatever this fellow's done, you can't blame him for the Canterbury rush hour.'

'It's his fault we're having to go through it,' she pointed out.

'We'd have to anyway.'

'No we wouldn't. We meant,' she reminded him, 'to eat at the Crossed Keys. We were already on the right side of town for that.'

'I see what you mean. We'd have been out into the country in a minute or two.'

'Instead of struggling through the worst of the town traffic to pick up the road to Maidstone.'

'Well at least we're doing it in one car, not two.'

'Yours, and I'm grateful for it.' Amy almost smiled. 'But aren't you taking positive thinking a bit far, to find a bright side to having one's car stolen?'

This time he did laugh but, hemmed in on one side by a removal van and on the other by a motorbike, he made no comment.

'Anyway,' she said, 'thanks to you, it hasn't hit me as hard as . . . as I suppose he meant it to.'

It was true; Paul's company and support had spared her the worst of the loss. Maybe it would be different in the morning when she needed the car to get her to school, but please heaven they would have it back by then. Meanwhile, at least she had her driving license, purse, school papers, everything she really needed, with her in her big school bag. It was tiresome not to have her driving shoes, or the maps she kept in the glove compartment, or the daily paper she had left on the back seat, but those were minor items easily done without.

What she couldn't have done without was Paul, his calm, his authority, his generosity in making her cause his own. It was no small thing to be willing to drive a round fifty or so miles on what might be a wild goose chase, for they had no way of knowing if Robert would be at home. They had considered telephoning, but agreed that he must be tackled face-to-face, and there was no point in warning him in advance.

'If we'd gone to the police,' Paul said as he threaded through a roundabout, 'they'd probably have kept us busy until rush hour was over.'

'We don't need the police. Unless Robert refuses to deliver, that is.'

It was an argument she had already used. They knew Robert had the coat and the car, she had reasoned, so they might as well go straight to him and get them back. She hadn't mentioned her dread of having to explain her bungled, discreditable private life in the hard, cold light of a police station.

And that would only have been the beginning. Suppose Robert were to be prosecuted for the theft of the car, and the case got into the papers? She hated to think of the effect that would have on her relationship with her classes; perhaps on her career itself. Who knew if the school would want to go on employing someone who got into such a sordid mess? It seemed all too possible that parents would complain . . . No, she wouldn't think about it any more.

Bad enough that I'm having to face Robert himself, she thought in renewed depression. At best he'll make me out to be crazy, at worst a lying troublemaker.

'Anyway we'll soon be out of it now,' Paul said. 'How about the Half Moon?'

'What?' She peered up at what she could see of the sky, black and moonless beyond the lights. 'What about it, then?'

'It's at Hurnfield, just before the M2 . . .'

'Oh, a pub!' she exclaimed, enlightened.

'Run by a friend of mine. They do a great roast beef and Yorkshire.'

'I'd sooner have a . . .' She broke off. I'd sooner have an omelette, she had been about to say, or something else that I can easily get down. But before the words were out, a vision of the perfect Yorkshire pudding floated into her mind. Fluffy-light and deep gold, it smelt deliciously of the tender roast beef which her imagination at once put with it. Why, she could even see the plate, blue willow-pattern, and a big chased-silver knife and fork which she couldn't wait to pick up.

'I haven't had roast beef since I was last in Northumberland,' she said. 'You're sure your friend's place does it right?'

'Right enough for me to enjoy it.'

'Do they roast carrots and parsnips round the joint as well as potatoes?'

'I can't remember,' Paul admitted. 'But there are lots of trimmings.'

'Cauliflower maybe, and broccoli, steamed, not boiled . . .' She broke off, the vision fading. 'Roast beef's a meal for Sunday dinner,' she told him sadly. 'They won't be serving Sunday dinner on a Tuesday evening.'

'Let's see, shall we?'

From the outside the Half Moon was a traditional, cosy Kent pub, white-walled and gabled, standing by itself at the end of the village. Its sign intrigued Amy. Its painted, star-flanked half-moon had flying across it the last creature she would ever have expected to see over the peaceful, Kent-style hills painted below it.

'A dragon?' she murmured, staring up at it.

'Brings good luck,' Paul told her. 'This way.'

After the cool night of the car park, the inn's bar greeted them with a luxurious warmth. As she and Paul picked their way through various groups who sat on squashy black leather benches round low white tables, Amy slowly took in pale walls with gilt-framed seascapes, a grey-green carpet, dark blue velvet curtains, and concealed lighting which somehow stilled the place, so that she felt like a fish swimming through an aquarium.

The slender barman was busy mixing a drink for a waiting customer. He was ivory-skinned, with polished black hair and tilted dark eyes; not a person she would expect to serve roast beef. He put the drink he had mixed on a small lacquer tray with two others and accepted payment with an intense seriousness which made him seem very young, like a child playing shop. Only when he had finished the transaction did he see Amy and Paul.

'Larky! Long time no see.' His wide smile made him look about sixteen, but his voice was incongruously clipped and authoritative, like an army officer's.

175

'Sorry, I mean Paul,' he corrected himself. 'If you came and saw us more often I might find it easier to get used to.'

Amy turned to stare up at Paul. 'You changed your name?'

Paul's mouth pulled together in what might have been distaste. 'Larky's what they used to call me at school.'

'From Clark, I suppose?'

'Sort of.'

'They called me Inky,' said the barman.

'That's ridiculous.' Amy surveyed his immaculate white shirt, dark-red velvet jacket, and black bow-tie. 'I can't imagine a spot of ink daring to come near you.'

'It had its own logic,' said the barman. 'So had Larky's.'

Whatever the logic of the nickname Inky, it had nothing to do with his real name, which when Paul introduced them properly turned out to be Owen Rees. Amy began to feel she was losing her grip.

'You're Welsh?' she ventured, embarrassed to be asking when he was so conspicuously something else.

'My father is,' Owen confirmed in his clipped, un-Welsh voice. 'My mother's Cantonese.'

'Could that,' Amy asked, 'be why your inn sign has a dragon on it?'

Owen nodded. 'Brings good luck.'

'Is it a Welsh dragon, or a Chinese one?'

'Chinese,' Paul put in. 'Welsh dragons are red.'

Having got so far, Amy floundered on. 'But you don't sound Welsh either . . .'

'Ah well,' Owen said with a sideways glance at Paul, 'our school trained us to talk born-to-rule.'

Amy hadn't heard the phrase before, but recognized it at once. It was a perfect description of those particular tones, so confident, so loud, so fitted for command. She glanced curiously at Paul, wondering how he had kept that soft, slightly hesitant voice after such a training. Perhaps he had resisted it, or perhaps it just hadn't worked on his vocal chords.

'I can't picture you two at school together,' she commented. 'Were you one of those child prodigies, Owen, studying with pupils years older?'

Paul laughed. 'He's thirty, same as I am. He's just wearing better.'

'You're wearing all right yourself,' Owen said.

Amy lifted her gaze to Paul's olive-dark face. In this strange, muted white light the blue eyes seemed very dark, almost black, the pupils enormous, all-seeing . . . She hastily looked away.

'I had no idea,' she told him, 'that you were as old as that.'

'Maybe we're just late developers,' Paul said.

'You speak for yourself,' Owen told him. 'I have a wife, children, a flourishing business – if that isn't development, I don't know what is.'

Paul smiled, and bowed his head in mock contrition. 'How are they all?'

They chatted for a moment about Owen's wife, who seemed to be called Heidi, and his children, of whom Amy lost count but he seemed to have at least three.

More customers appeared at the door, and Owen returned to his duties.

'Can I offer you two a drink?'

Amy and Paul exchanged a quick glance, then shook their heads as one.

'Thanks all the same,' Paul said, 'but we, er, we need to keep our wits about us this evening.'

Amy was silent, recalling with a sense of shock where they were heading and what they meant to do when they got there. How could she have forgotten, even for the brief time they had been here? And now it had come back to her, it seemed the heavy weight of dread within her had lifted a little. Perhaps, she thought, it's because this place is so . . . surprising.

'Have you come for the carp?' Owen asked. 'A lot of people are here for the carp tonight,' he added with modest pride. 'We put a sign in the window.'

'I promised Amy roast beef,' Paul said.

'That's on too. Not everybody likes fish.'

The restaurant turned out to be across the corridor from the bar. Already at half past six it had customers, and Amy could see why. Leaf-green cloths covered the roomy tables, each with a leaf-green candle in a silver candlestick and a silver vase of freesias whose freshness lightly perfumed the air. The lighting came from silk-shaded lamps on the white walls, and in the middle of the big room stood a riot of potted plants round a central table holding a cairn of cunningly arranged fruit on a huge silver platter.

Three tables were taken, and two more had reserved signs. One group was already eating gold-brown slices of something-or-other from which rose a seductive aroma of spices.

'Could that be the carp?' Amy murmured as a dark-haired young waitress showed them to their table and lit its candle.

'I expect so,' Paul said. 'Would you like to try it?'

'Another time maybe,' she said regretfully. 'My palate's expecting roast beef.'

Her palate was not disappointed. The waitress took their order without fuss, and perhaps deduced from its sober simplicity that this was a travel stop rather than an evening out, for their food arrived almost at once. The beef proved to be thinly sliced across the grain and so tender they hardly needed their knives, the Yorkshire pudding meltingly light, the roast potatoes crisp on the outside and fluffy within. The carrots were steamed rather than roasted round the joint but full of flavour and bright as jewels, and so was the broccoli in the other half of the partitioned silver vegetable dish. The gravy in the silver sauce boat tasted like the kind Amy always made herself, using the juice of the meat and little else.

She didn't know where her appetite had suddenly come from, but for a meal like this she hardly needed it. It seemed no time at all until her plate was empty, and long before she had finished she was astonished at how much stronger and more optimistic she felt. She knew it was days since she had eaten properly, but she

179

had never realized how the lack of food had been pulling her down.

Her system had been needing this fuel far too long, so long that she felt it had gone straight to her nerves and bloodstream like alcohol. She looked across at Paul, who was still eating, and loved the careful way he held his knife and fork, the neatness of his curly, lowered head as he concentrated on his food, the olive-dark tones of his skin which the candlelight turned to gold, the sweep of his long, dark lashes, the firmness of his straight nose which seemed much shorter when his head was lowered like this.

I'd like to hug him, she caught herself thinking, for bringing me here, for everything, for being such a love . . .

Dismayed, she sought to divert her own attention from the rush of feeling the idea produced in her by saying the first thing that came into her head. She glanced down at her green-and-gilt porcelain plate. 'These are different.'

'Hm?' Paul looked up, his eyes suddenly revealed like a light focusing on her from beyond the candle flame. 'What are? Different from what?'

'They were going to be willow-pattern,' Amy said nonsensically. 'And the knives –' she lightly touched the bone handle of hers – 'were going to be solid silver . . .' She burbled to a halt, looked down at her empty plate, and set her knife and fork together. 'Sorry. It's been a long day.'

'Good to see you eating properly.'

'It was marvellous, Paul. I don't know when I've enjoyed food so much.'

'Yes, Heidi's a great cook.'

Soothed as always by the softness of his voice and his air of serenity, she watched him methodically work through the last of his own portion. 'Heidi doesn't sound an English name either.'

'That could be because she's Swiss,' he teased, slicing a piece of Yorkshire pudding. 'They met when she was spending a year here to learn English.'

'What a league of nations. How come she does English food so well?'

'I expect she just learnt it. She and Owen are a remarkable pair; make a success of anything they tackle.'

Amy smiled, liking the way he could admire his friend without a trace of envy. 'What did he mean about your nicknames having their own logic?' she asked. 'I can't believe he was an inky kid?'

'He wasn't, not in the least.' Paul finished the last morsel on his plate, and put his knife and fork together. 'I wasn't all that larky, either.'

'Yours does sound a bit like your real name, though.'

'Coincidence.'

'So why Larky?'

'Perhaps I'll tell you about it some time. When we've less on our minds.'

'I suppose that makes sense.' But she couldn't resist probing further. 'What was this place that trained you to speak born-to-rule?'

He named a well-known public school. Amy was intrigued; working as she did in the state system she was always interested to hear about schools outside it.

'And they really teach boys to speak in that confident way?'

'Not formally. You pick it up by hearing and imitating.'

'Only you didn't, did you?' She knew she was being too personal, but she so much wanted to know more about him. 'Did you actually decide you wouldn't?'

'I don't know.' He ate the last of his food without much interest. Then he shrugged, his wide shoulders moving in the moorland-brown tweed with that special, graceful ease all his own. He wasn't looking at her but down at the candle flame, seeing pictures in it perhaps. Cheerless pictures to judge by the lines of his face which, gilded by the flame, stayed sombre. 'I hated the place.'

Amy was realizing with a shock how little she knew of Paul. They seemed to understand each other so well, she found it difficult to remember that it was barely twenty-four hours since they had first met.

'Were you really so unhappy at school?' she asked, full of sympathy. 'Right through from start to finish?'

His brows drew together a little as he considered the question. 'It got better as you grew older.'

'It still must have seemed like a life sentence . . .' She let the words trail off, picturing him as a sad little boy sent away from home to the brutalities of an all-male establishment 'I suppose your parents thought they were doing their best for you.'

Paul nodded. 'When my father was . . .' he hesitated, choosing his words, 'when he was – in funds – he set up a trust for my school fees. In his own way –' Paul put his knife and fork together with an abstracted air – 'that was a big sacrifice for him to make.'

'And your mother? She must have hated sending you to a place that made you so unhappy.'

'I didn't let her know. Stiff upper-lip and all that . . . Besides,' Paul added a little grimly, 'I think she was quite glad to be left alone with her new husband.'

So his parents had divorced. 'Did you get on with him?' she asked. 'Your stepfather, I mean.'

'He was all right. I didn't see much of him. He had this estate in Scotland . . .' Paul broke off, and looked around for the waitress. 'I need to ring Felicity, she'll be expecting me to pick up Jim. Time we went.'

But the restaurant had gradually filled, the little waitress hurrying from one table to another taking orders and delivering them. She muttered an acknowledgement of Paul's request for the bill, and disappeared towards the kitchen.

Amy was considering the new things she had learnt about Paul. He had gone to an expensive school, and his stepfather had an estate in Scotland. In other words he came from a backgound which took money – plenty of money – for granted. Now why did she find that so surprising?

She briefly wondered if she believed him, and quickly decided that she did. He had given the facts so reluctantly, and only in response to direct questions.

And there were his clothes, those old but grand tweeds for instance, that beautiful hand-painted tie, even the coat they now pursued. There was also Owen, who had been to the same school and spoke born-to-rule.

On the other hand there was that battered old van, the cheapest vehicle he could possibly have driven. As she thought of it a picture of it came into her mind. Then she realized that it wasn't Paul's van she was picturing but another she had recently seen, one with *Harold Clark, Heating Engineer* lettered on its side . . .

'That's it,' Amy said aloud. 'Where does Harold fit into your family, Paul?'

'Father's brother's son,' he responded promptly.

'And did *he* go to a public school?'

'Of course not!' Paul seemed amazed that she could ask such a question. 'Whatever made you think that?'

'Well, he's your cousin . . .'

'His father and mine were chalk and cheese.'

'So yours was the one who made the money?'

'No,' Paul's voice was suddenly cool, austere, warning. 'Harold's father was the steady one.' He twisted in his seat, signalling once more. 'The bill, please.'

This time the little waitress hurried over to their table. Amy waited, feeling snubbed for her inquisitiveness. Squinting upside-down at the figures the waitress scribbled on her pad, she was relieved to see that they were quite reasonable. Very reasonable indeed, in fact, for such a feast.

'I'm sorry, I forgot to ask if you wanted a pudding,' Paul said. 'Or coffee . . .'

184

'Nothing more, thank you.'

He paid the bill from an ancient, battered wallet of some soft leather from which the gilt flourish of his initials had almost worn away. The waitress, apparently satisfied with her tip, picked up their plates and departed.

'Right.' He put away his wallet, and started to rise. 'Let's go . . .'

'Wait.' Amy stayed firmly where she was. 'I . . . I'm sorry I've left this till now,' she began, still awkward from his coolness of a few moments ago. 'I suppose it's because I've had a lot on my mind . . .'

'You want to pay your share?'

'Something like that,' she said, relieved to have the words spoken. 'How did you guess that was what I wanted to say?'

'I've had supper with one or two women before.'

'Oh.' Amy wondered why she should find that so surprising. He was an attractive man, of course he would know lots of women. She badly wanted to hear if he was currently seeing anyone, but even without his recent put-down she couldn't possibly ask that. Nevertheless she couldn't leave it.

'And these women all wanted to . . . to share the bill with you?'

'The nice ones did.'

'Oh.' Amy turned the words over in her mind, gradually realizing what they meant. She wasn't at all sure she liked the idea of being described in such a lukewarm way.

'So you think I'm one of the nice ones?'

'You?' Paul smiled that sweet, bright, surprising smile. 'You're just . . . you.'

Now that, she thought confusedly, that I *do* like. She couldn't mistake the special warmth in the soft voice as he spoke the words, and the tenderness in his eyes which seemed so dark in the gold-tinted shadows . . . She dragged her mind back to business.

'So can I share the bill, please?'

His smile grew teasing. 'Supposing I said no?'

'Depends on the way you said it. The main thing,' she continued, refusing to be diverted, 'is not taking it for granted that the man has to pay every time.'

'OK, we'll agree on that.' His gaze never left her face. 'But for this time, shall we call it my invitation?'

She looked down at the green tablecloth, beyond him to the leafy chintz curtains, sideways to the white walls with their silken lamps. Finally, irresistibly, she had to return to that dark, intent gaze, and when she did she had the oddest sense of having settled at last where she belonged. 'Thank you for a marvellous meal,' she said humbly. 'Thank you from the heart.'

He was silent for a moment. 'That's a lot of thanks for a small thing.'

'It was a big thing . . .' She broke off, knowing she was speaking too vaguely, and tried again. 'It was a . . . a turning point. The first time I've been able to eat properly since . . . since all this started happening.'

Try as she would, she couldn't be more specific about the events of last Friday and their consequences. Instead she focused on the strength the meal had given her.

'I feel I can face anything now.'

'So let's.' He stuffed the bill in the side pocket of his jacket, and together they left the restaurant. A pause in the corridor pay phone for the briefest of calls, a moment in the bar to thank Owen for the quality of the cooking, and they were in the car park.

'Well,' Amy said glumly as she settled beside him in the van, 'here goes.'

In the dimness she felt, rather than saw, the sharp glance that Paul gave her. 'I thought you said you could face anything now?'

'Being able to face it isn't the same as looking forward to it.'

He started the engine without further comment, guiding them out of the car park, through the village, and back to the now much quieter A2. Soon they joined the M2, and settled to a steady sixty. She listened to the rattle of the engine, and tried not to feel each turn of the wheels bringing her nearer to Robert and a reckoning for past foolishness.

'You've heard about my schooldays,' Paul said presently. 'What about you? What were yours like?'

'Hm? Oh,' she came out of her gloomy imaginings, 'very ordinary. I and my brothers went to the local comprehensive on the school bus . . .'

'How many brothers?'

'Four.'

'And you the only girl?'

'The only woman. My mother died when I was eleven.'

'Ah,' he said as if she had given him a vital clue to something. 'And your brothers are all younger? And your father never remarried?'

She confirmed both facts. 'I think my parents were . . . very close.'

'I think you all were.'

'I suppose we were.' She suddenly saw her childhood in a completely new light for its contrast with his. 'I suppose we were a pretty close family. Still are.'

'I can tell that just by being with you. And I'll tell you something else, too.' He slowed for a road works. 'Your family adore you.'

'What?' Amy turned to him inside her seatbelt, blinking in surprise. She couldn't see his expression, only his strong, capable hands on the controls and a little of his profile touched by the thin, coloured light from the dashboard.

'No no, you've got that wrong,' she said, shaking her head. 'We were all fond of each other of course . . .'

'But you were the only girl, and the eldest.'

'The bossy eldest, always chasing them. They must have hated me sometimes.'

'You saw that your brothers did their homework? That they had clean clothes, packed lunches, sports gear, whatever?'

'Oh yes, I did all that,' she admitted. 'And it seemed I was forever badgering my father to eat enough,' she added from her memories of the unhappy time after her mother had died. 'He went right off his food for ages. That's when I learnt to cook.'

Heavens, she'd only been the same age as the year sevens. The same age as Tracy Norris, Martin Sullivan, Tim Horner. She wondered briefly at the problems eleven-year-olds too often had to cope with. Martin, for instance. What was it that had made him cry . . .

'There it is then,' Paul was saying as if he had proved a case. 'You fed them, cleaned for them, cared for them, saw them right. No wonder they adored you.'

'But Paul, they *didn't*! I don't know where you got such an idea.'

'Then I'll tell you.' The road works past, he brought the car back up to speed. 'There's a kind of . . . of gloss on you. A confidence, a queenliness almost.'

'But Paul . . .' She floundered to a halt. She wanted to remind him of their first meeting, her fear, her injury, the miseries that had afflicted her since. How on earth could he see her as confident, now of all times?

Perhaps he didn't need reminding. 'It's always there, whatever happens to you,' he said as if he too were thinking of the trials of the last few days. 'Right inside, without needing to think about it, you respect yourself even when you've made mistakes . . .'

'Do I really come across as so conceited?'

'No,' he said simply. 'Confident people never have to be conceited.'

'I . . . I see.' And at last, she did. 'Like a big man not having to throw his weight about.'

'That's it. I bet you're a marvellous teacher.'

'I don't know about that . . .' She interrupted herself with directions. 'We turn off at the next exit. He doesn't live in Maidstone itself, it's a village on the outskirts.'

They trundled through the motorway exit, out into the dark countryside, through it to a lit thoroughfare and at last, inevitable as fate, into the quiet, leafy street where Robert lived. Amy peered through the windscreen, examining the occasional parked vehicle as they passed it.

'I don't see my car anywhere.'

'He'd hardly leave it outside his own . . .'

'Stop here,' Amy instructed, feeling dread within her like a crouching animal. 'That's the house.'

And there it was, the massive front door through which she had escaped, the circular drive whose asphalt she could almost feel again beneath her bare feet. There was the window from which Robert had threatened his revenge, it and all the other windows in darkness.

'I . . . I wonder if he's home.' She tried to keep her voice steady.

'Somebody is.' Paul said.

She saw what he meant as he drew along the kerb and her angle of vision changed. On the other side of the low bushes, an off-road vehicle was parked to one side of the driveway. She didn't think it was Robert's, but so little had she learnt of him in those cloistered weekends that she couldn't be sure.

'I . . . I don't know if that's his,' she said. 'It doesn't seem likely, somehow.'

'If it isn't his, then someone else is there.'

'Maybe. I don't know anything about his . . . about what he does on weekdays.'

Only what he did at weekends, with me, she thought. Oh, if only I'd taken more interest in him, if only I'd found him out, if only . . .

'If it's his night for tenpin bowling,' Paul said, 'he'll be home presently.'

In spite of her savaging dread, Amy couldn't help laughing. 'It'll be squash rather than bowling. Unless the head of his firm goes bowling,' she added on second thoughts. 'Then he'd . . .'

She gulped. A warm hand had closed over hers. She supposed he meant to quiet her fears, but she didn't know whether he had or not, so great was the tumult of feeling that rushed through her now. It was as if her whole being whirled to him, drawn to his depths and tossed to his heights like a leaf on a fountain. She didn't know who made the first move and didn't care, she only knew that they were close, close, their mouths together, their arms holding one another, their souls entangled . . .

She pushed at his shoulders and pulled herself away from him, as far away as she could in the narrow space. 'This is all wrong.'

'It feels all right to me.' But he didn't try to draw her back, only lifted a lock of her hair and kissed it.

She brushed it out of his grasp. 'You don't know . . . you haven't heard . . . I haven't said . . .'

She floundered to a halt. Last night she had told the Clarks only the barest outline, that a man had proposed marriage to her, that she had rejected it, and that he now

191

seemed to be harassing her. She hadn't touched on her three-month affair with Robert, the selfish limits she had set to stop it interfering with her work, her lack of interest in her lover except as a means to her own pleasure.

And now she was paying for it, really paying in a way that made Robert's childish revenges seem trivial in comparison. Now a real man wanted her, a man strong enough to be tender and wise enough to be good. And thanks to her treatment of Robert, she felt unworthy of such a man.

'Would you mind not doing that?' She flinched away as he kissed the sensitive flesh below her ear. 'It makes it hard for me to think.'

'I agree this isn't the time or the place.'

But he kissed the same place again, and then her cheek, and when she turned to him he took her shoulders between his two strong hands and kissed her lips. This time however it was the briefest of kisses, quick and firm as the imprint of a signet ring on wax.

'Remember I'm here,' he murmured in her ear. 'Right here with you.'

Yes, but for how long? How much would he . . . like her, want her, continue to support her, after he had learnt what she was really like? And he would learn it, in the worst light possible; trust Robert for that.

'All right,' she said with a sigh. 'Let's go.'

CHAPTER 9

'I wonder if it always seemed as spooky as this.'

Amy stood on the pavement and surveyed Robert's domain. In the half-moon shaped flowerbed at the front of the drive, the professionally pruned rose bushes stood like prisoners, each tied to its stake and ruthlessly clipped to uniformity. The side beds held shrubs with poison-red berries. One side of the house was closed off by a flat-roofed double garage and an iron-barred gate; the other by laurel bushes whose leathery leaves shifted and rattled in the soft, wet wind.

'I never did like those laurels,' Amy added. 'They make a noise like a vampire's wings . . .'

'Enough of that,' Paul interrupted from the road where he was locking up the van. 'We're not up against anything supernatural, so stop scaring yourself.' He came to join her on the pavement. 'The person who lives here is just an ordinary creep . . .'

He broke off as if he regretted the word, and Amy could see why. It conjured a picture of

193

Robert creeping up on her, plotting by stealth to do her evil.

'. . . is just an ordinary, inadequate human being,' Paul corrected himself. 'We ought to get over to that porch, out of this rain.'

But he made no move in that direction. Instead he put his arms round her, there in the thin-lit street with the rain drifting about them, and drew her close. She rested her head on his shoulder and wondered how long it would take for his suit and her jacket and skirt to be soaked, and what Robert would say if he were to come out and find them like this, and didn't care about either.

No, that wasn't true. She didn't care about the rain, but she did care about what Robert would say. But then he would say awful things whatever happened, so she might as well try and forget him while she drew strength from this moment of closeness. She inhaled one of her deep, calming breaths, then buried her nose in Paul's shoulder and inhaled again.

'You smell different today,' she told him. 'Sort of mossy, heathery, ferny.'

'I expect the rain's bringing it out. It's a feature of this kind of tweed.'

'It's nice.' Amy drew in another breath of it. 'What happens when it meets your coat?'

'I take care it doesn't. Listen now.' He drew away from her and took both of her hands in his. 'There's a lot needs sorting out between you and me . . .'

'Is there?' She stared up at him, loving the way the street light from across the road highlighted the firmness of his jaw and the fullness of his mouth. Oh, if only she could forget the reason they were here, the squalid affair with Robert . . .

'You know there is. But for now, all you have to remember is that I'm with you. All right?'

'All right.'

He let go of one of her hands, but kept the other and raised it to his lips. Then, still holding it, he drew her across the pavement and into the semi-circular drive. The security light flicked on, startling Amy so that she jumped and her heart pounded. Paul squeezed her hand a little, just enough to show that he sympathized, and they kept up their steady progress across the drive. The glaring new light threw deep, distorted shadows across the red-brick gables, and made the berries on the bushes glisten like drops of blood.

'Does he really live alone in this great place?' Paul asked.

'I agree it's miles too big for one person,' Amy said. 'He doesn't use half the rooms . . .' She broke off, hating to show that she knew the house from the inside, hating herself for knowing it. As she limped along at Paul's side, treasuring the warmth of his hand round hers, she wondered why her knee should suddenly feel so much worse. Could fear really have such a specific effect? But she wouldn't be afraid, she wouldn't.

'He inherited it from grandparents, I think,' she added, trying to keep her mind on everyday things. 'He says it has happy memories of his childhood.'

There, that helped, picturing Robert as a little boy with adoring grandparents. But the relief lasted only until she lifted her gaze to the broad window above and to the right of the entrance, the window of the bedroom where . . .

No, she wouldn't think about that. Trying to keep her mind away from it, she stared instead at the little niche, sharp-edged in the hard white light, which decorated the brickwork above the porch. In the past she had laughed at that niche, put there as if to hold a tiny votive statue to guard the house, but now it didn't amuse her.

It's the people outside this house who want guarding, she thought.

Apart from the security light, the place was still in darkness. For a moment hope flared in her that Robert wasn't here, that she was going to be let off seeing him. The sensible part of her mind extinguished the hope at once.

She had to see Robert. Even before he stole her car she had to see him, though she hadn't been able to admit it. She had to do something to persuade him to stop this stupid, evil campaign he was waging against her.

The deep, brick-pillared porch, not reached by the outer security light, lay in heavy shadow. As they stepped into it Amy felt as if she were putting herself into the mouth of a huge, predatory animal, but the feeling abated a little as the porch's own security light came on. It showed her the heavy front door, its two glass panes patterned with red-glass lozenges like bloodstained teeth. Once she entered that door the animal would have swallowed her and the teeth might chew her up, but the light also showed something quite different and cheering. Two handsome earthenware pots flanked the door, one holding a tiny bay tree and the other a miniature rosemary bush. There was something so brave and sweet about those little plants, each in the middle of its big pot with a lot of busy growing required of it to fill the space it had been given, Amy felt better just looking at them.

'These are new,' she said, indicating the plants and glad to find that she could speak without a tremor. 'Looks like he's decided to grow herbs.'

'May they flourish,' Paul answered. 'A person who grows bay and rosemary can't be all bad.'

'I suppose not,' she murmured, unconvinced.

Paul pressed the doorbell, and its two-tone chime sounded deep within the house. Would Robert answer it? Would he be at home?

He would. Somewhere at the back of the hall a door opened, shedding white light which reached the front door's glass panels and changed the red lozenges to blooded spear-points. Robert must have been in the kitchen.

'I'm letting go of your hand now,' Paul said, and did.

Amy could understand why. Their attraction to each other was too new and vulnerable to be displayed, especially to an enemy, and besides it mustn't be allowed to distract them from the business in hand.

Nevertheless she felt somehow diminished as they separated, cold and small and lonely and useless, an inadequate challenger waiting at the door of the ogre's den.

'But never forget I'm here,' Paul said. 'Here and with you.'

The yellow hall light came on, and Amy stiffened for the awful moment of confrontation.

It didn't come. The door was opened, not by Robert but by a woman in a checked lumberjack-style shirt, jeans and trainers, her long dark hair caught up in a pony-tail secured with a rubber band.

'Here it is.'

She had a deep, velvety voice, a beautiful voice which Amy found soothing even now, in this place. She was offering a charity envelope, firmly gripped between strong, work-stained fingers. Her pink unpainted nails would have been filbert-shaped had they been allowed to grow, but were cut as short as they would go.

It's not that she bites them, Amy thought, looking for the tell-tale raggedness and finding none. She's just trimmed them to be out of the way.

'He told me you'd be coming,' the woman went on, presumably thinking she was speaking to a charity volunteer. 'Come on,' she added with a trace of impatience, 'let's have your bag where you collect these things.'

Amy turned her head to look at Paul, and found he had turned his to look at her. Recognizing that he meant her to start the talking, she cleared her throat.

'We . . . we didn't come about that . . .'

'Oh.' The beautiful voice cooling, the woman let the envelope drop to her side. 'I hope you didn't take me away from my baking just to convert me to the True Path or something?'

Amy shook her head, licked her lips, and drew a deep breath. 'I . . . My name's Amy Hammond.'

'Oh.' The voice was now icy, not an echo of the velvety tones remaining. 'I wonder you've the nerve to show your face here.' The woman's eyes, dark as a gipsy's, took in Amy's companion. 'It hasn't taken you long to find yourself a new boyfriend. Or were you two-timing my husband all along?'

'Your *what*?' Amy wondered if she had heard right.

'My name is Paul Clark.'

Awash with confusing thoughts, Amy discovered one of them to be that maybe Paul's school had done something for his voice after all. It still had its softness, but now carried an undertone of steel which somehow forced one to listen. Paul was not about to let himself be spoken of as if he weren't here.

'I,' he went on, 'am one of the people who've had their time wasted by hoax phone calls.'

'Oh.' The woman bit her lip, looked down at the doormat, looked up again and met Paul's gaze full on. 'Well . . . well it served her right . . .'

'Some of those calls were made by a woman,' Amy put in. 'Was that you?'

'And did it serve the rest of us right?' Paul asked. 'Me and all the other Clarks who were sent chasing non-existent work in the middle of nowhere?'

'Here, wait a minute,' Amy began. Stribble isn't as isolated as all that, she wanted to say. Luckily, she realized in time that the size and location of Stribble had nothing to do with anything, and that she mustn't on any account argue with Paul. Not that she could have anyway, seeing he was taking no notice of her.

'Well . . . well I'm sorry,' the woman said. Her deep, melodious voice sounded subdued, but she glared towards Amy. Embarrassment had brightened her eyes and cheeks and she looked younger than before, softer and more unsure in spite of her continuing hostility.

'But not about *her*,' she added like an embattled eleven-year-old crossing her fingers behind her back. Once more she was speaking exclusively to Paul. 'I . . . I know I shouldn't have brought other people into it, but I was so angry with her –' another rancorous glance towards Amy – 'for the way she treated Robert, I got carried away.'

'Will you tell me what I'm supposed to have done to Robert?' Amy didn't have much hope of an answer, but at least she could use her classroom voice and remind them both that she was also present. 'In fact, there's a whole lot of questions I want to ask you . . .'

'We need to see him. Urgently.' Strange how Paul's soft voice could so easily ride down any other. 'Could you fetch him, please.'

In spite of the 'please', it was more of a command than a request. The woman hesitated, influenced in spite of herself by the tone, then shook her head.

'He's not in.'

He's not in, Amy's mind echoed in an uprush of unreasonable joy, he's not in, he's not in. I don't have to see him. Unless – the joy sank away like a turned-off fountain – unless she's lying to get rid of us. Robert could have told her to say that.

'We'll wait,' Paul said, quiet but implacable.

'Don't waste your time.' The woman stepped back and grasped the door, preparing to close it. 'He has nothing to say to either of you.'

'You're wrong there.' Despite the flat contradiction, Paul's voice stayed soft as ever. 'He has a lot to say, either to us or to the police.'

'The police?' The woman's eyes widened, and her work-stained hand gripped the door tight. 'You wouldn't go to the police about a harmless practical joke? Why, they wouldn't take you seriously.'

'They will when we report a stolen car.'

'What?' Her head jerked up, her pony-tail bouncing and swinging. She swayed backwards a little as if from an assault, then looked from Paul to Amy and back.

'Whose car?'

'Mine,' Amy said.

'He . . . he'd never do that.' But her certainty had been shaken.

She knows things about Robert, Amy reflected, that make her think he might steal a car, if it happened to suit his purpose.

'The car's gone.' Paul drove his message home without heat or malice. 'It'll have to be reported, unless we can get it back.'

'So you've only just lost it?' The woman revived. 'Then it can't be Robert, he's been with me since seven.'

'I discovered the loss about half past five,' Amy said. 'It could have been taken any time during the afternoon.'

This was clearly another facer. The woman could alibi Robert for the evening, but not for the afternoon. 'It . . . it could have been taken by anybody,' she stammered.

'That's what we need to find out,' Paul said, treating the idea more seriously than Amy thought it deserved. 'And here on the doorstep is no place to settle anything. Can we come in, please.'

Once more the soft, polite request came out as a command. The woman looked them over, frowned, peered beyond them into the night as if hoping for rescue. None came.

'If we can't,' Paul said, 'we'll wait outside, in that.' He gestured back to indicate his van drawn up against the pavement. The woman bit her lip, stared down at the quarry tiles of the porch, then straightened as if she had made up·her mind.

'He's only gone out to the pub for some wine,' she said, stepping back to admit them. 'He'll be here any minute.'

So she hadn't been lying. Robert really wasn't in the house. In the renewed surge of relief that washed through her, Amy felt almost light-hearted. Paul indicated that she should go ahead, and she limped across the threshold into the big, square hall.

Then she saw the stairs, and it was as if the events of last Friday happened all over again. She felt the pile of the Turkey stair-carpet under her bare feet, the polished oak of the banister under her fingers, the panic as she fled, gathering up her clothes as she went . . .

'Remember I'm here,' a soft voice murmured in her ear, and a strong, gentle hand briefly touched her arm.

Strength flowed into her from the touch. Her breathing quietened, and she could walk past the foot of those terrible stairs without another glance in their direction. She could even *think* again, for what felt like the first time since Paul had pressed the doorbell.

'You're Sarah, aren't you?' she said to the woman ahead of her. 'That's why you called Robert your husband.'

The woman, laying the charity envelope on the hall table, looked up sharply. 'What do you know about me?'

'That you used to be married to Robert.' Amy cast her mind back, and realized there was quite a bit more. 'That you're Cornish, and after the divorce you studied to be a vet,' she continued. 'And that you're probably good, because the local practice took you on. Robert seemed annoyed about it . . .'

'Did he?' Sarah's eyes took on a surprisingly goofy, lovelorn expression, and she actually smiled. 'He isn't now.'

'Is that why you didn't go home to Cornwall?' Amy asked. 'Because you wanted to stay near Robert?'

'This way.' Sarah returned abruptly to her task, pushed open a door, and disappeared beyond it.

'Well done, Amy,' Paul murmured before they followed. 'For a minute there she nearly forgot she hates you.'

Amy had no time to reply, but she smiled her thanks for the encouragement.

As she entered the front room into which Sarah had led them, she realized with relief that here at least she would suffer no frightening memories. Robert tended to live in a den at the back of the house, looking on to the garden, and when she visited at weekends their activities had centred round that and the bedroom and kitchen. She had been inquisitive, of course, about the rest of the house, but had never explored it, and though this room was on the ground floor, she had never even glanced into it.

She found it surprisingly unlike anything she could imagine Robert wanting. For one thing its square-patterned Axminster carpet, sprigged wallpaper, chintz curtains and chair covers, and scattering of lace-hung, ornament-littered tables made it far too fussy, and far too ordinary. For another it had flowers, which Robert had never bothered with in all the time she had known him. But there they were, a tall vase on a bureau holding winter-flowering jasmine, and a bud-vase on a side table with one graceful rose.

'Those pots at the front door,' Amy said in sudden enlightenment. 'The bay and the rosemary. They're yours, aren't they?'

But Sarah, busy switching on various porcelain-based lamps, was not to be softened again so quickly. 'Please sit down,' she said coldly. 'I invited you in here to talk about this stolen car.'

Amy exchanged a glance with Paul. Oh, how much, how very much, she wanted to sit next to him on that couch facing the unlit fire, rather than away in this chair to its right.

But it was not to be. She sank to the chair alone, and looked again at the room from this lower, more relaxed position.

Family photographs, yet! A whole flight of them hung on the wall of the alcove to the right of the fireplace. At Amy's present eye-level, the nearest was a black and white studio portrait of a white-haired couple with a handsome little boy – could that be Robert with the grandparents who had left him this house? A little higher was a coloured one of a golden labrador dog, and a picture of a middle-aged couple who might have been Robert's parents, celebrating something at a table laden with glass and silver. Prominent on the other side of the room hung a big coloured picture of Robert in late teens or early twenties, distractingly gorgeous on a horse.

Why, he's got a family like anybody else, Amy thought, a family who have anniversaries, keep a dog, are proud of their son. Then she noticed, here and there about the room, conspicuously empty hooks where other photographs might once have hung.

And there aren't any photos of their wedding, she thought.

At first she scolded herself for the silly idea. Why on earth would one expect to see wedding photos on display after the couple had divorced? Then she knew why she had expected it.

'This is your room, isn't it?' she said to Sarah. 'Robert's kept it exactly as it was when you lived here.'

That lovelorn expression reappeared in Sarah's eyes. 'He says he couldn't bear to come in here . . .' She broke off, aware that she was lowering her guard again. 'Now, what's this nonsense about a stolen car?'

It was Paul who answered that, with his usual even firmness. 'I think we'll leave that until we can ask your . . . your husband about it.'

Amy noticed the hesitation on the word husband, and well understood it. Were Robert and Sarah married or weren't they? Whatever Robert's faults, surely he had been speaking the truth about his divorce, and the two could hardly have remarried in the four days since last Friday. Amy longed to ask what had happened, and what their plans were, but of course that was quite impossible. Instead, she nodded to indicate the dust-pan, brush and duster which had been left on the hearth.

'I'm sorry we've interrupted your dusting,' she said, polite as a visiting vicar. 'I don't suppose you get much time for chores, with your busy life.'

'I'd done most of it,' Sarah admitted ungraciously. 'You should have seen the dust and cobwebs – it was like Miss Havisham's wedding.'

'It . . . it certainly looks nice now,' Amy offered. 'Very welcoming.' She spoke from an half-conscious desire to conciliate, but quickly realized that what she said was true. Though the room might not be to everyone's taste it had a timeless, traditional charm which eased the eye and the spirit. With the fire lit and a trolley of homemade cakes and scones, it would be an agreeable place to be invited for afternoon tea.

Sarah acknowledged the compliment only with an indeterminate noise, but dipped her head and regarded Amy from below thick, dark, untrimmed eyebrows.

The idea of tea inspired Amy to another gambit. 'You said you were baking?'

'Sponge cake,' Sarah answered.

I knew it, Amy thought, amused in spite of her worries. This woman is the complete home-maker. Robert was a fool to let her go.

Sarah remained stiff-backed, hands clenched in her lap, but her dark eyes sought Amy's. Clearly she was torn between continuing antagonism and a desire to . . . to impress? To deliver a put-down to one she regarded as an enemy? Or maybe simply to mention the name of her beloved, and show how she could please him.

'Robert says he hasn't had a decent sponge cake since I left five years ago.'

Yes, she loved saying the name. Her beautiful voice lingered on it, and the austerity of her expression softened into something distant and dreamy. Amy decided to trade on it.

'So you two are together again?'

'No thanks to you,' Sarah flashed back, all softness gone. 'It might have happened a lot sooner, if you hadn't been leading him up the garden.'

Amy wanted to retort that she had never done such a thing to any man; that she was always careful to promise only what she could deliver, and what she promised, she always delivered. She managed to hold it back.

'Is that what I'm supposed to have done to him?' she asked instead.

'You made him think you were serious, didn't you?' Sarah demanded. 'You led him on until he proposed to you, and then you turned him down. Turned him down!' she repeated on a rising note of indignation. 'The best a man could offer, and a man like my Robert, and you turned him down.'

Strangely, Amy found herself almost sympathizing. However much of a monster Robert might seem, Sarah was still or again in love with him. It must have galled her to hear of another woman rejecting him, especially one she considered unworthy of him anyway.

'I'd honestly no idea he was thinking like that,' she found herself protesting.

'Then you damn well should have. You'd been . . .' Sarah paused, searching for a phrase. 'You'd been having sex with him long enough, hadn't you?'

Amy bit her lip, not daring to look at Paul.

'I know he only proposed to you to get back at me,' Sarah began, apparently quite happy with the story

Robert must have told her, 'but surely you knew the
. . . the affair –' she pronounced the word with distaste
– 'was going somewhere?'

Amy studied the half-moon shaped, ivy-patterned
hearthrug.

'Well didn't you?' Sarah persisted. 'What did you
think you were doing?'

Still Amy didn't answer. She couldn't. The only
honest answer was that she hadn't thought about it
at all. For three months she had visited and
enjoyed Robert every other weekend, and when
the weekend was over she had gone back to her
busy life in school and never given him another
thought.

'I . . . I can see why you're angry with me,' she said
at last. 'And why Robert was too . . .'

'You're damn right he was. The poor love didn't
sleep a wink all night after.'

'He wasn't the only one,' Amy murmured, driven to
defending herself. 'He did some pretty nasty things to
me, you know.'

'Whatever he did, you deserved,' declared Sarah,
her pony-tail bouncing with passion. 'Of all the hard-
faced, supercilious bitches . . .'

'Steady on,' said Paul.

'Also,' Amy put in, still intent on defending herself,
'his idea of marriage is different from mine.'

'More fool you, not knowing a good thing when you
see it.'

'Yes, well, the way he reacted . . .'

'And what about the way *you* reacted?' Sarah demanded. 'Physically attacking him, *hurting* him, and then running off and leaving him like that?'

Amy stared at the other woman in silence, taking in this partisan version of events. She supposed, when she thought of it, she wasn't really surprised. Maybe by now Robert believed it himself.

Sarah tossed her head, presumably believing she had won the argument. 'Well at least good came of it,' she went on in a quieter tone. 'On Saturday the poor darling was so down he had to talk to somebody . . .'

So he had talked to Sarah. Remembering Robert's scowling resentment whenever he spoke of his ex-wife, Amy wondered how on earth that had come about. He could hardly have sought her out.

'. . . and when we met in the post office,' Sarah continued, 'it all just came tumbling out.'

'The post office?' Paul must have decided it was time he came in again. 'That would he when he sent the conker, then.'

'I suppose I really ought to be grateful to you . . . Conker?' Sarah stared at Paul. 'What on earth are you talking about?'

At the memory of that innocent-seeming package and its ugly contents, a new weight of dread settled on Amy. She controlled it, keeping her hands still in her lap and forcing herself to meet the eyes of the woman on the other side of the fireplace. At least they were now more puzzled than hostile.

'It . . . it had been smashed with a hammer,' she said. 'It . . . it frightened me . . .'

'What?' And Sarah laughed, briefly but genuinely, with a display of splendid teeth. 'You scare easy, don't you? A silly old conker?'

'He . . . he used to talk about my hair . . .' Amy began, but got no further.

'I wonder what you'd have done,' Sarah cut in, 'if he'd sent you your wedding photos, all torn in pieces?'

So that was what had happened to the pictures which must once have hung on those empty hooks.

'And the wedding book too,' Sarah continued. 'He'd used scissors on that – like confetti, it was.' The dark eyes went misty and unfocused with pure, unadulterated infatuation. 'He tells me he took the frames out to the garage, and smashed them with a hammer like your conker.'

She speaks as if he'd given her a present, Amy thought. A proof of love.

And maybe it was, of a certain sort of love. But no, not really. Like the conker it was proof only of a violent temper out of control. She glanced across at Paul, and couldn't imagine him doing anything like that. Paul had a temper all right, but he would never let it lash about in such wild gestures. He knew how to harness it and make it work for him.

'I can understand why he did it.' Sarah sighed and shook her head, not, it presently emerged, at Robert's actions but at her own. 'Before I left I poured all

211

twelve bottles of his precious Sancerre wine down the loo. He'd just found out.'

Amy let out her breath in a long sigh, and discovered that she was more relaxed than she had felt in days. 'Sounds like you're well-matched, you two.'

'I got back at the little tart who took him away from me, as well,' Sarah reported with satisfaction. 'I had half a ton of horse manure delivered to her front doorstep . . .'

'Another hoax phone call.' Paul made it a statement rather than a question.

'And I rang all the papers, pretended to be her, and offered the story of my affair with our local MP.' Sarah heaved a gratified sigh. 'They besieged her for days.'

'So that's where Robert got his ideas,' Amy said. 'I'm beginning to think you let me off lightly . . .'

'But they didn't,' Paul told her. 'They didn't let you off anything.' He turned to Robert's wife. 'Why Clarks?'

Sarah shrugged. 'There are a lot of Clarks in the Yellow Pages. We meant to ring every one of them, but . . .' She paused, the goofy look back in full force '. . . but we sort of got distracted.'

'And you really think it's funny,' Paul said, 'to pull a silly stunt about somebody who's just been killed in a road accident?'

'What?' The goofy look abruptly left Sarah's face, to be replaced by what seemed like a genuine frown of bewilderment. She stared from Paul to Amy and back.

'Somebody told the undertaker I'd be dealing with the funeral arrangements,' Amy explained, 'as I'd been engaged to the dead man.'

For a long moment, Sarah sat in silence. 'I agree that was going a bit far,' she said at last. 'I can see I'll have to take him in hand.'

'The undertaker told me it was a woman who'd made the call . . .' Amy broke off, wishing it unsaid. If Sarah was acting her ignorance of that particular hoax it was a convincing act and Amy for one believed her. But if Robert's ex-wife hadn't made the call then another woman had, and the manner of his connection with this third woman seemed all too easy to guess. She wasn't sure she liked Sarah, but she certainly didn't dislike her enough to want to upset her.

And upset she certainly was. Her lips had tightened, her dark eyes narrowed, her capable, short-nailed hands descended to spread flat and square on the knees of her jeans. She looked more like a gypsy than ever, and a formidable one.

'I'll get it out of him,' she murmured more to herself than to her companions. 'He'll tell me, if it's the last thing he ever does . . .'

'That's between you and him.' Paul brought the conversation back on course. 'We're here to talk about the way he's been threatening Amy.'

'Threatening?' Sarah's frown turned to a scowl. 'That's a bit strong, isn't it?'

'My call was from a man, him, I presume,' Paul informed her. 'It said Amy had died after an accident with a piece of electrical equipment.'

'I agree Robert's humour's a bit on the . . . the black

213

side,' Sarah admitted, 'but you surely don't think he'd do anything to make that happen?'

'Are you absolutely certain he wouldn't?' Amy asked.

'Of course I'm certain!' Sarah declared, pink and passionate. 'It's one thing to have a laugh at your expense . . .'

'Stealing my car goes a bit beyond a laugh.'

'I don't believe he did that.' Sarah's tone was far less sure than her words, but gained conviction as she rushed on. 'But even if he did it's only theft, not even that, if he only meant to tease you . . .'

'Theft is theft,' Paul put in quietly.

'Not if he gives it back,' Sarah retorted, 'and if he's got it, he will give it back. But this other thing you're talking about,' she went on, returning to her theme, 'that would be murder . . .'

She stopped speaking, clearly appalled by the word. It dropped into the comfortable room like a stone, spreading ripples of shocked silence. Amy heard the little whirr of the battery-driven clock, a distant gurgle that might be an air lock in a heating pipe, the approach of a car. The car drew nearer, slowed, came nearer still, and dropped abruptly to silence just outside the window.

'There he is,' Sarah said with obvious relief. 'Now he'll be able to tell you himself that these awful things you're saying aren't true.'

CHAPTER 10

So this is it, Amy thought. Enter the fiend.

She glanced from one of her hands to the other, spread along the flower-patterned arms of her chair. Then she inconspicuously raised them a fraction, keeping hands and forearms parallel with the chair arms. Though the position was not a natural one and needed some slight effort to maintain, both hands held steady, without the least suggestion of a tremor.

The fact is, she thought, I've stopped being scared.

She looked across at Sarah almost with affection. It wasn't any dramatic battle which had cut Robert down to size but something far more effective, the defence of him by this besotted, hard-working woman who had been his wife. With her displayed photographs, her loving care, her indulgence of his tantrums and her unconscious authority over him, she had changed him from a terrifying force into a mere spoilt brat, unpleasant but manageable. Amy, who managed spoilt brats along with every other

215

kind of pupil, almost felt disappointed that, after all her fears, he should turn into something so paltry.

Neither of them had bothered to argue with Sarah about the truth or otherwise of their charges. With Robert so near it made far more sense to wait until he appeared, and take up the argument with him directly. So they all listened in silence as, beyond the bay window, the car door opened and closed.

A moment later the key turned in the lock of the front door, and that too opened and closed. From the hall issued the medium-to-light baritone which Amy had last heard threatening revenge.

'I'm back, Saucybums,' it called.

The ever-ready pink appeared in Sarah's cheeks, heightening the darkness of her eyes as she stole a sideways glance at Amy. She raised her chin, so determined not to be embarrassed by the pet-name that she looked like a scornful gypsy princess.

'I've got Bulgarian for tonight, shall we take it to bed with us?' Robert carolled, still unaware of being heard by any but Sarah. 'I know a thing or two you can do with wine besides just drink it out of a glass . . .'

'In here, Rob,' Sarah hastily interrupted. 'We've got visitors.'

'O-oh.' The single syllable rose to a self-conscious second note. 'That'll teach me to check before I speak.' A muted rattling followed, as of wine bottles carefully placed on the hall table. Then the door opened, and there he was.

And there he is, Amy thought, Robert the spoilt brat. Robert the player of silly practical jokes. Robert the menace.

He looked like none of those things. As casually dressed as his ex-wife in jeans and an autumn-gold sweater, what he most resembled was an ad in a colour supplement. Drink this coffee, drive this car, buy from this outfitter and you too can be as smooth and handsome as this.

Though caught by surprise, he didn't look foolish. His dropped jaw only drew attention to its perfect shape and proportion, and his widened eyes, lit by the frilly-shaded lamp on the table near him, shone a haunting, tigerish amber.

Amy glanced at Sarah and saw her transfixed and adoring, staring at Robert as if she had never seen him before. Even at this strange moment, with so many questions needing answers, all she wanted to do was just gaze and gaze at him.

'It's you.' He spoke to Amy almost as if he had been expecting her, and turned at once to Sarah. 'Why the hell did you let her in?'

'Hm?' Sarah gave herself a little shake, rousing from her trance. 'Sorry, my darling, but they're telling the most awful lies about you . . .'

'She let us in because if she hadn't we'd have gone to the police.'

It was Paul's soft, powerful voice which had supplied the answer. Amy shot him a grateful glance, and was intrigued to see how relaxed he looked. Relaxed, yes, but also ready for action. Long legs drawn against the flowered couch, hands quiet on his tweeded knees, dark blue eyes steady, candid and alert, he made Robert seem suddenly weak and flashy.

He's not such a conventional dreamboat, Amy thought, but he's good to look at and much, much stronger.

Especially now, when Robert was giving that phoney laugh at the mention of the police. Remembering how contemptuously he had always spoken of her drama lessons, Amy reflected as so often how much he could have learnt from just one of them. He really was a lousy actor.

'Police? I don't think so,' he said. 'Anyway, who the hell are you?'

He strode into the circle of chairs round the fireplace, turned his back on the empty grate, and belligerently straddled the hearthrug facing the couch. With his hands half-clenched at his side he loomed over the seated Paul as if he might any minute pull him up and knock him down.

'What makes you think,' he demanded, 'that you can come into my house and threaten my . . . my wife like this?'

'I'm one of the Clarks,' Paul responded, coolly stating his interest.

Robert's mouth set in a mulish line. 'I don't know what you're talking about.'

'Oh, come on . . .' Amy began, but caught Paul's eye and subsided.

'I think you do,' he said, still without heat, 'but leave it. We've come about something far more serious.'

'Ah yes, the police.' That forced laugh again. 'And what do you think you have to tell them?'

'Let's see now.'

Paul paused, setting his thoughts in order as if he had all the time in the world. From his place on the couch he had to look quite a long way upwards to face the other man, yet his whole manner spoke of confidence and control. He might have been on his own home ground rather than Robert's; the head of some business enterprise interviewing a job applicant.

'Let's start at the beginning,' he went on. 'First, there's sending abusive material through the post . . .'

'What abusive material?' Robert snorted. 'What are you accusing me of now?'

Amy sighed. 'You know damn well . . .' Once more she subsided at a glance from Paul.

'Then there's the fraudulent phone calls,' he continued, methodically adding to his list, 'including a specially nasty one about a man who had just died in a road crash.'

'I don't know what you're talking about,' Robert repeated. 'What phone calls?'

'The dead man was another Clark,' Amy put in, wearied by the automatic schoolboy denials. 'The actual call was made by a woman, but it's got your fingerprints all over . . .'

'Yes, and who was she?' Sarah shot to her feet and confronted Robert. 'I made the other Clark calls but you got somebody else to do that one.' She tossed her head, pony-tail flailing. 'If you've been two-timing me again . . .'

'You haven't bloody admitted to the calls, have you?' Robert accused in his turn. 'For heaven's sake, woman, haven't you any sense at all?'

'Don't be so stupid,' Sarah countered. 'How can I enjoy getting back at her if she doesn't know it was me? Now then,' she returned to her ferocious point, 'what little slut made that call for you?'

'I tell you I know nothing about it.' Robert sent a hunted look from one face to another. Amy began to feel almost sorry for him, trying to stonewall and being let down by his own side.

I can see why they split up, she thought. Doesn't she know better than to start on him at a time like this?

'If it's somebody you knew before we got back together,' Sarah kept up her attack, 'then you can finish with her now. At once. Or I'll . . . I'll have your balls for ping-pong.'

Amy, recalling the particular way she herself had disabled Robert in order to make her escape last Friday, couldn't resist an inward giggle. But Sarah could talk a whole campaign of assault; she would never take action against this man whose body she so idolized. Perhaps she realized that herself, for she followed up the threat with a far more convincing one.

'I'll find out who she is, you know. And when I do . . .' She let the idea trail into ominous silence.

'There isn't any other woman,' Robert protested.

How the mighty were fallen. Under this onslaught Robert seemed even more troubled and pathetic. His fine head turned one way then another as his amber eyes sought the far corners of the room as if for a means of escape. Amy thought of the poem about 'tamed and shabby tigers'.

However, he struggled gamely on. 'Now for heaven's sake, sit down,' he said to his tormentor, 'and let me deal with these two . . .'

'Sit down yourself,' Sarah retorted. 'You're making the place untidy, stuck there on the hearthrug. Take your own chair,' she added, indicating the one she had just vacated, 'and I'll fetch another.'

Without waiting for an answer she bustled to a plush-covered grandmother chair in the bay window. Amy saw Paul stir in his seat, ready to leap up and help, but Sarah lifted the chair as if it were no weight at all, and returned at once to set it down next to the one she had directed Robert to take.

She must be physically strong as well, Amy thought.

Robert had ignored the order to sit down. 'Stop fussing me, woman,' he said without looking at her, and to Paul, 'Please leave. Now.'

'Believe me, we don't want to hang about here,' Paul answered easily. 'We'll go the minute we've got things sorted out.'

'You'll go now. Or I'll . . .' Robert sought, and found, a suitable threat. 'I'll call the police.'

'But that's exactly what *they* say they're going to do,' Sarah protested, settled on the chair she had fetched. 'Do sit down, love, and tell them it isn't true.'

'Tell them what isn't true?' Robert turned on her irritably. 'I wish everyone would stop talking in riddles.'

'They've told me about the conker, that has to be you,' Sarah went on. 'And I've told them about the phone calls I made, so we can forget those.' She paused, then took a resolute breath as if to say something unpleasant. 'And I'm sure the undertaker call was you, it being a Clark and everything.' Her dark eyes lengthened to an an indulgent sternness, like a mother correcting a beloved child. 'You shouldn't have done that, darling.'

Robert glared at her. 'I tell you I . . .'

'Somebody really died. That's not funny. Now do sit down,' Sarah repeated with growing impatience.

Amy's laughter almost bubbled to the surface. This woman might be crude and vengeful, but in some ways she had a lot of sense, and she was making Robert look more and more like a mutinous little boy. However, he stayed on his feet and tried to keep at least the appearance of still having the initiative.

'I'm waiting for these people to go.'

Sarah sighed, shook her head at his obstinacy, and resumed her case. 'This guy here,' she began, nodding towards Paul.

'Paul Clark,' he interposed, refusing to be dismissed as 'this guy'.

Sarah tossed her head impatiently, but complied. 'This Paul Clark had a call saying *she* –' with a scornful jerk of her head towards Amy – 'had died.'

'You asked me to clear Amy's cottage,' Paul said, effortlessly back in charge.

Robert folded his arms. 'How many more times . . .'

'There's worse.' Armoured in his calm contempt, Paul thrust aside the attempted denial like a cobweb. 'Last night a potentially dangerous dog was left in Amy's garden.'

'What?' This time Robert wasn't acting. His mulish expression vanished, to be replaced by an astonishment which had to be genuine. He stared across to Amy, then back to Paul, then to Amy again. 'I don't know anything about a dog.' His tone now was quiet, puzzled, with none of the false emphasis he had put on his earlier denials.

'What a strange thing to do,' Sarah observed with innocent detachment. 'If the dog was dangerous, why didn't it hurt whoever brought it?'

'They could have doped him,' Amy suggested, though Jim hadn't shown the least sign of it. 'Something that wore off quickly?'

'The poor darling,' exclaimed Sarah the vet. 'I hope you looked after him?'

'We did.' Amy found herself warming to this compassion for an unknown animal. 'Actually, he's a nice dog . . .'

'Dangerous or nice, he's nothing to do with me,' Robert cut in irritably. 'I'd never do a thing like that, so stop trying to pin it on me.'

'He wouldn't, you know,' Sarah confirmed. 'He loves animals as much as I do. It's one of the things we have in common.'

Amy glanced up at the picture of the labrador, and then across at the picture of Robert on a horse. Yes, it could be true. With acceptance of the possibility came

223

a new worry, small but growing fast. If Robert hadn't left Jim in her garden, then who had?

'Right.' Paul pressed on, quiet but relentless. 'Then there was the soot . . .'

'So you did set that booby-trap!' Sarah interrupted, talking to Robert. 'Why didn't you tell me?' She turned to Amy, bright-eyed as a pet offered a treat. 'Did it make a lovely mess of you?'

'Of me it did,' Paul admitted, and added blandly, 'Pity you weren't there to enjoy it.'

'I can enjoy the idea of it,' Sarah answered. 'But I wish it had been *her*.' She jerked her head towards Amy. 'I don't have anything against *you*,' she told Paul kindly. 'I'm sorry you're mixed up with that red-haired trollop . . .'

'Steady on,' Paul said. For the second time, that quiet command brought Sarah to a halt in mid-flow. The last time it happened Amy had been too taken up with her own defence to notice the effect, but now, facing the other woman across the hearthrug, she saw the ready flush, the lowered gaze, the chagrin.

So Sarah could be reached. She was strong, but she knew she got out of line sometimes, and the right person with the right approach could show her she was doing it, and stop her. Paul had made her behave by sheer moral force.

And he's done it to prevent her calling me names, Amy thought, flashing him a grateful look. The idea was at once followed by another, bitter one. Oh, if only I deserved it!

Witnessing this instant taming of his wayward partner, Robert seemed first taken aback, then downright pathetic. He looked down at Paul again as if taking a new measure of an opponent he had underestimated. When he finally spoke, his voice was quieter, and held a new wariness. 'All right. I did the soot.'

Perhaps the story of the dog had also shaken him. Along with his pretence of complete innocence, he had given up some of his bristling animosity. However, he retained enough to thrust his hands in his pockets and look defiantly across at Amy.

'I took an afternoon off and drove to your place yesterday,' he informed her.

'You didn't break in,' she stated rather than asked.

'For heaven's sake, Amy . . .'

'What is he, a burglar?' Sarah rushed to the defence of her beloved.

'How would I know?' Amy countered. 'You prowled round my home, why stop at a break-in?'

'Say that again,' Sarah declared, bolt upright and bristling, 'and he'll have you up for slander . . .'

'I took the soot with me from here,' Robert said. 'I thought I might . . . I don't know,' he hesitated, '. . . rig it up at your gate or something. Then I found you'd left your shed unlocked.'

Amy checked back in her memory, and realized it was true. 'So there's no question of you having got in and tampered with my electrics?' she asked, anxious to be sure. 'That stuff about my having an accident was just to scare me?'

For a moment, almost by reflex, Robert's mouth set to that stubborn, denying straightness. Then he took a deep breath, let it out, and nodded. 'Yes. I wanted to scare you, but I'd never really hurt you.'

'Or anybody,' Sarah chimed in, dark eyes snapping.

Amy put her hand to the bruise on her neck, but stayed silent.

'So that's the phone calls and the soot dealt with,' Paul said, and looked enquiringly at Robert. 'And the conker?'

Robert hesitated, then nodded again. 'It's hardly a punishable offence.'

Paul ignored the comment. 'But you deny the dog?'

'I most certainly do.' Robert gave Amy a malicious glance. 'That must have been *another* –' he lingered on the word for emphasis – 'of your enemies.'

'I bet she has lots of them,' Sarah agreed enthusiastically.

Amy looked across at Paul. Drawing strength from his continuing, effortless composure, she repeated what he had suggested last night. 'Somebody must have dumped him. On their way to Dover or the Chunnel, to go abroad.'

But would this notional Jim-dumper really bounce along all the little roads through Stodbean Wood to Stribble? Wouldn't he – they, whoever – be more likely just to tip the dog out on the motorway, or near it? Or if they wanted to shut Jim into a garden, perhaps to save him from being run over, wouldn't they have picked a more accessible garden than one in end-of-nowhere Stribble?

'So now we come to the really serious thing.' Paul brought them all back to the point in his massive, methodical way. 'The theft of Amy's car.'

'*What*?' This time there was no doubting the genuineness of Robert's amazement. His perfect features whitening under the tan, he took his hands from his pockets, turned sideways, and slowly sank at last to the chair Sarah said was his. He sat there for a moment recovering, then rallied his defences and leant forward.

'I hope you don't think I had anything to do with that?'

Paul sat impassive. 'So you deny it?'

'Deny it!' Robert's voice lifted in outrage. 'I don't damn well have to deny a charge like that, it's you who should be ashamed of having made it.'

'A minute ago,' Paul pointed out, 'you were pretending you knew nothing about any of the other things either . . .'

'And anyway,' Amy broke in, unable to hold back any longer, 'who else would have done it?'

'Anybody else,' Sarah waded in. 'Cars are stolen all the time, every day.'

'But this one was stolen during a . . . a campaign of harassment by you two,' Amy countered. 'If you play silly tricks to upset someone,' she added with some satisfaction, 'you can't be surprised that when something more serious happens, the finger's on you.'

'And that's where it is,' Paul said, backing her. 'Right on both of you.'

'What, on me too?' Sarah's pony-tail swung with the force of her outrage. 'Why, I never heard anything so . . .'

'When did the car go?' Robert asked.

He's changed completely, Amy thought. He's not blustering any more. This has really shaken him. Aloud, she told him the notional time the car must have been taken, and when she had discovered the theft.

'This afternoon?' In his relief he slumped back like an unstrung puppet. 'I was in a meeting all afternoon. Two till five.'

'Who else was at it?' Amy asked.

'Julius Drew.' Robert sat up straight again, and brought out the name of Lang and Drews' chairman with a certain grandeur. 'And his son Tommy. And some of the other branch managers.'

'Phew! Thank goodness for that.' Sarah demonstrated her relief by fanning herself, a huge gesture that involved her entire forearm.

She does everything on a big scale, Amy thought, and just as she feels it. No wonder she loves animals, she's as instinctive as they are. It came to her that Sarah's admiration for Robert's looks was another aspect of her feeling for animals. She appreciated him much as she would have appreciated the beauty of a horse, say, or a dog.

'I never thought those stuffed shirts at Lang and Drews would be good for anything,' Sarah continued, 'but I see now they have their uses.'

Amy wondered how even she dared say such things in front of Robert. Sure enough he reacted at once.

'Would you mind not talking about my company like that?'

'What? Oh.' Sarah laughed, showing those splendid teeth again. 'Nothing personal, lover. *You* aren't a stuffed shirt . . .'

'That's enough.' But Robert spoke without conviction, as if he had little hope of persuading his wife, ex-wife, whatever, to be more discreet.

She just doesn't give a damn for his snobberies and pretensions, Amy thought. They roll off her. She wondered how long this reconciliation would last. A long time, she guessed, for Sarah would hang on like a limpet. No, like a lioness to its prey, for she was by far the stronger of the two. She must always have been so, and the years of study plus success in her chosen job would have boosted her confidence. Poor Robert, alas for his dreams of a company wife to help him achieve that place on the board.

On the other hand she'll be good for him, Amy decided. She'll look after him, and protect him, and massage his ego, and make him behave. In fact, she would in all ways keep his feet on the ground, and surely that was a good thing? She hoped Robert would think so, since his chances of getting away seemed so slight.

'So what about you, Sarah?' Paul said.

Hearing him speak the name, Amy realized that it was the first time he had used it. And he had never, at any time, used Robert's.

'Mm?' Sarah had stopped laughing, but the smile still lingered on her handsome face. 'What d'you mean, what about me?'

'Your – er – husband seems to be in the clear. Are you?'

Sarah sat up, bristling as she understood what he meant. 'Now look here . . .'

'You made the phone calls for him,' Paul pointed out inexorably. 'You could have done this too.'

'Well I didn't.' But Sarah had taken the point; some of the self-righteous vigour had gone out of her.

'The easiest way to settle it would be if . . .' Paul glanced at Robert, and left a pause which subtlly conveyed distaste, 'if like your husband you were with other people this afternoon.'

'As it happens I was,' she retorted. 'But I'd never, ever do such a thing anyway.'

'Could you tell me . . . tell us,' Paul corrected himself with a glance at Amy, 'who you were with?'

'Yes I bloody can!' Sarah leapt from her grand-mother chair and shot out of the room, her pony-tail following like a comet's tail. She returned in seconds waving a brown-covered, much-thumbed profes-sional diary which she opened to the appropriate date. She thrust it at Paul and plumped down again in her seat.

'I was on house calls all afternoon,' she informed him. 'They're all written down there, names, ad-dresses, animals . . .' She broke off in a new bout of wondering, outraged innocence. 'The nerve of it, to suggest *I'd* steal a car.'

Paul had taken a small diary of his own and a pen from his pocket, and was jotting down something from Sarah's.

'What are you doing?' she demanded.

He looked up from his writing, a little surprised that she needed to ask. 'We have to check these, of course.'

'Of all the damn nerve . . .' Robert began.

Sarah quickly rode him down. 'I'll do it for you.' She held out her hand. 'Give that back, and I'll call them now.'

Paul took no notice either of the command or of the outstretched hand. 'You surely see we'll have to speak to these people ourselves?' He turned his blue gaze on Robert. 'I'll also need the name and phone number of someone who was at your meeting.'

'I'll see you in hell . . .'

'Sh, darling.' Sarah held up a hand in a gesture both imperious and placating. 'He's right, alibis have to be proved.' She turned to Paul. 'He won't want you disturbing either of the Drews, but there'll be others.'

She leapt up and disappeared again, returning this time with an elegant, gilt-leafed address book. 'Was Sorenson there?' she she asked, riffling through the book.

'He was,' Robert answered, 'but I'm not having him or anybody else bothered about something so preposterous . . .'

'Here he is.' Sarah found the name she was looking for, and thrust the book at Paul. 'You'll be tactful, won't you?'

Tactful! Amy almost laughed aloud. Talk about pot and kettle.

Paul accepted the address book, and passed the brown-covered diary to Amy. Sure enough it held a series of appointments, all fairly close together and all here in the locality. Nobody who kept all these could have found time to drive to Canterbury and steal a car this afternoon. Amy let her eyes wander over the neat, round writing and thought how compact and open it was, and how like Sarah.

'Do we really need to do any checking?' she asked, handing the diary back to its owner. 'I'm beginning to think the theft of the car is just an unrelated coincidence.'

Still copying, this time from the address book, Paul didn't reply.

'It certainly is an unrelated coincidence,' Sarah declared, 'but you're going to be absolutely sure of that before you leave here. Where's your mobile, Robert?'

Robert tried again to be stubborn. 'I'll be damned if they . . .'

'On second thoughts, you can do it from the den.' Sarah looked from Paul to Amy. 'Which of you will make the call?'

Paul finished his writing, clipped his pen back in an inner pocket, and let his thoughtful blue gaze rest on Amy's. She stared back, wondering how she could begin to resist this proposal of Sarah's. The porcelain-faced clock on the wall told her it was well past nine; how could she possibly intrude at this hour into the evenings of complete strangers to ask police-like questions about alibis?

Paul could do it capably and tactfully, she was sure of that. But if he went out to the telephone in the den, she would be left here alone with these two. Or worse, alone with just Robert, as she had been last Friday. He might seem tamed at the moment, but Amy found she didn't at all want to discover what he would be like when Sarah wasn't with him.

Some of her feelings must have shown in her face. Paul too glanced at the clock, then assumed a business-like air, put away his diary, and rose to his feet with that springy ease which characterized everything he did.

'Thank you for the offer,' he said to Sarah, 'but we'll do our checking in our own time, in our own way.'

'Oh no you won't!' She confronted him, hands on hips. 'We're going to settle this here and now . . .'

'Excuse me.' He stepped round her neatly and carefully, as if she were one of the lace-covered tables, and offered Amy his hand. 'Let's go.'

Amy accepted without a word, and let him help her to her feet. Having got her hand he kept it, leading her through the clutter of lamps and nests of tables and plant pot holders, past the porcelain clock and the bureau with the winter-flowering jasmine and the table with the rose, and so at last to the half-open door of the room.

Once there he paused and looked back. Amy did the same, and saw Robert twisted uncomfortably in his chair to stare after them. His fine features were a battleground of different emotions, envy and malice and a continuing, sulky resentment, but perhaps the principal one was renewed shock at this quiet, cour-teous defeat of Sarah.

He can't manage her at all, Amy thought, and then this stranger comes in and just . . . walks round her.

Sarah herself was a study in astonishment. She stood frozen with hands on hips, her mouth still opened to insist that Paul check their alibis here and now. Even her pony-tail hung limp over one shoulder as if strangled by its rubber band.

'There won't, of course,' Paul said from the door, 'be any more hoaxes, booby-traps etc.' He was telling, not asking. 'I take it Sorenson is a colleague?' he went on to Robert. 'He'd probably be interested to hear about all this. And so would the people whose pets you visited, Sarah.'

'Why, you . . .' Robert had shot to his feet, and stood with legs braced apart and fists clenched, a picture of baffled rage. 'Get out, both of you. I don't want to see or hear from either of you, ever again.'

'The point is,' Paul answered, calm as ever, 'that Amy doesn't want to hear from *you*. Especially not indirectly, from somebody else whose time you've wasted.'

'She won't, not from us.' Sarah had at last roused herself to retaliate. 'But you mark my words, nasty things happen round a woman like that Amy.'

'Good night,' Paul said, 'and thank you for your time.' He turned his back on the room, and drew Amy into the hall.

Sarah's deep voice followed them. 'Nasty things will happen because she's a nasty piece of work, and people won't put up with it . . .'

Paul deftly closed the door, cutting off the denunciation. Feet thumped the carpeted boards on the other side of it, then it was torn open again to show Sarah fuming within.

'You'll see,' she intoned like a gypsy laying a curse. 'She's trouble, that woman.'

By now Paul had the front door open and was ushering Amy through it. He followed her, and closed it behind him. She hurried through the sudden brilliance of the porch safety light and into the circular drive. Sarah's intense enmity had shaken her, and now she wanted nothing but to get away from it.

'Do you think she'll come to the front door as well,' she asked, 'and go on with her insults out here?'

'If she tries to,' Paul said, his soft voice calm and reassuring as ever, 'her . . . her familiar will stop her.'

The outer safety light flicked on, making Amy jump. She turned her head to stare at Paul, wondering at the distaste that had entered his voice. It showed even in his choice of that word 'familiar', as if Sarah were a witch and Robert her demon-pet. In the new white glare she saw that Paul's full mouth had clamped tight, as if he might be keeping a difficult hold on himself. He opened it for a brief word of explanation.

'That man won't want her putting on a show for the whole street.'

'He won't, will he.' Amy slowed her pace to a mere quick walk. 'And he won't want his colleague knowing what he's been up to, either.'

'Not that I'd ever actually tell,' Paul said with more of that intense, bitter distaste. 'But he doesn't know that.'

'Oh Paul,' she burst out, reckless with gratitude and relief, 'I'm so sorry I let you in for all this.'

'You didn't.' He drew her past the imprisoned roses. 'He did.'

Amy felt a huge relief as they reached the neutral ground of the pavement. They crossed the road to the van, he opened the passenger door, and she folded herself into it with a sigh. This was last Friday's escape all over again, but better, because now she had Paul at her side fighting her cause and winning it.

He took his place at the wheel, and started the engine. Here they went, down the tree-lined street between the dark gardens, and out to the sodium-lit main road. It was really, really over. Really over for good.

Except that it wasn't. As the lit streets gave place to the dark countryside, her elation subsided and certain ideas began to take shape.

For instance, the way Paul avoided speaking Robert's name. His indirect references, as when a moment ago he had used the word 'familiar' and the phrase 'that man', showed something worse than distaste. They showed disgust.

Yes, Paul was disgusted by Robert.

And with me for having got mixed up with him, Amy thought. And rightly.

And besides that, she still didn't know who had stolen her car. Or who had put Jim in her garden.

CHAPTER 11

'The question is,' Paul said, 'where now?'

'Hm?' Jolted out of her gloomy musings, Amy stared through the van windscreen at the terraced houses beyond the Canterbury police station car park. It was nearly midnight. Here and there a downstairs light still glowed through a patterned curtain, but by now many windows were dark both upstairs and down. Soft rain drifted into the lamp light and out of it; polishing the asphalt and running in jewelled streaks down the windscreen. Reporting the loss of her car seemed to have gone on forever, and now that it was over she felt so worn out she could hardly think, let alone make sense.

On the way back from Maidstone they had hardly talked at all. Just to break the silence, Amy had tried the odd neutral topic. The lateness of the hour, how pleased Jim would be to see Paul again after all this time, the final fair copies of school reports which she now had to write, all met with the same courteous, brief replies. Only her apologies for having so completely forgotten the theft of the coat inspired any real response.

'That's all right,' he had answered with his usual good-natured ease. 'It would only have distracted us from the more important stuff.'

Changing gear to overtake a Spanish truck decorated at every angle with coloured lights, he had stopped speaking for a moment to concentrate. However, once they were well past the truck he resumed the subject.

'With so much to get through back there, I even forgot the coat myself.'

'It's such a strange thing to steal,' Amy had offered, glad to be talking. 'A car, yes. Thieves do steal cars. But breaking into your van and taking something so . . . so special . . .'

He kept his eyes on the road, but his voice held the hint of a smile. 'I'll miss it.'

'You . . . you don't think you'll get it back, then?'

Again that hint of a smile. 'I don't think it's even worth reporting.'

'Sad, though, that you've lost it.'

'I'll get over it.'

She had tried to keep the talk going from there, but without success, and at last she had given up. After that, every turn of the wheels had added to her gloom. Every motorway mile seemed to take her further from that marvellous closeness she had felt with him earlier this evening.

It all seemed to have happened in a different, happier age. In that other age he had spoken of things that needed sorting out between the two of them, but now he showed no inclination to sort anything. Probably he had just lost interest, she had reflected dismally as the weary miles rattled by . . .

Suddenly she realized he was asking her a question. So he hadn't lost interest after all. He was asking where they went from here, which showed he thought they were going somewhere. I've got to get this right, she told herself desperately, and did her best to brush away the cobwebs of fatigue.

'I . . . suppose I was sort of wondering that myself.'

'I could just take you to Stribble . . .'

'To Stribble?'

'It's where you live,' he reminded her with gentle sarcasm.

'Yes.'

Her new hope collapsed like a burst balloon. She had been wrong. He didn't want to talk about their future together, just about the simple, practical matter of where he should drive next. He wanted to know where he should take her before he put her down and left her, presumably forever.

'That's right, please take me to Stribble,' she said, trying and failing to keep the leaden flatness from her voice. 'Thanks to you, I don't think I've anything more to fear from the Dawlishes.'

'Not from them, no.' He made no move to start the engine. 'But if we believe them that they had nothing to do with putting Jim in your garden . . .'

'Which I think is probably true.'

'I think so too. But that leaves the question, who did?'

'The thing is, Jim turned out to be a *nice* dog.' Amy flogged her tired brain to make sense. 'I mean, it was frightening at the time, but . . .' She broke off, wondering if she would ever in all her life be able to express herself clearly again.

'But after we found out that Jim wouldn't have hurt you,' Paul supplied the words for her, 'it stopped seeming as if someone was out to get you.'

'That's it,' she said, grateful to him for working it out for her. 'It's still a mystery, but not such a worrying one.'

'And you don't think there was any connection between Jim appearing and your car disappearing?'

'I don't see how there can be,' she said, for indeed she had racked her brains on this one for much of that silent journey from Maidstone. 'One happened in Stribble, the other in Canterbury.'

'They both happened to you.'

'Cars are stolen all the time. And you heard what the sergeant said in there.' She gestured to the police station. 'Kids in the estates round Oakland are always taking and driving.'

'All right; maybe it was just kids, and the police'll find the car wherever it was left.' He didn't sound as if he really believed that, but rather as if he were letting it go for the moment because he had other things to discuss. 'That still leaves you in back-of-beyond Stribble with no transport.'

'That's right, I won't have,' she agreed, more depressed than ever. 'I . . . I just hadn't got round to thinking that far ahead.'

'So how,' he continued, patiently keeping her to the point, 'would you get to school in the morning?'

'How kind you are, Paul.' She meant it. She turned her head and saw his impassive profile dark against the dim-lit street beyond the car window. She appreciated his considering her difficulties like this, but she knew it was no longer personal. He would have done the same for his cousin Harold, for brash Dave, even for headstrong Sarah. Though perhaps not for Robert, she decided with a tiny flutter of black amusement.

'Never mind about me being kind.' He must have given up waiting for an answer. 'How will you . . .'

'Don't worry, I'll be all right. There's a bus if I walk to Smeddle.'

'And how far is that?'

'Let's see.' She cast her mind over the route, trying to work out its length. 'About a mile, I suppose.'

'That's absurd. Have you forgotten how lame you are?'

She hadn't; her knee ached at the very idea of a mile walk.

'If I came and stayed with you again,' he said slowly, more musing aloud than communicating, 'I could take you to school in the morning. But that would be another night away from my stock . . .'

'I couldn't ask you to do that,' Amy cut in quickly. 'It . . . it's good of you to even think of it,' she added in all humility. 'You . . . you don't have to look after me like this, Paul. I can take care of myself.'

He shifted in the tiny space of his driver's seat, moving his long legs to a new position. 'On the evidence so far, that's debatable.'

'You haven't exactly seen me at my best,' she retorted, stung. 'But anyway, thanks, you've been very helpful.'

What a weak, lukewarm way of putting it. She recalled how last night, within seconds of their meeting, he had supported her into her cottage after she fell. How once inside he had made her an ice pack, and thereafter done everything he could to save her from having to put weight on the injured knee. How he had stayed the night in her spare room so that she would have help if she needed it. How he had coaxed her to eat breakfast this morning, and treated her to a splendid meal this evening.

I didn't deserve him, she reflected in renewed depression.

Her sluggish brain presented her with a new thought, or rather, it reminded her of something she knew well but had forgotten till now. Her good friend Kate Campbell, Oakland's Head of English, lived in the nearby village of Bleanwold.

'I'm sure Kate'll give me a lift to school,' she said.

'That's more like it.' He glanced at his watch. 'I suppose it's too late to ring her tonight?'

'This morning, you mean.' Her own watch now showed five past twelve. 'No, I'll get to Kate before she sets off for school.'

Still he made no move to switch on the engine. 'So you really can manage for tonight and tomorrow, then.' His voice sounded as soft and unemphatic as ever. Amy assumed he was politely concealing his relief that he could at last be done with her and get on with his own life.

As she must get on with hers, one way or another. Heaven knew, she had plenty to do, and plenty of people who mattered to her. For a moment it had seemed that Paul might become one of those, but that was not to be, and she would just have to be sensible and accept it.

But good sense failed before her yearning memory of those few minutes outside Robert's house. How right, how perfect it had felt when he put his arms round her, and how safe when his hand clasped hers. Looking back on it now, from the metallic darkness of this little van with this new great divide between them, she felt that for the rest of her life her memory would treasure every last sweet second of that vanished, never-to-be-recovered closeness.

But since that happened, he had learnt the worst about her, the loveless affair with Robert which had brought her such troubles. None of her other affairs had been so wrong-headed, so stupid, so wilfully blind. Certainly she hadn't loved Andy or Kev or Philippe either, not enough to make a life commitment, but she had at least liked them and enjoyed their company.

But then I enjoyed Robert's company sometimes, she thought in mounting despondency. I must be totally lacking in judgement.

'I was going to suggest you could stay the night at my place,' Paul said. 'But if you're not worried about anything else happening, and if you can fix a lift . . .'

'There's no need,' Amy said, and then, noting the dreariness of her tone, repeated it with all the energy she could muster. 'Absolutely no need at all.'

It came out too emphatic this time. Perhaps that was why his response was so subdued as he settled into driving position.

'Right then. Let's get you home.'

And home they went through the drizzling dark. The outskirts of the city passed in an exhausted blur, and the narrow road to Stribble closed in round them like the walls of a cell, the walls of her miserable life as it would be after Paul had taken her to her door and gone away without her. Through the deeper darkness of Stodbean Wood they rattled, rain on the windscreen like tears, leaves drifting through the headlights like unhappy ghosts, near-naked branches raising their dismal, crooked shadows against a half-moon that came and went behind rags of cloud. It was almost a relief when the lights of Stribble blinked in the distance ahead.

Amy wondered how she could ever have found them cosy. As the van bounced past the flint walls of the church and then between the darkened houses of the Canterbury Road, she felt more suffocatingly shut-in than ever. For a moment she wondered if she should sell the cottage, but she knew that would answer nothing. It was herself she wanted to get away from, not her blameless, beloved home.

'This is the first place I was ever able to live alone,' she said as they came into the ring of light shed by the Nelson's white-lit inn sign. 'Fine mess I made of it.'

'It'll seem better in the morning.' Paul edged the van round the dilapidated estate car which stood against the further pavement from her gate.

'That'll be young Joe Gudgeon's latest banger,' she commented. 'He might at least park it by their own gate.'

Even by young Joe's standards, this was a banger indeed. Any hint of patina had long gone from its paintwork, and one of its wings, presumably replaced from a scrapyard, stood out congealed-blood red in the street light against the dysentery-yellow of the rest. Its number plate was so mud spattered as to be unreadable.

'What a wreck,' Amy said, and then, in weary indignation, 'Really, Joe might think a bit, blocking the road like this.'

'I dare say he wasn't expecting much traffic at this time of night.' Paul eased his van into Amy's empty parking place and switched off the engine. 'I'll help you to the door and make sure everything's all right.'

'There's really no need . . .'

He wasn't listening, already he had left his seat and closed his door. He came round to her side of the van, opened her door, and took her school bag from its place at her feet. By the time she had emerged into the night he was already opening her garden gate, its tortured shriek tearing the darkness.

'I must get that thing fixed.' As she spoke Amy had a vision of her empty future. Soon she would be alone again, and have to deal with things like a creaking gate or a piece of obstructive parking all by herself. She wondered why she had ever felt that to be a good thing.

'Off you go.' Paul hitched the school bag over his shoulder. Now he gestured her through the gate, and after she had obeyed he stepped through it after her. She didn't hear it shriek again, so she presumed he had left it open for his return.

He wants to make his escape as quickly as possible, she thought, and who can blame him?

'I'll stay with you,' he told her as he followed her down the path, 'until you've opened the door and put a light on.'

'Thank you.' But Amy stopped walking and turned to face him, feeling bound to protest again. 'You really don't need . . .'

'Come on, you're wasting time.'

He must be eager to be done with her. Without trying to argue any more, she turned away and continued her progress ahead of him up the uneven path. Only at the door did she speak again.

'My key's in my school bag . . .'

She got no further. In the rustling shadows of the garden, a deeper shadow detached itself from the square bulk of the shed and made for the open gate. It reached the road, and the street lights showed it to be a slight figure in jeans and a dark, high-necked sweater, a dark woolly ski-bonnet pulled low over its face.

Its movements were smooth and quick. Paul, reacting much faster than Amy, dropped the school bag with a thump and loped along the path, but he was too late. Before he reached the gate the figure had leapt into the banger and slammed its door. Paul rushed through the gate and across the pavement towards the car, but its engine must have been in better condition than its carriagework; it started first time and rattled off along the Canterbury Road at astonishing speed.

Jerked out of her torpor of fatigue, Amy listened to the noise the engine made. Its peculiar, regular bang-scratch, as of some ill-fitting part grating as it turned, made it all too identifiable. As she watched the piebald car disappear towards Stodbean, she knew without a shadow of doubt that it was the same vehicle which had brought Jim to her garden.

Paul had run to his van and reached out to open its door, but now he changed his mind and straightened. Clearly he realized that by the time he got his engine started and had manoevred out of the tight parking space, the other vehicle would have vanished down any one of the dozen twisting lanes which surrounded the village. He wheeled through the still-open gate and hurried back up the garden.

'Come on,' he said as soon as he came within earshot. 'Let's get in there and see what damage he's done.'

Still numb with shock yet awhirl with conflicting ideas and emotions, Amy picked up her school bag and drew her keys from their special pocket. She opened her front door with a sick feeling in her stomach. Would the place have been vandalized? Would her electric goods have been taken? She couldn't think of anything else a thief might want, but no doubt she would soon find out.

She switched on the hall light and peered fearfully about. It showed no sign of having been disturbed. She limped to the kitchen, dumped her school bag on the draining board, and switched on its light too.

On-off, on-off went the kitchen neon, then steadied. Its white brilliance showed that here also everything was exactly as she had left it this morning. Her eye flicked over breakfast things washed and left to dry on the rack, coffee and tea and marmalade all in a neat row on their shelf, the cafetiere in its corner with the toaster beside it.

'So they haven't stolen the toaster, anyway.'

Oh dear, was that small trembly voice really hers? She had meant it to come out cool and whimsical, but had only succeeded in sounding like a frightened little girl.

'Or the radio.' Paul nodded to the little shelf where her kitchen radio sat undisturbed. 'Let's have a look at the living room.' His soft voice offered guarded comfort. 'With any luck he didn't get in here at all.'

And so it proved. The living room was undisturbed, its curtains open as Amy had left them this morning, the television untouched in its corner, the exercise books from Monday's English lesson piled where she had put them on the table.

'So now what?'

Amy sank to the bench of her dining corner, suddenly so tired she could hardly see. With a huge effort of will she lifted her weary gaze to Paul.

'I thought it was all over when we settled Robert, but it isn't.' She stated her predicament in plain words so that she could hear the worst for herself. 'Somebody else is after me.'

'Tea,' Paul said.

Amy blinked. 'What?'

'I'll make it,' he assured her, and disappeared to the kitchen.

'There you go again,' Amy muttered after him. 'Taking over . . .' She trailed to silence. From the kitchen came the companionable sound of the kettle filling, then the soothing rattle of crockery. She let her head droop towards the table, and found its grey-gold surface immensely inviting. If she folded her arms like this, and laid her head on them like this, it made a wonderful place to rest.

The pile of exercise books beyond her folded arms reared up and became a scaly beast with Robert's head. It collapsed, dead maybe, but that was no use, a host of little leather-winged creatures at once flapped out of it. She recognized Richard Ablett, Tracy Norris, Martin Sullivan, Jill Gann, Joanna and Ella together as usual, Carl Stevens, Kate Campbell . . .

Kate Campbell? I must be going mad, Amy decided.

'But what have I ever done to any of you?' she asked the little flying things.

'Tea,' they answered in Paul's soft voice, and rattled their hard wings close to her ear with a noise like thunder.

'Wha . . .' She lifted her heavy head above the exercise books and blinked, glad to be awake again. Gradually she managed to focus on the mug of dark amber liquid Paul had set before her on one of her green and gold placemats. He must have taken the mat from the table drawer right under her ear, that would explain the thunder noise.

'Where's the milk?' she asked.

'It helps better with shock if you have it without.'

She turned to him with blurry indignation, the last of her nightmare fled. 'I'm not shocked.'

'Drink up,' he urged, quiet and steady as ever.

'I never have tea without milk . . .' She stopped because she sounded so childishly crotchety, yet this was a serious objection. 'Without milk it'll be too hot. I won't be able to drink it for ages.'

'I cooled it.'

'How did you do that?'

'Added cold water.'

'You put *cold water* in my *tea*?'

There she went again, that childish whine. To cover her embarrassment she sipped the tea. Finding it surprisingly palatable and exactly the right temperature, she drank in silence until the mug was half-empty.

And it worked; her head began to clear. She could even sit up straight, and look across the pile of exercise books at Paul with something near to intelligence. He had seated himself opposite her on one of the chairs, and held his own mug of tea between his two hands. She watched him empty it, and set it on the placemat in front of her.

'Now,' he said with a business-like air, 'go and pack.'

Amy stared at him. 'Pack what?'

'All you'll need for the night. You're coming to stay with me.'

'But my house,' she began, incoherent with surprise.

'I'll bring you here for a visit after school tomorrow,' he assured her, massively unarguable as with Robert earlier this evening. 'You'll be able to check it's all right.'

'And if it isn't?'

'You won't make it any better by staying here on your own.'

'I might.'

'And you might get knocked on the head . . .' He broke off and bowed his own head, staring down at the pile of exercise books or at the grey-gold table beneath them. Amy could see that he had compressed his lips in – anger? Yes, anger with himself.

'Sorry, I didn't mean to frighten you. Just go and pack what you need, there's a good girl.'

Amy flung back her head and summoned all her remaining energy. Within her surged a heady, idiotic delight which had to be concealed at all costs.

'I've told you before,' she said, 'about condescending to me.'

He sighed, and glanced at his watch. 'It's getting late, Amy.'

'I don't even know where you live,' she pointed out, a little surprised by the fact. 'Where is this antique shop of yours?'

He returned her gaze for a moment, but didn't glance at his watch again or make any further reference to the time. Instead he pushed the exercise books aside and spread his hands flat on the table in that gesture which was beginning to seem so characteristic. Perhaps it helped him to concentrate, or perhaps he just needed to feel the solidity of the real world under his palms.

'It's in Hythe,' he told her, staring down at his hands.

'But that's *miles* away.' Once more she heard her voice go up to that embarrassing squeak of protest.

'It may be further from Canterbury in miles, but it's far, far easier travelling. No woodland tracks.' Paul raised his gaze to hers once more. 'To get to school in the morning you'd have an easy run along Stone Street.'

Amy stared at him in silence for a moment, then bit her lip and wondered what she was arguing about. Did she really want him to go away and leave her here? She had a brief, vivid picture of herself alone in the cottage trying to sleep. The slightest sound would jerk her awake, and she would spend all night miserably counting the hours till morning.

'I'm . . . I'm sorry,' she said with difficult humility. 'You're going out of your way to help me – to go on helping me – and I'm grateful . . .'

'So go and pack.' He rose to his feet. 'I'll take the torch, and check that the shed's all right.'

'Oh dear.'

Having dragged herself to her feet beside him, Amy drooped. How near he was, yet how far. How marvellous if she could just put her head on that damp, tweedy shoulder, and feel those tweedy arms around her, and close her eyes. And how impossible that it should ever, ever happen again. She gathered her wits, and struggled with this new problem.

'I'd quite forgotten the shed.'

'I don't suppose the intruder got into it,' Paul soothed her. 'He was probably just using it to hide from us.'

'But what if someone's still hiding there?'

'Not very likely, seeing their transport's gone. And that car –' he smiled with what seemed like genuine amusement – 'we'd certainly hear if it came back.'

She agreed, remembering that characteristic bang-scratching engine note. 'Paul, did you recognize . . .'

'If you're quick,' he interrupted her, allowing himself to look at his watch again, 'we should still get a few hours' sleep tonight.'

There you go again, she thought with distant, exhausted resentment. Ordering me about as usual.

Remembering her earlier complaints, and how weak and futile they had sounded, she didn't voice this one aloud. Instead she silently accepted that he didn't want to talk about the intruder just now, and made her way without another word through the hall and up the stairs to her green and gold bedroom.

Here too, all was as she had left it this morning. Her primrose-patterned duvet and pillows lay exactly as she had straightened them, and the plain green curtains were still open. Amy wandered over to the darkened window, debated whether to close the curtains or not, and decided not

Below her the front door opened, shedding a rectangle of yellow hall light which framed a tall silhouette. She remembered the first time she had seen that silhouette – heavens, was it really only last night? – and how scared she had been of it. How things had changed.

Or perhaps not. Paul was moving along the garden now shining her heavy torch ahead of him towards the shed, where all seemed as undisturbed as in the house. He would soon have finished and come back, she reckoned, and if she hadn't packed by that time she would be keeping him waiting once more.

Not that he'd complain, she thought as she took her suitcase from the top of the wardrobe. He doesn't have to. He can make me do what he wants just by being so . . . so good, so easy-going, so nice.

She tumbled into the case what she thought she might need for tomorrow. Her grey pleated skirt would do, it was non-crush, and she could wear the new moss-green sweater with it. A change of underwear, toothbrush, shower brush, hairbrush and comb, make-up in its little bag, and that was it, she hoped. She took the suitcase to the little landing, and started down the stairs with it.

'I'll take that,' Paul said, coming back through the front door and mounting the stairs to meet her.

'Thank you,' she said, and surrendered it. 'So the shed was all right,' she stated rather than asked as she followed him down the stairs.

'Still locked, and completely untouched as far as I could see,' he threw back over his shoulder.

Returning to the living room, she looked around her with a painful sense of guilt. Her dear cottage was under attack and she was running away from it, leaving it to the enemy, whoever he was, to do whatever he wanted to it.

'Believe me,' Paul said softly, 'I wish it were different.'

Of course he did. She had already been nuisance enough to him and now, just when he thought he was done with her, he was having to take her home with him. To hide her fresh wave of misery as the understanding hit her, Amy walked to the table and pretended a great interest in the pile of exercise books.

'I wonder if I should take these to mark?'

'I'll be nearly two o'clock when we get in.' His soft voice held a suggestion of controlled patience. 'Are you really about to sit down and mark books before you go to bed?'

'It's got to be done . . .'

But not till next Monday. I'm being difficult again, she thought.

'No, you're right,' she admitted, not turning to face him. 'Even in the ordinary way, I wouldn't have done them this evening. I'll just get my school bag.'

Keeping her back turned to him, she moved through the hall and into the kitchen. There stood the bag on the draining board where she had left it. At least that didn't require any special packing; it always contained everything she needed for her day. She felt in its key pocket and was relieved to find her keys there; she must have automatically returned them in that fearful moment when she first opened her door. She took them out, shouldered the bag, and returned to the hall.

'I'm ready,' she called into the sitting room. 'Shall we go?'

He picked up the suitcase and came out to join her. 'Stand back, I'll go first.'

'Th-thank you.' She stepped backwards into the kitchen to let him pass. How good he was, she reflected anew, and how miserably inadequate she herself seemed in comparison. He had already investigated the garden, but something might still be skulking there, so he went ahead of her to put himself between her and possible trouble.

However, when she stepped out of doors after him she found the garden pattering in rain-washed innocence. Small night creatures rustled among the shrubs and shook faintly-glittering drops from the leaves, and damp, earthy scents drifted up from the wet flowerbeds.

The rain had come on heavier, which perhaps was just as well. Amy still felt like a traitor as she relocked the mortice from the outside and turned away from the house, but the feeling was overlaid by something more urgent, the need to reach the shelter of the van as quickly as possible.

Paul moved ahead of her, slowing his pace to hers, and they traversed the garden with no further incident. He opened the gate for her, then the van door, all with characteristic speed and neatness. And here she was in the passenger seat at last, buckling her seatbelt while Paul put her suitcase in the back.

When he started the car she leant back against her headrest and thought once more about her poor little abandoned cottage. Please keep it safe, she asked whoever there might be to ask, and shut her eyes to make the prayer, or whatever it was, more effective.

The car stopped almost at once. Amy opened her eyes and peered through the windscreen, but the darkness was too deep for her to see anything. She could just make out the five-barred gate by which they were parked, and the hedge beyond it, but nothing more.

'Why have you stopped here?' she asked, yawning. 'We can't have gone more than five yards.'

'We've gone five miles, to Feldor Kennels,' Paul answered, opening his door. 'I'm collecting Jim.'

'At this time of night?'

'They told me there's always somebody on duty.'

He left the car, closed its door, and set off along the road by the hedge, presumably heading for some entrance concealed from here. Amy sighed, and closed her eyes again. The rain had lightened, but still went pat-pat-pat on the roof of the van . . .

'Back already?' she murmured as she heard the rear door of the van open. 'You were hardly gone a minute.'

'All of fifteen,' Paul informed her, invisible at the van's rear opening. 'It was Felicity's partner Doreen, and she wanted to chat. I'm glad you could sleep while you waited.'

'I didn't sleep . . .'

'In, Jim.'

The van rocked on its wheels and filled with a powerful smell of wet dog. Amy felt a cold nose investigating her hair and ear, and put a hand back to stroke the long wolf-muzzle.

'Hi, Jim. Lie down.' Jim fussed and turned for a moment beside her suitcase, then settled. 'It's lovely to see him again,' Amy said, eyes closed once more.

Though in fact she hadn't seen him, had she? Oh well, they would both know what she meant. Here was Paul back in his driving seat and away they went, next stop Hythe . . .

'Wake up, Amy.'

She blinked up to where Paul stood at her open passenger door with Jim at his side. 'What do you mean, wake up? I told you before, I wasn't asleep.'

Paul leant in, took her school bag, and stood up. 'Welcome to Gemini.'

CHAPTER 12

'Friday night at last.' Amy flopped into one of Paul's old leather armchairs, and caressed Jim who had sauntered across the carpet to greet her. 'There were times when I stopped believing it would ever come.'

'I know the feeling.' Paul took her school bag from her lap, and set it on the pedestal desk in the corner. 'Don't . . .'

But she couldn't summon the energy to make her usual protest. Any school week was tiring, and with reports, rehearsals and a parents' evening this one would always have been tougher than usual; with all her other problems it had become barely endurable. She had managed to keep going until it finished, but now it was over she just wanted to sit here and do nothing for the rest of her life.

'What's that delicious smell?' she asked, breathing in more of the spicy, winey scent that had greeted her the moment she entered the flat.

'Jill made us *coq au vin* for supper.'

'So she can cook as well?'

'Better than she cleans.'

'Marvellous.' Amy wondered if she would ever meet the invaluable Jill, who came in three times a week. 'Makes me realize how hungry I am.'

'It'll be a while yet.' His velvety voice drifted through her haze of fatigue. 'I'll bring you some tea.'

Behind eyelids too heavy to lift, she could feel herself relaxing into a smile. 'You're a great believer in tea, aren't you?'

'It works.'

'Well, thanks then.'

No answer, except presently the distance muffled noise of a kettle filling. Jim's furry head had slipped from under her fingers; he must have followed Paul to the kitchen, perhaps in the hope of being given something to eat. Or maybe he had already eaten? Maybe Jim had his main meal at lunch times? She realized that she didn't know even this detail of their daily routine, in spite of having stayed here for two days.

But then, she hadn't so much stayed as simply spent two nights in Paul's austere little spare room. She had left at eight each morning and returned at ten each night too tired to do more than drag herself to bed; so tired that tiredness seemed a way of life; so tired that events and ideas and imaginings ran together in her brain and would not be separated into their individual parts.

If she worked at it she could dredge up a vague memory of her first arrival here. Paul had helped her out of his van and guided her across the narrow street, and the outside air must have brought her round a bit. She could remember the wet pavement, and the shuttered shopfront, and the question she had asked about the name on the fascia.

'Why Gemini? Is it your birth sign?'

She was fairly sure he'd said no, he just liked the sound of it, but after that it all went vague again. They must have gone through the side door and up the walled-in stairs to the little landing, but she couldn't remember. He must have shown her into his spare room, but was the bed already made up with that sailing ship-patterned duvet, or did she make it up, or did he, or did they both together? She couldn't remember.

And then she must have unpacked and cleaned her teeth and so on, but she could recall none of it. The first thing that came back to her with any real clarity was waking hours later to find she had seriously overslept.

From then on, life had been like running up a down-moving staircase. She had scampered through her preparations for the day, swallowed a hasty breakfast in a welcoming, surprisingly roomy kitchen, and then drowsed by Paul in the van where the salad-and-mothball smell seemed to have got stronger, perhaps because of her overnight rest from it. At school that morning she had dragged herself through some of the worst lessons she had ever taught.

Break time and strong coffee had helped. At lunch time the police had phoned to say her car had been found in a nearby street, and that piece of good news had positively brought her awake at last. She had immediately phoned the garage where the police had towed it; then rung Paul to say that she didn't after all need him to come and pick her up at eight as they had arranged.

'Great news about the car,' he'd commented. 'Is it much damaged?'

'The thief hot-wired it, and broke the steering lock,' she had told him. 'The garage is repairing it this afternoon. They say the inside, er . . .' She paused, feeling somehow guilty. 'They say it smells of salad and mothballs.'

'Of . . . I see.' A brief silence at the other end of the line. 'Only the smell? No sighting?'

'None, I'm afraid,' she said, wishing it were otherwise. 'It looks as if whoever stole your coat used my car to take it away, then dumped the car.'

So however unwittingly and unwillingly, she had helped in the theft of Paul's coat. That explained her sense of guilt, unreasonable but persistent and strengthened by the fact that she had the car back while the coat was still missing.

'As if,' Paul's soft voice speculated, 'they wanted the coat more than the car.'

Amy, tried to imagine who could feel like that. 'Strange, isn't it.'

'Not everyone would think so,' he replied, his voice infused with mock dignity. 'Unless you mean it's strange for a thief to show such good taste.'

But she couldn't treat it so lightly. 'I'm sorry they haven't got it back for you.'

'Nice to know it's valued,' he had observed, philosophical as ever. 'I gave you a key to the flat, didn't I?'

Amy confirmed it, feeling in her jacket pocket where she had put the key in this morning's rush. More guilt; she might easily have lost it from that pocket. She must remember to transfer it to the part of her school bag where she kept her own house key.

'Good, so I won't have to rush back to let you in.'

'You're going out?' she had asked, her spirits dropping even further.

'Seeing I don't have to fetch you, I'd like to visit my g . . .' His voice came to a halt as if he had said more than he meant to. 'I'd like to pay somebody a visit.'

Tired and distracted though she was, Amy could easily guess the word which began with g. So he was going to see his girl. The idea made her want to burst into tears, or throw the handset across the staff room, or jump up and down and scream. Luckily she remembered something important she needed to know.

'I'm pretty vague about how to drive back to your place,' she said in a carefully controlled voice. 'Can you give me your address?'

As it turned out, in practical terms she was thankful he didn't need to fetch her from the Chaucer Centre that evening. Her after-school meeting was late starting, and by eight o'clock, the time Paul would have appeared, she had nowhere near finished organizing the lighting, sound effects, scenery, costume, make-up, and front-of-house which were its purpose.

Before she could get there at all she had to beg a lift. Tom Birchill, the bearded woodwork teacher who was to build the town square and market stalls of the set, drove her to the garage to fetch her car. Then when they finally arrived at the Chaucer Centre, they found the studio not just overheated in its usual way but ferociously hot, so hot that the pupils already there seemed able to do nothing but sit about and pant.

'I'll find the caretaker,' Tom announced. 'He must be out of his mind.'

He returned fifteen minutes later to report that someone had put up the thermostat as high as it would go. 'Perishin' kids, eh?'

Even with the thermostat properly adjusted, the place took its time cooling. In the sweaty heat where every decision seemed difficult and every discussion to go on forever, Amy could only be thankful Paul wasn't here waiting for her to finish. If he had been, she might very well have skimped or postponed. Without that complication, at eight she organized sandwiches and hot drinks for everyone who wanted them, allowed a twenty-minute break to consume them, and finished at half past nine with everything satisfactory tied up.

Her feeling of achievement lasted no more than the time it took to leave the building. Before she said goodnight to the others her worries were back, first about her car, and when she found that in good order, about her poor abandoned cottage.

I ought to go and make sure it's all right, she thought as she edged through the Canterbury traffic.

But . . . alone? In the dark? And if it wasn't all right, what good could she do? And if she surprised the intruder again, what might happen to her? No, there was nothing to be gained by going to Stribble.

So instead of her own besieged home she would head for Paul's empty flat. Some choice. And it was empty because he was out seeing his girl. Why had he never told her he had a girl?

You know perfectly well why, she reasoned with herself. It's because you've only known him five minutes, and in that time you've hardly stopped to breathe, let alone chat. Their only interlude of quiet had been when they had supper in his friend Owen's pub – was that really only last night? And Paul had mentioned then that he knew other women. A marvellous man like him *had* to know other women.

Only . . . a regular girl, a woman who had become part of his life and meant something to him; that was a real facer. Amy wondered what she was like. A fellow antique dealer maybe, with whom he would have so much more in common than he could have with an overworked schoolteacher? A cool blonde, a dashing brunette, another redhead?

I bet she's young, she reflected, feeling every one of her twenty-nine years. And I bet she's calm and sensible. I bet she'd never get into the kind of mess I'm in . . .

A car hooted, and she found that the light had turned green. Pulling away from it, she wondered in mild panic whether her present state of distracted fatigue made her unfit to drive. From then on, she did her best to give all her mind to the road.

Paul had told her how to find the town car park near to his flat. She manoevred into it with a feeling of relief, and had no difficulty in finding tiny, ancient Hop Lane off the High Street. Since Paul's was the only shop in Hop Lane, that was easy too. His living room had a light in it; she supposed for the same reason as she habitually left one in her own home when she went out on winter nights, to make the place look occupied.

'Hullo old lad,' she greeted Jim, who bundled down the stairs to her the moment she opened the door. 'So he didn't take you with him.'

'Yes I did,' Paul said as he appeared on the landing. 'Here, Jim, you clown, you're blocking the stairs.'

'You're back, then?' Amy limped up after the dog, cursing the wave of happiness that washed through her on seeing Paul again. 'I thought you'd be much later than this.'

'No, she doesn't keep late hours . . .' He broke off, just as he had earlier on the same subject. This time however he had revealed, clearly and finally, that the person he had visited this evening was a woman. Amy swallowed hard, and looked down at the two stairs she still had to climb. The pain in her knee had intensified almost beyond bearing.

'Come and sit down.' Paul indicated that she should go before him into the living room. 'You look all in.'

'Thanks.' She made it to the yellow-lit landing and just stood there, too tired to raise her head. 'But I think I'll go straight to bed.'

And she had, and had fallen asleep almost at once, and wakened at the reasonable hour of seven the following morning. So Thursday had been a little less of a scramble, but no happier.

'I'll be even later tonight,' she had told Paul as they breakfasted at his scrubbed kitchen table. 'Parents' evenings always go on forever, and this is for the kids who have exams in the offing.'

'So you won't be able to visit your cottage today either.'

'It won't run away.'

'Cheer up.' He filled the exquisite, wide gilt cups from his silver coffee pot. 'Leave me your house keys and I'll go this afternoon when Aminata's here.'

Aminata? An Asian woman? Could this be the girlfriend? Amy's mind at once produced a graceful sari-clad figure with shining black hair and peachy-gold skin. How could he bear to sacrifice time with such a goddess to do yet another favour for her?

'She does afternoons in the shop,' Paul explained, 'so I can get out on the other things I need to do.'

So he worked with Aminata. Well, he still might want to see her of an evening, but more likely the girlfriend was someone else. Someone perhaps who could look after him, instead of constantly having to be looked after . . .

'Key?'

His patient reminder brought Amy to herself. 'I'm sure you've enough to do . . .'

'I'll enjoy the outing. So will Jim.' He leant sideways in his kitchen chair, and looked under the scrubbed table to where Jim sat in his favourite position leaning against her leg. 'You'll like Stodbean Wood, Jim.'

'Well . . . thanks,' Amy said.

How nice of him, and how like him, to make out it would be a pleasure to go to Stribble, when she knew it would be a burden and an imposition. And yes, she would be glad to be reassured that the cottage was all right.

'Thanks,' she repeated with more enthusiasm, and half-rose. 'The keys are in my school bag . . .'

'Don't move.' As usual he was on his feet long before her. 'I'll fetch it.'

But her house keys weren't in her bag. Not in their own special front pocket, not loose in the main part of the bag, not in any of its other sections. After five minutes of ever more frantic searching, she had to admit that she must have lost them.

It was the last straw. Tears of self-pity welled up, and she wanted nothing but to put her face in her hands and sob and choke and hiccup like a two-year-old. Jim must have sensed her distress; he emerged from under the table with a clatter of claws, laid his head on her lap, and looked up at her. She took a hasty gulp of her coffee, and stroked him.

Then suddenly Paul was there too, kneeling at her other side, his arms round her and her chair together. 'Want to cry it out?'

It felt so good to have him close again, so warm and safe, that she was almost tempted to accept the offer. She could press her cheek against his, and he would comfort her, and maybe they would kiss again . . .

And she would be late for school. And anyway, he belonged to someone else. She drew a deep, ragged breath and pulled away from him.

'No thanks. I'd only have to redo my make-up.'

He knelt back and regarded her with his head on one side. 'Might you have put the keys down in your room last night?'

'Why would I take them out of the bag?' Unwilling to see how much he pitied her, she refused to return his gaze.

'So maybe you dropped them at school somewhere?'

'They're always zipped up tight until I need them,' she explained. 'I had your keys in my pocket, so yesterday I never opened that part of the bag. Oh, Paul!' Stricken, she turned her head at last and met the dark blue gaze. 'Someone must have deliberately stolen them. The same person who tried to break in the other night . . .'

'I'll get your locks changed straightaway.' He rose to his feet. 'The Hythe locksmith's very good; I'll get on to him as soon as he opens.'

'Thanks,' she said humbly, and strove to gather her battered wits. 'May I use your phone?'

'Of course.'

'The Norrises at number 21 keep a spare key for me.' She finished her coffee, and rose to her feet. 'I'll ask them to give you it.'

The call made, she had been left with barely half an hour to get to school. And when she returned to the flat at ten that evening, she had been so tired she only just found the strength to accept the new set of keys Paul gave her, and listen to his reassuring account of how everything in her house seemed all right.

'I brought those exercise books you so much wanted, as well.' He gestured over to the desk where he had piled them. 'You did say they wanted marking . . .'

'But not tonight.' Amy stared across at them, the last thing in the world she wanted to see. 'I'll do them over the weekend. Er, thanks,' she added, remembering her manners as she dragged herself to bed.

Which left only Friday to be got through, and now that too was over. Thank heaven for the tradition that kept Friday night clear of all school events. She had nothing to do now, and nowhere she needed to be, for a whole marvellous evening. Her school bag held three sets of report blanks to be filled, but she would worry about that tomorrow. For tonight, she was just going to sit here and *be*.

'Tea.'

'Hm?' She opened her eyes with a start. 'I must have dozed off.'

'Feel free.'

She blinked up at him. He carried a gleaming silver tray which held the silver milk jug and sugar bowl, the gilt cups and saucers she already knew from breakfast times, and a patchwork tea cosy which no doubt covered a silver tea pot. He set the tray on the little oak coffee table, and yes, the tea pot was silver, all smooth, beautifully balanced curves and pouring with never a dribble. He brought her tea to the carved hexagonal table next to her, and offered her the milk jug.

'Thanks,' she said, declining it, 'but I've been taking it without since . . .' She trailed off as a faint memory came back to her. 'Didn't I make a fuss about that, some time recently?'

'You were a bit fractious, yes.' He returned the milk jug to the tray. 'You'd just had a bad shock.'

'Nice of you to make excuses for me.'

'I'm not making excuses.'

'Well anyway,' she said, raising her tea to her lips, 'after that I tried it again without milk, and found I like it better.'

'It means you really taste the tea.' He settled opposite her with his own cup and saucer. 'I've been having it like that for years.'

Try as she would, Amy couldn't resist a little thrill of pleasure that they now had this habit in common. Strengthened by the tea, she told herself not to be absurd, and to distract herself started looking back over her day.

'I saw Kate in the staff room after school, to clear some reports,' she said. 'Then she seemed to want to talk, so we stayed and chatted for a bit.'

Though in fact Kate hadn't said anything much. They had exchanged trivialities about the reports, and about various pupils, and about last night's parents'

271

evening, and between those Amy had let several long silences develop in case her friend was looking for an opening, but in the end nothing out of the way had emerged. Drinking more of her tea, she wondered what it had all been about.

'I'd have been in the shop if you'd come back any earlier,' Paul said. 'I started my Friday night accounting while I waited for you.'

He nodded over to the pedestal desk, and Amy saw that it held a litter of papers and a calculator. She wondered why he didn't use the computer he kept in the tiny third bedroom, but perhaps he just liked being here in his living room.

And it is nice here, she thought, glancing round at the pale walls with their brilliant pictures of exotic places, the floor-length curtains of sapphire-blue velvet faded at the edges to dove-grey, the unpatterned toast-brown carpeting which had seen better days. Nothing's what I would have chosen and none of it matches, Amy decided, but it feels right somehow.

Lamps made from tall Chinese vases stood, one on the floor by the overloaded bookcase, the other on the desk. Their fringed, pale-amber silk shades cast a muted glow which bounced back from the the bright surfaces of the tea tray.

'Is all that silver stuff from your shop?' She asked idly.

'Heavens no.' He glanced down at the gleaming collection. 'It's family. Ma doesn't much care for it.'

'But it's beautiful,' she said in surprise.

'Could be it's too modern for her.' He drained his cup, and returned it to the saucer. 'Or it could be because my father bought it.'

'How sad.' Amy thought of her own parents, so close that nothing but death could part them, and of all the things in her home made sacred by the mere fact that her mother had used them. 'Where is your father now?' she asked.

Paul stared down into his tea cup as if reading his fortune there. 'He died in Los Angeles five years ago.'

'I'm so sorry . . .'

'Don't be. We'd lost touch for years by then.'

Amy sighed, for him and for all children of such careless parents. 'When was the last time you saw him?'

'In my first year at Oxford.' Paul sipped his tea, remembering. 'He was on a lucky streak for a while, and had a flat in Baker Street.'

On a lucky streak for a while. Amy turned the phrase over in her mind. 'He gambled?'

'Yes,' Paul said simply. 'He was hopeless about money. He'd dine at Claridges, then not be able to pay the rent.' Paul glanced again at the silver tea service. 'I expect he bought that with money we needed for shoes.'

'That does make it easier to understand,' Amy said slowly, 'why your mother doesn't like it.'

What a wretched, insecure childhood he must have had. She and her brothers had lost their mother, and their father had been angry and grief-stricken for many years, but at least they'd always had enough money.

They'd had each other, too, which brought another question to mind. She asked it carefully, wanting to know more, hoping this subject wouldn't become too painful for him to speak of.

'Were you their only child?'

He nodded. 'Ma probably made sure there wasn't another.'

So his mother hadn't trusted his father enough to bear him any more children. Amy wondered how Paul had emerged from such a childhood with so much balance and good temper.

'How old were you when they split up?'

'Ten. She put up with it far longer than she should have.'

'She must have loved him.'

'I think she did, at first.' He finished his tea, leant forward, and took her cup to place beside his own. He didn't speak again until he had finished pouring from the beautiful silver tea pot and returned her refilled cup.

'I think she did love him at first,' he repeated, settling back in his chair at the other side of the coffee table. 'But by the time I was old enough to take notice, all that kept them together was her pride.'

'Her pride?'

'And her obstinacy. She was determined not to let her people know they'd been right about him.'

Amy glanced across at the door, where Jim had just strolled in licking his chops. Paul must have fed him as she had guessed; food was the only thing which could have kept him from their company for so long. He took up his usual place at her feet, and she stroked his head absently, thinking of what Paul had just told her.

Her people, he'd said. She supposed he meant his mother's parents, his own grandparents, but what a cold, distant way to put it.

'So your mother's . . .' she hesitated, seeking her own word, '. . . your mother's family didn't approve of your father?'

'They were right about his being shiftless.' He rattled his cup back to its saucer. 'But being right isn't everything.'

Yes, he had used that word *people* intentionally. He didn't like his grandparents, she could see it in his sudden expression of distaste. She had last seen that expression when he had turned it on Robert.

'You mean,' she began carefully, 'they got other things wrong?'

'I never thought of it like that before.' He glanced across at her, the distaste replaced by an approving warmth which acted on Amy like champagne. 'Yes, they did get other things wrong. When Ma married Pa, they stopped speaking to her.'

'How terrible.'

Amy was used to the idea of life without grandparents. Her mother's parents had both died when she was small, and her father's while she was in her teens. But to have grandparents who didn't want you, grandparents who never spoke to your parents, that was indeed terrible.

'They came round when she married again,' Paul said. 'Hamish – my stepfather – is much more their sort. But that was too late for me.'

'Too late?' She felt she knew the answer, but she wanted to hear it from him.

'I never got to know them very well.' Yes, that was what he had meant. 'Or like them.'

Amy could have wept for the picture of his childhood that was building up. No brothers or sisters; no security over money, then no father, endless years at a school he disliked, and grandparents who had disowned his mother.

'What about your other grandparents?' she asked. 'Your father's lot?'

'Now that was a completely different story.' He smiled that sweet, brilliant smile before which all sombreness fled. 'They were great. Not rich, but . . .' He frowned, searching for a word,' . . . but sort of *solid*. Stable, kind, loving – like Harold and his family.'

'Ah yes.' She recalled their conversation in Owen's pub.'You said Harold's father was the steady one.'

He held up his cup and saucer in an enquiring gesture. 'More tea?'

'Yes please,' Amy said promptly. She didn't really want the tea, but she did want this conversation to go on. When he talked to her like this, so freely and honestly, she could forget that he had a girlfriend, and that she and her home were under threat from someone unknown. She could even forget that the threat was the only thing keeping her with him, and that the moment it was resolved she must go back to her own home and probably never see him again. She could forget all those things and think only about being here with him.

'I must get some mugs, and put these fiddly little cups away,' he said as he returned her cup with its third refill. 'I seem to be forever refilling them.'

'My father can't be bothered with cups either. I suppose that's where I got the habit of mugs.' Amy accepted her unwanted third cup with a murmur of thanks, and returned at once to the fascinating subject of Paul's earlier life. 'Did you see much of Harold while you were growing up?'

'Very little.' He sipped his tea reflectively. 'My mother believed we hadn't anything in common,' he went on with an air of restraint, even of strain. 'I had to wait till I grew up to find how wrong she was.'

'I hardly know Harold.' Amy recalled the serious young man whose inner core of confidence meant that he never needed to pretend or show off. 'But I'd have said his temperament was perhaps a bit like yours.'

'He's ten years younger than I am,' Paul said, 'but yes, we get on well. One of his sisters is great, the other's more like –' he broke off, then continued with an air of making himself say it – 'more like my father.' He sighed. 'Maybe there has to be one in every generation.'

Amy glanced round the room again, a theory forming. 'Did you get the rest of your furniture from your mother's place, as well as the tea service?' she asked.

He nodded. 'Ma scoured the attics for me.' He put his hand on the battered leather arm of his chair. 'These chairs belonged to her grandparents, would you believe. They must be sixty or seventy years old.'

'I won't say they're as good as new,' Amy said as she inspected the scuffed leather of her own chair, 'but they're still very comfortable.'

A picture was beginning to form in her mind of Paul's mother and her side of his family. Those gilt cups, the silver tea service, the absurd Chinese vase lamps, the rich, faded curtains and the ancient, superbly made armchairs all spoke of opulence. So did the casual mention of attics – not *an* attic, but attics in the plural – into which such goods could be stowed and forgotten until needed to help out a son who was starting his own home.

It all seemed a long way from Harold Clark and his small family business installing central heating. Could Paul's mother's family be snobs? Could they have resisted the marriage because they had decided the Clarks weren't good enough? 'They came round when she married again,' Paul had said, meaning presumably that his stepfather was rich and well-connected enough to be a good match.

She didn't feel strong enough to ask the question direct, but she could try a roundabout route. 'What does your mother think of you running an antique shop?'

'It worries her, of course,' he admitted readily. 'She doesn't say so, but she fears I may take after my father.'

'And do you?'

'No.' The single word came out serene and unassertive, a simple statement of fact. 'I take after the Clarks, but not my father.'

'It must be a bit uncertain though?' she offered cautiously. 'As a way of earning a living?'

'I don't need to earn a living.' He smiled, with a certain edge of irony. 'My father left me three million dollars.'

'What?' Amy put down her cup, suddenly weak. 'Real money? In the bank?'

Paul nodded. 'He financed movies. It seems that after a while, he got a reputation as somebody who could pick winners.'

'So in the end, his gambling paid off.' Amy sat back, taking it in. 'That means you're rich.'

'It certainly means I've got enough.' He regarded her over the gleaming tea things. 'Do you mind?'

'Me?' She screwed up her eyes, and shook her head to clear it. 'Why do you ask that?'

'I said the other night that there are things to sort out between you and me.' He went on watching her intently, his expression hard to read. 'That's one of them.'

Amy caught her breath. What could he mean? Did the things he wanted to sort out include the fact that he was seeing another woman? Did he mean to break that off, she wondered, and felt acutely uncomfortable at the idea. And if he didn't mean to break it off, how could she and Paul possibly form any relationship at all?

'What . . . what are the others?' she asked, stammering a little in her tension.

He shrugged. 'One of them was obvious at the time . . .'

'You mean Robert,' she said. 'Do you think that's settled now?'

'I'm not entirely sure. But if it is –' his open blue gaze met hers – 'then there's another problem, isn't there?'

'Someone else harassing me, you mean?'

He nodded. 'Have you any idea who it might be?'

'I wish to heaven I had,' Amy burst out. 'I suppose all the things that have happened might be coincidences,' she went on, voicing the thoughts that had gone round and round in her head in the past few days. 'Jim appearing . . .'

The dog turned his great head at the mention of his name, and she stroked between his ears.

'The car and the coat,' she went on, 'the late-night intruder, my house key disappearing, even the heating being turned too high . . .'

Paul leant forward, alert to this new information. 'What heating?'

'Somebody tinkered with the studio thermostat on Wednesday.' She realized that she had simply been too busy to tell him of such things. 'It might have been just a kid fooling about, or . . .' Depressed, she let the sentence trail off. This was her first evening off after a hell of a week, and for a while there, relaxing and drinking tea and learning more about Paul, she had begun to enjoy it.

Perhaps, with his usual perceptiveness, he had picked up her thoughts. When he spoke again, his soft voice was even gentler than usual, so gentle that she had the feeling of being stroked and soothed by it.

'There are other things you need to know about me, too. Important things.'

'Yes,' Amy said simply. 'Are you going to tell me them?'

'I can tell you some of them.' He paused, perhaps sorting out his thoughts. 'You know that Harold and his family live in Hythe?'

It was the last thing Amy had expected. She shook her head, disoriented. She liked Harold, and had been glad to learn that Paul got on so well with him and his family, but what had that to do with the relationship between her and Paul?

'Tomorrow afternoon, when Aminata's here,' he continued, 'I'd like you to come with me, and pay them a visit.'

CHAPTER 13

'I can't just sit still all morning,' Amy protested. 'I've too much to do.'

'None as important as getting better. Here.' Paul gave her the Saturday edition of his paper. 'You can spend the time reading that.'

She accepted it unwillingly. She never read any paper, let alone these overblown weekend affairs. She put it down on the octagonal table and stroked Jim, who had sensed her dissatisfaction and laid his head on her lap to gaze earnestly up into her face.

'See how well his cut's healed?' Paul observed. 'That's what you're aiming for. Complete cure by Monday.'

'My knee's better,' Amy responded, still mutinous. 'Last night's rest . . .'

'Was good, but not enough. You're still limping.'

'Only the least little bit.'

But she knew he was right. Her knee was much improved after Friday's quiet evening, but it wasn't yet healed. A morning sitting down would probably help it a lot, and after the difficulties of the past week, a little more rest would probably do her more good than anything else she could think of.

'I could make a start on my reports, I suppose.'

'No you won't,' he said implacably. 'That's not resting.'

'They've got to be done.'

'You'll do them a lot better after a day off.'

It was so true that she couldn't argue further. If she tried to tackle those reports today she would probably take forever and make all sorts of silly mistakes. If she left them until tomorrow she would not only write them better but faster, and might even enjoy it.

'I'll put your chair by the window so you can see down into the street,' Paul told her. 'And I'll leave you Jim for company.'

'Big deal.' But to show it was nothing personal, she pulled Jim's ear. 'Poor old lad,' she added standing up to let her chair be moved and seeing how Paul had to edge it round the dog. 'You know, don't you, that he's far too big for this place?'

'And he needs a garden as well,' Paul agreed. 'I'm working on it.' He set the chair by the window. 'Come on, sit.'

His voice stayed low, but carried such authority that Jim turned his head sharply. Still standing where he had risen to let the chair be moved, he lowered his haunches to the carpet and waited, surprised and expectant.

'You see, you've got us both terrorized,' Amy observed, smiling as she moved to obey. 'Over here, darling,' she added to the dog. 'He didn't mean you.'

283

While she settled to her new position Paul glanced at the gilt wall-clock, another family piece to judge by its angular nineteen-thirties styling. When he spoke again he was already moving to the door, the heathery tweed suit moulding itself to his supple movements.

'Time I went down to open up. Call if you need anything.' He paused to look back. 'If I hear you move I'll . . .' He broke off, presumably seeking a dire enough threat 'I'll withdraw sympathy.'

'Not that!' Amy flung her hands up before her face and cowered back. 'Anything but that!'

He smiled, but insisted. 'I will, though. I'll start wondering how many of your problems are self-inflicted.'

'They all are,' she said, abruptly sober. 'I don't know what I would have done without you this past week, Paul.'

'Neither do I,' he retorted ruthlessly. 'So do yourself a favour and sit still.'

'Bully,' Amy muttered, but obeyed.

The paper took her through the first two hours. She prolonged the time a little by trying the crossword, but could make no sense of it. And Paul's books were no use; she had already established that his shelves contained nothing but biographies and travel books, neither of which she ever read, some big illustrated books on period furniture, and some heavy stuff about architecture.

So she was left with nothing to do but stare out of the window. And while she appreciated Paul's moving her chair so she could see down into Hop Lane, it wasn't exactly a bustling thoroughfare. The windows opposite offered glimpses into store rooms and empty offices, and the street itself, its old red bricks gilded by thin November sunshine, seemed deserted except when the occasional pedestrian cut through it to the High Street. There went a group now, an old woman and two children, someone taking her grandchildren Christmas shopping perhaps . . .

'The excitement will be too much for me,' Amy murmured to Jim.

Jim's ears went up then flopped again, the doggy equivalent of a shrug.

'Oh, all right,' she said, shamed by his patience. 'I know I have to do this to get better. I'll stop moaning.'

But try as she would, she couldn't keep the uncomfortable thoughts at bay. Like how depressing she found it that Paul turned out to be rich. She had no use for such a large sum of money; all it did was to make a huge barrier between them.

'And goodness knows,' she thought, 'there are enough of those already.'

He must very much regret having talked to her so freely last night. He had spent the rest of the evening keeping her at verbal arm's length, chatting carefully about nothing in particular. When the time came to eat the *coq au vin*, he had made the distance physical, putting her at one side of his scrubbed kitchen table and himself at the other. He'd said it would give them more space to spread out and enjoy their meal, but she hadn't believed him, and hadn't enjoyed the meal at all.

He had refused to say why he wanted her to visit Harold and his family. She hadn't asked again, but she wondered about it, a lot. She was sure the girlfriend came into it somewhere. Could Paul be attached to one of Harold's sisters? He'd said how much he liked them . . .

'But they're his cousins,' she objected to Jim. 'It's not healthy, cousins marrying . . .' Heavens, what had she just said? Who had ever mentioned anybody marrying?

It was then that she knew, with a certainty that clenched her stomach, that it was her own idea entirely. She had thought of it because she wanted to marry Paul.

Which is absurd, she argued with herself. I only met him six days ago.

But that really wasn't the point. It was true that until last night she had known little of his family and background, but in the ups and downs of this last week she had learnt a great deal about his character.

He's kind, cool, strong, brave, and a hundred per cent reliable, she reflected desolately. He'd make a marvellous husband. And I must stop thinking such things.

Because he already had someone else. Never in any of the affairs she had indulged in since she left home – those affairs which now seemed so paltry and cheap – never had she knowingly accepted a man who was committed to another woman. It was one of her rules.

I never poach, she told herself, and I'm not going to start now. Even if I could.

Which, she had to accept, she probably couldn't. Heavens, Paul had only kissed her once, and that had probably been a brotherly way of giving her courage to face Robert. If it hadn't felt brotherly, that was because of her feelings about him, not his about her. Let's face it, she thought, I don't *know* how he feels about me.

She lay back in the big armchair with closed eyes, misery dropping over her like a heavy grey cloak. In vain she told herself that she had never meant to marry at all. From where she was now, that seemed mere empty posturing.

I only ever felt like that, she realized with blinding clarity, because I hadn't met Paul . . .

A small sound made her open her eyes. Jim sat up, ears erect and muzzle pointed to the stairs where the light footseps pattered on upwards. Could it be Paul to ask if she wanted anything? No, his tread was firmer, and anyway he always took the stairs two at a time. So who?

The steps reached the landing and a moment later the visitor stood framed in the doorway. Amy blinked, shook her head, and looked again. No, she wasn't dreaming; the vision in the doorway was really there.

She at once realized two things with sickening certainty. First, that this must be Aminata, and next, that she need look no further for the mysterious girlfriend. If Paul worked every day with this woman, he just had to be in love with her.

She wasn't Indian as Amy had imagined but African, a smooth mahogany brown. She had great leaf-shaped eyes, a high forehead, and perfect cheekbones just touched with peachy-pink. Her hair was hidden by a face-framing, indigo and scarlet silk scarf tied at the back of her long neck, and she wore a navy cloak like a nurse's, partly unbuttoned so that it flared out as she moved and showed its scarlet lining. Beneath the cloak she wore some more complex, almost floor-length garment. She must have raised the skirt to climb the stairs; she still clutched it, showing ankles clad incongruously in fur boots and scarlet ribbed tights.

'*Ooh la la*!' Charmingly dismayed she fended off Jim, who clearly knew her and had padded over to greet her.

French? Did I really, Amy wondered, hear her speak French? Her depression deepened, if that were possible.

Seeing the newcomer's way barred by welcoming Jim, she came to herself and called the dog back to her side. The woman let her skirts drop to their full length and regarded Amy a little uncertainly.

'I call in to see Paul, but 'e 'ave customaires.' Her voice was low and lilting, her phrasing careful. 'So I zink, instead I will meet Mees Amy.'

Amy cleared her throat. 'Sorry, I didn't mean to be rude . . . you're Aminata?'

The bright-bound head dipped gracefully, and white teeth showed in an engaging smile. 'Paul 'ave told you about me?'

Amy nodded. 'Forgive me for not getting up . . .'

'No no no!' It came out enchantingly Gallic as Aminata vigorously shook her head. 'You must not. Not on any account.'

Amy recognized a familiar echo. 'Did Paul say that to you?'

Again Aminata shook her head. 'I 'ave no chance to speak to 'im.'

So she had decided to come up here while Paul was otherwise occupied. She must have heard him speak of me, and wanted to see me for herself, Amy thought. Well she needn't worry, I can't compete and if I could I wouldn't.

'Do sit down,' she said aloud. As she spoke, she looked doubtfully across at the other armchair. It stood at the far side of the room, and seemed far too heavy for this delicate creature to haul within a sociable distance.

Aminata appeared to have no doubts, and glided purposefully towards it. However, when she reached the armchair she ignored it and instead picked up the tiny black three-legged stool beside it. Returning to Amy she set the stool opposite her at a sociable distance.

'You're surely not going to sit on that?' Amy asked. 'It can't be comfortable.'

'It is very comfortable.' Aminata spoke matter-of-factly, as if used to having to explain this preference. 'It is exactly what I like. Paul, 'e bring it from the shop specially for me.'

So Paul kept an item of furniture here just for his beautiful assistant, friend, and . . . mistress? Amy had to crush down a wave of the purest, most painful jealousy.

Aminata had returned to the unwanted armchair to drop her cloak over it. The complex garment beneath turned out to be three garments, a kaftan-like robe whose sea-green silk was shadow-striped with indigo and gold, a long skirt of the same material, and a scarlet silk shirt. The copious sleeves of the kaftan dropped in supple folds over the long scarlet sleeves of the shirt, and the whole effect was so brilliantly exotic that Amy found herself staring again.

'You like?' Aminata stroked the kaftan complacently, making its shadow-striping ripple like water. '*Maman*, she make ze dressmaker to sew, and she send it to me.'

'It's *gorgeous*,' Amy sighed, feeling suddenly ordinary and colourless in her grey pleated skirt and moss-green sweater. 'You look like a queen.'

'*Tiens*!' Pleased with the compliment, Aminata grew confiding. 'Really it is for Christmas. I will wear at ze parties. For everyday –' she made a gesture which set the silk rippling and floating, – 'I wear ze cloze like yours, ees more *pratique*.'

She swept across and settled on the stool, straight-backed but with every sign of ease and comfort. The sea-coloured silk drifted about her, then dropped into graceful lines from which she seemed to rise like a mermaid from the waves. She smoothed it fondly. 'Ees present from *Maman*. It arrive today in ze post, so I come 'ere today to show it to Paul.'

Amy struggled with a painful picture of Paul inspecting and approving both the splendid outfit and the beautiful wearer. 'I'm sure he'll love it. Did your mother design it?'

'*Mon Dieu, non!*' Aminata laughed at the idea. 'It is what my people wear all ze time, only zees –' she indicated the shirt – 'would be different. Low neck, no sleeves, little frill at ze waist.'

Amy tried to imagine a whole population going about in such dress. It must be like living in the middle of a yachting regatta.

'Is not really *pratique* for zis cold country,' Aminata admitted. 'If it rain I must wear raincoat, and zese –' she raised her arms with the great sleeves floating and billowing – 'zey would crush.'

Amy nodded. She could see the difficulties of trying to bunch those sleeves under a conventional coat.

'But today ze sun shine, so I can use my cloak zat I buy from Oxfam,' Aminata prattled on. 'So I think, although it is not Christmas, I will wear my present.'

'But if everybody dresses like that where you live,' Amy began, framing her question carefully for the girl's uncertain English, 'doesn't it ever rain there?'

'Only in ze ouet season, September to December. Zen dry, dry, dry.'

'And hot?'

'Yes, *Le Mali* is 'ot. Often too 'ot.'

Le Mali. Amy cudgelled her brains, but couldn't remember ever having heard of the place. She tried not to look too blank, but it must have shown. Or perhaps Aminata was used to having to help people out.

'It is in *l'Afrique du Ouest*, on ze river Nigere. You 'ave eard of Tombouktou?'

'Tombouk . . .' Amy unravelled the French pronunciation. 'Would that perhaps be Timbuktoo?'

'Zat is one of our cities,' Aminata informed her. 'Also on ze Nigere, and so is our capital Bamako, where I live.'

'Bamako,' Amy repeated, blank once more. 'I'm sorry . . .'

'It is far off,' Aminata excused her. 'And ze connections are all to France.'

Clearly it often happened that nobody had ever heard of the place. Presumably that was why she mentioned Timbuktu, because apart from the river Niger it was the only thing in *Le Mali* that the English had ever heard of.

'I speak good French,' Aminata explained unnecessarily 'Now my family send me to stay ouiz *Tante* Marie to learn English.'

So she had a relation here in Hythe. Cosmopolitan Kent, Amy thought, they come here from everywhere. Even so, a French-speaking African lady was something special, doubly exotic.

'Your English is very good,' she said politely.

The elegant head dipped again, accepting the compliment. '*Tante* Marie she say I learn bettaire if I see people, so I 'elp Paul in ze shop.'

'So you know about antiques as well?' Not knowing the first thing about them herself, Amy felt another stab of jealousy.

'I learn, a little,' Aminata told her. 'But Paul 'as few antiques now. Mostly we sell ze carvings *Malien*.'

'Malian carvings?' Amy queried, automatically translating.

'*Biches* – gazelles,' the girl corrected herself. 'Masks, birds, *gris-gris*. You 'ave not seen?'

Amy shook her head. 'The shutters are up when I leave in the morning, and when I get back at night.'

'But you see zees one?'

'Which . . . oh.' Amy turned to stare where the girl was indicating. Inconspicuous on the dark corner of the desk next to the jointed lamp stood a black wooden figure perhaps the height of one-and-a-half handspans.

Aminata jumped up and fetched it, and when Amy took it into her hands she saw that it was a carving of a woman. The limbs were too short for realism, the body too long and the hands too big, but the final effect was of pattern and intent. The arms were raised to frame the elegant head, leaving the small, pointed breasts and pregnant belly to form their own springing lines. Hips and belly were each carved with a band of chevron-stripes which echoed the slanting lines of the eyes and mouth.

'She's wonderful,' Amy said, cradling the little figure in her two hands. 'So mysterious, and so powerful.'

Aminata clearly regarded this as another compliment. 'She is from *Les Gemaux*. Ze Tvins,' she translated. 'My sign.'

'Gemini?' Amy queried. 'The same name as Paul's shop?'

Aminata confirmed it. 'Papa and Paul choose it because of me.'

Amy's spirits dropped ever further at this revelation of the depth and strength of the relationship between Paul and this beauty. He knew her father, and he had named his enterprise after her birth-sign. He must be serious about her.

When I asked Paul about the name he said he just liked sound of it, she reflected gloomily. I suppose he didn't want to go into all this with me. She looked down at the little black figure. It was made of some kind of white wood which showed here and there through the uneven dark stain.

'So Paul sells things like this,' she said slowly, 'from West Africa?'

'Only from Les Gemaux. My papa, 'e is in charge of ze packeeng and ze transport. 'E is vairy good at it,' Aminata announced, complacent once more. 'Nozzing is ever broken.'

Amy wondered how Paul came to be selling carvings from the back of beyond. How had he got the idea, and once he had it, how had he organized it?

'And zey sell vairy well,' Aminata added proudly. 'As zey should, for zey are vairy good, and not dear.'

Amy looked down into the goddess's huge unpupilled eyes. Come to think of it, they slanted upwards over the cheekbones exactly as Aminata's did, and the high forehead was the same too.

'Do you model for these carvings?' she asked.

'*Pardon*? What is zis model?' When it was explained

294

to her, Aminata laughed. 'No no, ze men do not need models. Zey follow *le tradition*, or zey make up out of ze 'eads.' She glanced at the clock. '*Mon dieu*, so late! I am to lunch early today, and I 'ave not yet made ze shoppeeng.'

'Thank you for coming to see me,' Amy said with mechanical politeness.

Taking the words completely at surface value, Aminata smiled her brilliant smile. 'I too enjoy. We will meet again.'

I wonder, Amy thought in renewed depression. Paul didn't know she'd come up here – I wonder if he'll let us meet again?

When she was alone once more, the November sun seemed cold and colourless. She shut it out by closing her eyes and leant back in blank misery, holding the little black figure. What was this mysterious Mali where the women looked like Aminata and the men carved enigmatic little black versions of her? She pictured a jet-black, jet-shiny river flowing through dense green rainforest where many Aminatas drifted bright as butterflies . . .

'That's a good girl,' said a familiar, velvety voice. 'This is exactly what you should be doing.'

'Hm?' Amy opened her eyes, astonished that she could have slept when she was so unhappy. 'I was in *Le Mali*,' she said, gathering her fuddled wits.

Staring up at Paul, she saw something in his face tighten. Was it the muscles round his mouth? Yes, he had somehow closed up.

So it's true, she thought miserably. Aminata's his girlfriend, and he didn't want me to know about it. And yet, he didn't act at all guilty. Instead, she had the strongest feeling that it was not he who was being tested but herself. For some reason this moment was important to him, so important that he needed to deal with it now, before anything else. As if too preoccupied to interrupt himself fetching a chair, he sank to Aminata's black stool, his dark blue gaze holding hers.

'So Aminata's been here,' he said softly, guardedly. 'She must have come and gone by the back way, when I was busy.'

'I . . . I . . . was glad to see her,' Amy said, choosing her words with care. 'She's . . . very interesting, and very beautiful.' She caressed the little black figure, which still rested on her lap. 'She makes me feel like a sparrow beside a bird of paradise . . .'

'Not a sparrow.' Mysteriously, he relaxed into that tender, transforming smile. 'A woodpecker maybe.'

'You're calling me a woodpecker?' Amy gazed at him, unable to look away. 'Red crest, harsh call, habit of banging on?'

'Bright colours,' he contradicted her. 'Strong voice, never shows off but you always know it's there.'

Oh dear. He shouldn't be looking at her like that, or speaking in that special, soft tone as if to a lover. Amy looked hastily to one side and blurted the thing she had to talk about. 'Is Aminata your girlfriend?'

'Good heavens.' The blue eyes widened in amazement which had to be genuine. 'Whatever makes you think that?'

'You didn't tell me how beautiful she is.' Amy felt she was stating the obvious. 'And you called the shop Gemini because of her . . .'

'She told you that?' He paused, sorting out his thoughts. 'When I bought this shop it was called Gemini. All I did was keep the name.'

'And this place in Mali?' Amy held up the little figure. 'Where this comes from. Les . . .' She floundered, unable to remember the French.

'Les Gemaux,' Paul completed it for her. 'Adrissa – that's Aminata's father, who runs it – liked the idea of calling it by the same name as the shop.'

'Not because it's Aminata's birth-sign?'

'It's news to me that it's also her birth-sign.' Another smile, this time indulgent. 'What a little madame she is.'

'A little . . .' Amy broke off, considering the phrase. She and colleagues often applied it to pupils, especially girls round about the time of puberty. A new suspicion rose in her mind.

'How old is Aminata, then?'

'Fourteen.'

'But . . .' Feeling unutterably foolish and at the same time idiotically light-hearted, Amy tried to explain herself. 'She seems so mature. So sure of herself.'

'It's true,' he admitted, 'that in Malian terms she's a fully-grown woman.'

'Well then . . .'

'Do me a favour, Amy.' Though he spoke reproach-
fully, something seemed to have pleased him. Whatever the test he had been putting her through, she
seemed to have passed it, she couldn't think how.

And clearly he wasn't about to tell her. He rose from
the stool as if a heavy weight had just dropped from his
shoulders, and made for the kitchen with a spring in his
step. 'I'll just put something on the table, and we'll eat.'

Now what was all that about? Amy wondered. But it
really didn't matter, nothing mattered against the wonderful, marvellous fact that the beautiful Aminata was
out of the running, not a threat, a mere schoolgirl . . .

'Is she still at school?' she called through the open
kitchen door.

'Who? Oh, you mean Aminata.' Clearly he had
forgotten all about her, further proof if proof were
needed that she wasn't an important part of his life.
'Yes, she's staying on at school till she takes her
Bachaud, whenever that is . . .'

'So how come she can be here in term-time?'

'It isn't term-time in Mali,' he answered amid the
clatter of plates. 'They close for the rainy season. They
have to.' He appeared briefly in the doorway, smiling.
'Malian children won't go to school when it rains. They
act like the English do about snow.' He disappeared again,
and the meal-preparing noises renewed themselves.

Malian children. Amy treasured the phrase, staring
down into a Hop Street which seemed to have grown
suddenly, spectacularly sunny. He really did think of

298

exotic, beautiful, elegant Aminata as a child, classing her with the other children who wouldn't go to school when it rained. Called to the kitchen, she rose with an appetite she hadn't known she possessed.

She was halfway there before she realized two things. First, that she was now hardly limping at all. Second, that she still held the little blackened Aminata-figure. Perhaps it was helping to make her well, she thought as she set it by her place opposite Paul.

The something he had promised to put on the table turned out to be paté, several kinds of cheese, and crusty French bread.

'Proper meal this evening,' he told her as he pulled out a chair for her. 'When we've time to enjoy it.'

Amy glanced down at the little black figure. 'Tell me about Les Gemaux.'

'It's a profit-sharing co-operative.' He pushed the salad bowl towards her. 'I spent some of my father's money establishing it.' He cut them each a piece of the crackling bread, passed her the paté, and took the cheese for himself. 'The Malians are a gifted people. I hated to see them wasting their time carving fakes . . .'

'Fakes?' Amy lifted salad on to her plate. 'How do you mean?'

'Ceremonial masks, drums, stools, *biches* . . .'

'Aminata mentioned the *biches*. Gazelles, she said. Are they something special?'

'They certainly are, and specially Malian too.' He took the salad in his turn. 'When these things are genuinely old, and have been used in rituals down the ages, they fetch high prices internationally.'

'I see.' Amy nodded, spreading pate. 'So modern carvers try to make their work seem old.'

'After they've carved them out of bits of packing crates,' he confirmed, 'they stain them and drill worm-holes.'

'And they succeed? I mean, the things end up seeming old?'

Paul nodded, his mouth full. 'Tourists and dealers buy them as antiques,' he explained when he had swallowed, 'take them back to Europe or America, and sell them for a huge profit.'

'Having bought them for peanuts?'

'Just about. And for those peanuts, all that marvel-lous talent –' he nodded down at the figure by Amy's plate – 'gets pinned down copying the past, instead of finding its own way.'

Amy stared at him in admiration. What a wonder-ful way he had found to spend his father's money. Not only was he providing employment in a poor country – she was sure Mali must be poor – he was also helping craftsmen. No, she corrected herself, he was helping artists find the best way of using their talents.

'So in Les Gemaux,' she began, expressing it in her own words to make sure she had it right, 'the carvers don't copy, they –' she sought for the right word – 'they create.'

'My people carve whatever they want to,' he agreed. 'They develop their own individual talents.'

300

'And yet –' Amy nodded down at the little figure – 'this seems very traditional to me.'

'It is. That tradition's their strength and their starting place.'

'I see.' She picked up the little figure and weighed it in her hands, impressed once more by its power and its purposeful, thrusting patterns. 'This is where they start, and but for Les Gemaux, this is where they'd have to stay.'

'Exactly. In Les Gemaux they explore the different directions they can go.'

'Still with the bits of packing crate?'

'That's the medium they're used to working with. And it keeps the prices down.'

'So the craftsmen carve, Aminata's father packs and sends, and you sell.'

'And you might be surprised how well they go,' Paul told her with rising enthusiasm. 'Hythe's exactly the right place – people come here for speciality shopping.'

'So you're showing a profit?'

Amy tried not to sound too cast down. She liked the sound of Les Gemaux and wished it well, but if it made a profit Paul must be as rich as before, or richer.

And he's still got a girlfriend, she thought as one idea led to another, even if it isn't Aminata. Still, she was with him, and would be with him this afternoon meeting the part of his family that he liked best. What was more, the sun was shining and she was enjoying this simple meal very much. She drew the salad bowl towards her for a second helping.

'Who mixed this?'

'I washed the lettuce. Jill leaves the dressing ready in a jar.'

'It's marvellous.'

Paul took his own second helping. 'How's that knee after a proper rest?'

'Much, much better,' Amy admitted. 'I could almost take Jim for a . . .'

'Don't say it, he knows the word, and no you couldn't. We'll take him with us,' Paul added, clearly having thought it out, 'and I'll walk him round Cliff Road while you're talking to my g . . .' Exactly like the other night, he bit off the word as if he hadn't meant to use it. He stopped meeting Amy's glance too, and instead became extraordinarily interested in his salad.

Amy tried to eat hers, but found it suddenly tasteless. So this was going to be it, then. This afternoon she was to meet his girlfriend, and so put an end to any chance she herself had with Paul. Just to be sure, she put down her knife and fork and questioned him in a voice gone suddenly husky.

'Wh-who's that I'm going to be talking to?'

'My family,' Paul said. 'You'll see.'

CHAPTER 14

'**A**nd that's another thing,' Amy said as she crossed the narrow pavement of Hop Street to Paul's van. 'You're rich, yet you drive this grotty little thing . . .'

'It isn't grotty,' Paul said, pretending to be hurt. 'Never mind, Albert,' he added, lovingly adjusting the twisted coat-hanger that served the van as an aerial. 'She didn't mean it.'

Amy blinked. 'You call it Albert?'

He nodded, opening the door for her. 'Harold's is Archie.'

Amy recalled that Harold drove an identical van. 'Did you buy them together?'

'Yes, from the same dealer. They're like members of the family now. Come on.' Paul gestured her to the passenger seat. 'Don't keep him waiting.'

'Couldn't a Rover or something be just as much a member of the family?' Amy persisted as she obediently tucked herself into the van.

'Maybe,' he agreed, and shrugged. 'I'm just not interested.' He patted the van's top. 'Albert's hyper-reliable. Not a minute's trouble, all the six years I've had him . . .'

The words were cut off as he closed her door and went round to the back to put Jim on board. The van – Albert – did its usual rocking motion as the dog jumped into the back and settled. Amy waited, considering what Paul had just said.

Six years he'd had this van. So he already owned it when his father died five years ago, and never saw any need to trade up. She wasn't sure why, but she liked him for that.

It's so cool, she thought. The money didn't go to his head and he just isn't interested in showing it off. Instead he's using it to do some good in the world.

So here was another reason for liking Paul, and a lot of good it did her. Her depression deepening, she stared through the windscreen to where a little wind played with dust and dead leaves in the chilly, sunlit street.

'Right.' Paul opened the driver's door and settled beside her. 'Here we go then.'

In contrast to her own black mood, he seemed strangely light-hearted. Ever since lunch time he had hummed to himself, cracked silly jokes, clowned over the washing-up, even made Amy hold a horizontal broomstick while he limboed under it with a grace and suppleness which made her catch her breath. Now, guiding the van through the busy road at the end of Hop Lane, he laughed aloud.

'Fancy you thinking Aminata was my girlfriend.'

So who *is* your girlfriend, Amy wanted to burst out, but held it back. If he told her, if it all came finally out into the open, she would have lost him for good.

'It'll be dark when we come back this evening,' he said as he negotiated the roundabout, 'so we'll stop off now for you to see the canal.'

'What canal?' She felt unable to summon up much interest, but at least it put off the evil hour. 'Is it supposed to be something special?'

'It *is* special.' He turned into a quiet, tree-lined road leading down to the sea. 'Come and look for yourself.'

Already he had driven as far as a road-bridge and brought the van to a halt at its kerb. Amy heard Jim's eager stirrings in the back and turned to soothe him with a hand between the great wolf-ears. 'Are we taking him with us?'

'We're only going across the pavement,' Paul pointed out. 'It's not worth the time it'd take to let him out.'

'Poor old lad,' Amy said to Jim.

'He'll soon be having his turn. Stay, Jim.' The dog settled, and Paul got out and came round to open her door. 'Come and have a look.'

She pulled up the collar of her Cossack coat against the funnelling cold wind, thrust her hands deep into her pockets, and walked with him to the railing. Below it she saw a strip of dark brown water gilded by the late, low winter sun and disappearing beneath another bridge in the tree-crowded distance. Willows and beeches and chestnuts lined its grassy banks, and wide asphalt footpaths held inviting benches. It must be cool and shady in hot weather. Even now, with the branches bare and the cold wind freezing her ears, it still made an agreeable view.

'There it is, the Royal Military Canal.' Paul made a flourishing gesture. 'They hire out boats in the summer. And look.' He pointed along the water. 'Even though it's winter, and cold, people still come here to enjoy themselves.'

Amy saw what he meant. In the distance by the next footbridge, two muffled-up anglers sat surrounded by tackle and protected from the wind by green umbrellas. Opposite them two small children, supervised by women she took to be their mothers, threw bread in the water. Fleets of ducks appeared from under both bridges, bustling towards the bread. Behind the children the town of Hythe, its cosy houses cushioned with trees, climbed the hill to the church and beyond.

'It's nice,' she conceded as Paul joined her. 'But . . . military?'

'Dug by the army in 1805,' he confirmed, 'to help keep out Napoleon.'

'What?' Amy stared down at the ten-foot strip of water, and wondered if she'd heard right. 'Do you mean Napoleon Bonaparte?'

'The man himself.'

'Let me get this straight. If Napoleon had ever got his army over the twenty miles of Channel –' she gestured down the road to the blue line of the sea – 'he was supposed to be stopped by this ten-foot wide canal?'

'Absolutely.' Paul put on an accent like Aminata's. '*Mon Dieu*, I cannot cross zees!' he exclaimed with well-acted, squeaky dismay. 'I must take my *armee* back over ze sea to France.'

Even in her black mood, Amy couldn't help smiling. 'The people who built this thing really thought that was how it would go?'

'Maybe it would have, who knows? But anyway, digging it kept the troops out of mischief.' Paul straightened from the parapet and turned to face the view across the other side of the bridge. Amy turned to join him, and saw that from here the canal, as if done with the town, curved like a country river between thick elder-hedges and grassy, unpaved footpaths.

'See?' Paul said. 'Kent's short of rivers, they get lost in the chalk. The military have left us something just as good or better.'

'I do see.' Amy turned again, this time towards the sea. On one side of the road lay a golf course, on the other playing fields, pleasure parks, tennis courts, allotments and a wealth of trees, a green patchwork between town and sea. 'It's lovely here,' she said. 'Thanks for showing it to me,' she added, the polite little girl again, and shivered.

'You're cold,' he said, quick as ever to care for her well-being.

'I suppose I am,' she admitted, glad of the excuse. 'I haven't had much exercise today to get my circulation going.'

307

'Let's go.'

And that was it. The brief interlude over, the ordeal was almost upon her. Their next stop would be Harold's family home, and waiting there for them would be Paul's girlfriend.

Amy returned to the van with dragging footsteps, and sat in miserable silence as Paul turned it towards the busier traffic of the town through-road. Much too soon, a mere second or two later it seemed, he turned off into another quiet street and drew to a halt at its pavement. This street was hilly, she noted through the car windows, and so thick with old trees that each house seemed to stand in its own wood. She felt the cold air on the back of her neck, and the familiar bouncing of the van on its wheels as Jim jumped down from it, and now there was no putting it off any longer. Paul had opened her door.

'Come on into the house,' he said like a welcoming host.

Alert and tail-wagging at his side, Jim seemed to back up the welcome.

Amy rose from her seat, and found the street even prettier than it had seemed from inside the car. Uphill it ran into yet more trees; downhill it ended at the busy road, but across that lay a pine-fringed track to the sea. The few houses she could see were big and prosperous looking, and long drives with name plates indicated others out of sight which were probably richer still. Nothing here remotely resembled the nineteen-thirties semi she had imagined they would be visiting. Clark's Heating must be doing better than she had realized.

'This way.' Paul indicated the entry nearest to where he had parked.

Together they crossed a short drive, Jim padding beside them. This house was perhaps thirty years old. Though the smallest and simplest of those within view it was still big, a long rambling frontage under a low, spreading roof. Somewhere inside it, a bell responded to Paul's finger on the button.

The girl who opened the door was tall and slender, with short, fluffy dark hair, round cheeks, and a wild-rose complexion. Amy thought she noticed a resemblance to Harold and her spirits sank even further. So here she was, the one who had prior claim on Paul, and just as Amy had feared, she turned out to be one of Harold's sisters.

'Hi!' The voice was not girlish but womanly, warm and confident with cockney overtones. 'Nice to see you, Paul. And you –' she offered her hand – 'must be Amy?'

He's told her about me and she isn't in the least worried, Amy thought as she took the proffered hand. She's just so sure of him . . .

'Amy it is,' Paul confirmed. 'And Amy, this is Betty, Harold's mother.'

'M – mother?' she stared at the other woman, and for the second time that day felt incredibly foolish. First she had taken a child of fourteen for Paul's girlfriend, and now a woman who must be at least forty even if she didn't look it, and who was also his aunt. Now that she knew, she could see the tracery of fine lines round the woman's sparkling brown eyes, but just the same . . .

'You don't look old enough to be anybody's mother,' she blurted out before she could stop herself.

'Nice of you to say so.' Betty, who had bent to greet Jim, straightened to accept the compliment. 'I sometimes feel a hundred . . . do come in out of the cold.' She stepped back through a glass inner door, adding over her shoulder as they followed, 'Marie's expecting you.'

So she's called Marie then, Amy thought, and wondered why the name seemed vaguely familiar. Surely she had heard it before, quite recently?

The outer lobby led into a big square hall, itself windowless but with doors leading off it to rooms bright-lit by the late-afternoon sun. A wide, handsome staircase rose to one side, and at the end of a short corridor another glass door showed through its frosted pane the outline of kitchen cupboards. Scents of coffee and baking drifted through the warm air.

Paul commanded Jim to sit and the dog obeyed, though with a beseeching, walk-hungry stare. While Betty took their coats and hung them in a built-in cupboard, Paul strolled across and put his head round one of the doors. Presumably not finding what he sought, he tried another.

'Where is everybody?'

'Harold's team's playing at Romney,' Betty informed him. 'His dad's gone to cheer him on, and you already know Aminata's at the shop . . .'

'Aminata?' Amy looked from one to the other. 'She lives here?'

'Of course.' Betty turned to Paul in surprise. 'Didn't you tell her?'

'Tell me what?' Amy asked, dreading some new revelation.

'Aminata's parents only let her come here because we were here to look after her,' Betty explained, and to Paul: 'Doesn't she look something in those new robes her mother sent!'

Paul nodded in agreement. 'And doesn't she know it.'

'Oh well, teenage girls . . .' Betty let the words trail off, as if everyone knew what teenage girls were like. Amy, who often said such things herself as a teacher, remembered something else she knew about Betty.

'You have two daughters, haven't you,' she ventured. 'Is –' she swallowed hard, and got out the dreaded name – 'is Marie one of those?'

Two pairs of eyes, blue and brown, turned the same wondering gaze in her direction. Now what had she said?

'My daughters,' Betty told her, 'left home years ago.'

'Oh,' Amy floundered, lost once more. 'I'm sorry to hear that . . .'

'Don't be,' Betty assured her with practical kindness. 'Jen's doing well in London, Mandy's getting married in time for the baby to be born. Haven't you,' she demanded of Paul, 'told her *anything* about us?'

'I've made a start,' Paul said with his good-natured smile. 'There's a lot to tell.'

'All the same, me about to be a grandmother . . . Oh well.' Betty laughed, mostly it seemed at herself. 'I suppose it isn't as important to the rest of the world as it is to me.'

Amy was trying yet again to get her bearings. So Paul's cousins – Mandy and Jen – were out of the running. Who then was Marie, and what was she doing here with the Clarks? Then she remembered where she had heard the name before. Of course, it was this morning, from Aminata.

'This Marie we're going to see,' she began. 'Is that Aminata's aunt?'

The idea made her feel better. It was such a dignified title, aunt, it didn't at all fit with being a girlfriend.

Then she remembered that she herself had been an aunt for three years, and didn't feel at all dignified about it. Certainly she didn't believe it would rule her out from being Paul's girlfriend should she ever be so lucky . . . Anyway, here was Paul casting her down anew.

'Aminata calls her Aunt, but they're not related. It's a courtesy title.'

'But it is the same person?' Amy persisted, determined in spite of her misery to get it right at last. '*Tante Marie* is the person you've brought me here to meet?'

'She is,' Betty confirmed, and nodded towards the door on the other side of the hall. 'That way. I'll take this hell-hound to the kitchen,' she added, patting Jim, 'and find him something to cheer him up while he's waiting.' She moved towards the glass kitchen door, Jim eager at her side. 'When I've done that,' she called back over her shoulder, 'I'll bring some tea.'

Paul and Amy decorously apart as always, crossed the hall in the opposite direction to the fateful closed door. Amy tried not to drag her feet as she thought of the glamorous French or French-speaking Marie in the next room, waiting for them.

I wonder why she hasn't come out to meet us, she thought. Is she so important that she can sit in state and wait for privileged people to approach?

Paul gave the dreaded door a soft, respectful knock.

'*Entrez*,' called a voice from within.

'Oh goodness,' Amy hissed, 'I do hope she speaks some English.'

'Don't worry,' he assured her. 'She does.' He opened the door and stood back to let her go in ahead of him. Seeing that was what he seemed to want she stepped through it, wondering what she and Marie could possibly have to say to each other even if Marie did speak English.

The room she entered was big, low-ceilinged, and filled with sunlight from a wide, chintz-curtained window which looked across a garden to the sea. Near the window a two-bar electric fire, both bars glowing, warmed a sitting circle of two chintz-covered armchairs and a two-seater couch. Among them in another, higher armchair sat an old lady.

313

So where was Marie? Amy let her eyes discreetly search the room. Was she maybe beyond that other door, waiting to make an entrance? Before she could speculate further, Paul led her to the old lady, apparently the only person in the room.

Amy saw that though old she was also beautiful. She must be Malian like Aminata; though her skin was dark honey-gold rather than mahogany, she had Aminata's high forehead and modelled cheekbones, and wore a silk scarf in the same way, covering her hair and knotted at the back of her neck. The scarf was anemone-pink and violet, and another exactly like it filled the neck of her anemone-pink woollen cardigan.

To Northumbrian, east-wind-reared Amy the room felt uncomfortably hot, but it didn't seem to be warm enough for the old lady. As well as the scarf at her neck she had a crocheted blanket over her lap – all in anemone colours of violet and pink and indigo and cream, she noted wonderingly – which covered her entirely to the floor.

Such was her dignity that Amy almost felt she ought to curtsey. Instead she ventured a tentative smile. Perhaps that was the wrong thing to do; certainly the old lady made no pretence of returning it. Her dark, tired, leaf-shaped eyes continued to measure her with distance-keeping caution.

Can she be Aminata's nurse, Amy wondered, here to chaperone? She'd certainly keep any fourteen-year-old in order, even one as bubbly as Aminata . . .

What was this? What was going on? Paul had bent to kiss the old lady's cheek. And what was that he had just called her? Something foreign sounding . . .

Too late, Amy thought, I've missed it. I'll have to stay more with it, and hope he says it again.

'This is Amy,' he said, and suddenly for no reason at all smiled widely and joyously. 'I'm pretty sure she's going to be all right.'

'I 'ope so.' The old lady's manner remained stiff and guarded but she did offer a frail hand. Amy took it uncertainly, afraid of hurting the thin, honey-gold fingers tipped, she noticed, by perfect filbert nails, unpainted but a beautiful pink-gold.

'Welcome to my 'ome, Amy.'

Her home? Oh well, it was her home for the moment. Amy gathered her thoughts and told the necessary polite lie.

'I'm happy to be here.'

Where on earth had Marie got to, and when was she going to appear?

'Forgive me for not rising.' The old lady gestured down at the rug which covered her. 'I am supposed to keep warm for ze next day or two.'

Only for the next day or two? Winter would be a lot longer than that, and so would Aminata's stay in this cold climate. At the very least she had talked of being here at Christmas.

'*Grand'mere*'s malaria's been troubling her again,' Paul explained. 'The fever's died down, but we have to be careful.'

315

Grand'mere. So this lady was Aminata's grand-mother. What devotion, to travel so far and endure an English winter to take care of her grand-daughter.

'Please sit down.' The lady Paul had called *Grand'mere* gestured gracefully at the chintz-covered chair opposite.

'Thank you.' Amy sank into it and waited for Paul to be given a similar order. However, he stayed on his feet.

'I'd better go and give that poor dog his walk.'

'Ah, bah!' The old lady exclaimed. 'Why you must keep zees dog . . .'

She left the idea hanging in eloquently implied disgust. So that was why poor old Jim had been taken to the kitchen, because Aminata's grandmother didn't like dogs. Paul didn't comment, only smiled with his usual tolerance, bent to kiss the old lady's cheek again, and moved to the door.

Amy gazed after him, and noted with her expert drama teacher's eye that he wasn't as easy as he would like to seem. The set of his shoulders showed tension, and when he turned for a final glance into the room, his blue glance went questioningly from Amy to the old lady, and back to Amy.

But what was the question? What on earth was going on? Why was Amy being left alone with Aminata's grandmother, and why did these two seem so . . . so watchful? The old lady, though she had welcomed Amy in words, still hadn't offered the least beginnings of a smile.

316

'Cheer up, *Grand'mere*,' Paul said from the door. 'It's going to be all right, you'll see.'

'What is?' Amy asked, more and more bewildered.

'I'll be about an hour,' Paul told her.

Then he was gone, the door closing after him and leaving her alone with this formidable, unsmiling old lady. Aminata's grandmother – *Grand'mere* – seemed in no hurry to start a conversation.

Meeting that cool, measuring gaze, Amy fought down a rising sense of panic. Jim had to have his walk, and it had to be now because the short winter day wouldn't last much longer, but she did wish Paul hadn't left her here like this. Once more, as with Paul earlier today, she had the strongest feeling that she was being tested, though she couldn't imagine how, or what would happen if she should fail the test.

And where, oh where, was Marie? Well, at least that gave her something to talk about.

'I understood,' she began tentatively, 'that I was to meet someone called Marie.'

Now what was the matter? The old lady had straightened so firmly that her high-backed chair might have been the seat of judgement, her crochet rug a robe of office. Her long neck had stretched, her chin raised itself to a scornful angle, and her beautiful, tired old eyes had gone from cool to cold. What power she suddenly had in her – she must certainly make Aminata behave.

But what on earth have I said, Amy wondered.

For a wild moment she found herself picturing Marie as Paul's secret, mad wife, locked in the attic

317

like the demented Mrs Rochester. Getting a grip on her fantasies, she sought a way to clear up whatever misunderstanding this was.

'I'm sorry if I've said anything to offend you, *Madame* . . .'

She broke off, intrigued to hear herself using the French form of address. She had even pronounced it in the French way. She hadn't thought about it, just used the word that seemed best fitted for this frail, powerful, dignified woman.

'I am Marie.' The stern old voice offered no forgiveness. 'But no one calls me zat vizzout my permission.'

'I . . . I'm sorry . . .' Amy floundered to silence. Then, calling on all her reserves of voice, manner and acting experience, she managed a statement that was entirely sensible and coherent, if a little stilted.

'I'm sorry I misunderstood. I would never – *never*,' she repeated for emphasis, 'wish to be impertinent or to give you offence.'

'You would not?' Some of the coldness melted a little. 'Betty uses my name. She is after all my *belle-fille* . . .'

Belle-fille? Amy racked her brains, trying to remember what it meant. *Fille* on its own meant daughter, which Betty clearly wasn't. Stepdaughter perhaps? Had Betty's father taken this beautiful Malian woman as his second wife? Was that why such an exotic creature was here in the household of Harold Clark, Heating Engineer? That would certainly explain why Paul called her *Grand'mere* . . .

'. . . To ozzers, I prefer to be what you have already called me,' she continued. 'It is a good title, *Madame*. Nicer zan your ugly English Meeses.'

Meeses? Oh, she means Mrs, Amy realized.

'Yes, *Madame* is much prettier,' she readily agreed.

'Vairy well.' The old lady seemed positively to relax, almost to smile. 'Now, *Mademoiselle*, Paul 'as already told me much about you.'

'He has?'

Amy wondered why he would do that. Perhaps this lady didn't get out much, so the rest of the family made a point of keeping her up-to-date with what happened in the outside world?

'I suppose,' she began cautiously, 'he's seen a lot more of me this last week than he has of his girlfriend.'

'Girrl-friend?' *Grand'mere*'s beautiful, winged eyebrows drew together in puzzlement. 'I know nozzing of any girl-friend but you.'

'Me!' Amy could hardly keep the longing from her voice. 'He's certainly been a good friend to me,' she went on in explanation, 'but I'm not his girlfriend in that sense, *Madame*.'

'You are not?' The eyebrows drew closer, the frown more angry. 'You do not like my Paul?'

'Oh, I do!' It was out before Amy could stop it, the words seeming to jump from her mouth with more words after them. 'I like him more than I can say. I like him so much . . .' She managed to break off at last, but already it was too late. The unguarded passion in her voice, which must have appeared in her face too, had given her away completely.

Yes, the old lady knew exactly how Amy felt about Paul now, and it pleased her. Slowly at first and then ever more surely she smiled, a brilliant smile which lifted all the tired old lines of her face and showed the captivating young woman she must once have been.

''E likes you too,' she said.

'Do you think so?' For a brief moment Amy let herself hope, then crushed it. 'He doesn't behave as if he . . . liked me in that way, *Madame*.'

'No, 'e would not.'

Amy looked up, surprised by the certainty in the deep, soft voice. 'You seem very sure of that.'

'I am very sure. 'E would not do or say anyzing until 'e knew . . .'

A knock interrupted her. Amy heard the light, welcome rattle of tea cups, and jumped to her feet to open the door.

'Ask 'im,' *Grand'mere* instructed after her, 'to tell you about Carol.'

Amy stood still. So that was her name. 'His girlfriend?'

'Ask 'im.'

Amy shot a beseeching glance back over her shoulder, but didn't dare persist in her questioning. Instead she finished her journey to the door and let in Betty with the trolley. The next few minutes were taken up with the organizing of little tables, the filling and passing round of wide, delicate tea cups, and tiny, delicious egg and cress sandwiches.

320

'Nice to have somebody to make them for,' Betty said. 'Marie eats hardly anything, and the men would demand sausage rolls.'

'Paul too?' Amy asked, reflecting again how little she knew of these small details of his everyday life.

'They're ready in the kitchen for when he comes back,' Betty answered.

The talk continued at that level, comfortable, undemanding, leaving Amy's mind free to wrestle with what she had just heard and try to make sense of it.

Carol. Somewhere in Paul's life was a woman named Carol.

Yet *Grand'mere*'s absolutely positive that he likes me, she reflected. It was difficult not to draw hope and strength from the old lady's certainty, but she must be mistaken. Surely if it were true Paul would by now have shown his . . . his liking . . . one way or another?

Whereas he avoids touching me, she thought, except for that one time when he was sorry for me . . .

'. . . in zose days,' *Grand'mere* was saying, '*Le Mali* was French Ouest Africa. Zey were terrible, colonial times, but zey brought *Maman* and *Papa* togezzer.'

'Here's a picture of Marie's parents.' Betty went to a walnut side table full of silver-framed photographs, and handed one to Amy. It proved to be an old-fashioned, formally-posed wedding picture. A moustached, shiny-haired groom who might have been French cradled his top hat and proudly displayed his bride, another Malian beauty in a magnificent robe of broderie anglaise.

'Marie's father went to Mali from Marseilles to set up as a studio photographer,' Betty explained to Amy. 'Her mother sold eggs . . .'

'She worked zere.' *Grand'mere* indicated a painting on the wall. 'In Bamako market.'

Amy studied the picture, brilliant against the white wall. It showed a striking red crenellated structure like a desert fort, but with more and wider openings than a fort could have. Now that she was giving the painting her attention she could see that it showed people busy in and around it – blue-robed men in shallow, pointed straw hats, bright-robed women with baskets on their heads, an old man robed but bareheaded, in earnest conversation with a young one in French-style safari clothes.

'When *Papa* saw *Maman* at the market, 'e said, zat one and no ozzer,' *Grand'mere* went on with her story. 'Zey were married for fifty years.'

'She certainly was beautiful.' Amy returned the photograph to Betty, and added, greatly daring, 'Like you, *Madame*.'

The old woman acknowledged the compliment only with a brief nod. She seemed to have something else on her mind, something which kept her dark, newly sombre gaze on Amy. Betty, who had risen to clear the tea things, sat down again with the task unfinished. A silence fell on the comfortable room as if they were all waiting for something to happen. The test, whatever it was, seemed about to begin.

'You do not zink it wrong,' *Grand'mere* said at last, 'for a white man to marry a black woman?'

Amy blinked, then shook her head vigorously. 'Of course not. I hadn't even thought about it.'

The two women stayed silent, both focused on Amy as if unconvinced. Nettled by the double scrutiny, she knew that if she didn't speak her mind calmly now, she would speak it angrily at some future time.

'I . . . I'm a guest in your home,' she began as smoothly as she could manage. 'And I . . . I think you should . . .' she hesitated once more, seeking the least offensive way of putting it '. . . should trust me not to be a racist.'

The old woman frowned, and Amy quailed. Who was she to lecture someone twice, three times her age, on the courtesy due to a guest?

And yet what else could I do? she asked herself. I *do* think she should trust me – they both should. Then she saw that it was all right. *Grand'mere* and Betty exchanged glances and now the old woman's frown cleared, driven out by that rare, brilliant smile.

'Forgive me,' she said. 'It is only that I 'ave learned to be cautious for my grandchildren.'

Amy smiled back. 'That's very understandable. You have other grandchildren?' she went on, hoping to turn the conversation in an easier direction. 'Besides Aminata, I mean . . .'

She stopped, realizing that she had it wrong again. She had learnt so many new things in the past few minutes that they were all going round in her head.

'I'm sorry,' she said. 'When I first came in here, *Madame*, I thought you were Aminata's grandmother . . .'

'But I am Aminata's *Tante* Marie,' the old lady pointed out.

'I know. It's sort of a question of linking it up,' Amy floundered. 'Of course it's Harold who's your grandson . . .'

'And Paul,' said *Grand'mere*. ''Arold and Paul are cousins. Sons of my sons.'

CHAPTER 15

'Why on earth didn't you tell me?'

Amy put the question the moment they reached Paul's living room. She had held on to it all this time and could hold it no longer. Using all her self-control she managed to keep her voice low, but none of her acting skills could conceal the anger and . . . yes, the hurt . . . she felt.

And she had a right to be angry. He had put her in an impossible position. Bad enough that he had taken her to visit his grandmother without saying what he was doing, but not to tell her before he left her alone with the old lady . . .

Only he probably did, she reprimanded herself. I was wool-gathering when we first went in there. All the same . . .

Betty and *Grand'mere* must have seen at once how stunned she was. Astonishment, hurt and anger with Paul had kept her speechless, not knowing where to start. She didn't dare look at *Grand'mere* but knew, somehow, that the old lady's chilly, distant manner had returned in full force.

It was Betty who had come to Amy's rescue. At first she only offered more tea, but her voice was warm with sympathy. When Amy refused, Betty rose to her feet and gathered plates and cups and saucers to be piled on the trolley. Amy shot up to help, and when her offer was accepted, found the small domestic task did something to help restore her calm. When it was done she returned to her seat, conscious of the continuing frosty silence from the old woman. She half-expected Betty to escape by wheeling the trolley away, but no, she too reseated herself.

'He should have told you,' she said. 'I don't know why he didn't. He always told the others . . .'

'Others?' Alert as ever to the subject of other women in Paul's life, Amy faced his grandmother for the first time since learning of the relationship. 'He's brought people here before, *Madame*?'

'Many, many,' the old lady told her through tightened lips. ''Arold also . . . and my grand-daughters, before zey left 'ome.'

'Marie,' Betty explained, 'likes to meet the young people who come to the house.'

For 'meet', Amy thought, read 'vet'. To make sure they're worthy, I suppose. What happens when she decides they aren't, I wonder?

She felt the heat rising in her cheeks, and struggled with her resentment. Who did this old lady think she was, that she could have a say in the . . . the friendships of her grandchildren? Well, if she rejects me it isn't going to be on the grounds of racism, Amy decided with new resolution.

'You're right,' she said to Betty, 'I didn't know that *Madame* is Paul's . . .' No, damn it, she would come right out and speak the problem. 'I didn't know that Paul is partly black.' She turned, straightening in her chair the better to look the old lady full in the eyes. 'I hope you don't think that makes any difference whatever to the way I feel about him?'

In the long silence that followed Betty made a move, then stilled. Amy, conscious of how dark the room had grown, wondered if she had meant to put on a light, then left it to a better moment.

Outside the window a blackbird whistled softly. Dusk was settling over the room, blurring outlines, dimming colours, shadowing the old woman's stern features so that it was difficult to see how she had reacted to Amy's challenge. When she spoke at last her voice was gentle as the dusk-softened voice of the blackbird.

'It really, truly, makes no difference?'

Amy felt her indignation wane like the daylight. The quiet, sad question seemed too general to be resented. It was life itself which Paul's grandmother feared, and how could you blame her for wanting happiness for her grandchildren?

'His being partly black makes no difference to me,' she answered slowly, thinking it out as she spoke. 'What does matter is that he didn't tell me, though he must think it's important.'

'I agree.' The old woman's voice warmed and strengthened to its usual certainty. The dusk-faded moth colours of her blanket stirred about her as she leant urgently forward. 'You must take it up with 'im,' she went on, 'when you are next alone togezzer.'

She surely doesn't think I'd take it up right here in front of her, Amy thought, resentment rising again.

She looked once more from the window to the darkening sky, and once more her irritation faded. This lady was a matriarch, used to guiding and forming her family's behaviour. If Harold and Paul were anything to go by they did her credit, and certainly made it possible to forgive a little bossiness.

The new peacefulness had stayed with her until Paul's return. As soon as he appeared – without Jim, who must have been put back in the kitchen – her anger flared anew, reinforced now by her sense that the two other women were on her side and blamed him for her embarrassment. Both were a little reserved with him as they chatted of small things; the walk; the weather for tomorrow; Harold and his father who would soon be home from Romney and wanting their tea. On leaving, Amy had taken *Grand'mere*'s hand in farewell, and been rewarded with a silent, significant glance. Yes, she certainly had to talk to Paul of what she had just learnt, and as soon as possible.

Nevertheless she had held it in after they left the house. Seeing she couldn't think of anything else, and presumably neither could he, they had driven back to his flat, let themselves into it, and climbed the stairs in ominous silence.

Amy had gone to her bedroom first, to take off her coat and drop it on the bed. Stronger for those few minutes by herself, she had resolved to stay calm, cool, rational. She wouldn't raise her voice, she wouldn't accuse him, she would simply point out the embarrassment he had caused her, and ask for an explanation.

So she was surprised and chagrined at the way her simple, rational question came out. She did manage to keep her voice down but the words hissed like steam escaping. So forceful were they that Jim jerked his ears up and stared at her, then skulked over to where Paul knelt by the floor-standing Chinese vase lamp.

Paul however seemed unmoved. He didn't answer, only put a hand down to pacify the dog and then clicked the switch on the floor. When the lamp blossomed into light his olive-dark features seemed impassive as a carving, and Amy shot an involuntary glance at the little black figure on the desk

Yes, she thought, I could have seen it if I'd known to look.

She turned back to Paul. He hadn't inherited those huge, tilted eyes so striking in Aminata and *Grand'mere*, but he had the same elegant, powerful, high-crowned head. He straightened, and for a moment the unshaded light from the top of the lamp cast hard, shifting shadows over his high cheekbones, his straight, broad nose, his wide, strong mouth she so longed to . . .

Amy closed her own eyes and gave herself a mental shake. When she opened them she saw that perhaps he wasn't so impassive after all. His full lower lip had caught between his teeth, and his blue, un-African eyes were rueful.

'I nearly did tell you . . .'

'You didn't,' she interrupted, hearing the high, child-ish note in her voice but powerless to bring it down to a more reasonable level. 'You told me you were taking me to meet your *girlfriend*. You *know* you did.'

'Girlfriend?' Standing at the other side of the room, lit by the silk-shaded lamp, the dog pressed against his legs, he frowned. 'What girlfriend?'

'How would I know? She's *your* girlfriend, not mine.' A part of her hated her whining, over-emphatic tones, but she couldn't stop. 'You've mentioned her *twice*.'

'When?'

'Last Wednesday, when I rang you from school.' She cast her mind back over the past week, and pulled from its pell-mell events the one she needed. 'When I said they'd found my car so you needn't come to Canterbury to fetch me . . .'

'So I decided to visit *Grand'mere* instead, seeing she's been poorly.'

'Then this lunch time,' Amy tore on, too wrought-up to take in what he was saying, 'you said you'd walk Jim while I was talking to her.'

'Talking to who?'

'Your *girlfriend*, she yipped, angrier and more confused than ever. 'Haven't you been *listening* . . .'

'Amy, you're raving.' He took a step towards her and stopped, hampered by clinging Jim. 'You must have a fever or something.'

330

'But that's what you said.'

'I said I'd walk Jim while you were talking to my grandmother. At least,' he added, the rueful expression back in his blue eyes, 'I nearly said that.'

'You said your g . . .' Amy stopped in mid-flow. Girlfriend. Grandmother. Yes, that was right, he hadn't finished the word either time. So now they were right back to her opening question. 'So why didn't you *tell* me?'

'That I'm part African?' Paul shrugged. 'Can't you guess why?'

'No I can't,' Amy snapped. 'Unless it's more of what I got from your grandmother, that I might be racist about it.'

'You'd be surprised how many people are.'

He moved to switch on the other Chinese lamp, his back to her. Then he unwound the yellow scarf which, now he had lost his coat, seemed to be all he needed to keep warm, and with his usual long-legged grace flung himself into what she had learnt was his favourite armchair. Jim kept close to him, settling at his feet with a wary eye on Amy.

'Sit down.' Paul indicated the other armchair. 'And we'll talk about it.'

She stayed where she was. '*Talk* about it . . .' She stopped, distracted by an angry twinge from her knee. So it wasn't entirely better then, and her present tensions must have tightened it and made it worse. She glanced at the comfortable chair he had indicated, glared at him in defiance. Then she limped to the pedestal desk, turned its wooden-armed chair outward into the room and eased herself into that.

Paul, now sideways to her, only smiled infuriatingly as if at something funny. He didn't bother to crane round to face her but stared ahead, his straight, strong profile lowered in thought. When he did speak, he took her by surprise.

'You remember my friend Owen Rees?'

'Who runs that marvellous pub –' she dredged her memory for its name – 'the Half Moon?'

He nodded. 'Can you remember our school nick-names?'

'I can remember that they didn't make any sense.' Amy frowned. 'What has this to do with . . .'

'He was Inky.'

'That's right, and the un-inkiest person you could ever hope to meet . . .'

'I was Larky.'

'Like Clarky without the C.'

'No. Like Darky.'

'D . . .' Amy let the word go unfinished.

'You know what kids are,' he went on evenly.

Yes, she knew. 'But why?' Remembering her thoughts of a moment ago, she glanced again at the little figure on the desk. 'I can see now that you do look Malian in some ways . . .'

'Peule,' he put in absently.

Amy stared at him in bewilderment. 'Pearl? What on earth . . .'

'Or Fulani. It's the name of our particular African race.'

'I see.' She nodded sideways at the statue. 'Like that?'

'That's a stylized version of how a lot of us look, yes.'

'But not you, or only in –' she paused, looking for the right phrase – 'in sort of secondary ways. And you're no darker than many Europeans,' she added, remembering what he had just told her, 'so why Darky?'

'My father came to visit me once, early on.'

'And?'

'He's . . . he *was*,' Paul corrected himself, 'much darker than me.'

'Little beasts. And Owen?' she asked. 'Inky?'

'From the day he started, he was Chinky.'

Amy silently contemplated the boundless cruelty of children.

'So we got together and worked out a compromise.' Paul grinned with a certain relish. 'Then we enforced it.'

'You mean you fought about it?' she enquired, already knowing the answer from her teacher's experience of small boys.

'Took on all comers,' he confirmed. 'Owen's mother had taught him karate, and he taught me.'

'You know karate?' She looked at him with a new respect. 'That must make you handy in a brawl.'

'Now I'm grown up, I try to keep away from brawls.'

'I'd noticed.' She spoke dryly but, she noted with relief that her voice sounded quieter. Had he taken her on that detour to his school days expressly to calm her?

If so, he had succeeded. She knew she ought to be grateful, but she could feel a new wave of irritation building at the way he could always make her do what he wanted. To stem it she returned her thoughts to the small boy he had been.

'You say your father looked African,' she began, slowly and carefully. 'Is that why your mother's parents objected to the marriage?'

'To be fair to them, I don't think so. Not that I knew of, anyway.' He stared down at his elegant old tweeds, perhaps re-running memories of his English grandparents. 'After all, there was plenty to object to without that,' he said at last.

Amy put aside her pity for that small boy whose father had so signally failed to take care of him. 'You still haven't answered my question,' she reminded him. 'Paul, why? Why didn't you tell me?'

'There's been so much going on.' But still he didn't turn towards her, still he didn't meet her eyes. 'We haven't had much time . . .'

'We had ample time last night and today.'

Amy recalled their leisurely supper last night, where she had spoken of her life on the farm and her reason for staying there so long. At the time she had believed it was fair exchange, that she was telling him about herself in return for learning so much about him. Only, he hadn't told her as much as she then thought. He'd left out a significant item which clearly meant a lot to him. She remembered the twice-unfinished word she had so painfully misunderstood.

'You didn't just not tell me,' she said. 'You deliberately kept it back. As if . . . as if you thought it would make a difference to the way I . . .' She closed her mouth abruptly, snapping off the sentence before it could give her away. To the way I feel about you, she'd almost said, and she wasn't getting into that, not while he kept this immense, cold distance between them.

However, when he turned his head to look at her, she knew that she might as well have said it anyway. His blue eyes studied her with a gaze so intense, so penetrating that she shifted uncomfortably on her hard chair, caught as if in a search light.

'Are you sure it doesn't?' he asked gently.

Amy took a deep breath, then answered with a new steadiness. 'I'm sure.'

She wanted to say more, but restrained herself. She wouldn't protest, or reproach him further, or pour out pledges and assertions to prove how much she meant what she said. That would only lessen the effect. Those two small, quiet words were all she needed and all the answer she would give.

They hung in an amber-lit silence that went on and on. She heard the tick of his angular wall-clock; the far-off drone of a car; from the kitchen the muffled whirr of the refrigerator; from Hop Street below a man's voice raised to greet a friend.

Perhaps it was that greeting, called out in the street by someone they didn't know and who didn't know them, which broke through Paul's reserve. It was such an unmistakably friendly noise. It was followed at once by a sigh from Jim, who lowered his ears and settled couchant, and then it was Paul who sighed.

'Yes, I should have told you,' he said, head still turned uncomfortably towards her so that he could look her in the eyes. 'I'm sorry.'

'Oh Paul . . .'

Oh hell! She had breathed his name like a holy word, and she was sure that she had looked at him with all her soul in her eyes. If only he'd get up and draw her to her feet and take her in his arms . . . but he wouldn't. Whatever his grandmother believed, he didn't feel about Amy the way she did about him and if she wanted to salvage any pride at all she had to stop giving herself away as she just had.

She stared down at her grey pleated skirt, knowing that she must speak and wondering how to begin. Well, for a start she could accept his apology.

'Like you said,' she began, 'there's been a lot going on.'

It came to her then that if he had held something back, so had she. Yes, she had told him of her childhood and early womanhood. She had also spoken of her enjoyment of college, and of how much she liked her job at Oaklands, but she too had left out something important, something she knew disturbed him. She gathered her courage to speak of it.

'I suppose,' she began bitterly, 'I can hardly blame you for not trusting me, once you'd met Robert.'

'Robert?' Still awkwardly sideways because of the distance-keeping place she had chosen to sit, he stared at her. 'What's that buffoon . . .' He trailed off, restraining himself. 'What's he got to do with anything?'

'You said it yourself,' she told him bleakly. 'Robert's a buffoon – too vain and trivial and silly to take seriously. I *didn't* take him seriously,' she hurried on, anxious to pour it out now she had started. 'Not from the moment I first met him.'

She stared down at her lap. How miserably grey this skirt was, why had she ever bought it? And these pleats, long lines that came together then ran apart, ever further apart until there was no hope of their ever meeting again.

'I never liked him,' she burst out, 'yet I still . . .' She jerked her head to one side, instinctively recoiling. 'I can't bear the thought of it.'

Another silence. When she dared to look across the room, she saw that Jim had raised his head to stare at her once more, ears alert. Paul buried a soothing hand in the dog's gold ruff, then slowly turned his head back towards Amy, arched brows drawn together in a small frown.

'I must admit,' he began, 'I did wonder what you saw in him.'

'Only his looks.' Amy spoke with a self-loathing all the more vehement for the way she had suppressed it in the past few days. 'Can you believe that? I didn't like him, but I . . . enjoyed . . . his looks.'

Paul shrugged. 'We all make mistakes.'

'And I've been making them ever since I first went to college.' Amy realized that this was the first time

337

she had ever admitted it. 'And they were getting worse. I was getting more and more . . .' She paused, seeking the word. Careless? No, that wasn't it. Undiscriminating? Nor that . . .

'*Loose!*' Lighting on the right term at last, she spat it out with contempt. 'I thought I was such a free spirit, but I wasn't free, I was loose. Out of control.'

'Oh, come on now . . .'

'I was, though.' She took a deep breath. 'After being at home buried in family chores, I kind of went mad when I got away to college.'

The words dropped away into another long silence. She glanced across at him anxiously, and saw that he was once more looking ahead into space. When he turned back towards her it was she who looked away, fearing to meet the contempt she had seen in his dealings with Robert. However, his voice was cool and neutral.

'Do you want to talk about it?'

'No,' she said. 'But I need to.'

'So let's have it.'

'Well, I worked hard, and I didn't do drugs – I mean, I tried them and didn't like what they did to me . . .' She trailed weakly to silence, realizing that she was talking to put off the evil hour. 'What I did like was sex. With anybody I fancied. Sometimes, while I was at college, two at a . . .'

'I don't want to hear any more.'

She sensed a distance, a held-back force in his even tones and drooped her head, letting her hair swing forward to hide her shamed cheeks. 'I . . . I'm sorry.'

338

'Don't be. We all have to find our own way. The important thing is . . .' He broke off. 'Amy, could you do something for me?'

Anything, anything in the world! 'What?' she asked aloud.

'Come and sit over here –' he indicated the leather armchair opposite him – 'before I get a terminal crick in my neck.'

'All right.' She got up and crossed the floor on leaden feet. She would have flown to the moon for him, gathered the stars in a basket to lay at his feet, cut up the rainbow to weave him a tie, and all he wanted was for her to sit where he could talk to her more easily . . .

An anguished yelp from Jim cut short her silly fantasies. The dog shot up, his poor tail still under her foot. She shifted her weight quickly, too quickly for her weakened knee, which buckled under the sudden strain. Her hands, extended in apology to Jim, had to clutch the arm of Paul's chair instead. Choking back tears of shock and humiliation at her own clumsiness, she slowly sank to her knees.

'Don't cry, Amy.' Paul's voice was low, hoarse, urgent, close to her hear. 'Don't cry, my darling . . .'

He raised a hand and gently stroked the tears from her eyes. Then – could it really be that his arms were round her at last? They were, they were, strong and warm and sensual while his fingers played on her spine, then on her neck, then in her hair. Still on her knees by his chair she raised her face to his, and waves of delight crashed through her as his mouth, his dear, dear mouth, came down on hers.

It was the sweetest kiss she had ever known. At first it was soft and gentle, a mere tasting. Then the tip of his tongue parted her lips, her tongue rushed to meet it, and they were engulfed in each other, lost to everything but the urgency of their need to know each other at last in the blind, headlong, unreasoning world of the senses. When they drew apart, both were gasping.

'Sit, Jim,' Paul said dreamily.

Amy glanced down, and saw that the dog had been pawing at Paul's foot. 'I expect he wants his supper,' she said, somewhere a long way off.

'I'll give it to him —' Paul put her gently aside, and stood up — 'while you . . .' He broke off, gazing down to where she still knelt. 'I was going to say, while you take your clothes off,' he said with a wicked gleam in his eyes, 'but on second thoughts, I want to be the one to do that job.'

'There you go again,' Amy gave a small, distracted laugh. 'Taking over.'

'Wait here.' He stood up. 'I'll be right back.'

Amy waited in a daze. It seemed forever before he returned, carefully closing off Jim, his supper, and his new beanbag bed in the kitchen. She rose at once from the armchair where she had been impatiently waiting, and they met standing upright in the space between the desk and the armchairs. When they kissed again he pressed her close and she exulted in the strength of him, the warmth, the hardness, the hot, compelling thrust of his arousal . . .

'Now Amy Hamilton,' he said when at last they drew apart. 'Hands above head.'

Laughing at the instruction, so like one she might have given in a drama lesson, she obeyed, and he lifted her sweater over her head.

'You shouldn't ever cover those.' He stared down at her breasts, white against the black of her bra. 'They're too beautiful to hide.'

'They wouldn't exactly help classroom discipline . . .'

'Turn round.'

She obeyed once more, and felt the bra's catch released. Its straps slid gently down her shoulders, and as it fluttered to the carpet he cupped her breasts from behind and pressed his thumbs against their hardened tips. She turned back to him and he slowly, reverently bent down and kissed each flaring pink crest. Amy caught her breath as new longings coursed through her.

'I don't know that I can wait much longer, Paul.'

'You'll wait. And like it.'

He traced a pattern on one breast with his tongue, an agonizing little spiral. Around and about his tongue circled until finally his lips closed once more on the deliriously demanding centre. Then he raised his hand to it and teased it with merciless gentleness between his fingertips while his mouth dealt with the other. She buried her fingers in his hair, just as she had wanted to do for so long, and surrendered herself to the delight he was giving her, hating it when he drew away.

'Oh, don't stop!'

'I won't,' he told her, and undid the fastening of her skirt.

It slid to the floor in a jumble of grey pleats. Slowly, sweetly, tantalizingly he pushed down the black briefs which were all she wore under it, down over her thighs under his stroking fingers, down over her knees, down, down to her feet.

'So soft,' he said, looking down at her. 'So bright . . .'

While she stood with her feet tangled in discarded garments, he knelt before her, drew her body towards him, and buried his face between her thighs. Amy felt herself opening, gushing, overflowing, so urgently that she had to plead with him.

'Can it be now, please? Now?'

Somehow he was naked. Before she had time to savour his lean darkness, he had snatched her up in his arms, hurried her to his bedroom, and flung her on the double bed. Then he was over her, and as the heat of his manhood slid into her she felt her entire self rush to meet it, her whole world concentrated and completed as she would never have believed possible.

'Steady,' he murmured, kissing her shoulder. 'I want to please you, Amy.'

'Oh you do please me, you do.'

But she knew the word was inadequate. It was more than pleasure that she felt as he began to move in her, it was a sense of rightness, as if she had been made and

342

put into the world only for this. She moved with him, guided by him, running her hands down the smooth skin of his back from broad shoulders to narrow waist, then pressing her fingers urgently into his flesh as their rhythm quickened, tightened, lifted, until she and he soared together into a place where she had never been before. Somewhere in the room she heard a strange, animal cry. Only when they lay still, joined but quiet, did she realize that she had made it herself.

For a long time they lay like that without speaking. Then he shifted his weight off her and lay beside her, still close, still without speaking, and raised himself on one elbow. She put a finger on the hard, wonderful curve of his shoulder, and traced a line down to the swell of his biceps, which moved and rippled as his hand played some delightful game with her navel.

'I thought you didn't like me,' she said at last.

His hand stole from her navel to her breasts. 'I . . . like you very much.'

'I thought after you met Robert . . .'

'Amy, darling, living is making mistakes. I've made them too.'

'With women?'

He didn't answer, but his hand left her breasts and pushed her damp hair away from her face.

'*Grand'mere*,' Amy said, 'told me to ask you about someone called Carol.'

He turned abruptly away from her and sat up against the old-fashioned mahogany bedhead. 'She was nobody. It was a long time ago.'

Amy lay back, staring up at his straight, strong profile. Something had happened to her in the last hour which would change her life forever, and part of the change was a new understanding of this wonderful man she loved.

'She hurt you,' she said with absolute certainty. 'When?'

'Five years ago.' He stared back into his own past. 'I . . .' He swallowed. 'I loved her. Very much.'

Amy felt a ferocious twist of jealousy. 'And she didn't love you?'

'At first she did.'

'And then?'

'She found out I was part African.'

'But that's horrible.' Amy jerked up to sit beside him, head turned to stare at him in shock. 'Racial prejudice is bad enough, but to stop loving someone . . .' She let the thought die away. 'I didn't know there were people like that.'

'Well there are.' He spat out the words as if he hated their taste. 'And she was one of them.'

'No wonder you shied away from telling me.' She thought of the way they had kissed, just once, and then never again until now. 'Is that why you . . . you suddenly got all . . . all cold, and distant with me?'

'I suppose it is.' He spoke as if with difficulty, still turned away from her. 'I've known a lot of women since then. They all had to –' he gave a short, strained laugh – 'to pass the colour test.'

'And did they?' Amy had to ask, and to go on asking, though she feared what she might hear. The thought of them twisted in her like a knife, but she had to find out all she could of these other women he had known. Perhaps he had brought them here, to the very place where he and she had just come so momentously together . . .

'Some did, some didn't. I see they're settling down.'

He seemed to be speaking of her breasts, whose tips he touched one by one. They immediately proved him wrong by thusting up with a new urgency.

'Amy,' he said in pretended shock, 'you are one fiery lady. So it's true what they say about red-headed women . . .'

'I'm not red-headed women, I'm me,' she protested, and then, because she had to ask, 'So you haven't . . . done this . . . with any other red-headed woman?'

'Not one.'

That was something, she supposed. Then she stopped thinking, about that or anything else except the delicious movements of his hands over her body, and then of her hands over his body. When their bodies joined once more, as they had been made to be joined from the beginning of time, she stopped thinking at all.

When it was over they slept. Somewhere in the timeless dark she was aware that he had left her, and lay half-awake until he returned to rouse her to a long, slow, dreamy rhythm of love. Then she lay close to him, waiting for sleep, and had fleeting, blurred thoughts of the other men she had known.

They always wanted me to take care of them, she thought. Like I took care of my brothers. I suppose I'm used to ordering men about . . .

She woke to find the place beside her empty and light filtering through the edges of the heavy velvet curtains. The sound of the flat's outer door opening and shutting, and a small, friendly wuff from Jim, told her what Paul had been doing. A dog's bladder couldn't hold out forever.

It must have been for the same reason that Paul had disappeared last night while she slept. She had quite forgotten Jim's needs, she realized with a pang of guilt, but Paul hadn't. He would never forget anyone who depended on him.

All the same, he can't go on keeping that poor dog here, she thought sleepily. We must work something out . . .

She sniffed. Coffee! Even the smell brought her round, reminding her that today she must write her reports. She leapt out of bed, and ten minutes later arrived in the kitchen fully dressed and ready for business.

'And you were right,' she nobly admitted to Paul as they breakfasted. 'I'll be able to do them a lot more easily today than I could have yesterday.'

Paul smiled, and went on eating cornflakes with the hand that wasn't holding hers. 'Would my computer be any help to you, or would you rather work at the desk?'

'Desk, please. My bag's still there where you put it on Friday night.'

'I'll walk Jim while you're doing them. Poor old lad hasn't had much company in the last –' he glanced at the clock – 'fourteen hours.'

'Were we really in bed that long?' Amy marvelled. 'Doesn't the time go quickly when you're enjoying yourself.'

After he had departed with politely impatient Jim leashed in one hand and a poop-scoop in the other, she made herself another coffee. The pain in her knee, she realized as she moved about the kitchen, had completely gone. Better than that, she felt relaxed, alert, ready for anything. If I work as well as I feel, she thought, coffee balanced on her way to the desk, then I'll polish this lot off this morning and have the afternoon for myself.

True, Paul hadn't spoken any specific words of love. But his body had loved hers, and she knew now that he had no other woman.

It's going to come out right, she told herself as she zipped open the various pockets of her school bag. Here was her favourite pen, here her register; she set them to hand. Then she opened the main part of the bag to take out the reports, and stared down at them in disbelief.

Someone had torn them into a million pieces.

CHAPTER 16

'You can't do your job properly as a teacher without making enemies.'

As she spoke, Kate Campbell set about her grilled trout. Amy tackled her lasagna at least with more appetite, though not much more, than the Monday exactly a week ago when they had last lunched at the Crossed Keys.

'And schools like any community have their share of nutters,' Kate went on between mouthfuls. 'Can you think who you've upset lately?'

Not *if* you've upset anyone, but *who* you've upset, Amy noted, and admitted the justice of it. Pupils must learn to fit in, and to accept criticism as well as praise. In any class someone at one time or another stepped out of line and had to be dealt with. She had hoped she never dealt with them too harshly, but it seemed all too possible now that she had at some time been harsher than she realized. She rested her knife and fork and stared sideways, out of the window at the end of their table to the rainwashed, sheep-dotted sweep of the north downs.

'I was a bit heavy with Tracy Norris, at rehearsal on Tuesday . . .'

She let the sentence trail off. Tracy's parents had divorced and remarried; she, their youngest child, was in the adoring care of grandparents. Her grandmother embroidered kneelers for the cathedral; her grandfather guided weekend tourists over it. Under such a home influence Tracy accepted authority so willingly that it seemed wildly unlikely that she would attack school reports, one of authority's most potent symbols.

Amy sighed, and checked back on that rehearsal. 'I suppose I might have annoyed Carl Stevens as well. He was wearing this silly scarf . . .'

'Carl's thrilled to be doing his song in the play,' declared Kate, his form-tutor. 'He'd never put that at risk.'

Amy nodded, and considered the rest of her previous week's teaching. 'There's Richard Ablett.' She had a vivid picture of cozening, green-eyed Richard, object of Joanna Larkin's thirteen-year-old passion. 'He got his whole group in trouble last week for doing the wrong improvization.'

'He's trouble, certainly,' Kate said. 'But I don't see him tearing up report blanks, it's not his thing.' She looked up from her plate to stare at Amy, grey eyes thoughtful. 'Are you sure your demon draper's out of the frame?'

'Pretty sure,' Amy confirmed. 'He's back with his wife. Besides . . .' She didn't finish the sentence, but knew Kate understood. First this was unlike any of Robert's hoaxes earlier last week, and second, to do it he would have had to come to Oaklands some time on Friday to gain access to her bag. She had never guarded it much and clearly somebody had got to it, but surely not Robert, unknown in the school and too noticeable to be overlooked by man-mad teenage girls.

'So who does that leave?' Kate asked, putting her knife and fork together.

'Only a school full of people, that's all,' Amy responded gloomily, and glanced down at her friend's bulging handbag. 'Have one of your cigarillos if you want.'

Kate's gaze also dropped to her handbag, but she didn't touch it. Almost she might have been looking at it simply to avoid having to look anywhere else.

'I, er, I don't smoke any more.'

'Really? When did you stop?'

'Oh, some time last week . . .'

Kate went on staring down at her bag. Amy recalled how, last Friday after school, her friend had hung on in the staff room talking about nothing. She would have had ample opportunity to open a school bag and damage its contents . . .

I'm getting paranoid, Amy thought, and quickly spoke aloud. 'It's such an odd list of . . . of difficult things that have happened to me.'

She cast her mind back, listing yet again. An apparently dangerous dog left in her garden; her car and Paul's coat stolen; an intruder using a car with a distinctive engine; her keys missing; the Yates Centre drama studio badly overheated . . .

'Though heaven knows,' Amy said, thinking aloud, 'that could just have been the cleaners being careless.'

'Hm?' Kate blinked and gave her head a small shake. 'What was that?'

'Nothing.'

Nothing I haven't said a hundred times already, Amy meant. She looked more closely at her friend and saw her cigarillo-free hands loose on the table, her cheeks a little flushed, her grey eyes wide and unfocused as she stared out to where a new curtain of rain swept over the downs.

'I begin to think,' Amy said carefully, 'that I might not be the only one who's got troubles.'

'Hm?' Kate came back from far away. 'You mean me?'

Amy nodded.

'No no,' Kate said. 'No troubles. No troubles at all.'

'Something on your mind though,' Amy said. 'I wish you'd tell . . .'

'I'm pregnant.'

Stunned, Amy stared across the table. 'Is that what you wanted to talk about last Friday?'

Kate nodded. 'You looked so tired, I decided not to bother you.'

'Oh Kate!' Amy exclaimed, guilt-stricken. 'I'd have wanted to know, honest I would.'

'It's all right, it worked out fine.' A Mona Lisa smile played about Kate's long, sensible mouth, combining with the new colour in her cheeks and her softened looks to make her almost pretty. 'I decided it was the . . . the father I should be telling.'

The father. A thousand questions chased each other through Amy's mind, but before she could decide which were permissible to ask, Kate spoke again.

'Tom Birchill and I are getting married as soon as we can fix it.'

'Why Kate, that's marvellous.' Amy thought of the stocky, good-natured woodwork teacher. 'He's such a *kind* man.'

Six years ago, when she came to Oaklands on her first teaching practice, Tom had helped her a great deal with difficult pupils. Most of her discipline problems had been with older, rougher boys, and often woodwork was the only item on the timetable that gave such boys any sense of self-worth. That made Tom an important person in their lives, and when he told them to behave for Amy, they behaved.

Speaking of him was a sharp reminder to Amy of what real trouble was like. Almost four years after that, returning to Oaklands as a regular teacher, she found Tom thinner and sadder, with new lines scored downwards from his mouth and eyes. She had learnt that his wife and daughter, his only child, had been killed in a road accident two years earlier.

'Oh, it's marvellous to think of him having another chance to be happy,' Amy told Kate. 'Will you go on teaching?'

'Probably not. I'll want another baby as soon as possible after this one . . .'

They chatted of Kate's plans, and for the first time Amy found herself envying her friend. With Paul, she felt as much in limbo as ever. In spite of the marvellously special, the unique pleasure he gave her in bed, she still had no idea how he felt about her. She didn't know if they had any future at all, let alone the secure future that Kate now had with Tom. She didn't even know if she wanted one.

'I see now why neither you nor Tom answered the phone to me yesterday,' she said. 'I suppose you were out together, celebrating?'

Her mind wandered back to the events of the day before. Once she had found her vandalized report blanks she had spent an hour on the telephone. She had still been using it when Paul returned from walking Jim, the two bundling up the stairs and entering the living room windblown and smelling of the sea.

'Westerly's blowing, you must come and see the waves . . .' Seeing that she was on the phone, he stopped and waited till she had finished her call. 'What's the matter?' he asked when it was over.

She told him. 'And tomorrow's the deadline for handing completed reports over to form teachers for collating.'

'So you won't make it?'

'I will. Luckily this lot were blank, or it would be more complicated.' She gestured uncertainly down at the phone. 'I hope you don't mind . . .'

'Of course not.'

'Thank you,' she said, meaning it. 'I've been ringing round the staff, finding who's got blanks to spare.'

'And?'

'Sue Norman at Faversham has, and Jane Gordon at Whitstable, and Dennis Hirst at Grove Ferry.' She paused, working out the best way to make the journey. 'If I drive to Faversham first, then to Whitstable, then to Grove Ferry . . .'

'That's some drive. Can I do any of it for you?'

Amy shook her head. 'Thanks, but there's still my place to be checked.' She paused and glanced up at him, accepting that his day as well as hers had been wrecked. 'Would you mind going to Stribble on your own again?'

She could have wept for their bright plans. She had so much looked forward to the time when, reports safely written and packed away, she would go back to her cottage with Paul late in the morning. They had meant to finish the contents of her refrigerator in a scratch mid-day meal, and then give Jim another run in Stodbean Wood. Then they had planned to come back to Hythe and have their evening meal in the Italian restaurant nearest to Hop Street . . .

But crying about it wouldn't help. She stood up.

'I don't know who did this to me,' she said as she went to her room for her coat, 'but they aren't going to beat me.' She looked back to Paul, sure she had heard him murmur something. 'What was that you said?'

'Nothing,' he said in louder tones. 'It'll keep.'

A moment later they all descended the stairs to the street together. Amy, tense as a drumhead and gradually hoisting in the fact that once more someone out there was trying to harm her, issued voluble instructions.

'Don't just look in the rooms, do the roof-space as well,' she told Paul, going through the street door ahead of him. 'And then there's wardrobes, laundry box, sink cupboards, cupboard under the stairs. Outside there'll be the dustbin . . .'

'You think someone might hide in that?' he asked as he locked the street door behind them.

Amy didn't smile. 'They might leave something in it.'

'I suppose they might,' he agreed with a small sigh, and opened the back of his van for Jim.

'Oh, and bring back the stuff from the fridge,' Amy ordered as she made for her own car. 'We'll use the eggs up for supper.'

And so they had gone their separate ways.

Five hours of careering across Kent yielded Amy the number of report sheets she needed. With the help of her book of street plans she hadn't too much trouble finding each place, but once there she had to explain what had happened to her own blanks, and the explanations, brief though she tried to keep them, cost her more time.

When she returned to Hop Street it was well after three, the November darkness already closing in. Paul didn't seem to have returned; he must be checking her

355

place as thoroughly as she could have wished. Knowing that though she didn't feel hungry she must eat, she made herself a cheese sandwich and got straight to work on the reports.

What with tension and fatigue from the efforts of the long drive, the task went with painful slowness. When the telephone rang at four she picked it up at once, hoping for Paul's voice and glad of the break.

'What the hell do you think you're up to?'

It was her father. Amy imagined his friar's fringe of white hair dancing with the force of his explosive words, his lined, weatherbeaten face creased with the worry beneath the anger. In all her six years away from the farm, first at college and now working in Kent, she had never once forgotten the vital Saturday call home to assure him that she was well. Never until now.

'I've tried and tried to get you,' he went on. 'I rang you till midnight last night, and again this morning . . .'

'I'm sorry.'

'. . . and when I finally get an answer it's from a man, and he says you're at his place. What's going on, Amy?'

'Didn't he tell you?' Amy asked, playing for time. 'I'm er, I'm staying with him. He's called Paul . . .'

'He told me his name, for what it's worth,' the impatient old voice interrupted. 'What I want to know is, who *is* he?'

Amy swallowed hard. She had always been careful to shield her old-fashioned countryman father from her earlier, over-active sex life, but this was different. She wasn't going to lie about Paul, now or ever.

'He's . . . he's someone I care a lot about, Dad.'

A long pause. 'About time too,' said her father at last. 'I was beginning to think you'd never settle down.'

'There's nothing settled . . .'

'I just hope he's good enough for you, that's all. Tell me about him.'

'Not just now, Dad. I've . . . got a lot on my mind . . .'

'Well, here's something else to put on your mind,' her father cut in, autocratic in his concern for his only daughter. 'I want you and that fellow up here at the farm as soon as possible, d'you hear?'

Amy almost smiled. She might have known that he would be as determined to vet Paul as Paul's grandmother had been to vet her. The brief amusement faded as she wondered apprehensively what, in his worry, surprise and indignation at hearing a man answer her phone, he had already said to Paul.

'I told you Dad, nothing's settled . . .'

'He seems a nice young chap as far as I can tell,' her father admitted, 'but I need more than a minute on the phone with him.'

'It's far too early . . .'

'Christmas'll do, if you can't make it sooner.'

She finally managed to ask about the family, and heard their news for that week. Gareth had passed his motorbike test first time, little Kirsty had cut her first tooth, Jenny and Lynne were busy with the Christmas puddings, her father and David had finally mended the fences at Top Field, Adam had a new girl from over Wooler way . . .

Some time during the call, Paul came back. 'Glad to see you've put his mind at rest,' he observed when Amy put down the telephone. 'He was in a right old state when I spoke to him.'

'He worries about me,' she explained. 'He's never got used to me moving so far from home.' She glanced at her watch. 'I can't talk, I have most of these –' she gestured down at the pile of reports on the desk – 'still to write.'

She finished them some time after seven. Then there were the exercises and stories to mark for her Year Seven English class, in preparation for today's written lesson with them.

'Can't you leave those for once?' Paul asked.

Amy shook her head. 'If you don't keep up with their written work they lose interest.'

The marking took her until after eight. When it was done they ate the bread and eggs from her refrigerator, respectively toasted and scrambled by Paul, and speculated endlessly and fruitlessly, just as Amy and Kate were speculating over lunch, about who the new persecutor could be. After supper she had felt fit for nothing but bed, and once there, she and Paul had found more urgent things to do than talk. So nothing had been settled between them, nothing, nothing.

It was too big and difficult a subject. A part of Amy wanted passionately to spend the rest of her life with

Paul, another part told her she didn't want to be with any man permanently, even him. Her heart yearned when she thought of bearing his children, then sank at the memory of washing nappies, coping with childhood illness, supervising homework, and watching beloved infants turn into grumpy teenagers. It seemed only yesterday that she had escaped from such responsibilities.

Besides, she so much enjoyed teaching, and wanted to go on giving all her mind to it. Sipping the excellent coffee provided by the Crossed Keys, she tried to put the whole problem from her and think only of this afternoon's school.

Tracy Norris says her sister's typing classes are teaching her not to inset the first lines of paragraphs,' she told Kate as Head of English. 'I said I'd ask you about it.'

'Blocking's for business letters only,' Kate said firmly. 'Make her inset.'

'Thanks. And listen, how do I stop them putting apostrophes everywhere . . .'

Amy's first lesson after lunch was Year Nine drama, a double period in her school studio. She hated having to lock her school bag away in her little office, and hated it more when the pupils grouped for their improvizations and she found herself wondering if any were taking the chance to plan something against her. When she moved among them it seemed clear that all were working hard on the exercise, and the lesson passed without incident.

Next came Year Seven English, another double period. In spite of her other commitments and worries she had prepared the lesson thoroughly and the class tackled it with their usual eleven-year-old eagerness, but during their written exercises her glance strayed without her will to the bright, lowered head of Tim Horner. Could he be the one? Might he not resent all the times she had checked him, and want revenge?

Some time near the end of the lesson, she glanced at her watch. At exactly this time one week ago she had been fetched to the telephone to talk to George Kensing, Funeral Director . . . But that had been Robert's doing, and Robert had been dealt with. What was more, living with Sarah he would stay dealt with . . . She wished she could find more comfort in that.

I'd almost rather this was Robert still, she told herself. At least I knew then who it was.

Eventually the lesson passed, and she was ready to go to the Yates Centre. She had no rehearsal tonight, thank heaven, but needed to check that the coloured gelatins had been put on the lights as she had directed, and that the resulting colours could all be worked from the switchboard according to plan. She must also just look into the costume cupboard; it should be empty now and ready to receive the *Hurnfield Market* costumes, but sometimes things got dumped there.

She drove to the centre and parked her car. A few minutes more, she thought as she opened the door into the drizzling rain, half an hour at the most, and I'll be free to go home . . .

Home? Climbing out of the car and locking it, she wondered at how easily she could forget that she had been driven out of her cottage.

Yet a part of her continued to rejoice. Home's where Paul is, it carolled. Being home and being with Paul are the same thing.

'Hi Debby,' she said, sliding off her damp coat as she entered the Yates ladies' cloakroom. 'Working hard as ever, I see . . .'

She broke off. At the sound of her voice Debby had jumped, the plastic spray bottle of cleaning fluid dropping from her hand to wash basin with a muted clatter. She didn't pick it up, or check the porcelain for damage. Instead she turned her strong, slow-moving body to face Amy, who waited, puzzled at the effect of her casual greeting.

'Oh, er, hello Miss.' Debby pushed back her corn-gold hair, showing freckles oddly prominent on her pale cheeks. 'I, er, I wonder if I could have a word, some time? Some time soon,' she added quickly.

'Of course.' Amy hung up her coat and glanced down at her watch. 'Now, if you like.'

'Wish I could, Miss.' Debby turned away, rescued the spray bottle, and moved on to the next wash basin. 'But I'm on here till five,' she said as she applied the next lot of spray, 'and the new caretaker's a terror.' She rubbed at the basin as she spoke. 'He says there's plenty more cleaners where we come from.'

Amy bit her lip. She hated the thought of hanging about here till five, but she was fond of Debby, whom she had taught during her first year at Oaklands. That had been a bad time for sixteen-year-old Debby and her family; and through it all she had shown herself endlessly steady and sensible. Now she seemed to want help.

'All right,' Amy said. 'See you in the coffee bar at five?'

The so-called coffee bar was only that during productions, though with so many schools and dramatic societies using the place, that was often enough. The rest of the time it was simply a counter and a few seats and tables by the entrance to the studio; a good quiet place to talk. Amy decided that as soon as she had finished her brief chores she would settle there and mark the latest set of exercises she had brought with her from her Year Seven English class.

Then when I do get in I'll have more time to spend with Paul, she thought as she made her way to the pay phone in the lobby.

How strange it felt, wanting to be done with school work and not take it home with her. And even stranger, she realized as she put her coin into the slot and tapped Paul's number, to be ringing a man to say he mustn't worry, she would be a bit later than he expected.

However, Paul didn't answer the phone. She tried again, this time careful to push the right numbers, but still no result. He must be out somewhere – Aminata too, since the same number rang in both shop and flat.

She replaced the handset, surprised at her own disappointment. Had she really set such store just by hearing Paul's voice for a moment? Heavens, she'd be seeing him soon, and for now she had other things to think about. Yet as she crossed the lobby the curious blank emptiness stayed with her. And if she felt it over such a small thing, what would it be like if she were never to see him again . . .

No, no, no! I can't let that happen, ever, ever, ever.

She found that she was shaking her head so vigorously that her hair flew about her shoulders. She looked round, hoping nobody had seen her arguing so furiously with herself, but it was all right, she was already out of the much traversed lobby and into the corridor which held the costume cupboard. It was quiet here. Between productions, few people went further down it than the caretaker's cleaning cupboard, which now stood with its door wide open . . .

Amy stopped, and sniffed. Could it be? A confusion of scents eddied from the open shelves; in just one brief glance she saw household soap, carpet cleaner, air freshener and window cleaner. Something here must have a similar scent to the one she thought she had noticed. It couldn't be . . .

She sniffed again. Hell, it couldn't *not* be. Whatever the domestic pungencies around it, nobody could mistake the singular mixture of linseed oil, vinegar and mothballs.

Heart racing, she continued along the less used part of the corridor. The oil, vinegar and mothball smell grew stronger. She reached the door of the walk-in costume cupboard, and threw it open. The smell billowed out at her, a palpable presence as she threw on the light switch.

However, when the overhead neon flickered to life it showed the little room empty. Deep shelves filled one side of it, all empty. Opposite them stood the clothes rail with not even a coat-hanger, let alone a coat. Yet in the confined space the smell was everywhere and overpowering.

Amy put out the light and tried to reclose the door. Only when her fingers missed its handle did she realize that she was trembling.

It's only an empty cupboard, she told herself. Nothing's changed, except you've learnt that the coat's been here.

Trying to tread even more firmly than usual, she made her way back along the corridor. The smell seemed to move with her, but it was so sharp, and so mixed with the other scents from the still-open cleaning cupboard, that she couldn't be sure if it were really still there or if it were only that her nose couldn't shake it off. It stayed with her, or seemed to, while she traversed the barely-lit coffee bar, pushed through the swing door into the empty drama studio, and flicked on the house lights.

They immediately went off again.

She pressed the switch a second time and the same thing happened; the place was lit for only a fraction of a second. In that fraction however she had time to glance up beyond the red-carpeted, stepped audience tiers and see a flicker of movement within the smoked glass corner booth which held the lighting controls.

So he's up there, she thought, whoever he is, and wanting the place dark so as to get away without being seen.

She tried the lights a third time. Nothing happened; she presumed that whoever was in the lighting booth had turned off the master switch. From now on, the studio would stay dark.

How huge it felt, a whole lightless world of space. Somewhere in the vast limbo she heard a quiet click which must be the lighting booth door opening. Then came a patter of feet on the steps, and with them a weird rustling and slithering like the movements of a giant snake. The smell of mothballs and linseed oil and vinegar was suddenly overwhelming.

The coat, Amy thought. He has Paul's coat.

The pattering and the slithering went on, coming lower and nearer while adrenalin-fuelled ideas zig-zagged across her mind like lightning flashes. She must get some light in here somehow. Apart from this main entrance where she stood, the studio had several other ways out, she must get a look at this person before he (or she, but somehow Amy knew it was a he) managed to reach one of them and disappear.

She pushed back the swing door behind her and the footsteps stopped. He must have frozen where he was, still on the steps and well beyond the reach of the square of thin, filtered light which was all she had managed to let in from the economical dimness of the coffee bar.

She glanced back to the distant main lobby, but nobody was in sight to help. She put down her school bag, hoping it would prop the door open, but even weighted as it was with exercise books it was too light to resist the door's powerful spring. She held the door open a moment longer, pinning her adversary on the stairs while she worked out what to do.

A picture came to her of the great red sliding doors which made up most of the wall furthest from her. If she could cross the darkness and slide those doors apart she would have light, plenty of it, from the brilliantly-lit room beyond.

She knew from her brief glimpses a moment ago that the studio was free of the odd tables, chairs or bits of scenery which sometimes littered it. Nothing would trip her up. Without further thought she launched herself into the dimness, which turned at once to darkness as the door behind her swung shut.

There went her unseen companion, continuing his way down the stairs. What on earth was he doing to make that strange noise that went with him? It sounded like he was dragging something and if he was, so much the better, it would be slowing him down. The noise helped her keep her bearings in the blackness; she moved swiftly on with hands spread before her, and in a moment felt beneath them the painted surface of the wooden doors.

A heave, and the door slid back as far as it would go. Fluorescent light from the further room flooded over her, hurting her eyes. She turned away from it and, still dazzled, saw a short, curiously misshapen figure scamper into the chasm of shadow between the tiers of steps and the wall. So he was making for the side entrance then, and she still hadn't got a proper look at him.

She darted after him, but all she saw was the side door swinging uselessly, her quarry already beyond it. She shot through it herself, into the dressing room on its other side, but that too was empty. The other door which led back to the coffee bar was still swinging, so through that she went and there he was, not misshapen after all, just wearing a jacket too big for him and burdened with the clumsy bulk of that wretched coat which he clutched determinedly in his arms as he raced for the lobby . . .

Where a tall man and a huge, handsome dog happened to be strolling towards the studio.

'Grab him, Paul,' Amy shouted.

But Paul didn't need to grab him.

'Jim!' the boy shouted. 'Oh, *Jim*!'

He let the coat flop to the ground and flung his arms round the dog's neck. Jim wuffed with delight and stood on his hind legs to set his great paws on the boy's shoulders and lick his face. The boy, too small to bear the weight, fell on top of the coat and the dog with him, so that by the time Amy reached them it was hard to tell boy from dog from coat.

'I guess we've found where Jim belongs,' Paul said.

'I guess we have.' She stared down at the shaggy, sandy head, and at what she could see of the battered, over-large leather jacket, the checked shirt and faded jeans.

'And now, Martin,' she said, 'you're going to tell us what you think you're playing at.'

CHAPTER 17

'Poor Debby,' Amy said. 'I hate the idea of having to break this to her.'

Debby's brother Martin, wrestling with Jim on the black, composition-tiled floor of the coffee bar, gave no sign of having heard. Perhaps he really hadn't. Since Paul and Amy had brought him in here he had taken little notice of anyone but Jim.

Amy, waiting for Debby to finish her cleaning job and keep their appointment, had seated herself well away from the boy. With the round black table between them, she might better be able to resist her overwhelming urge to shake him till his teeth rattled.

At least she had discovered the reason Paul was here. 'Betty took Aminata to visit a friend in Canterbury,' he explained. 'Trade's always slack on a Monday, so I closed early and hitched a lift with them.'

'And why,' she asked carefully, 'did you do that?'

He turned his fine, close-curled head towards her. The wall lights, switched on when they came in here, were red-shaded, and in their softening glow his eyes seemed deep, dark, almost violet.

'It meant half an hour more with you.'

Amy sighed, torn between pleasure and regret. 'Only it turned out to be with me and . . .' She nodded towards the oblivious Martin.

'It's still half an hour more with you.'

For a whole minute after that she hadn't wanted to shake Martin at all.

The urge came back now though, and stronger, as she tried to question him. Only her sternest classroom tones could persuade him to pay her any attention, and then he gave the briefest answers.

Paul's careful, patient approach yielded slightly better results. They gathered that on the Thursday before last, Jim had trodden on a broken bottle and badly cut his paw. As they couldn't afford a vet Debby had tried bandaging the wound, but Jim kept pulling the bandage off. The following Monday night Jim had vanished; Debby said he must have run away.

And yes, Martin had stolen Amy's keys; yes, he had overheated the studio before Wednesday's rehearsal; yes, he had torn up the reports in her bag.

'Deb makes me come 'ere wiv er when she cleans,' he told Paul, 'to keep me out o' trouble, she says.' He ducked his head, clearly aware of the irony. 'Gets borin'.'

Paul went on with his questioning, Martin with his answers. Yes, he had hot-wired Miss's car, a trick he had learnt from older boys, and yes, he had used it to take the coat away . . .

'But *why*?' Amy broke in. 'What on earth did you want it for?'

'Dunno.' Blind to everything but his dog, Martin didn't spare a glance for the coat odorously draped over another table. 'You c'n 'ave it back if you like, Mister.'

'Good of you,' Amy snapped.

'He took it as a comfort blanket,' Paul observed quietly. 'Now he has Jim back he doesn't need it any more.'

Amy sighed in agreement, regretting her hasty sarcasm. She hadn't known Martin two years ago, but Debby had told her of his grief and bewilderment at their mother's sudden death. Since then his father had failed to cope and eventually drifted right away; his sister would certainly have done her best but she was young and not very bright. He would need his comfort blanket, especially after he lost Jim.

'And why,' she asked, trying to take her cue from Paul's gentleness, 'did you put it in the costume cupboard?'

Martin shrugged. 'Nobody goes there.'

'Yes they do . . .'

'Only for rotten plays. That's why I 'ad to take it out, for your rotten play.'

So much for *Hurnfield Market*, which was costing Amy so much time and trouble. Perhaps Martin felt he had gone too far, for he volunteered more.

'Took it 'ome first, but Deb would've wondered.'

'She'd have smelt it,' Paul said. 'Was it always that strong?' he asked Amy.

'Stronger,' she confirmed. 'Some of it's wearing off.'

'I must have got more used to it than I realized.'

'Will you wear it again?'

'Maybe next winter, if the smell's worn off by then.'

'It's worn off already from the van.' Amy turned back to Martin, a new question welling up. 'And why take *my* car? Why not drive the coat away in the van where it already was?'

'Dunno.' Martin didn't look up from his inspection of his dog's almost-healed paw. 'This is doing fine, ennit, Jim?'

'Martin,' Amy burst out in exasperation, 'we're talking about a criminal offence here . . .' She broke off, aware through that new, unnameable sense that Paul silently disapproved. In the glance they exchanged, she tacitly admitted that he could do this better than she, and let him take over.

'It does seem strange, Martin,' he began in his deep, soft voice, 'to go to the trouble of breaking into two cars instead of one.'

For Paul, Martin looked up. 'Jus' thought I would.'

Amy had been casting her mind back over the events of the week before. They had been so many and so momentous that she had given little thought to her two short encounters with Martin, but she could recall them clearly.

'On Monday when the police picked you up in the cathedral,' she began, 'you were doing your sunwise dance to make somebody better.'

'It worked too.' Martin offered Jim's paw for inspection. 'Might've worked straight away if they'd let me finish.'

'Paul took him to the vet,' Amy said.

'Still worked.' Martin set the paw carefully to the ground.

'So on Tuesday when I saw you here at the Yates,' Amy went on, 'you must have been thinking about Jim a lot? Missing him?'

'Yeah.' The boy kept his head down, suddenly motionless.

'So that,' Amy blundered on, 'is why you cried . . .'

'I never!' His head whipped up, hair in angry, sandy spikes, eyes so wide they showed the reflections of the red wall lights. 'I never cry, never, never . . .' He broke off, distracted by Jim's nose, which the surprised dog had thrust into his hand.

'All right, boy. You ain't never goin' away, ever again.'

Silence followed. Martin once more had eyes only for his dog.

'Was anyone else there when he cried?' Paul asked Amy.

She shook her head. 'Just us two.'

'That's it then. He'd know your car?'

'Must do. He picked on it because it was mine, you mean?'

'Straight after you'd seen him cry.'

'Yes,' she answered from her own hard-won understanding of tough little boys. 'He had to show me he's not really a softie.'

'And had to go on showing you . . .'

Paul broke off as Debby hurried in, her trainers pattering across the solid floor. She carried her winter coat over her arm, and her discarded overall lay folded in the basket which bumped against her jeans and shabby white T-shirt.

How pretty she's become, Amy thought. Or rather, her mind corrected because 'pretty' seemed too slight a word for Debby's strong comeliness, what a fine looking woman. Too pale though, poor love, and even paler now she's seen Martin.

'What's he done now?' Debby asked in a resigned tone.

At the sound of her voice Jim, who had been temporarily invisible under the table, poked his head above it and wuffed a greeting.

'Oh God.' Debby sat down heavily in the chair Paul had pulled out for her, and looked at Amy. 'If you only knew how I wish I hadn't done it.'

'Done what . . . Oh.' Amy remembered the old car with the bang-scratchy engine. That was exactly the kind of car she would expect the Sullivans to have, or to have access to.

'So it was you,' she said.

Debby drooped. 'I didn't know what else to do. 'E was 'urt, an' Col said . . .'

'Col?'

'Colin Morgan. My feller.' Debby revived at the thought. ''E 'asn't a job yet, but 'e's tryin' ever so 'ard . . .'

'And where does he come into this, Debby?'

'. . . works 'is allotment an' sells the stuff to market traders, does up old cars . . . eh? Oh.' Debby's pallor warmed to a slight, becoming blush. 'Well, 'e lives with us now, don' 'e? For keeps.'

'Worse luck,' Martin growled from the floor.

'Go on, Marty, Col's good to you. Takes 'im fishin',' Debby explained to the others. 'An' to football, when we c'n afford it . . .'

'Don' like Jim, though.'

'Yes 'e do, Marty, you know 'e do. It's just . . .' Reminded of what she had to explain, Debby sagged again as she spoke to Amy. 'Col says it ain't fair keepin' such a big dog in a tenth-floor flat . . .'

'Took 'im out every day, didn't I?' Martin reran what must be an old argument.

'That's another thing.' Debby nodded down at her brother. 'Bunkin' off school to take Jim out. An' the feedin'. This job don' pay much –' she indicated the overall in her basket – 'an' neither does Col's vegetables, though they 'elps us eat better . . .'

'But you must have known before you got Jim how expensive he'd be?'

Amy spoke from a sense of disappointment. In her two-year teaching career she had met many ill-kept children from homes which also featured large, well-kept dogs. She would have expected better of dear, sensible Debby.

'We didn' know 'e'd grow so big, did we?' the girl protested. 'An' Martin did want that puppy, an' I thought it'd 'elp . . .' she faltered. 'It was just after Mum . . .'

Amy reached out and laid a hand on the girl's sturdy shoulder. 'I know,' she said softly, regretting yet again her impatience. 'I expect it did help, too.'

Debby gave her a timid, grateful smile. 'But then Col says it ain't fair to Jim, an' then Jim's 'urt, an' then Jill Gann next door . . .'

'Jill?' Amy had a brief vision of the lanky thirteen-year-old who last Monday in the drama room had eaten the crisps which were her entire lunch. 'How is she?' Amy asked, knowing now that the poor child had to eat for two.

Debby shrugged. 'All right.' As well as can be expected, she meant. 'She memorized your address from a envelope you threw away.'

'Why did she do that?'

'She thought she'd write to you if she got desperate.' Debby's forefinger drew sunwise patterns on the black shine of the table. 'Seeing you're a soft touch . . .'

'A *what*?' Outraged, Amy jerked upright in her chair. 'I am no such thing!' She turned on Paul. 'What are you smiling at?'

'Nothing. Maybe,' he told Debby, 'you could have put that a bit more tactfully.'

The girl stared back at him, out of her depth. 'Miss gave Jill a pound . . .'

'She was hungry,' Amy said.

'She spent it on cigarettes.'

Amy looked down at the table and sighed. She should have known better.

Debby added in her fussy, motherly way. 'I tell 'er she shouldn't be smokin' in 'er condition, but she don't take no notice.'

Paul brought her quietly back to the point. 'So she gave you Miss's address.'

'Yeah. An' Col took Jim there . . .'

'What?' Martin must have tuned in again. 'You *bitch*! You *cow*!' He scrambled to his feet, one hand protective on the dog's ruff, his little, un-formed face white with fury. 'I ain't never speak-in' to you again,' he informed his sister. 'An' neither's Jim.'

'But Marty, look 'ow good Miss's been to Jim,' Debby protested with her own brand of logic. 'She's 'ad 'is foot seen to, an fed 'im well, look at 'is coat, an I bet she's walked 'im . . .'

'He's *my* dog, it's for me to do things.' Martin turned towards the exit. 'Jim an' me's goin' away an' we ain't never comin' back.'

He stumped off, pulling Jim along with him. The dog gave an uncertain glance back at the others, then allowed himself to be walked away, claws rattling.

'I'm sorry, Marty,' Debby wailed after him. '*Please* don't . . .'

She broke off as Paul rose and loped after the two. He overtook them easily, and sank to a springy crouch before them with a hand out to Jim. Amy, trained in the use of differing heights to convey dramatic meaning, marvelled at his sound instinct in bringing himself down to the same physical level as the boy.

'This is the best behaved dog I've ever met.' His voice drifted back soft, unthreatening, easy. 'Is that your doing?'

Martin hesitated. 'Dogs 'ave to learn.' He sounded a little calmer.

'Did you take him to obedience classes?'

'What's those?'

'So you taught him yourself?'

'Spent hours on it,' Debby confirmed from her place at the table. 'Our Marty's a good lad if 'e'd give 'isself a chance . . .'

'You shut your mouf, our Deb!' Martin whirled to face his sister. 'Sendin' my Jim away an' tellin' me lies!'

'I know Marty, an' I'm sorry, honest I am.' Debby looked from her brother to Amy, shamefaced. 'When you was so upset I sent Col to try an' get 'im back . . .'

'Late Tuesday night?' Amy exchanged a glance with Paul, both recognizing the intruder in her garden who had made off in the car. 'Debby, have you any idea of the worry you've caused me?'

'Sorry Miss.' Debby wilted once more, half-hidden in her sandy-gold hair. 'Marty were so miserable.'

'He was worse than miserable . . .' Amy began.

'Come on, Martin.' Over by the door, Paul rose and put a hand on the boy's shoulder. 'You know you've got to face what you've done.'

Martin stared upwards, suspicion in every line of his body. 'What's it to you?'

Paul thought for a moment. 'You know the way Col is with your Debby? Well I'm like that with Miss.'

Oh are you, Amy thought, and then as a wave of joy washed over her, are you really, Paul? For keeps?

'You've given her a bad time the last few days,' he continued. 'The least you can do is say you're sorry.'

Martin thrust his hands back in his pockets. 'Ain't sorry.'

'Then it's time you were.' A touch of steel entered the soft tones. 'Because I'll tell you something else. Jim's with us now, and he's staying with us . . .'

'No 'e ain't!' Martin's hand shot back to Jim's ruff, grabbing it so tight that the dog grunted in mild protest. 'You ain't got no right . . .'

'We've got every right. Debby left him for us to take care of, and we have. Better than you could.'

Martin dropped to wrap both arms round Jim's neck. 'He's *my* dog.'

'He'll still be that.' Paul thought for a moment. 'It's dark nights now, but in spring you can come to Stribble in the evenings . . .'

'I'm not waiting all that time.'

'I'll bring him to school,' Paul offered, 'and we'll walk him lunch times.'

'Every day?'

'Can't promise that. Often, though.'

'How often?'

'Tomorrow, for starters.'

Martin found a serious objection. 'That means I gotta be in school.'

Amy and Debby exchanged glances. Amy saw that the girl had untwisted her hands on her lap, and crossed her fingers.

'You 'ave to anyway, Marty,' she said.

'You can stay with me some weekends, too,' Amy began on impulse. 'That'll be two days you and Jim can be together all the time.'

Almost before she finished speaking she regretted the words. What on earth was she doing, saddling her already overcrowded life with a small boy at weekends? A criminal small boy, for heaven's sake . . .

Martin threw back his shaggy head to look up at Paul. 'Will you be there?'

'Certainly will.'

For keeps, Amy's heart sang, for keeps.

Martin stared upwards a moment longer, still tightly grappled to his dog. Then he slowly, reluctantly unclasped himself, rose to his feet, resumed his hold on Jim's ruff, and marched with him back to the table. Having reached it he didn't sit on the floor as before, but pulled out the fourth chair and established himself in that.

Paul followed, directing a glance at Amy over the boy's head.

She accepted the signal. 'Now, Martin. Which of us is going to tell Debby what you've been doing?'

Jim had taken up his favourite pressed-close position against Martin's leg. The boy looked down at him, away from everyone at the table.

'You can.'

Amy accordingly began the weary catalogue. Long before she had finished Debby was exclaiming in horror. When she heard of the hot-wired car she clutched her head as if it would burst. 'Oh Marty,' she exclaimed, half-guilty, half-angry. 'This is what comes of 'angin' round that Trevor Fagg and 'is gang. We'll 'ave to tell the police . . .'

'No!' Amy threw it like a gunshot.

Three pairs of eyes, four counting Jim's, trained on her. Martin's held surprise, Debby's shame mixed with hope, Paul's . . . What on earth was Paul *smiling* at? The smile hadn't reached his mouth but it was there in his eyes, a kind of fondness . . . But she couldn't think of that, not just now.

'I – I'd rather forfeit my no-claims bonus,' she said, trying to conceal her embarrassment. 'I . . . I don't want Martin getting a police record because of me.'

'It wouldn't be because of you,' Paul softly pointed out. 'It would be because of what he did himself, of his own free will.'

'He was unhappy . . .' Amy broke off, unwilling to risk another angry reaction from the boy. 'Well, there it is.' She knew she sounded more stubborn than she meant to, but went on anyway. 'I don't want the police told.'

'You 'ear that, Martin?' Debby said.

Her brother stayed silent, staring from one woman to the other.

'So just for a start, what 'ave you to say?' Debby demanded.

Martin ducked his head sideways.

'Go on,' merciless Debby insisted. 'Say it.'

Martin let out a garbled mutter.

'That won't do. You look Miss in the eye and say it proper.'

Martin shot her a hunted glance. Then he finally obeyed, looking straight at Amy and speaking as if the word were dragged out of him.

'Now then. You cost Miss money, 'ow you goin' to pay 'er back?'

Martin stared at his sister in alarm. 'I ain't got no money, you know I ain't . . .'

'It doesn't matter, Debby.' Aware of the ways Martin might get money if he had to, Amy spoke urgently. 'I don't want it. I wouldn't take it if you offered . . .'

'Suppose Martin pays it,' Paul suggested, 'after he's grown up and got a job?'

'That's a long time,' Debby objected. 'An' jobs is 'ard to find, you ask my Col.'

'They're easier,' Paul said, 'if you have a good school record.'

'That's right, I got on 'ere 'cause I'd a good report from school. I'm always tellin' Marty . . .' Debby broke off, her slow mind grasping where this was leading, and turned to her brother. 'This means you got to go to school every day.'

'Aw Deb!'

'An' work 'ard when you're there.'

'An' if I don't?'

'Col won't take you to see Jim, an' this gentleman 'ere –' Debby indicated Paul with a flick of her head – 'won't bring Jim to see you.'

'I bet you could get good marks if you really tried,' Amy joined in to soften the blow. 'And when you do . . .'

'When you do,' Debby interrupted, grabbing Amy's intention and running off with it, 'you can go an' stay the weekend with Jim. All right?'

Martin turned to Amy, his eyes wide, his small face suddenly childish and pleading. 'Can I really come and stop weekends with Jim?'

Amy thought of her home, her sanctuary, invaded by a part of her working life. Her neat little spare room messily occupied, her lavatory seat left up, shaving cream unrinsed in her wash basin . . . Well, that at least wouldn't be Martin, or not for a year or two. And anyway, Paul would help. For keeps, for keeps . . .

'You 'ave to get the good marks first,' Debby announced implacably.

'Let's try it from here to Christmas,' Amy offered. 'If you go to all your classes *and* work hard . . .'

'Okay.' But Martin slumped at the prospect.

'. . . then you can have Jim for the holiday. We have to go to Northumberland for Christmas.' Amy glanced sideways at Paul, but ignored his surprise. 'You can have Jim while we're away,' she went on. 'And when we're back, you can stay in Stribble the rest of the holiday.'

'Chrismas.' Martin kicked moody feet under the table. 'A 'ole month I 'as to be all goody-goody.'

'But you'll see Jim lots, in that time,' Paul reminded him.

Martin blinked up at him. 'Can I take him home now? Just for tonight?'

'No you can't,' Debby said crossly. 'Take no notice Mister, it's a try-on.'

'Tain't much to ask,' Martin muttered, 'fr a 'ole month bein' goody-goody.'

'It'll take more'n a month to make up for what you been up to.'

'But he's right, one night isn't much.' To her own surprise Amy found herself pleading the boy's cause. 'They've been separated for a week.'

'All right then.' Debby gave in with unexpected ease. 'For you, Miss. Just the one night, mind,' she told Martin.

'Thanks, Miss!' A brilliant smile transformed Martin's blunt features. 'I'll give 'im back tomorrer, honest.'

It only remained for Paul to write down the Sullivans' address, so that he could go there at lunch time next day to pick Jim up. From there he would go on to the school gate and meet Martin, and the two of them would give Jim his walk.

Martin's smile stayed with him for the rest of the time they were all together. When they left the coffee bar he and Jim ran ahead along the corridor, two exuberant young friends reunited. By the time Amy and Debby reached the main lobby with Paul and his regained coat, boy and dog had already crossed to the door.

'Night, Miss, night Mister,' Martin said. 'See you in the mornin'.'

'I'd better catch them up quick,' Debby murmured. 'I'll need to be there when they get 'ome, to tell Col what's 'appened.' She hurried after her brother, but paused at the door. 'Night, Miss, Mister. An' thanks again.'

'Do you really think it'll work?' Paul asked after the girl had disappeared. 'Do you think that young tearaway will learn to behave so he can see his dog?'

'I don't know. Debby was crossing her fingers.'

'Maybe we all should.'

She retrieved her coat from the ladies' cloakroom. Fastening and belting it, she moved with him to the outer lobby, where they paused for a moment to stare through the glass doors at the pelting rain.

'I'll miss Jim,' she said. 'I hope they feed him right.'

'They did before we got him.' As he spoke, Paul arranged his own rescued coat over his shoulders. 'Handy that I've got this back.'

She shivered as she stepped into the rainy night. Paul followed, and with a hand on her arm, brought her round to face him under the shelter of the canopy. With infinite gentleness he turned up the collar of her raincoat so that it cradled her head, then took her hand. Thus joined they walked to the car.

'Your place or mine?' he asked.

'My place,' she murmured, contemplating rather than answering. 'It is mine again, isn't it?' She tried to get used to the idea. 'The Sullivans won't be bothering me any more, or not like that . . .' She turned sideways in the seat to look at him. 'You told Martin,' she began carefully, 'that we're the same way as Debby and her Col.'

'Well, aren't we?'

'They're living together . . .'

'So are we.'

'You mean,' she asked softly, 'you want us to go on doing that?'

'I've already set it up. That's why I came here, to tell you as quick as I could. That is,' he added as an afterthought, 'if you agree, of course.'

There he went again, organizing her life for her. But he did it so well, and at least he was consulting her.

'Agree to what?' she asked.

'Harold wants a place of his own. He'd be happy to take over my flat . . .'

'So you'd move in with me.'

The lavatory seat left up. Shaving cream in the wash basin. Paul to come home to . . . The night seemed suddenly, unaccountably bright; the rain on the windscreen glittered like stars.

'We'd need your double bed,' she told him, thinking of her own chaste single.

'Maybe we'll even buy a new one.'

Paul and me in a double bed every night, her heart sang. Paul and me together every day, helping each other, sharing our problems, always there for each other. It was all she ever wanted, yet when she spoke she surprised herself with her caution.

'You're good with children, Paul.'

'So are you.'

'Only, I'm not sure I want any of my own.'

For a long moment he stared ahead through the rain-streaked windscreen. Rain pattered on their little tin roof, assaulting their cosy bubble of dryness. Somewhere in the distance, a heavy goods vehicle changed gear.

'Do you want to talk about it?' he asked.

She didn't, but knew she must. 'I . . . I don't want to give up teaching.'

'You needn't. For a start, we can afford plenty of help.'

'It isn't that simple.' She told him of her father's bad experiences with housekeepers. 'And even while they were there I had to do a lot for my little brothers. There were times,' she added, staring through the rain-glittering windscreen, 'when I wore to school whatever clothes I could find with no baby-burp on the shoulders . . .' She turned at some murmured comment. 'What was that you said?'

'I said oh, my love.' He took her hand. 'So brave, so loving, so everything I've always wanted in a woman.'

Amy sat motionless, her hand in his, rainbow colours circling her world. 'You never said that before.'

He leant towards her. 'Shall I say it another way?'

'I love you too, Paul. Very much. But . . .' she resisted his urging '. . . children?'

'It matters, I can see that.' He sighed, sat back, and faced ahead as she was doing. 'Supposing I said I'd share the baby-burp?'

She turned to stare at him. 'You'd wash nappies? Wipe up spills? Stay with them when they're poorly. . .'

'What do you think?'

She saw at once what he meant. So far, he had proved himself well able to do any domestic chore that came his way. A series of pictures flashed through her mind, of Paul bathing an olive-dark baby, picking up after a curly-haired toddler, answering the eternal questions of a dark-blue-eyed seven-year-old, keeping in order a lanky, springy, limbo-dancing teenager. Yet still she objected, even though she now saw a picture of herself in a hospital bed holding a newborn baby. She was smiling down at the downy-haired bundle as Paul wrapped both of them in his strong arms and bent to kiss her . . .

'You've a business to run. Two businesses . . .'

'One. The antiques were just something to do,' he added in explanation. 'The carvings are where the action is.'

'You mean you can live just on selling those?'

'You're forgetting my father's money.'

'Yes, but surely you're not just going to . . .'

'I'll be busy enough. Somebody in America wants all we can supply, and there are other markets to try out . . .'

'So how would you find the time to look after children?'

'I'll find it. Work from home if need be.'

'Home,' Amy said softly. 'My cottage, home for both of us . . . and for our children.'

'Speaking of which, why have I to go to North-umberland for Christmas?'

'My father wants to meet you.'

'Right. We might as well go on to Scotland, for you and Ma to get acquainted.'

'That's not fair,' Amy protested, smiling. 'You've already put me through one ordeal by relatives . . .' She broke off, sobered. 'Do you think your mother will like me, Paul?'

'*Grandmère* and Betty do.'

'That's different.' Amy thought of his English mother who after her aberrant marriage had reverted to type and married a Scottish landowner. 'She might not approve of me.'

'She'll have to,' he answered with typical honesty. 'You're my woman now. Now and always.'

Now and always. While she took in the excitement of it, the comfort of it, the endless togetherness of it, he drew her into his arms, and she no longer resisted. Their kiss was gentle, both holding back in this public place, but behind the easy meeting of their lips was the thought of a lifetime together with the man she loved.

'Now and always,' she repeated as they drew apart. 'If that's how it's going to be, I suppose we might as well get married.' She felt the laughter rippling through his chest, and drew away indignantly. 'What's so funny?'

'Yes, do let's.' He smoothed her hair from her face. 'I thought you'd never ask.'

**THE EXCITING NEW NAME
IN WOMEN'S FICTION!**

PLEASE HELP ME TO HELP YOU!

Dear *Scarlet* Reader,

As promised, I have some excellent news for you this month – we are beginning a super Prize Draw, which means that **you could win 6 months' worth of free Scarlets!** Just return your completed questionnaire to us (see addresses at end of questionnaire) before 31 July 1997 and you will automatically be entered in the draw that takes place on that day. If you are lucky enough to be one of the first two names out of the hat we will send you four new Scarlet romances every month for six months, and for each of twenty runners up there will be a sassy *Scarlet* T-shirt.

So don't delay – return your form straight away!*

Sally Cooper

Editor-in-Chief, *Scarlet*

*Prize draw offer available only in the UK, USA or Canada. Draw is not open to employees of Robinson Publishing, or their agents, families or households. Winners will be informed by post, and details of winners can be obtained after 31 July 1997, by sending a stamped addressed envelope to address given at end of questionnaire.

Note: further offers which might be of interest may be sent to you by other, carefully selected, companies. If you do not want to receive them, please write to Robinson Publishing Ltd, 7 Kensington Church Court, London W8 4SP, UK.

QUESTIONNAIRE

Please tick the appropriate boxes to indicate your answers

1 Where did you get this Scarlet title?

Bought in supermarket ☐

Bought at my local bookstore ☐ Bought at chain bookstore ☐

Bought at book exchange or used bookstore ☐

Borrowed from a friend ☐

Other (please indicate) _____

2 Did you enjoy reading it?

A lot ☐   A little ☐   Not at all ☐

3 What did you particularly like about this book?

Believable characters ☐   Easy to read ☐

Good value for money ☐   Enjoyable locations ☐

Interesting story ☐   Modern setting ☐

Other _____

4 What did you particularly dislike about this book?

_____

5 Would you buy another Scarlet book?

Yes ☐   No ☐

6 What other kinds of book do you enjoy reading?

Horror ☐   Puzzle books ☐   Historical fiction ☐

General fiction ☐   Crime/Detective ☐   Cookery ☐

Other (please indicate) _____

7 Which magazines do you enjoy reading?

1. _____

2. _____

3. _____

And now a little about you –

8 How old are you?

Under 25 ☐   25–34 ☐   35–44 ☐

45–54 ☐   55–64 ☐   over 65 ☐

cont.

9 What is your marital status?

Single ☐   Married/living with partner ☐
Widowed ☐   Separated/divorced ☐

10 What is your current occupation?

Employed full-time ☐   Employed part-time ☐
Student ☐   Housewife full-time ☐
Unemployed ☐   Retired ☐

11 Do you have children? If so, how many and how old are they?

_____

_____

12 What is your annual household income?

under $15,000	☐ or	£10,000	☐
$15–25,000	☐ or	£10–20,000	☐
$25–35,000	☐ or	£20–30,000	☐
$35–50,000	☐ or	£30–40,000	☐
over $50,000	☐ or	£40,000	☐

Miss/Mrs/Ms _____

Address _____

_____

_____

Thank you for completing this questionnaire. Now tear it out – put it in an envelope and send it to:

Sally Cooper, Editor-in-Chief

USA/Can. address
SCARLET c/o London Bridge
85 River Rock Drive
Suite 202
Buffalo
NY 14207
USA

UK address/No stamp required
SCARLET
FREEPOST LON 3335
LONDON W8 4BR
Please use block capitals for address

Scarlet titles coming next month:

MASTER OF THE HOUSE   Margaret Callaghan
Ella has just started a new life as housekeeper to the wealthy,
newly engaged Fliss. But when Fliss's fiancé comes home,
Ella's troubles really begin! For Jack Keegan is Ella's ex-
husband – the only man she's ever loved . . .

SATIN AND LACE   Danielle Shaw
The last proposal Sally Palmer expects to hear from her
boss, Hugh Barrington, is 'Will you be my mistress?'
Surprising even herself, Sally embarks on the affair with
consequences which affect everyone around her!

NO GENTLEMAN   Andrea Young
When Nick comes back into Daisy's life, she's convinced
she's immune to his charm. She's going to marry safe,
handsome and loving Simon. So let Nick do his darnedest
to persuade Daisy that it's excitement *not* security she
desires. She's already made her choice, and nothing will
change her mind . . . or will it?

NOBODY'S BABY   Elizabeth Smith
Neither Joe Devlin nor Stevie Parker tell the truth when
they meet. He thinks *she's* a writer, she thinks *he's* in PR.
After a wonderful night together, Joe leaves with no
explanation. So Stevie takes her revenge . . . then Joe
plots his!